MW01205695

The Naturalists

C. G. Haberman

Acknowledgements

Thank you all who diligently work and continue your work preserving the unique south-central Nebraska Rainwater Basin wetlands. To the area agricultural producers who have not destroyed these unique acres, God bless you.

I have special memories of Richard Fuehrer and our traditional Thanksgiving morning pheasant hunts along the grassy marsh edges. Together we took March drives to watch and enjoy nature's magnificent waterfowl migration before the birds moved north. This book is written with you in mind. Your passing still saddens me.

Special thanks to Dr. G., Dr. B, Jerry J., and my daughter for their comments. Finally, to my mother and my wife—thank you, and God rest your souls.

About the Author

C. G. Haberman is the author of CJ Hand Mystery novels:

Dead Man's Run

Mill Creek Malice

Deadly Circles

He resides in Nebraska.

Excerpts from the previous novels, samples of his photography, and more information at *cghaberman.com*

Job 12:7-10 - *But ask the animals, and they will teach you, or the birds of the air, and they will tell you; or speak to the earth, and it will teach you, or let the fish of the sea inform you. Which of all these does not know that the hand of the LORD has done this? In his hand is the life of every creature and the breath of all mankind. (NIV)*

Hayman Family Tree

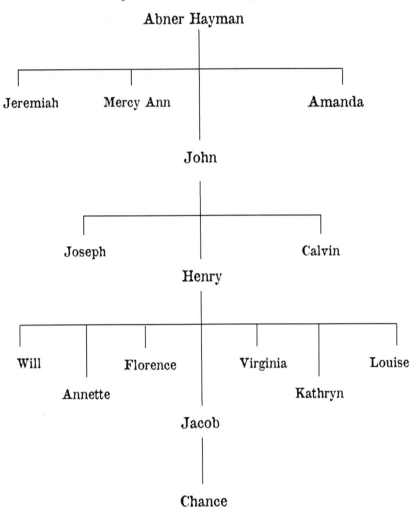

The Naturalists

*A Historical Novel of
the Hayman Family*

Volume I

1827 – 1899

The Beginning

The Journey

The Settling

The Murder

The Trial

The Discovery

The Beginning

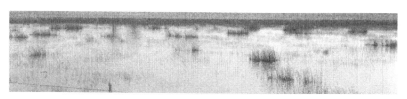

Let all regard themselves as the stewards of God in all things which they possess. Then they will neither conduct themselves dissolutely, nor corrupt by abuse those things which God requires to be preserved.

John Calvin, 1554, Commentary on Genesis, from the English translation of 1847. As reprinted by Banner of Truth Publishers, 1965.

The marble is cool to the touch as I stand to watch the glorious scene, unfolding as it has for ages. The sight never fails to send a chill down my spine. The ducks and geese dominate now, but they will soon leave—followed by the shore birds. The sound floats in the air, gracing my ears with mesmerizing tones and harmonies.

My name is Chance Hayman. I stand on the native prairie sod within the fenced acreage above the Hayman Marsh in the Rainwater Basin of south-central Nebraska. This ground awaits my remains—a return—to nourish the grasses and forbs. My wife, Karin, who stood by my side for nearly thirty-five years, now rests in the assigned plot alongside where I will eventually begin again. Karin's memorial, unlike the lichen-encrusted marble on which my hand rests, is a medium-sized granite block engraved with cattails that border the chiseled lettering. It is of wonderful clarity (like her mind) and smoothness much like her lifelong complexion.

The marble memorial, where my hand rests, is that of my great-grandfather, John Hayman. It is he who began our family appreciation of this marsh nestled in the hollow to the east. It is where he first came in 1855. A land he loved, nurtured, and protected until the day he died. There is no wife's grave. None of us Haymans know what became of our great-grandmother. I know she was born in the 1840s, fled the Oregon Trail, and married John in Fillmore County. Placed beside John's grave there is a small bronze plaque attached to a marble slab commemorating Maggie. Etched on the plaque are the words *Thank you, dear Mother.*

Henry Hayman, my grandfather, rests slightly downslope from John's grave. The gravestone beside him inscribed, Aletha Jones Hayman with the numbers: 1903-1960. I did not know my grandmother for she left Nebraska on my grandfather's death. What little I do remember of her was the long black hair. A hint of lilac followed wherever she ventured. And endless gossip about Aletha churned in the small town's quiet parlors and hushed church circles. Aletha returned as ashes, sent by her lawyer.

Dad, Jacob, died in 1981. My friends and their parents still hold him in high esteem. My mother, Lillian, peacefully died in 1994, a woman of God with an enduring conviction of honesty, and held a strong work ethic instilled by her father and mother.

Mom always had time for us, my three sisters and I. Her patience, with her sometimes-rebellious son, allowed me to become a modestly successful person with an appreciation for life—every day.

The roar of flapping wings and honking geese breaks my thoughts. A bald eagle soars above the marsh seeking the genetically weak and ailing among the flock. I watch as the stately raptor rides the warming morning air and uses the powerful wingspan to assure this bald eagle will remain atop the food chain.

Another of the great white-headed birds sails over the flock, suddenly peels back, and dives into the mind-numbing waterfowl numbers. Two more eagles soar around the flock, joining in the dizzying disturbance.

A slight breeze eddies past me carrying with it the marsh odor, an earthy smell of shallow, aged, and murky water. Thawing, from the body heat of the massive flock, provides much of the open resting and dabbling spots on this fine March morning, a morning that begins with an unrivaled crispness. A smile tugs at my face.

So many times, Karin and I came to this spot to watch similar spectacles unfolding before us. The peace and quiet of this family plot gave us many hours of pleasure. This is a refuge from the never-ending negativity—a place away from mouths of those who must be unhappy to be happy.

Karin died last year, two years after my mother's death. I am finally healing, still, my heart aches. As I wait in the cloudless morning, I now wonder at the path I might follow. I can, if I so choose, work with the bureaucrats. I am critical of them and have been for many years. My familiarity with the governor brings her aides to me. They seek help with a problem: wetland restoration and preservation.

Not many people know or understand this state, the State of Nebraska. It offers greater diversity than meets the traveler's eye. Here in the Rainwater Basin country—an area mostly known by wildlife biologists, birders, and hunters—is a force that must stop. To me, this marsh country is part of my drive, my existence, and my soul.

I owe all this to my great, great-grandfather. It all began because of him, Abner Hayman, a tyrant in his own right.

4

The Journey

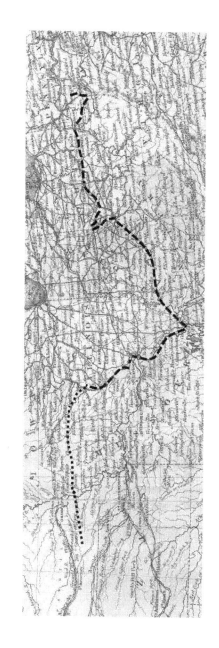

Abner Hayman Journey– Dashes

John Hayman Journey – Dots

Chapter 1

His silver-streaked, black hair flowed over his clerical collar and a worn, faded Bible lay open in the right hand. His left hand clenched and unclenched in the space above his head as he quoted the scripture. This minister extolled the virtues of God, a well-educated man of the cloth, coming to this county from the halls of Yale and the New Brunswick Theological Seminary.

Abner Hayman paused to scan the congregation, sitting in polished pews hewn from the deciduous forest near the church. His dark-brown eyes met each of the parishioner's, finally resting on his wife, Mary, seated in the front. He stepped from behind the pulpit. Shuffling feet broke the dramatic silence Reverend Hayman had elicited.

"Before I offer the final prayer, I'm pleased to announce Mary and I will be parents by this time next year."

Mary, a surprised look on her face, dropped her head. She slowly lifted it while several hands from the pew behind her graced her slender shoulders.

Abner continued, "We are proud to settle in south-central Pennsylvania where the Lord works his ways through the Reformed Church, providing you with strength, guidance, and wisdom. Reverend Heidt has built a strong following." He turned to face the Reverend. "Thank you, Pastor Heidt, for your dedication to the Lord." Abner pivoted, returned to the pulpit, and completed the liturgy for the third Sunday in Lent.

It was his first year of ministering to followers in the church started by the Reverend Josiah Heidt. Abner's energetic preaching style at first shocked his senior pastor and the staunch German congregation of the Zion Reformed Church in Franklin County, Pennsylvania. The word spread of the dynamic minister and his attractive wife. Attendance continued to increase, especially on the Sundays Pastor Hayman preached. The number of young families doubled since his arrival the previous May. With each passing week, new followers came to join the church. Overflowing pews and collection plates started the call for a new church building.

An unfamiliar face appeared the First Sunday of Lent. Since his first arrival, he sat in the same spot and always dressed in expensive, black woolen suits and black tie. This Sunday the man sat in the third pew next to Mr. Dressler.

After the church proceedings, the stranger stopped to greet, and congratulate Mary before he returned to his journey. He lingered, talking with Reverend Heidt, while Abner bid good day to church members.

Mary trailed the final crowd, waiting patiently, while they chatted with her husband. Two impish boys interrupted their parents and Pastor Hayman by tugging at Abner's jacket.

"Pastor, you gonna play hoops with us this afternoon?" asked the red-haired, freckled-faced boy. The father started to admonish his son, but Pastor Hayman interrupted.

"Levi," Abner said, "only if you promise to let me win."

Levis' friend said, "But you always win."

Pastor Hayman patted the boy's shoulder. "Ah, but you two are improving so much I'm starting to worry."

Levi grinned. "Thank you. I promise not to bring my sister."

"Levi, your sister is always welcome to join in—every day."

Before Levi could protest, his parents ushered him down the steps.

Abner watched the family climb into their buggy pulled by a well-groomed horse. Levi's father owned and clerked the hardware store in the small community of Mercersburg. Abner felt someone touch his arm.

Mary slipped her hand into his. "Levi likes you, Abner." A smile creased her face, showing the first hint of pregnancy.

The stranger from the third pew took his leave from Reverend Heidt and stepped over to Mary and Abner. "Reverend Hayman, I'm Samuel Carnes." He smiled at Mary and continued, "I introduced myself to your wife after the service." He held out his large hand.

Abner grasped it and said, "Welcome to God's church, Samuel."

As Reverend Heidt busied himself with the collection plate, Samuel softly spoke, "Reverend Hayman, I'm on my way to Washington. I've been in the area buying and selling land to individuals moving west from the Atlantic shores." He paused as a young boy leading two packhorses rode up on a sturdy black horse. "Aha, the young man is on time." Samuel signaled to tie up the three horses. "After a year in Washington, I'll stop again on my return to western Ohio." He eyed Mary. "I would like to spend time visiting with both of you about your vision for the future." Samuel shook Mary's hand, put on gloves, and donned a hat hanging near the church door. After easily stepping into the saddle, He tipped a finger to the hat brim and led his packhorses south.

Mary took Abner by the hand and led him inside the church. "Come, Abner, we must clean before the evening service. Then I'll prepare the evening meal while you entertain Levi and his friends."

"I forgot about the boys." He frowned. "Samuel Carnes rather unsettled me."

Mary looked up at him. "How, Abner?"

"He's so well-spoken ... his manner isn't like most people we know."

Mary studied Abner's troubled face. "We'll probably not see him again."

"I don't know," Abner reflected, "but I won't fret about it. Let's finish here. I must get on with outlining the evening sermon."

"Why do you change the sermon? Why not preach the same?"

"My dear wife, I don't want to bore those who come twice on Sundays and sin on those days between." A grin broke the troubled expression.

Chapter 2

The Monday after Trinity Sunday, Abner, and Josiah traveled to forest land owned by Calvin Deirks, the church head elder. Calvin, an astute man, now owned several farms in the area, which nicely supported his growing family. He, his wife, and three of his five boys worked the seven farms around the small stream draining to the West Branch of the Conococheague, a tributary of the Potomac River. The more land Calvin cleared the more acres he owned to pass on to his sons. Water for the Deirks Farms came from the clear-running streams fed by springs in the mountain range to the west. Forest wildlife flourished on the farms, feeding in the small, interspersed grain fields between the thick stands of trees.

Josiah and Abner needed wood for the church and family uses so they asked permission from Calvin to clear the land. He agreed and offered the services of his oldest sons, plus wagons, horses, and the cost for log processing at the Chambersburg sawmill.

Abner sought a straight, tall oak tree to build a baby's rocking cradle for their firstborn due in a few months. For Mary, he planned a new rocking chair to match the cradle. He had access to the smithy shop in Mercersburg and wanted the expertise of his friend, working in the woodworking cabin to hone his budding craft.

Calvin's two older boys, awaiting the ministers, sat next to the trail alongside the farmland he wanted to clear. A large wagon pulled by six draft horses, with heavy leather harnesses shimmering in the mid-morning light, stood ready to haul fallen logs. With his foot against the wheel brake, a younger Deirks boy relaxed on the wagon seat. Tethered to a makeshift hitching post stood two loosely harnessed draft horses.

"Good mornin', Pastors," the eldest Deirks boy said. He held two axes.

"Mornin' to you, Esau," Josiah answered.

"Ready to drop a few big ones?" asked Matthew, the second oldest.

"We're ready," Abner said and whacked him on the arm.

The two Heidt boys jumped from their father's wagon and trotted over to Mark Deirks seated on the plank behind the wagon tongue.

"Mark, what're ya doin'?" Obadiah Heidt asked.

"I'm waitin' for my father. He's gonna bring the two big oxen to pull the logs outta the forest and load 'em on the wagon."

Obadiah asked, "Can I help him?"

"Don't rightly know, but you kin ask." Mark shifted slightly to watch his brothers sharpening the axes fetched from under the wagon seat.

A short distance off—in second-growth stands near the edge of a previously cleared forest—ruffed grouse drummed. A harness squeaked and rattled as a lead horse shook off the first of the pestering flies emerging in the warming morning.

Abner watched the horses tails switching. "Reckon the female flies are feeding."

"How'd you know they be females?" Josiah's second son, Jobe, asked.

"Learned about horseflies in a college science class," Abner said. "The males lack biting mouthparts."

Josiah smiled, "I'm glad the good Lord sent you and Mary to us, even with your rather unorthodox sermon delivery and unusual science knowledge." Josiah slapped Abner on the back. "You're becoming family here in Franklin County, Abner."

"Thank you, Josiah." Each passing week Abner and Josiah became more comfortable with each other's style, teaching and preaching the Reformed Church liturgy. "Your wife ... Rebecca ... has been a wonderful help."

Esau motioned for his brother, the two pastors, and the Heidt boys to follow him. He stopped a few feet into the forest and surveyed the trees marked for clearing. "That big hickory goes first. We'll fell the trees along the line we marked," he said to the older men and his brother, "and the boys can do the limbing."

Matthew stepped up to the hickory, propped his second ax against a maple tree, and began the laborious chopping to fell the big tree. Esau began chopping on a white ash. The harvested timber would make for good use on the farms, church, and parsonage. The ringing axes carried through the morning. Calvin's boys planned on a modified domino harvest to speed clearing. The big hickory would fall first. Esau and Matthew made the wedge cut so the hickory tree would crash into the white ash, which, in turn, would fall on the trees Abner and Josiah had made wedge cuts.

The Deirks boys made the wedge cut on the final large tree in the line. After finishing the cuts on all five trees the boys returned to the hickory. They chopped the back cut, making the hickory the first domino to fall. If Esau calculated correctly it would drop the next tree, the ash, and all five trees would be down in several minutes. When the creaking and cracking of the falling trees stopped, and the timber rested on the forest floor, Josiah, his boys, and Abner began the limbing task. The youngest boys chopped and hauled off the smallest limbs.

A sideboard wagon stood ready to haul the larger limbs to Mercersburg for use in furniture construction, after drying. Carter Kranz, the blacksmith, employed Abram Schneider, an expert woodworker, to manage this part of his business. From the limbs harvest today, the talented carpenter would select only the best for his furniture orders.

Sweat poured off the men and boys as they worked into mid-afternoon. Calvin arrived with food prepared by his wife and a neighbor's widow. They all broke for lunch, looking forward to the rest.

"Father," Mark Deirks said, "I'll drive the rig down the lane to the trees that need loading." The young boy untied the reins and moved the log wagon down the trail. "Save me something to eat."

"The boys had felled trees several months back and piled all the slash for burning, as soon as we get favorable weather." Calvin carried a large basket to the shade of a basswood tree and handed out food and tin cups. Rebecca Heidt, Calvin's wife, had prepared a hearty stew and brewed coffee and tea for the day. "Abby Holtz made the biscuits. Best cook in the area."

"Yeah, so good Dad might want to add her to his list of sweeteners." Matthew grinned at his father.

Calvin scowled.

Matthew ignored his father's icy stare.

Josiah said, "Let's bless this food by having a short prayer."

The tense moment between father and son passed after the prayer.

"The oak you wanted is down the lane, Reverend Hayman. A proper log that'll make excellent furniture, including a rocking chair and crib," Calvin said over his tin plate full of stew and biscuits.

Chapter 3

Mary sat quietly while the baby moved within her. The sunlight inched from her left to right through the open cabin door and the single window. Her mind drifted, like the sun crossing the room, slowly and with warmth. She thought about her marriage to Abner at the seminary chapel.

Her parents, being of fine upbringing, had not approved her marriage to Abner Hayman, but acquiesced to her desire. Father Hilmar, as Mary called him, intimately involved with the banking community, played a major role in Philadelphia's rise to prominence by 1800. Hilmar Schmidt commanded the respect of the banking community with his genius and charm.

It was Hilmar's second wife who gave birth to Mary in 1808. The small girl inherited the beauty of her mother—blond hair, striking blue eyes, and a shapely figure. As Mary grew into maturity, many of Philadelphia's finest sons courted her. But she had other plans. Mary wanted a man with high intellect and the drive to succeed. While attending her final year at a preparatory school in New Jersey she met Abner Hayman. She fell in love with him and his suave manner, and his confidence of knowing what he wanted in life. Father Hilmar, an agnostic, had no concern about the religion, but her mother was a different story because she came from a staunch Catholic upbringing.

A hard kick snapped Mary from her daydreaming. Being a petite person, the weight of the baby created onsets of backaches and she easily tired while doing daily chores. A small smile formed as she remembered what her mother said, "Mary, a man loves eating good food and making love." She did not fail Abner.

"Mary," the voice announced, "are you ready for a walk?" Rebecca Heidt's handsome face appeared in the window.

"Yes. Please come in, Rebecca," Mary said.

The two women became close friends over the past four months when Rebecca learned there would be a Hayman child in the cabin. They visited many times over the past month about birth and attention to child rearing under difficult conditions of living in a rural area.

Rebecca stepped into the quiet of the small cabin. She always liked to visit Mary, admiring furniture Abner crafted and the furniture pieces Mary's parents brought with them on their visits.

"Oh my, what a lovely table and chair set. Did Abner make it?"

"He did. I'm amazed at his woodcraft." Mary pulled a chair away from the walnut table. "Have a seat while I find my walking moccasins."

Rebecca raised her eyebrows. "Where did you get moccasins?"

Mary chuckled. "Abner got them from the blacksmith in Mercersburg." She then groaned. "Ouch … that hurt."

"Baby gave you a healthy kick?"

"Yes, he or she, did." Mary arched her back and studied Rebecca. "Did you have high activity from your children?"

Rebecca snorted, "Before and to the present."

Both women laughed.

"To answer your question, Rebecca, the moccasins were a gift from Carter Kranz. He got them as payment for his services from a cook-wagon man accompanying one of the pack trains working between Philadelphia and areas west of Mercersburg. The cook got them from an explorer passing through the land of tall grasses—wherever that is."

Mary picked up one of the ornately-beaded, hard-sole moccasins.

"My, my … they are interesting. Made by the … savages you say?"

Mary flinched at the derogatory statement. "The Indian tribe … I don't know which," Mary said, surprised by Rebecca's word choice.

"I mean no disrespect, but you know … they don't believe in God."

"Feel the softness of the leather," Mary said.

Rebecca rubbed the side of a new moccasin against her tanned cheek. "My, they're so soft, Mary. How'd they do this?"

"No idea. Come let's walk." She slipped on the moccasins.

The Hayman cabin sat upslope, a half mile from the main trail leading to the mountain gap. Pack trains moved over the road every day of the month, weather permitting. Rebecca talked while they walked. "The pack trains are more numerous and longer. At least it seems like that." Rebecca watched the dust rising in the distance. "Do you ever wonder what it's like beyond the west mountain range?"

"No, but I think Abner does."

"We hope you'll stay as part of our ministry."

"Thank you, Rebecca. Abner's learned a great deal from Josiah. Your husband's a kind man." No acknowledgment came from Rebecca. "I don't know if Abner will want his own church, but I do hope our child can grow up in this beautiful valley."

Chapter 4

The polished, oak cradle gleamed in the dim morning light. Abner rolled over and hugged his wife. The summer had become a fleeting memory. Any day now Mary would give birth to their first child. He placed his hand on her abdomen and felt the small bumps against the distended muscular wall separating the child from the world Abner had come to love. The first signs of fall appeared in the valley resplendent with the mountain forest displaying yellows, reds, and purples above the drying cropland of tan and yellow-brown colors.

"Mary, you're feeling okay?"

"No, I think I swallowed a watermelon seed and it's still growing inside me." She giggled. "I'm fine. Maybe a little late with the birth, but you were so active last winter I don't know when conception happened." She groaned.

"Are you sure you're okay?"

"If you keep doting on me I'll probably become ill."

He laughed. "Okay, okay."

"You're not preparing your sermon for this morning?"

"I did it last night after you fell asleep," he said.

"How did I get to bed?"

"I carried you."

"No."

"Yes, I did. You are a mite heavy, but I persevered."

She elbowed him. "Abner—"

"Yes," he interrupted.

"I love you."

He sighed, "I'm fortunate to have such a wonderful wife."

Josiah cast his eyes on the surprised and worried faces. The church members expected Abner to preach this Sunday. "Don't look so downtrodden this morning. I'm standing in for Reverend Hayman for he is the proud father of a healthy baby boy."

A small chatter filled the expanded church, which was full, and turned into a rousing applause.

"What's the boy's name, Reverend Heidt?" a voice called from the elder's pew.

"Jeremiah Isaiah Hayman," Pastor Josiah replied. "Mrs. Heidt helps Mary and the baby while Pastor Abner gets his wits about him."

A quiet applause began and turned into a tumultuous handclapping before it reached the pulpit. Josiah warmly smiled and began clapping with the congregation.

Calvin Deirks turned to the elder seated next to him. "I do believe our senior pastor has learned from his young associate."

The first snow descended on the valley much earlier than usual for southern Pennsylvania. The pack trains two weeks earlier had churned up tons of dust along the trail, filling nearby cabins with an earthy smell. Even though the snow came early, the area people welcomed the moisture that settled the dust after the abnormally dry fall in the picturesque mountain country.

Abner sat reading his notes for the coming Sunday sermon. His left foot kept a steady rhythm, following his wife's pleasing humming. He peered at his soundly sleeping baby son. Abner glanced at his wife, rapidly regaining her normal figure. The last Saturday of October snow rode in with the southeast wind. The moist air bade nothing but bad news for the farmers who neglected their harvest, celebrating at taverns in Mercersburg and along Cove Trail.

"Abner, no one will be in church tomorrow. Why bother?"

"God will be there. I must prepare for those few who might come, so not to disappoint them."

His son neared six weeks of age, a healthy lad loved by both parents. By Christmas, Jeremiah would be past the age of three months. Abner looked forward to spring when he could walk in the woods, carrying Jeremiah and pointing out the wonders of nature. He watched his wife prepare the evening meal of grouse, potatoes, and the delicious bread Abby Holtz had taught her to bake. A chuckle escaped from between Abner's lips as he thought of the comment made by Matthew to Calvin about the sweetener. Many single men courted Abby, a fine-looking widow. Even he focused on Abby more than once during his sermons.

"Abner, what are you snickering about?" Mary asked.

"I'm thinking about Calvin's son, Matthew. Last spring, he teased his father while we ate. He made a suggestive comment about his father's attraction to Abby Holtz." Mary stared at him. "Calvin didn't like the connotation."

"Abner, Calvin's not the only one who admires Abby." Mary smiled at her husband. "I've noticed you gazing at her."

Abner sputtered, "But—"

"Come now, Abner … don't deny it. She's a lovely woman. While I was pregnant with Jeremiah I many times coveted her figure. It's only natural that men desire such a fine woman."

"Mary, you're as beautiful as she."

"Why thank you, Abner."

He nodded.

"And tonight, you will show me how much?" She smiled at him. "But only after a good night of your reading biblical passages for me and our son."

"Yes, but you must promise to sing afterward … to Jeremiah and me."

Mary wiped her hands on the towel, dropped it on the table, and sat on his lap. "Abner, I love you and our son. We have great days ahead of us."

"Here in Mercersburg?"

"Where else would we find such welcoming warmth?"

Chapter 5

Three weeks following the October snow, another storm roared in during early November, then a rapid melt and the streams ran bank full. The warming trend in the northeastern United States felt good as Abner sat aboard his buggy, maneuvering along the rutted road to Mercersburg. He had four weeks to finish the cedar chest, a surprise Christmas gift for Mary. Within the chest he would place the two wooden toys he carved for his son.

Located on the main road to Cove Gap, at the west end of Mercersburg, the Kranz & Sons Blacksmith and Wood Shop buzzed with activity. Carl had built a plank walkway with hitching posts, so customers wouldn't track mud into the shop where they worked on their projects.

Abram Schneider, the master carpenter, waited in the doorway for Abner. "Right on time, Pastor," Abram said. "Was it a rough ride?"

"Not as bad as I feared," Abner said as he stepped from the buggy.

"The brass clasps came in yesterday. The cedar chest is gonna look mighty fine." Abram raised the coffee cup to his lips and sipped. "I know Mary's going to love that chest. You do have a good touch with wood, Pastor." He stepped aside so Abner could enter.

"Thank you." Abner looked around the cozy room, the tobacco smell mingling with cedar wood.

"Pastor," Carl Kranz's booming voice came from the passageway connected to the blacksmith area, "you got an angel with you?"

Abner chuckled, "And a good morning to you, Carl."

Abram returned to his pedal lathe.

Carl took a cup from a hook near the stove, grasped the handle of the large coffee pot, and poured a cup of the dark fluid. He handed the steaming cup to Abner.

"Egg coffee, Carl?"

"None other, Preacher, you'll never have a cup in this place with grounds to foul your palate." Carl poured himself a cup.

"When am I going to get you to our church, Carl?"

"One in the family is enough. All I hear from the missus is Reverend Hayman this, and Reverend Hayman that."

"Is that impiety?" Abner chaffed.

"No, I'd swear she's in love with her wonderful minister, but she's a mite old for you. Besides you already have a fine wife."

"Carl, your wife's a wonderful person and rears good children, raising them knowing of God."

"There's good reason those kids are easy to get to church." Carl grinned at Abner. "The boys … they like the teaching your wife does in Sunday school and the girls, leastwise the eldest two, come to church to look at you. I ain't sure they hear what yer sayin', Reverend, but they do talk Bible passages with the missus, so somethin' soaked in."

"Good of you to notice the girls absorb the Lord's wisdom." Abner wiped away the sawdust created by the fine-toothed saw and blew away what remained. "Maybe there'll be a day I can get you to the church."

A raucous laugh erupted from Abram. "If the missus puts him in a casket and sees to a proper burial."

"I gotta get back to work; the forge is hot by now," Carl said. "Reverend, I have a hard time believing what ministers preach."

"It's not us, Carl, it's the Lord speaking," Abner said. "You're a good man, a good friend, and a good husband and father. God smiles on you even if you do not attend church."

"Thank, God." He smiled. "Did I really say that?" He was gone before Abner and Abram could respond.

The sigh of the plane on wood calmed Abner. A religion conversation with Carl mildly taxed his patience. He looked up to find Abram staring at him.

"Yes?" Abner asked.

"You know, Pastor Hayman, Carl is like a mule. He works hard ... but is so dad-blamed stubborn it hurts. It ain't you. You've brought him closer to God than anyone else."

Abner remained quiet, working at smoothing the cedar for lining the oak chest.

"Reverend, you've brought good and Godly teaching ... and learning to this area." Abram stopped to think about his next words. "Reverend Heidt is ... excellent, but you're the one who inspires when you preach. God's in you, no doubt. You talk to the children with love, and they know it. I hope you remain in our county."

"Thank you, Abram. You're too kind."

"My pleasure, Reverend Hayman," Abram responded.

"We hope to stay. My past eighteen months have been invigorating. Now we have a son who brings us much joy and we want to settle down."

Chapter 6

For the next few weeks, Abner helped Mary care for Jeremiah and preserve food for their pantry, and he alone chopped wood for the coming cold days. The cedar chest took one day from each week. With Abram's help, Abner would finish well before Christmas. The preaching load increased because Pastor Josiah developed a lingering cough and was slow in recovering.

The weather turned foul over the week before Christmas. Moisture fell as a mix of rain, sleet, and wet snow. Parishioners dealt with illness among their children and elderly, and faithfully slogged to church in the miserable weather.

This Sunday, Mary waited for Abner to hitch the horse to the buggy and arrange the blankets to protect Jeremiah from the damp cold.

"The Lord is testing the congregation," Abner said.

Mary held her son close. "He's testing all of us, Abner." She felt her son stir and cuddle to her bosom.

"With the Lord's blessing we've been fortunate, and so far, haven't succumbed to a cough and the illnesses surrounding us."

For the remaining ten minutes of the trip, Mary held her son tight and worried over Jeremiah catching the sickness that attacked the church members. She wanted to stay home to protect him, but knew Abner would not approve. The gray skies, intermittent rain and snow and cold temperatures grated on her normally patient self. Little Jeremiah sensed the unsettled demeanor within his mother. Mary marveled at how Abner stayed calm and held tightly to his faith.

This Sunday the congregation huddled in extra clothing against the damp cold. The well-fired stoves brought warmth, but not enough to hold their usual rapt attention. Rattling coughs sporadically distracted Abner from his sermon delivery.

"With this weather, I'm encouraged for our crop production next spring. With that positive thought, I will shorten the service by our singing one verse of each song. Please pray at home for those homebound, sick, in need of monetary help, and for the sunshine we so dearly need." Even he sighed with the reprieve of a shortened service.

Calvin Deirks was one of the ill, so his older sons helped with the elder tasks their father routinely carried out.

Before taking his place at the door, Abner spoke to Esau.

"Esau, could you help me?"

"Sure, Pastor, what do you need?"

"Please take Mary and Jeremiah to our cabin. Before you leave, ask Matthew to help damp the stoves and make sure we have enough wood for the evening service."

"Sure will, Pastor." Esau spoke to Matthew and Luke before he helped Mary and Jeremiah into the Deirks' large buggy. He bundled Mrs. Hayman and Jeremiah against the increasing cold with a blue woolen blanket.

Matthew damped the stoves.

Luke hummed quietly as he moved about. "Pastor," Luke asked, "you want all the hymnals gathered and placed to the side as usual?" He continued with Abner's nod.

At a table near the pulpit, Matthew worked with the collection plates.

It would be at least thirty minutes before Esau returned. Abner spent time checking the wood supply for the two stoves, one front, and one rear. Several elders had donated wood, stacking the cords a short distance from the church side doors. Hopefully, that supply would heat the church for the next two to three months.

Luke and Matthew carried several well-dried split logs to the back stove and placed them next to the kindling box. Luke held up two fingers indicating he would bring in two more loads. He searched for the driest wood and quickly loaded his log carrier. On his return, he found Reverend Hayman deep in prayer. As quietly as possible he placed the wood near the front stove. Someone had filled the kindling box.

Abner looked up. "Luke, where's Matthew?"

"Matt's outside covering the woodpile, and then is taking Mother home."

"Thank you, Luke. You're a great help." There was something about the boy that piqued Abner's curiosity, being very quiet for his age. "When you finish with the logs come sit and visit with me until your brother gets back."

Luke shyly finished rearranging the logs and came to sit with the pastor. "Am I in trouble, Pastor Hayman?"

"Far be it. I noticed you come to church and our house for Bible study … without fail."

Luke beamed. "I like Mary. She's kind and smart. I can understand what we're being taught."

"You mean you don't understand me or Pastor Heidt?" Abner asked with a grin when he noticed the boy's panicked face. "That's okay, Luke. That's why Mary teaches most of the Bible studies and I do the sermons."

Luke nodded. He added, "The little kids like you because you are a good man, Pastor Hayman. Like Mrs. Hayman, you're kind."

"Thank you, Luke."

The front church door swung open and Matthew signaled for his brother to come along. Abner could hear Esau's voice moments before he stepped into the church.

"Pastor, your wife, and son are home. We're going now. Your buggy is by the side of the church under as much cover as I could find."

"Thank you, Esau." The doors closed and Abner sat alone in the cooling building. No religious carvings, statues, or paintings adorned this church because of the teachings and beliefs that forbade images of any type. He sat for several more minutes deep in thought about his meeting with Samuel Carnes. What plan? Abner believed in a divine plan for all humans—he felt his unfolding—a growing membership, a growing family, and a growing personal closeness to God.

Chapter 7

Warmth spread through the cabin as Abner stoked the small stove that doubled for heating and cooking. When the Haymans first moved into the cabin, the fireplace was the only heating and cooking method. Even in the summer, there were evenings when Mary felt a chill. The woods surrounded the small cabin with just enough area for it and the barn, which housed the buggy, horse, and a small hayloft storage for the grain and hay. Surrounded by towering trees, the cabin shade was nearly continuous except in winter after the leaves fell and the sun curved along the southern sky.

Now, a year later, a stone walk led from the small roadway to the cabin. The parishioners had built an addition to the barn housing another stall, a work area for Abner's wood carving, and a large bin to store oats for the horse. Abner helped chink the cabin's north wall and install a cast iron stove, and they added a bedroom with nursery, doubling as a quiet study.

"Mary, is Jeremiah asleep?"

"I'm finishing with his feeding, why?"

"I'm returning to the church for the evening service."

"Abner, don't you think one service today is plenty?"

He thought about the question and decided to wait to answer until Jeremiah was in his cradle. A rustle of clothes, a tiny burp, and the hush of blankets signaled his son slept. No doubt Mary would ask again.

"Abner, we've had this conversation, you can cancel the service."

"You're correct, we had this conversation several times, and I always give the same answer."

She did not respond. Instead, she brought utensils from the small cupboard secured to the west wall. A large ladle followed. Mary removed the kettle lid and scooped helpings of venison stew from the bubbling pot.

They quietly ate, a mild tension filling the air.

Abner broke the silence with a prayer.

"Must you respond every time with prayer? Abner, can't we act like husband and wife rather than minister and woman?"

A small whimper came from the bedroom. Mary broke the icy stare with Abner. Her head turned toward the bedroom at the second whimper. The sudden, small cry made her quickly move from her chair.

Abner sat frozen at the table. He didn't move until he heard Mary talking to Jeremiah.

"What's wrong, Mary?"

"Abner, if I knew, I would be doing something other than rocking him."

"Will he be okay?"

She frowned and replied, "I'm not God."

Abner pivoted and left the room. He gathered his Bible, a pen, ink, and writing paper. He moved the dishes to the small basin where Mary washed the plates and utensils, and then returned to the heavy table to develop adaptations for his second sermon, this evening delivered in German.

The afternoon had an icy atmosphere. The time he spent hitching his horse to the buggy took much longer than usual for he did not want to face his wife who spent the afternoon with their son.

On arrival at the church, he found the Deirks boys had tended the stoves and placed hymnals at the end of the pew rows. Members filtered in and sat two rows back. Precisely at seven, he started the Reformed liturgy. Attendance was sparse with three pews to his left and four to his right only half-full.

The winds howled from the east-southeast, carrying with it heavy snow. Again, he cut short the service and the songs.

"Esau, how's your father?" Abner asked.

"Better, Pastor, thank you for asking," Esau said.

Luke and Esau together completed the after-service chores and hurried home. Abner bid them a safe trip and closed the church with a prayer.

At home, he found Mary seated at the table with Jeremiah in her arms.

"Abner, our son is seriously ill. I'm scared ..."

They spent the next half hour trying to decide what might help their boy.

"Fetch the doctor, Abner ... for Jeremiah ... and for me."

He hurried back to the barn, hitched the buggy to his now exhausted horse and whipped her onto the road to Mercersburg. Two doctors lived in the small, growing community. Abner stopped at the doctor Mary used for the pregnancy, although he did no real medical work. A midwife helped deliver Jeremiah. Abner rapped at the cabin door and shortly he peered at a drunk, craggy-faced man.

"Doctor, I need your immediate help."

The inebriated man squinted at him. "Get out of here, damn you. What're you doing out on a night like this?"

The cabin door slammed shut; darkness descended on Abner.

The other doctor, new in town, lived two blocks away. Abner flicked the reins against the horse's rump and the buggy plowed and swayed toward the young doctor's home. The whitewashed house loomed out of the darkness.

After waiting a minute, for an answer to his frantic knock, Abner stared at a slender male face.

"Yes?" the doctor said.

"I'm Abner Hayman. We're in immediate need of your help."

"What's the problem?"

"My wife and son are ill. I don't know what to do."

"How did you get here?"

Abner, frustration rising, said, "I'm driving my buggy. Hurry please."

The doctor looked at the beleaguered man and turned to talk to someone in the parlor.

"Give me a moment; I'll get my bag." He returned dressed in a heavy wool coat and sturdy boots. "Sir, can you bring me back?"

"I can and will do so, with God's blessing."

The wind began to whip the snow into drifts up to the buggy wheel hubs.

The doctor studied Abner. "You're the Reformed Church pastor?"

"I am," Abner said.

Chapter 8

Church bells pealed across the outskirts of Mercersburg the week following Christmas. The Zion Reformed Church congregation sat solemnly while the young pastor's tears trickled onto the small oak casket. Mary, pale and shaky, held tight to her husband's arm.

Reverend Heidt, with a tremor in his voice, spoke the words over the couple and the small box. Sobs from members overflowing the church punctuated his mournful words.

After the gray, wet weather of the past several weeks, a brilliant sun shone down on the cemetery and the burial site for the baby, Jeremiah Isaiah Hayman. The muscular Carl Kranz stood in the rear of the church, waiting to lead the mourners to the open grave. This self-proclaimed Godless man held the small casket on his shoulder as he waited for Reverend Heidt to finish the burial liturgy. After a brief moment of silence, he gently lowered the tiny Hayman casket into the open grave.

Mary, surviving the horrifying illness, needed physical support from her husband to rise from her kneeling position. No tears flowed from her eyes. She had cried herself dry over the past week. Mary stood straight, her breath rasped in the cold air, her face pallid, and of sober dignity.

Abner appeared emotionless at the cemetery, all his energy and tears spent at the church. As Reverend Heidt spoke the final burial words, Abner struggled to contain the fury rising within him. Why him? Why the innocent child? Why make Mary suffer the sickness and the loss?

The night Abner brought the young physician to the cabin he felt the morbid fear of death. The wind howled through the leafless trees, their gnarled, finger-like shadows ominously adding to the eerie, snow-ridden environment. The doctor called the sickness the "strangling angel of children." The young man worked feverishly over the child. Abner plainly remembered the physician's head shake and a tear inch down his face. He pronounced Jeremiah dead at daybreak.

The storm had subsided and the snow blanket sparkled under a blue sky. A ray of light shimmered off the small, white sheet, covering her son from head to toe. Mary's pleading eyes watched the young doctor depart with Abner, her physical strength and faithfully tested.

Ten days after the funeral, Mary's father loaded his large, ornate, carriage to take her to Philadelphia for an extended recuperation. The medical community, much larger there, would provide the care Mary needed to ensure her recovery.

"Abner," Mary said, "I want you to know I will return, but not until I have wrestled with my illness and thoughts. When I do return, I shall explain how I feel and what I see as our future." She coolly bade Abner a farewell and disappeared into the carriage.

Reverend Heidt met with Abner the day following the departure. "Abner, I'm sorry about you being alone. Rebecca told me of Mary's disappointment with the tragic events."

Abner stoically sat in his cabin, his eyes focusing on nothing. The Bible lay closed on the table, as it had for the past ten days. He had not preached a sermon since the last Sunday evening in December.

Josiah studied Abner for several minutes. "Abner, where's your faith? Where's your strength?"

Abner blinked, but did not move or respond.

"To the parishioners you've preached strength in the face of misfortune," Josiah said, "now you must do what you preached."

"Josiah," Abner said, "my son died, my wife has left this household, I'm unsure of my own faith, why should I—"

"Abner, you're feeling pity only for you. Do you not believe as you have preached; that is, destiny?"

Moisture filled Abner's eyes, "Why?"

Josiah felt his pain, trying not to allow it to overwhelm him. "Strength is in the Lord, Abner." He waited. No response came. "I'll not give up on you, nor will the Lord. I want you, and the congregation wants you, to resume your powerful ministry. Don't let me down, don't let them down, and most importantly don't let Him down." Josiah stood, placed a hand on the Bible at the edge of the table, and walked out.

The next morning Abner saddled his horse and rode west through the Gap. He found an isolated spot near a small spring bubbling from the mountainside. It flowed clear—cold to the touch—destined to become a lifeless, frozen creek. The sun played across the forest until dipping behind the west mountain range. He did not move. The air chilled and he sat, allowing the cold to penetrate bone-deep.

Then a vision of death became one of life as the moon crept heavenward. An owl swooped over his head and into the lifeless, deciduous tree branch directly above his head. He stared up at the large, horned owl peering down on him.

Abner violently shuddered. A moment later he emerged from his transfixed state, feeling a strange tug at his inner being, pulling him back toward Mercersburg.

Chapter 9

Nearly a month had elapsed since Mary returned to Philadelphia with her father. No news came from her or her family. Abner expressed his thoughts in a letter sent to the address of Hilmar Schmidt. The letter went unanswered. Whether Mary ever received the letter he did not know. Since her departure, Abner showed signs of weight loss, his cleric collar appearing loose and his black wool pants and coat hanging off his thin frame.

In the congregation, the first Sunday of Lent, Abby Holtz sat in the spot Mary occupied. She smiled up at him as he started the service. She had lost her husband nearly two years before, and many single men in the community of Mercersburg courted her. Several times over the past year the dry goods clerk, who recently moved to the community, escorted her to town events. Hushed rumors of Abby having designs on Pastor Hayman, after she lost interest in the clerk, swept through the church circles.

Abner looked over the congregation as he welcomed the nearly full church. As usual, all the men sat to his left, the women to his right, and the children fidgeted in the rear pews. A small smile spread across his lips when he saw Carl Kranz seated in the next-to-last pew. His eyes locked with Carl's, an amused expression covered the blacksmith's square face.

Josiah, now at full strength, wanted to conduct communion this First Lenten Sunday. Carl, not being a member, could not take communion from the senior pastor, but Abner vowed to personally bless his friend after the service.

Rebecca sat in her usual spot on the women's side of the church. She smiled at Abner as his eyes passed over her. He smiled back and continued, making eye contact with the parishioners. Rebecca watched Abby, sitting in front and to her left, noting the slight nod when Abner's eyes fell on the attractive woman. Rebecca knew she must talk to Josiah.

When Abby moved to the altar, Abner placed the bread in her hand. She stood with her head bowed, not looking at him. Josiah passed the group cup from one communicant to the next. A deacon wiped and turned the cup between sips. As Abner waited he felt a twinge while he watched them drink. Was it possible Mary's disease came through common cup sharing? Did she have the disease and pass it on to their son?

The service moved smoothly and speedily on the first warm Sunday in a long while. Josiah stood at the church door bidding good day on one side. Abner stood opposite, greeting and visiting with many of the young church members.

Abby waited at the end of Abner's parishioner line to visit with him. "Pastor, I noticed some curious looks when I sat in Mary's seat. I apologize. I wanted to talk with you today." She said.

"Abby, is something wrong?"

"Yes and no. I am concerned for your health. You're losing weight and your color is sallow." Her smile disappeared with his look of mild anguish. "Would you mind if I cooked some evening meals for you?"

"Well ..."

She again smiled at him. "I promise not to distract you from your love for Mary."

Abner stood silent for a few seconds. "I would like that ... and I promise not to stray from the teaching and preaching of the Lord."

"Thank you, Abner. As tomorrow is your usual day off, may I come for an afternoon walk, and talk, and a meal?"

"Please do." He held her hand a tick longer than normal. "Thank you, Abby."

Josiah and the two deacons cleaned the church in Mary's absence. The Deirks boys, who spent weeks recovering from the ailment that spread through their family, again assisted their father.

"Abner, may I speak with you a moment?" Josiah said.

"Surely," Abner said. He gave his stack of hymnals to the youngest deacon.

They walked to the front of the church and stood near the stove. "I want to ask if you and Abby are—"

"Josiah, she stopped to ask about my health and if she might stop with food several evenings a week."

"You do not receive food from other members?" Josiah frowned.

"I do, but I must warm the food myself and many times I forget to do so and fail to eat it, and it spoils."

"You know there will be talk with Abby's attention toward you."

Abner studied his senior pastor's face. "I trust her and I trust myself. God knows I will be faithful to my wife."

"I know you're strong, Abner, but ..."

"I will not succumb, Josiah," Abner said with a chuckle.

"But ... will she behave? Abby is a wonderful woman in looks and attitude and the ... uh ... the temptation might be too great." He stopped to find the right words. "I don't want to see either of you hurt. I want you to stay with me until I retire."

The words caught Abner off guard. He quietly spoke, "I promise you, and God."

Chapter 10

Rumors turned to heated talk when the congregation discovered Abby cooked for Abner and took long walks in the woods with him.

The weeks passed rapidly and still no reply to his letter. Abby was a Godsend. She helped him with wash, taught him how to cook, did the garden clearing and planting, worked the horse once a day, and walked daily with him.

"Abner, have you written your wife?"

He remained silent.

"Abner, are you listening?"

"I am."

"Well?"

"Abby, I cannot thank you enough." He stopped on the trail into the woods and turned to her. "Why do you ask me about my writing?"

"You are the husband. Why didn't you initiate contact?"

"I did, and no reply came."

"Abner, did you ever think the letter might not have gotten to her? Or maybe her father intercepted it? Or the reply lost?"

"No, I did not. Well … a bit."

Abby looked at this intelligent man and said, "You are a good man, do not take offense at what I am going to say." She waited for a retort. None came. "Abner, you have a woman who cares dearly about you, and will be good for your future."

He took her hands in his. "Abby, if I were a single man I would propose to you right now. Josiah warned me about my feelings."

"Shush, I do not wish to hear this. Mary and I are friends and hope to remain so."

"You talk as if she will return."

"I received this, this morning." Abby withdrew an envelope from her dress pocket and handed it to him.

He carefully opened it.

Dearest Abby,

I am writing to ask if you have talked to Abner. There has been no contact from him since I left the cabin with my father.

I am doing fine and regaining strength every day. As I have had no contact from Abner I am assuming he does not know I exist. I want to return to our home and to the Mercersburg area to rejoin my husband. If you see him, please let me know how he is doing.

Sincerely,

Mary Hayman

Abby waited and watched Abner as he stared into the forest tangle, lining the walking path. "Now you know why I asked you if you wrote. Something happened to your letter."

"I wrote it in the care of her father."

"Don't misread that. Perhaps someone lost … or even absentmindedly discarded it." She sighed. "Abner, do me a favor, please. Sit down and write her after we get back to the cabin. Do it every day if you love her … plead for her to come back."

The candle, flame flickering in the cabin draft, sat to his left. A paper lay in front of him, a pen squarely in the middle. He thought of Mary, of Abby, of Josiah and Rebecca, and of Carl Kranz. Abner rose from his chair and took a cup from the hook near the stove. Abby had encouraged him to drink tea for the relaxing effects. The jar of tea leaves and a strainer sat nearby. He placed the small strainer over the cup, added leaves and slowly poured the hot water.

Abner sat watching the small, dancing shadows cast by the flickering candle. The only sounds were the wind around the cabin and mice scurrying about below the floor planks. Periodically a loud pop and crackle came from the stove and the burning wood would settle. He had never felt so alone. His son now at rest and his wife gone to Philadelphia to wrestle with her health and feelings made him question his ministry.

He opened his Bible to Philippians 4:13 and read out loud, "I can do all things through Christ which strengtheneth me." He sat for a moment and turned to Ephesians 5:25 and again read to the cabin quiet, "Husbands, love your wives, even as Christ also loved the church, and gave himself for it."

He gently closed the worn Bible and began to write.

Chapter 11

Soft, plodding hoofbeats and wagon wheel squeaks interrupted his sermon preparation for Ascension Sunday. Abner rose from the table and peered out the south cabin window at the bulky wagon driven by a bearded, disheveled man. Next to him sat a small person covered in a blanket, the face shaded by a floppy hat. The wagoner reined in the horses after circling the freighter so the passenger side faced the cabin. His long, canvas coat fluttered as he scrambled from his perch and disappeared. A moment later he reappeared with a valise in his left hand and held out his arm to help the passenger climb off the large seat.

The floppy hat slipped back and dropped to her shoulders. The wagoner took Mary's hand and led her to the cabin.

Abner stood transfixed at the sight of his wife. She smiled at the driver when he said something to her. Her laughter filled his ears like the soothing call of a mourning dove. Mary smiled at Abner, and he silently thanked God.

She came into his open arms. "Abner," she quietly said, "it's good to be with you again."

Shuffling feet broke the moment. "This is Oliver ..."

"Reverend Hayman, good to meet ya."

Abner took the man's hand and firmly shook it. "Do you have a last name?"

Oliver shook his head. "It's just, Oliver, sir." He bowed ever so slightly. "It were my pleasure gettin' to know ya, ma'am." He turned back to Abner. "You be a lucky man, Reverend." He turned and hustled to the wagon, climbed to the seat, and snapped the reins. The draft horses lumbered down the lane. The reins snapped lightly on the animal backs as they turned onto the road.

Mary followed Abner into the cabin and surveyed the neat, orderly cabin interior. "Abby must have taught you well while I was away." She smiled at him. "She wrote me after you sent what seemed like a hundred letters."

"I didn't mean to overwhelm you with my letter writing."

"Abner, I have saved them all and reread them many times. I love every word, especially the poems." She kissed him. "I need to rest; do you mind?"

"Not at all," he said. "What route did you take from Philadelphia?"

"I traveled by stage to Chambersburg and then by the heavy wagon to here." She sighed, "It was sixteen, bumpy hours by stagecoach and after a restless night at a fine Inn, four hours from there."

"Did Hilmar pay for the trip?"

"He did … reluctantly." She frowned, the crows-feet at her eye corners had deepened. "He didn't want me to come back. He pleaded for me to return, and not stay here."

Abner didn't ask if it to be with or without him.

"I'll not return. Father Hilmar showed his true colors while I recuperated."

He started to ask a question.

"Abner, I don't want to explain. I want you to hold me after I've rested."

He helped her with the small traveling case, turning down the bed while she removed her travel garments.

Two hours later, Abner prepared fresh trout caught in the clear stream near the cabin. Potatoes baked in the stove coals and carrots brightened over water vapor. Abby had taught him so much while Mary was away. He now felt the urge to pray his thanks to God for the divine blessings placed on him.

"Abner, it smells so good. What is it?" A smile formed when she appeared in the main cabin room.

"I've prepared fresh-caught trout, baked potatoes, and carrots."

"Abby taught you to cook and …?"

"Oh my, yes, she taught me … to repair rips in my clothes—" He looked at her. "Mary, I love you. I would not stray from you or our God."

"Abner … I want us to have another child."

Chapter 12

Ascension Sunday inspired all members of the Reformed Church. Abner stood in front of the pulpit as he greeted the congregation. He motioned for Mary to stand. "I welcome back my wife, Mary. It is God's blessing she lives and thrives."

Carl Kranz loudly uttered, "Amen," from the rear of the men's side of the church.

"Thank you. Carl," Abner said. Carl's wife giggled from her seat in the pew across from her husband. "Abby, please stand." A quiet murmur rippled through the church. "God surprises us in so many ways with his kindness and his ways of delivering it."

"Amen," a deep voice came from near the church near the doors. Several people turned to see who uttered the word.

"Thank you, Samuel Carnes, and welcome back." Abner watched Samuel move to the spot he had occupied last year, always next to Mr. Dressler. The men slid toward center aisle to make room for him. Arthur Dressler shook Samuel's hand as he sat.

Abner continued. "Abby Holtz for me was a Godsend. She helped me and Mary through a traumatic time. Those of you who have lost a child know what I'm talking about." He stopped and looked over the congregation. "I learned to cook, wash, sew, and how to look at my inner self. She's an angel sent by God. Thank you very much, Abby."

Mary turned and hugged her friend.

"Also, to all who helped me through that very difficult time, God bless you." Abner turned and walked to the pulpit.

After the normal liturgy for this day he paused before the sermon and said, "I am starting the sermon with a reading from the Gospel of John."

He read, "But Thomas, one of the twelve, called Didymus, was not with them when Jesus came. The other disciples therefore said unto him, we have seen the LORD. But he said unto them, except I shall see in his hands the print of the nails, and put my finger into the print of the nails, and thrust my hand into his side, I will not believe. And after eight days again his disciples were within, and Thomas with them: then came Jesus, the doors being shut, and stood in the midst, and said, Peace be unto you. Then saith He to Thomas, Reach hither thy finger, and behold my hands; and reach hither thy hand, and thrust it into my side: and be not faithless, but believing. And Thomas answered and said unto him, My LORD and my God. Jesus saith unto him, Thomas, because thou hast seen Me, thou hast believed: blessed are they that have not seen, and yet have believed."

Abner looked over at Josiah. "Josiah came to me with his recent concerns, but he came openly. I say to you, who doubt, reflect on the passage I have read." With that said, he continued.

Samuel Carnes inquisitively looked at Arthur. The little man leaned over and said, "Mr. Carnes, I'll explain to you after the service." Art was one of the true Christians in the congregation, scorning rumors and vile talk.

Rebecca approached Mary and Abby. She first hugged Mary and then Abby. "Mary," Rebecca said, "it's wonderful to see you in church. And, Abby, you're to be commended for helping Abner through his sorrows." Rebecca glanced over Mary's shoulder at the tall, handsome man talking to Arthur Dressler.

Samuel noticed Rebecca's glance. "Excuse me, Mr. Dressler; I want to speak with the pastors' wives before they busy themselves with their morning duties."

Arthur grinned at Samuel and said, "That Abby is one fine woman. She would make a good catch for any man."

"You read me perfectly, Arthur." He shook hands with this delightful individual who possessed great knowledge of the area.

Abby admired the man speaking with Arthur. The dark hair with the neatly trimmed sideburns highlighted on the clean-shaved rectangular face with a strong jawline made her ask, "Mary, do you know Mr. Carnes?"

"Not really, he stopped and chatted for a bit after Abner announced my pregnancy."

"Mary, Mrs. Heidt, and …"

Mary said, "This is Abby Holtz, Mr. Carnes."

Samuel bowed slightly. "It's my pleasure, Mrs. Holtz." He took her hand and held it for a brief moment then turned to Mary. "I'd like to invite you and your husband for a meal at the Mercersburg Inn this evening. Abby, you and Pastor and Mrs. Heidt are most welcome."

"Thank you, Mr. Carnes, but Reverend Heidt and I have prior plans." Rebecca shook his hand and caught up with Josiah.

"Please join us, Abby," Mary said.

Abby thought for a moment and said, "I'm delighted. While the men talk, we can catch up on the past few weeks."

Abner finished visiting with a recently widowed woman from north of Mercersburg and joined his wife. "Welcome, Samuel. You've met Abby?"

"I have," Samuel said, "and with pleasure. Mary and Abby agreed to join me for dinner after your evening service. Would you care to join the three of us?"

Mary's laughter filled the church. The elders and deacons turned to look at the foursome. A deacon frowned at laughter in the church.

"Sorry, Abner, I might've caused a problem," Samuel said.

"You've provided me with a delightful moment. Mary's laugh is a refreshing sound." Abner grinned. "I'll be happy to join you, sir."

Samuel hugged Mary. "I'm sorry about your son. The positive is you live to bear another child or more." He smiled at Abner.

Abner's nostrils flared as he quietly inhaled.

Chapter 13

Two hotels built the past two years provided the respite needed after long days travel from the east of Pennsylvania. Based on Mr. Dressler's recommendation, Samuel selected the Mercersburg Inn located a block off the main road. It housed a drinking room of fine style and a dining room with a formal seating. The other hotel had been his first choice, but it mainly catered to male wants.

"Thank you, Samuel," Abby said as she stepped from the buggy he rented from the livery.

"Mary, be careful of the step. It's not in the best shape," Samuel said as he helped her from her side of the buggy. A boy in his early teens drove the buggy to the hitching area as they walked into the hotel lobby.

Abby asked, "Is this like Philadelphia hotels, Mary?"

"No, but it's a nice start." Mary turned to Samuel. "Mr. Carnes, the other must be much less expensive."

"Oh, it is, but ..." A mischievous smile inched across his handsome face. "You might not approve of the behavior in the other."

"Would you, Samuel?" Abby asked.

"Why, do you think I am a man of loose morals?"

"Not at all, but you look like a gambling man."

"It's that obvious?" He helped her with the chair and Mary with hers. "My," he said as he sat next to Abby, "you are astute. I do like to gamble, but not just for fun. My work requires taking chances on land and people."

"Mr. Carnes, what do you do?" Mary said.

"I cannot remember if I told Abner, but I'll tell you both ... I deal in land purchasing and sales ... and transportation." He briefly watched a couple across the room engaged in a lively conversation. "For example, the man and woman across the way might want to sell their land they bought some time ago. I would deal with them for the sale." He paused to sip his coffee. "The man I work for has much money and wants to expand his holdings.

"My work for him will end. I'll be managing the government land office in western Ohio to sell federal land."

"There are buyers after the 1819 crisis?" Mary asked.

Samuel sat back. "Mary, you know of the crisis problems?"

"I do, for my father's a banker in Philadelphia."

"What's his name?" Samuel asked.

"Hilmar Schmidt."

Samuel Carnes leaned back. "Hilmar Schmidt, the banker of bankers?"

"Yes," Mary said and turned to look at Abby. "And, Abby, he's the reason I left ... and returned."

Abby studied this fine-boned woman. She had wondered at Mary's refined nature. "Please explain what you mean by the reason you left and returned."

"My father's a demanding person and likes having his way. He did not want me to marry Abner and did not approve of the wedding." Mary toyed with the tablecloth edge. "He's a take-charge person and is hard to deal with. I became so distraught with Jeremiah's death I didn't have the energy to object when he took me to Philadelphia."

Abby said, "Where was Abner in all this turmoil?"

"I don't know. We had a disagreement and we weren't on the best of terms at the time."

"I'm sorry," Abby softly said.

Samuel sat quietly.

"Don't be, Abby, for I realized I wanted to be with Abner."

"May I ask a question, Mary?"

She nodded.

"Do you want to stay here?" Samuel asked.

"A fair question ..." She watched Abner enter the dining room and stop to chat with several church members who arrived before him. "It's lovely here, but it holds much sorrow."

Samuel stood when Abner came to the table.

"Please, Samuel," Abner motioned for him to sit, "it's not necessary to stand in my presence."

"It's a habit, Reverend."

"Abby, you're especially lovely tonight." Abner sat and placed a hand on Mary's shoulder. "It's wonderful to have Mary back and a thank you is due Samuel for inviting us." He smiled. "I shall have the roast quail and special vegetables at this fine place as Samuel is the buyer."

"Aha, a minister with a sense of humor; I like that." Samuel waved to the server he was ready to order.

The server apprehensively approached with a troubled look. She appraised the foursome and recognized one man as the pastor at the Reformed Church near Mercersburg. Samuel offered to order for the group and asked the young woman to place the bill on his hotel tab.

"What caused her hesitancy?" Abby asked.

"Many hotels or inns or taverns do not allow women in the same dining area. They serve them separately." He shook his head, showing his disagreement.

"Do you travel?" Mary asked.

"I do and I'm fortunate, for I recently spent two months in Europe, dealing with several countries wondering about our country beyond the Mississippi River." He took a small map from his vest-pocket and passed it to Mary. "This is a land of opportunity and we have a wonderful future before us if we don't fear our shadows."

Abner questioningly looked at Samuel.

"Many of us will not have a chance to explore and strike out on new paths." He turned to Abby. "Abby, you asked if I like to gamble. Moving out of comfortable surroundings is taking a gamble, especially in this growing and unknown land. Much awaits discovery." He waited until the server placed the food at table center and her assistant placed bowls, plates, and silverware in front of them. "The land is still wild to the west of Ohio, Indiana became a state a little over a decade ago, and more recently Illinois and Missouri joined the Union."

Mary appeared highly interested, Abner somewhat curious, and Abby looked at Samuel with admiration.

"Let's eat while the food is hot," Samuel said. "Reverend Hayman, will you bless this food?"

"Gladly," Abner said, "and ask the Lord's guidance for all of us; you, Abby, and especially my wife." He folded his hands and bowed his head. Samuel took Abby's hand.

Chapter 14

Abner and Mary rode to the cabin from Mercersburg as the sky paled to a golden glow on the pleasant spring evening, and dark shadows played across the road, causing the horse to step carefully.

Darkness descended on their home while Abner stored the buggy and fed the horse. He felt good about the meal and the conversation, but wondered at Samuel's bringing up new land exploration.

After settling down for the evening, Mary quietly said, "Abner, you and I are comfortable with everything except for the sorrow of losing Jeremiah. We have a good home, the church members respect you, and Rebecca and Josiah want us to stay so you can step in when Josiah retires. And, I'm out of my father's clutches in this scenic valley."

Abner put down the candleholder. "What do you mean, your father's clutches?"

"The time I spent with him was uncomfortable. He wanted to order my life, to make me his little girl again." Mary continued, "He has an abusive behavior." She noticed Abner stiffen. "I don't mean physically. Hilmar—father—likes to think for those people around him."

"Something troubles you, Mary." Outside, the pitch dark enveloped the Hayman cabin and barn. "What is it?"

Mary shook her head. "I'm not sure. It's something Samuel said tonight."

He walked to her and put his arms around her waist. "Welcome, home, Mary." Abner lit a candle and walked out to check on noises in the darkness.

"Oh, Abner, I love you," she said to the closed door. The candlelight passed the window. Mary prepared herself for bed then sat staring at the small rocking cradle. "Dear, God, please show us the way. Do we belong here?" Tears trickled from her eyes. Her sobs echoed in the room.

When Abner returned to the dining area he was surprised not to find Mary. He had thought she would be reading and they might talk more of her Philadelphia experience.

"Abner, are you coming to bed?"

"Soon, Mary, after I do some reading."

He heard her sigh. The rustle of the bed covers made him uncomfortable. Five minutes later her arms circled his shoulders as he leaned over his Bible. She softly said, "Lo, children are a heritage of the LORD: and the fruit of the womb is his reward." Her hair tumbled over his shoulders.

"Psalm 127, verse three to five," Abner whispered.

"Come to bed, Abner." She took his hand and led him into the other room.

The sunlight filtered through the open door to the dining area. Abner turned to his wife and said, "Shall I make some breakfast?"

"That would be delightful, Abner. I didn't imagine you to cook.'

"Abby taught me many things."

Mary sat up and looked down at him. A grin covered his whiskered face. "Be careful what you think."

"Abner, you offered up the leading sentence."

"Mary, I could never be unfaithful. I couldn't forgive myself, nor would, God."

She leaned down and kissed him. "Are you serving breakfast in bed?"

"Preparing the meal is enough. I don't want to spoil you."

She gave him a pouty look. "Off with you. What's for breakfast?"

"A surprise waits after you dress." Abner pulled on his trousers and boots. He slipped into the shirt hanging on the peg beside the bed.

An hour later, Mary came from the bedroom. She watched as he busied himself with breakfast preparation.

He bowed and extended a hand toward her chair. From a pot on the stovetop, he ladled mush into the bowls containing fresh berries.

"And Abby taught you this? Did she stay over and get up to teach you?"

"Mary, what did I say earlier?"

"I apologize, Abner."

"She's good with horses. Abby would ride over early and teach me how to prepare breakfast before we walked in the woods."

"And you wonder why people doubted you?"

He flushed. "I never thought of it that way. It was all innocent."

"You never felt something for her?"

"I did. I once said something and she said you are best friends; she did not want to risk that relationship."

"Thank you."

He inquisitively looked at her. "You are welcome."

They ate quietly with little conversation. Abner had the day away from the church. He wanted to walk and finish a chair caning.

The trotting horse coming up the lane caught their attention. Abner stood and peered out. "It's Samuel."

"Greetings to you, Reverend Hayman and to you, Mary," Samuel said as he slid from the saddle. He shook hands with them. "Have you any coffee or tea?"

"Please come in, Samuel," Mary said. "We can offer you tea prepared by the pastor himself."

Samuel returned to the horse, opened one saddlebag, and from it gathered a small bag. "A special gift for both of you," he said. He handed the gift to Mary.

"Come inside, Samuel." Abner motioned toward the cabin and said, "What brings you our way?"

"I," Samuel began, "hope you seriously think about what I'm proposing." He waited while Abner sipped the tea. "I would like you to start a church in western Ohio."

Abner smiled at him. "I don't think a church can begin without administrative approval."

"I've cleared that hurdle," Samuel said.

Mary asked, "How?"

"Contacts, Mary, contacts."

Chapter 15

Abner and Mary felt the exhilarating, yet frightening, emotion as they waited for the Carnes Carrier wagon to haul their meager belongings to western Ohio. A broad-tread, four-wheel freighter drawn by four horses appeared in their lane a few minutes after Josiah and Rebecca bade them farewell.

Mary stared at the two men seated high above the horses. Both wore brimmed hats that shaded their faces. The rider stepped down from his seat and approached. "Reverend Hayman?" he asked.

"Yes, I am," Abner answered. "And this is my wife, Mary."

The wagoner removed his hat and extended his hand. "I'm Billy Williams, a pleasure to meet you. Samuel Carnes sends his greetings." He looked over his shoulder. "My assistant Johnnie and I'll load your belongings for transport to Preble County, Ohio."

"I see you're about half full." Abner watched Johnnie lead the horses to the small stream near the cabin.

"We are. If you don't fill the wagon, we'll make a stop in Cumberland to fill it up. Gotta couple who bought some land from Samuel in Darke County and they have some goods." Billy eyed the barn. "You got any hay or oats we could give our horses?"

"We do. There are oats in the barn and you're welcome to all the hay you want."

Billy waved at Johnnie and pointed to the barn.

Johnnie led the horses to the log barn. He came over after putting the hay and oats in four large wooden buckets. "Howdy, I'm Johnnie Smith." He shook hands with Abner and Mary.

"Mind your manners, Johnnie."

Johnnie shrugged and removed his hat. "Sorry folks, I forget the hat after many days on the Pike."

Billy caught the Hayman's look. "Pike's what we call the road we'll take to Ohio, at least for most of the way."

Abner helped the two men load the wagon. The time to load took fewer than ninety minutes. While Abner and Billy covered, and secured the Hayman goods, Johnnie hitched the horses and checked the wagon wheels and underpinnings.

A covered buggy swung into the lane and pulled beside the wagon. "Johnnie, Billy," the young lad addressed the two middle-aged men, "you finished?"

"Yep," Billy answered, "just ready to pull out."

"Your goods will be safe with those two. Sorry, I'm Theo, short for Theophilus, and the last name's Bachmeier." He held his short-billed cap.

Mary shook his hand. "Good biblical name to go with your German last name." She liked his pleasant smile.

"I run a buggy for Mr. Carnes between Chambersburg and Hagerstown. I'm here to be sure you're on time for the westbound stagecoach." He took their luggage pieces, tied them securely behind the passenger seat, and helped the Haymans into the seat behind him.

The sun radiated off the buggy top as it dropped south toward the Potomac River in Maryland. The land, as they neared the National Road, had recent forest clearing.

"Theo, please stop before we cross into Maryland," Mary said.

"Will do, Mrs. Hayman," Theo said, "but we can't linger too long, or the stage will leave without you."

"Not to worry, Theo, I only want to say goodbye to my home state."

"Yes ma'am, I unnerstand," Theo said, and slowed for another buggy headed north. A young woman lightly held the reins as they passed. Theo tipped a finger to his cap.

Ten minutes later he pulled into a turnout. "The state border, Mrs. Hayman," Theo said as he stepped down from his seat.

Abner and Theo held Mary's arms as she moved from the buggy.

"Thank you," Mary softly spoke. "She pushed back her bonnet. "Can I have a minute to myself?"

"Mary ...?"

"I need a moment of peace before we start a new life, Abner."

Abner and Theo watched her slowly walk up the trail, with each step the bonnet lightly swayed side-to-side behind her back. When she stopped, Mary folded her hands and looked north. Her lips silently moved. Her face rose toward the cloudless, blue sky.

Theo cleared his throat and pulled a timepiece from his vest pocket.

Mary deeply breathed the clean air and turned toward the buggy.

The Carnes buggy waited at the tavern front where the rested stagecoach horses stood waiting for the next Carnes coach. The yard bustled with the activity of wagoners checking their loads, some heading east and the others heading west.

Ten minutes after Theo arrived at the Tavern, the Carnes Stage Lines reined into the station. The driver handed the reins over to a young assistant as he stepped down. The man sitting beside the driver swung down and another boy began to unhitch the horses. It took less than ten minutes to hitch the fresh team to the wagon tongue.

"Reverend, Mrs. Hayman, Godspeed to your destination." When Theo spotted the stage driver he shook hands with Abner and Mary and wished them safe travel.

The stagecoach driver looked over the crowd inside the tavern. He spotted Abner with Theo, walked their way, nodded at the buggy driver, and stepped up to the Haymans. "Reverend Hayman?" The lean, tall driver said. When Abner nodded, he continued. "Your bags are on the stage. Are you ready? We'll arrive in Cumberland by dark." The driver extended his arm to Mary and escorted her to the coach.

The couple seated in the coach smiled and returned to visiting as Mary and Abner moved into the seat facing rearward. The Haymans didn't expect pleated, cushioned seats more comfortable than the buggy. Mary stretched her legs and Abner found room for his knees.

"Abner Hayman," he said, "and this is my wife, Mary."

"Pleasure," the young man said. "My wife, Judith, and I'm Richard Thomas. How far are you going, Reverend?"

"We're moving to Preble County, Ohio." Abner smiled at Judith.

"We're bound for southern Illinois. Do you know the stagecoach owner, Samuel Carnes?" Richard asked.

"We do, and travel at his pleasure," Mary said.

"As are we," Judith replied.

The stage jerked as the driver snapped the whip above the new team. Richard pulled a small bag from between his knees and extracted a map. He studied it a moment and handed it to Abner. "It's a little dated but should give you an idea how we'll travel. At Zanesville, we take Zane's Trace southwest to the Ohio River and west by steamboat to the Mississippi River and north to St Louis."

"Do we pass through Columbus?" Mary asked.

Richard said, "You'll travel to the town, but the Pike's under construction and it'll be slow along the surveyed construction areas."

"How many miles a day does the stage make on such a modern road?" Abner asked.

"If no delays, we should travel sixty to seventy miles." He took the map from Abner. "We've traveled from Baltimore to Hagerstown and we'll make Cumberland this evening. The plan is to stop at the Tavern where President Washington stayed on the way to his land sale."

Chapter 16

Their stage left on time from Cumberland, bound for Uniontown, Pennsylvania. The scenery along the route caught Abner and Mary's attention as well as the history discussion led by Richard. The easy trip helped the couples become familiar with one another's backgrounds and their hopes for the future. The Johnson-Hatfield Tavern had become a popular spot; they spent the evening at this quaint layover.

An acerbic religious discussion between Abner and a Catholic priest, on the approach to belief in God, marred the evening. Mary watched in amazement at the priest's challenge and Abner's stuttering response. For the first time in their marriage, someone bested Abner when discussing religion. The evening left her husband as nearly unsettled as the night Jeremiah died.

During the night, Mary woke more than once to find Abner kneeling in prayer, asking for God's help. Before breakfast he returned to his assured self, the priest's absence in the serving area softened his disposition.

Before boarding, the driver stated he would watch for Whiskey Will. This young man became famous in Pennsylvania for scurrying between the towns of Washington and Uniontown, having himself a jolly good time. His escapades along the Pike had become a routine show for the regulars hauling freight and for the short-haul wagoners—known as sharpshooters—traveling between Cumberland and Wheeling.

Midway through the trip, the assistant driver leaned down and called to the passengers, "Whiskey Will headed our way."

The four craned their heads out the side windows. The man stood on the seat, grasping the reins, and whooping at the stagecoach drivers. A bottle of whiskey protruded from his fashionable jacket, which fluttered in the breeze created by the rapid pace of the two-horse buggy.

At the next four-horse team change, Abner cornered the driver and asked, "Is that young man always on the road?"

The driver chuckled. "Not always, but more often than not."

Abner asked, "How does he support himself and his carefree habit?"

The driver shook his head. "I think it's a wealthy father." The driver scrutinized the horse team exchange. "His father's a direct competitor to Mr. Carnes. Excuse me ... I need to talk to the hitch man."

Two other stagecoaches waited for their fresh horses. At least forty wagons filled the rest area at the popular site, carrying all types of goods and supplies. Buggies from the local area added to the liveliness of a growing nation.

Inside the building, the din of conversation carried from one room to the other. The colorful garb of various regulars and sharpshooters caught the attention of the two women. And the two attractive women caught the eye of many a wagoner.

Richard entered the tavern looking for Judith when he met a young man about to intercept his wife and Mary. He stepped in front of the nattily dressed traveler and asked, "Are you going the same way as my wife?" Richard took Judith's hand.

"Excuse me, sir?" The man stared at Richard. "I wanted to inquire of the lady with your wife if she might join me for the dance tonight in Wheeling."

Richard smiled at Mary. "You best ask the Reverend, her husband."

A wash of color appeared on the lad's face. "Sorry ma'am I didn't realize you're married."

Mary held out her hand. "No offense young man." She studied his fine facial features. "I'm sure you'll have no trouble finding someone."

He grinned at her. "Thank you, ma'am, besides a dance ... there's a spelling contest at one of the taverns in town." He held out his hand to Richard. "Have a pleasant trip, all of you."

Abner heard Mary's laugh in the room to the left, entered, and had to sidestep a young man scurrying out. Mary and the Thomas couple stood laughing and animatedly talking. "A joyful gathering," Abner said, "why all the laughter?"

Judith grinned at Abner. "Mary could have had a date tonight, other than you, Abner."

"Time to board, folks," came the call from the Carnes stage driver.

Richard stopped abruptly beside a tall man and his short wife before leaving the tavern. "So, how the heck are you doing?" Richard blurted out. "This is my wife, Judith."

Abner and Mary continued to the coach where the driver helped Mary inside the recently cleaned interior. After settling into their seats, Mary looked at Abner, his color pale, a frown deepening the brow lines.

"Abner, are you sure you're not having some problems?"

At first, Mary didn't think he heard her question.

Before she could ask again he snapped at her. "I told you before, I'm doing fine."

Chapter 17

The trip to Wheeling was uneventful. Abner spent most of the time napping. Judith and Mary talked softly with Richard about the terrain west of Columbus, Ohio.

"Samuel's working in Preble and Darke Counties, which border Indiana. He's trying to sell, and open, more Congressional land to settlers." Richard studied Mary as Abner slept. "You look concerned."

"Darke County sounds rather ominous," Mary responded.

Richard chuckled. "Mary, the county name is after a General William Darke who died shortly after the turn of the century."

"What's the area like?" Mary asked.

"I only know what Samuel has sent in a letter; I have it here." He handed Mary the one-page letter.

She carefully read and reread it. "It's forested much like our Pennsylvania, but it's flat. What of these prairies and marshes in the north of Darke County?"

"Samuel's concentrating on that area; it's been devilish to sell and is going cheap," Richard said. "The low value is because the marshes sent many a settler fleeing. They lost everything trying to farm the area."

Abner stirred and turned his head away from the conversation.

"Is Abner feeling poorly?" Judith asked.

"He says no. I'm concerned about his lack of sleep," Mary said.

Richard responded, "If Abner's anything like what Samuel described he'll snap out of it. Samuel talks about your husband's strength."

The stagecoach slowed and came to stop. The voice of the driver sounded worried as he called out, "Are you okay?"

Abner came awake. "What's wrong?"

"We don't know," Richard said.

A loud moan came from outside the coach.

"Reverend Hayman, there's been a buggy accident," the assistant said as he opened the coach door. "Can you help us? I don't know if she'll live."

Abner quickly stepped outside the coach and hurried to the road edge where the buggy lay on the young woman. "This must've happened no more than a few minutes ago. Richard, come help," Abner called.

The four men quickly evaluated the accident and decided to cautiously lift the buggy off the agonized woman. Abner took charge and directed Richard to calm the horse while he and the two drivers pulled the buggy upright.

"Oh-aah," the woman moaned. "Someone help me; I'm going to die."

With the buggy off the woman, Abner knelt beside her. Softly he lifted her head to his lap. "Ma'am I'm a minister. God watches over you."

The woman groaned. "I hurt terribly where the wagon fell on my chest and legs."

"Mary, come quickly, please."

Both women moved to help Abner.

"Check if she might have ribs broken from the impact. She might have a punctured lung." He looked up at Judith and asked, "Please check her legs to see if there might be a break."

Mary and Judith began the gentle probing, taking care not to cause her pain. Relieved looks flooded their faces.

"No breaks on either leg that I can tell," Judith said.

"Her pain might be a cracked rib or separation from her breastbone," Mary offered. "She doesn't have difficulty breathing."

The driver offered a cup with some water. "This might help. I took the liberty to add some spirits."

Mary took the cup. "Thank you."

Abner raised the woman's head; his other arm curled under her back.

"Drink ... it has spirits that will help dull the pain."

The woman took a sip, coughed and took another sip. "Thank you."

"You'll live," Abner said. "God smiles on you."

"There's a doc in the village at our next stop. Roads are good all the way." The driver took the buggy reins from Richard and swung up into the seat. "I'll test the wagon. If the horse and rig are okay, I'll have my assistant drive her on ahead of us." He snapped the reins on the horse's rump and the wagon easily rose from the roadside drainage ditch. He headed the horse down the pike, turned, and came back at a healthy pace. "Henry, take her to town."

The men lifted her into the buggy seat. "I'll ride with her," Abner said.

"Thank you," the injured woman said, "… any more of that water?"

Abner smiled. "I think we can get some."

Chapter 18

Rays of light lit the room where Abner and Mary slept. The morning started cool on the late summer day in Wheeling. He woke and gently turned to his back and watched the shadows creep across the room as the yellow-white, early morning light brightened the area. It took him a minute to realize they weren't alone. Across the way, he could see movement on the curtain surrounding the bed. Then he remembered they and the Thomas couple shared the small room.

A voice called through the canvas door, "Rise and shine or you'll miss breakfast unless you don't want any. Freshly washed breakfast tables await stagecoach passengers and drivers who follow the wagoners." The female rattled the canvas and moved on to the next room. This female-run Inn proved roomier than most, and it included a breakfast for stage passengers after the freight wagoners finished and headed onto the government Pike.

A curtain separated the couples and it fluttered when someone bumped the colorful material. Judith giggled when Richard fell back onto the bed. "Nice try," she said.

Outlined by the sunlight, Mary's profile revealed a smile. She leaned close to Abner. "I want another baby, Abner, don't you?"

Abner did not respond.

"Hurry, Abner and Mary, we don't want to miss the meal before we catch the stage to Zanesville."

"Abner ..."

He sharply yanked at his vest and walked out of the small room.

A tear trickled down Mary's cheek.

Richard and Judith sat across from two men, talking and laughing. They looked up and motioned to the spot they had saved. The room was noisy with passenger chatter and stage driver stories.

The man talking to Richard swung his left leg over the bench seat and stood. His sweat-stained hat rested on his back. He stuck out his hand to Abner and said, "I'm your new driver, I go by the name Zach. The ugly guy beside me is Cyrus." Cyrus touched a finger to his brow. After shaking hands with Mary and giving her a nice smile, he sat and finished his thick slab of salt pork.

"Abner," Richard said, "We'll part ways at Zanesville tonight. Zach and Cyrus will take you on to New Westville."

"Mr. Thomas," Zach said, "will take another stage to the mighty Ohio River. We'll overnight in Columbus and next day travel to Xenia ... overnight there. Next day we travel from Xenia ... to near Lebanon and stop for the night in Franklin. From there it is on to New Westville. The government road is under construction. If we go that way a long delay is likely." He slyly smiled. "Richard said he ain't in a hurry to get to southern Illinois."

Abner asked, "After Columbus how long before we arrive in New Westville?"

Zach thought a moment. "We'll stop each night at a tavern until we get to Xenia. A new driver takes over in Xenia. Depends on the weather and the Pike conditions, where we stop," he said. Cyrus loudly belched. "And if Cyrus don't make us stop too often," Zach said and slapped his partner's back.

"Zach, your teams bein' hitched," the female owner said.

"Thanks, Tillie." He stood. "C'mon, Cy ..."

Cyrus pulled his hat atop his head and pointed a finger at the two couples. "Hurry on up, we got to be on our way," he pulled a watch from his shirt pocket, "in 'bout ten minutes."

The ride to Zanesville took less time than planned. It gave Judith and Mary a chance to explore the bustling hub. Samuel had arranged a buggy for the women and horses for the two men.

The government road carried people to and from the new land even this late in the afternoon. Dust rose from the graveled surface and settled on storefronts, hitching rails, and parked carriages. Small dust devils agitated the fine, flour-like soil, adding to the grime stirred by the previous wagons and carriages. Eventually, the pancake-like deposits slid back to the walkways and roads before a disturbance again lifted it skyward.

Turnpikes radiated from the town center. The evening light began to dim, and the candle lighters appeared on horseback and bicycles like dancing fireflies. Judith and Mary returned to the inn full of conversation about the visits at the bookbindery; clockmakers shop; and the white, glassworks factory, all arranged by Samuel.

After the evening meal, the two couples visited about the growth and new businesses the government Pike brought for many towns along the route. Richard and Abner talked about the numerous men's shops in the city center and the tobacco shop Richard found that presented a wide array of cigars.

The pungent cigar smoke floated in the dining area, mingling with mixed smells of roast bear, elk, deer, and warm baked bread. For dessert, the couples enjoyed freshly-baked huckleberry pie.

"Does Samuel always provide such extravagant treats for persons he likes?" Mary asked.

"No, in fact, he reserves his best ... only for the best. That's why it's a pleasure to have you travel with us, Reverend and Mrs. Hayman." Richard tapped his cigar ash into a small, sand-filled crock located by the table leg.

A note, tied to the bottle of Madeira wine, wished the couples Godspeed, and Samuel looked forward to seeing all four of them. Richard reached over and carefully grasped the bottle. "My, my, Samuel must think you are real jewels ... imported wine."

Richard poured half a glass for Judith and Mary, a full one for Abner and himself. "Toast to successes for all of us."

"And God bless each of us ... now and forever." Abner touched the wine glass to the other glasses held above the table.

After consuming the entire bottle, the two men toured the inn while the women visited and discussed staying in touch.

"Judith, I noticed you studying Abner. What is it?"

"How well does Abner know ... Mr. Carnes?"

Mary flinched at the use of Mr. Carnes rather than Samuel. "We know him through his church attendance and over a meal. Why do you ask?"

"While we were in Baltimore, I happened to meet some people who asked about Samuel Carnes." Judith kept an eye on the dining entry. "Questions arose about his veracity and womanizing."

"Truthfulness about …?"

Richard and Abner appeared in the entryway.

"I can't say … for sure," Judith said, "it's like he has a hypnotic grip on a person … they believe everything he says." She stopped talking when the men came within earshot.

Chapter 19

Abner lay on his back staring at the ceiling. He felt Mary stir and then turn into him. His arm slid around her slender shoulder as she placed her head on his chest. It felt good to hold his wife and finally feel free to have a husbandly closeness. Something caused him to withdraw from their normal attraction over the last months in Franklin County.

"Abner?"

"Um...?"

"Are we doing the right thing?" Mary said.

He didn't immediately answer.

"Abner, did you hear me?"

"About our ...?" he chuckled. "That was pleasant tonight, Mary."

"Abner, it's wonderful to have some of your hidden humor reappear."

He kissed the top of her head. "I assume your question is ... are we doing right by moving from Pennsylvania?"

"Yes."

"Why are you asking? It seems we're okay with moving ... have you changed your mind?"

"No, something in my conversation with Judith made me skeptical about Samuel."

"And ..."

"We know so little," Mary said, "about him and his businesses."

"We trust in God ... don't we?"

"Yes," Mary answered.

"Then it's destined we make our way to New Westville."

"Thank you." She raised her head to face him. "Perhaps we should drink Madeira every evening."

The next morning, they ate without Judith and Richard because of different stagecoach schedules. From Richard's statement, Abner and Mary agreed the couple's activity in Wheeling meant they hoped for a first child. The Haymans likely would not see the couple for some time, if ever again.

The stage left the government road about halfway to Columbus. The bumping and swaying made Abner wonder at the words Richard spoke. He slipped his arm around Mary. "Shall we continue to try for a baby this evening?"

Her eyes brightened and she pulled his head to her bosom. "Oh dear, God, yes ... yes."

"**R**everend Hayman," a female voice called into their room as the morning light streamed into their sleeping quarters.

"Yes," he answered; his voice weak and raspy, awakening from a deep sleep.

"We're in need of a minister." The woman entered their room. "Are you decent?"

"One moment, please."

Mary woke and whispered, "What is it?"

"I don't know." He slipped into his trousers, tossed on his shirt and clerical collar, followed by a vest. He plucked his Bible from the small stand next to the bed.

"Yes?" He eyed the young woman.

"We have an elderly man who's seriously ill. Please follow me."

Abner followed her down a long hall and up steps to a room filled with candlelight. He eyed the old man covered with a wool blanket, the facial color resembling spent ashes.

"Fetch a wet cloth, please."

"Yes, sir." The girl poured water from a pitcher into a bowl on the stand next to the bed. She handed the damp cloth to Abner and folded her hands.

"How did you know he was in trouble?"

"I lost my grandfather last year, Reverend. He looked the same way, kind of gray and listless."

"What's your name?"

"Ruth."

"Ruth, God bless you." He touched her hands. "Is there a doctor staying at the Inn?"

"No, sir." She liked his touch. "I sent one of our stable men to fetch the doctor. He should be here in twenty minutes." Ruth looked at a small timepiece fastened to the black bib covering her white blouse.

"Why did you come for me?"

"The gentleman asked for a minister and your registration said you're a German Reformed pastor."

The elderly man stirred. He opened his eyes and immediately noticed the cleric collar. He asked, "Catholic?"

Abner shook his head and took the man's hands. "German Reformed, sir."

"Ach … güt." A faint smile appeared on the sweaty face. A quiet moan slipped from his lips. "I'm dying." He squeezed Abner's hands. "A bit of scripture, please."

"If we confess our sins, he is faithful and just to forgive us our sins, and to cleanse us from all unrighteousness." Abner felt the grip tighten.

The man looked at him and said, "1 John 1:9."

Abner nodded.

"The Apostles Creed, Reverend." The man closed his eyes and gripped Abner's arm.

As Abner softly recited the prayer the man's grip tightened and abruptly loosened at the last words. "Amen, and God rest your soul."

Ruth sniffed. "I wish I could've done something for him."

"Ruth, you did. You brought him close to God in his last moments."

Ruth confoundedly looked at Abner.

"No, I'm not professing to be God." He pulled the cover over the man's head. "He shared the word of God with us and his maker."

Ruth relaxed. "Thank you, Reverend."

An hour later Abner and Mary sat on a bench in front of the Inn. Zach came striding over. "Ready?" he asked.

Their meager cases sat beside them. "Yes, Zach. Where's Cyrus?"

"Checking the coach to make sure it's clean inside and out."

"Are you taking us all the way to Eaton?" Mary asked.

"No, Mrs. Hayman, I'll be with you to Xenia. A new driver takes you from there to Franklin and on to Eaton."

From the stable area, a loud curse erupted and Cyrus kicked at a young boy. "You didn't get the harness right on the lead mare."

"I'd better calm old Cyrus down before he gets his butt kicked by the stable master." Zach spun on his boot heel and stomped to the stable harnessing area.

"They do take their job seriously," Mary noted.

Abner nodded.

"You're quiet this morning, Abner. What's bothering you?"

"The death this morning rests heavy."

"Abner, you did what you could by bringing the word of God to the man."

"I know, but he seemed so knowledgeable about his maker. We could have shared more before he died."

Mary placed her hands on each side of his angular face. "Abner, you're a good man and minister."

"And a sinner ..."

"Abner, we're all sinners. Remember what you always say, God forgives." She kissed him lightly on the lips. A sound of a whip cracking and harnesses squeaking altered their attention.

He took Mary by the hand and led her to the boarding area for the coach ride to Xenia.

Chapter 20

They napped during the early morning as they traveled southwest toward London, Ohio. The second stop for the horse change evoked higher spirits for Mary and Abner as the countryside abounded with prairie and large oak, hickory, and elm trees. The gently rolling land pocketed with standing water, held ducks, geese, and ornate-winged blackbirds.

"The road is better than I expected," Zach said. "This time of the year is best to travel because we get periods where the uplands bake dry."

Cyrus led the new team to the coach and with help of an elderly, stooped man they hitched the horses to the wagon tongue and resumed the trip fifteen minutes after stopping.

As they neared Xenia, Abner said, "I like this country—even if it does not have the mountains and trees like Pennsylvania—for one can see the horizon."

Mary took in the prairies and the different birds floating above the tall grasses in the non-farmed areas.

"How many good souls live in Xenia?" Abner asked Cyrus as the assistant to Zach began unhitching the horses.

"Last count … maybe a thousand." Cyrus groaned as he straightened up.

"Are we staying here?" Mary asked as she took in the bawdy tavern.

Zach answered her question as he pulled up with a one-horse buggy. He stepped down, pulled the Hayman bags from the storage area at the coach rear, and plopped them in the small open box behind the buggy seat.

"Reverend, Mary, I'll take you to the hotel, which is very nice, and in the morning, your new driver will be back to fetch you and your bags for the stage to Franklin.

Mary admired the hotel, nearly as fine as some in Philadelphia. Delicate, glass ornaments dangled from the edges of a large chandelier, suspended from the lobby ceiling, musically tinkling in the air currents. She smiled at the nicely dressed man behind the highly polished oak desk. Key hooks and mailboxes for each room stood behind the gleaming wood structure.

He smiled back and said, "Do you have reservations?"

Zach gently placed the bags beside the Haymans and answered, "Yes they do. Reverend and Mrs. Hayman are guests of Samuel Carnes."

Mention of Samuel's name made the clerk stand straight and reached for a small bell beside the register. With his other hand, he rotated the large, ornately-bound book for Reverend Hayman to sign. The clerk shook the small bell while Abner penned his and Mary's name.

A stocky, well-built lad immediately appeared and swept up the bags. The clerk said, "Mr. Carnes' suite."

Zach laughed. "Enjoy your stay, Reverend. He gave a small bow and said, "Mrs. Hayman, you're a lovely woman. It has been my pleasure to meet you and your husband." He shook hands, pivoted, and walked out.

The young man carrying the bags waited by the hallway entry. "Follow the gentleman to your room. I'll be by in twenty minutes to show you the hotel dining, reading, and leisure time areas." The clerk snared a sealed letter from the large mailbox. "Mr. Carnes left this for you."

"He was here?" Abner asked.

"He was," he handed Abner the note, "I believe two days past."

The Haymans followed the young fellow to the room and waited while he unlocked the door. They stepped into a sitting room containing a large fireplace, a heavy walnut table surrounded by four sturdy chairs, and Oriental Rugs that covered the smooth, hardwood floors. Several bookcases filled with newspapers and two lounge chairs were placed next to a hickory settee.

Mary let her hands drop away from her mouth. "Abner, we can't."

"Why not, we'll not have many opportunities like this in the new town."

The lad carried the bags into an adjacent room, returned, and said, "If you desire anything just leave a note on the door. We try to meet all requests."

Abner reached in his pocket for a tip.

"Sir that is not necessary. Mr. Carnes adds a percentage to his room bill … for all services." He bowed slightly and left.

After gathering their wits about them they entered the bedroom. Mary gasped. A large four-poster bed with a canopy stood in the middle of the room. Candles sat on two reading chairs, a bureau with four drawers, and a mirror sat to the left of the large bed. The small fireplace built into the wall, covered with a screen, could be seen from the bed occupants.

"My, my … this rival the Inns where my father stays in Boston and New York." She shook her head in disbelief.

He took in the bedroom layout and wondered.

"Abner," Mary eyed him, "what all does Samuel own and operate?"

"I don't know. We both know he has the stagecoach lines, the freight lines, government land sales offices, but what else? Maybe inns and taverns are part of his portfolio."

A knock interrupted their conversation. Abner strolled to the door and the clerk stood ready to tour them around the hotel.

"Reverend Hayman, I must apologize for my crassness. I am Robert Higgins; I go by Dob."

"There's no need to apologize, Dob. Mary will be with us in a minute." Please step in."

"I hope the rooms meet your expectations." He looked over Abner's shoulder at Mary coming from the bedroom. "Mrs. Hayman, you are a fetching sight."

Abner turned to find Mary in the dress she wore when he first met her. He smiled at his wife, and said, "Mary," she held out her hand and Dob took it in both of his, "this is Robert Higgins."

"Mrs. Hayman," he briefly studied her, "that's a lovely dress." He turned and motioned them ahead of him.

"Thank you, Mr. Higgins," Mary said with a polite smile.

Chapter 21

Biscuits and honey accompanied the salt pork and fried potatoes served in the Xenia Hotel dining area. The chatter of children and adults mingled with the metallic clank of large pots and pans.

"Is Franklin far?" Mary asked.

Darius Lathrop, the stagecoach driver for the final leg of the trip from Xenia to Eaton, stopped to tell them the coach would leave in thirty minutes. "Not far," he said. "A man and his daughter will join us for the Franklin to New Westville run."

"Thank you, Darius," Abner said. "It'll be good to have company for the final miles. What's your estimate of time to travel from Franklin to Eaton?"

"It took us about seven hours two days ago, but it should be fewer as they're working on leveling the road." He chuckled. "A delay might happen if there's heavy traffic as the bridge is … uh … well, you'll see when we get there. Normally, it's about five hours."

"Are you saying it's not safe?"

"No, Mrs. Hayman, it's a mite strangely built. It curves downstream and then curves upstream." He gave her a reassuring smile. "It'll be okay."

As Darius walked away, Abner said, "Mary, they travel the route every few days and he doesn't appear concerned. He wanted us to know so the odd construction wouldn't surprise us."

She gave him a weak smile and nibbled at her biscuit.

The assistant driver finished hitching the horses and watched Darius stride toward the cleaned stagecoach. "Darius, you tell the passengers we're picking up crazy Chris?" he asked as soon as his partner stood beside him.

"No, Josh, I simply told them we're picking up passengers at Franklin."

Josh Means worked with Darius the last fifteen months and didn't question the head driver's decisions, which always were on point.

The two men climbed to the high-mounted seat and slowly guided the Carnes stagecoach to the passenger loading area. The Carnes Coaches used the stage station nearest the hotel. The Xenia city size and the number of travelers demanded two stations to serve coaches and freighters.

"Josh, take the buggy and pick up the Reverend and his wife."

"Why not use the kid?"

"Mr. Carnes said no one other than those in his employee group will tend the Reverend and his wife."

"Kinda unusual, don't ya think?"

"Suppose Samuel's become a true and staunch believer?"

Josh grinned. "Yeah, old Sam also just might like the Reverend's woman. Scuttlebutt has it she's pretty."

"Watch your mouth." Darius shook a finger at the young assistant. "I'd hate to see what Mr. Carnes might do if he thought you were starting stories."

"I'm not starting stories—" He noted the look on Darius' face and stopped. "I'm on my way."

The buggy kicked up dust as Josh urged the horse along Main Street to the hotel. He stopped under the canopy and hustled into the hotel lobby. The Reverend and his wife stood by the checkout desk; Josh understood the scuttlebutt about the minister's wife.

"Reverend Hayman, Mrs. Hayman, I'm Josh, the assistant to Darius. Are you ready for the ride to the stagecoach?"

Mary held out her hand. "Pleased to meet you, Josh. I'm Mary."

He blushed as he took her warm hand.

Abner smiled inwardly at the boy's shyness. "Josh, we're ready."

Several buggies waited near the hotel entrance. The hotel manager stood by their waiting buggy. "Reverend, thank you for your stay and we hope you'll soon return."

"It was wonderful," Mary said and took Josh's hand as she entered the buggy.

"I hope we can return, Dob," Abner said.

Darius waited by the stagecoach for Josh to bring the Hayman's to the last leg of their journey. This coach, with stylishly painted, white doors left the impression of elitist passengers traveling the road. The Carnes name boldly inscribed above the door contrasted with the oak-wood coach. Every wood and leather item gleamed from the recent cleaning.

Darius and Josh helped the Hayman's settle in the plush interior. The tufted, beige seats matched the interior wood color. Small footrests pivoted out from under the seats for the short-legged passengers.

Before closing the coach door, Darius said, "If all goes well we should arrive in Franklin shortly after one o'clock. Enjoy the trip. Stretch now … it'll be less roomy when the people board in Franklin."

The non-forested land held small log cabins and a few homes built of milled lumber. Stumps of old oak, hickory, and elm trees protruded from the recently cleared land. Fields of corn and vegetables filled the small acres where tilling proved profitable. Smoke plumes from burning trees drifted lazily in the distance, the ash eventually bound for lye soap production.

The slowing stage signaled the arrival in Franklin. They had made one stop between Xenia and Franklin to change teams and stretch. Josh took every minute to admire Mary.

"Darius, I envy the Reverend."

The head driver grinned at his apprentice. "You like her?"

"Yes, sir," Josh Means said with a wide smile.

"Maybe you can approach crazy Chris about his daughter when he boards." Darius slapped Josh on the shoulder and waited for a retort. None came. "You gonna try to give it a fling with the young girl?"

"Darius, I never did see a Injun gal so pretty."

"She's not full-blooded Indian; she got lotta white blood."

Josh shook his head, grinned, and took the reins of the new team.

Chapter 22

The old man's eyes blazed. "I'll be as I wanna be." Brown spittle flew from Chris Kreulfs' thick lips. "You mule's backside you ain't gonna tell me what to do. Samuel Carnes don't own me."

"If you can't behave," Darius paused, "I'll kick you outta the coach."

"Every time I ride with you, you damn ... you give me the dickens."

"Chris, you want me to keep you from boarding the stage?"

Chris shook his head. He calmed down so he could speak without swearing. "Is Carnes gonna be at the station in New Westville?"

Darius nodded.

"I'll behave if you let me get off this damn coach before we get there. My daughter and me, we can walk to meet my woman."

"Fair 'nuff, Chris," Darius said, "but remember if you make one disturbance, you're off."

Chris nodded, wiped the chewing tobacco from his cheek pocket, and deposited a fresh shred of chew. The old man bumped Darius as he stomped by on his way to the men's outhouse. Near the privy, he nearly ran over a lanky, well-dressed male. He scowled as he swerved off the path.

"Sorry, sir," Abner said.

Chris grumbled and threw open the outhouse door.

Inside the stage station, Abner located a water pitcher and soap. When he finished washing he turned and bumped into a young woman. "Excuse ... me," he said, his voice catching in his throat.

The oval-shaped face with the prominent cheekbones caught him off-guard. Abner could not take his eyes off her.

"Is something wrong?"

"No, not at all, I thought you were … sorry for bumping into you."

"I should've been more careful," she said. "I'm Chirtlain Kreulfs, Chirt for short."

He held out his hand.

"After I wash, sir,"

Abner felt like a gawky boy as he stood watching her. She must have French-Indian blood he thought. Her speech reflects a good education.

Mary appeared in the washroom. "Abner, you've met Miss Kreulfs?"

"We … uh … bumped into each other."

Chirt finished drying and took his extended hand. She held it as he began to let go. "I've not been to church in a long time, Reverend Hayman. I'm looking forward to hearing you deliver God's words."

"You know me?"

"Yes. Samuel … speaks highly of you."

"Are you of the Reformed faith?"

Chirt released his hand. "My mother is Catholic. My grandmother married a Frenchman. That's why most people are leery of me; it's the Indian blood, you know."

"Who're you talkin' to?" Chris blathered as he entered the washroom.

"These people are traveling with us, Pa," Chirt said.

Chris stared at Mary. "You be a mighty pretty lady; you belong to him?" Chris pointed at Abner with a tobacco-stained index finger.

Mary smiled. "I belong to God and … yes … I'm Abner's wife."

"Well, I'll be. You be the preacher Sam Carnes spouts about so much?"

Chirt jumped in. "Pa, this is Reverend Hayman and his wife Mary."

"Well—"

"Ready to get going folks; let's board now," Darius said. He stared at crazy Chris, shook his head, and walked away.

After settling the passengers inside the coach, Darius climbed into the seat and snapped the whip above the horses. The coach lurched forward.

Josh looked at his mentor and said, "Chris get feisty?"

"That crazy ass, he wanted to pick an argument with the preacher." He snapped the whip once more and the horses responded to his anger by picking up speed. "When we stop make sure this team gets more oats."

"You're the boss," Josh said.

"And get the new horses hitched fast as you can, record time, you hear."

"Sure 'nuff, boss." Josh held tight to his seat.

At the stage stop, Darius and Josh immediately unhitched the lathered horses. They led them to the pen and turned the team over to the stable hand.

"Hey, Darius, who put a burr under your seat?"

Josh said, "George, get the other team out to the stage fast, and make sure this team gets more oats."

George watched Darius rumble out of the pen area and stomp to the stage. "I do believe someone done upset Darius." George completed the harnessing and spotted Darius grab crazy Chris, roughly guiding him behind the horse barn.

Abner and Chirt watched the two men in heated conversation. "Must I intervene?" Abner said to Chirt.

She emphatically said, "No. My father has a tendency to irritate Darius; they'll work this out ... on their terms."

"Chris, what the damnation did I tell you about getting in people's face?"

"That man is not good ... he's evil, look at him slobberin' over my daughter when he has a fine-lookin' woman of his own."

"Chris, is your wife meeting you this afternoon?"

"Yeah, but you know her and her drinkin' problem."

"If she's not there I'll find someone to fetch you. Take a deep breath and gather yourself ... we're about to leave. I don't want to hear a peep out of you, or I'll dump you along the road and not send anyone to find you." He gripped Chris by his scrawny arm. "Understand?"

Crazy Chris started to give a smart retort and thought better when he saw the fire in Darius' eyes and felt the anger in his grip. He shook out of the grasp and tramped back to the stage.

"Damn you, old man," Darius muttered, "...you cause any trouble ..."

Chapter 23

Two miles outside New Westville, Darius reined in the horses. He passed the leather straps to Josh and said, "If I have any trouble with crazy Chris, you slap the horses and get on down the road."

"What you gonna do?" Josh asked.

"I gotta make sure the passengers are safe. You stop at the bottom of the draw if he goes nuts. I don't guess he'll do anything, but ..."

Josh sat with the reins in his hands ready to head down the road.

"Chris, come out." Darius waited, the coach door slowly opened.

The old man backed out and pointed a finger toward his daughter leaning out the coach window. "Listen up, gal. Tell that mother of yours, she is to get her fanny out here soon as your feet hit the ground in town." He turned to Darius. "You got some water while I wait?"

"No." Darius pointed the old man to the roadside. Chris stepped into the drainage channel and Darius mounted the coach. "Let's go, Josh." He didn't look back.

At the stage station in New Westville, Josh reined the horses to a stop at the Carnes Coaches designated area. An ornate buggy hitched near the door had an attendant standing ready to take on passengers. As the stagecoach dust settled, Samuel Carnes walked from the frame building and stood by the buggy.

One hundred feet beyond the building an old, gray wagon—two swayback horses hitched to it—stood in the shade of a large oak tree. An Indian woman sat on the wagon seat smoking a tiny cigar, peering through the settling stagecoach dust.

Darius hustled to the coach door, opened it, and waited.

Chirt stepped out first, followed by Mary, and finally Abner. Chirt looked around and spotted her waiting mother. She turned and said, "Mrs. Hayman, it's been a pleasure. Reverend, I'm anxious to hear your first sermon."

Samuel hurried to her side and gave her a brief hug. "Where's Chris?"

"Best ask Darius," Chirt said. She gathered her single bag from Josh and ambled to her waiting mother.

Samuel beamed at Mary and Abner. "Welcome to Preble County, the people await the Reverend Hayman and his lovely wife." He turned to the young coach assistant. "Josh, take their baggage to the buggy."

"Yes, sir," Josh said, picked up the bags, and trotted off.

Samuel shook hands with Abner and gave Mary a lingering hug. "We'll first get you settled in your home. When you've had a moment, we'll dine at the hotel. Tomorrow I'll introduce you to the newly erected church and our members." He waved at Darius and signaled he wanted to talk.

Abner and Mary walked to the buggy where Josh stowed their baggage. The old wagon, with Chirt holding the reins, squeaked and rattled by the Carnes buggy. She waved at the group and lightly slapped the reins to urge on the horses to find her father.

Crazy Chris had caught a ride on a freight wagon and sat tall beside the old man holding the reins. He spotted his nags, pulling the old wagon, slowly approach the small wood-plank bridge spanning Elkhorn Creek. The streamflow at this time of the year became nothing more than a small trickle, originating from upstream springs.

"Stop yer rig right here," Chris said.

The old freight driver reined in the horses just shy of the bridge.

"Thank ya kindly." Chris carefully crawled off the wagon. "You'd been the Carnes Carriers I'd never gotta ride."

The old man ignored the comment and eased the horses onto the road.

"Where ya been?" he stared up at the two women, "I coulda died."

His wife, Susanna, frowned. "Old man, you're nothin' but foul wind."

"Get in, Chris," Chirt said, knowing the use of his name would ruffle him.

"Girl, I told you not to call me by my first name, ya hear."

Chirt slapped the reins on the rump of the two old horses as Chris got one leg on the wagon floor. The jerk threw him off balance and he tumbled into a layer of manure-stained straw. She turned the wagon and headed back.

"Shee-it, girl, you coulda killed me."

"That would be our good luck," his wife slurred through gritted teeth.

When their old wagon slowly passed the stage station, Chirt noticed the absence of the ornate buggy. Samuel Carnes seemed rather distant toward her when they arrived. Was he that enamored with the minister or maybe his wife? The grumbling old man in the wagon bed broke her musing.

Samuel took the road northeast from New Westville to the site of the church and parsonage. Off to his left, he could see the Kreulfs' wagon headed toward the northern Preble County prairie.

The headwaters of Whitewater River flowed north and abruptly turned southwest, south of New Madison. The land above the headwaters he bought and sold many times, because the settlers were overwhelmed by the marshy country. Only one man tamed the land. crazy Chris had purchased those lands and conquered the problem by draining the swamps. Drained, the land became suitable for raising crops, except Chris never did, as he spent too much time being a horse's rear.

The frame church rising above the level horizon left the Haymans in awe. East of it stood a small frame house. Mary became drawn into the surroundings the nearer they came to the new construction. Someone had planted flowers around the door entry and along the house's west side. A large hickory tree to the east shaded the home and one-hundred yards north a tall forest filled the horizon.

Abner stared. "Samuel, when did all this happen?"

Samuel halted the buggy at the small stone wall fronting the church property. "I arranged it last year and hoped you would accept, if you didn't I would've had to settle for second best from Cincinnati." He stepped out of the buggy, hitched the horse to the closest rail, and helped Mary down.

Abner waited until Mary stepped safely to the turf. He stood in the buggy, not believing his eyes. The signs of autumn filled the air; asters and grasses had set new seed and yellow and red colors tinged the forest. Maples stood in stately splendor, their lobed leaves fluttering in the breeze.

"It's wonderful, Samuel."

"Thank you, the pleasure is mine." He felt the inner relief that Abner didn't know about the confusing Ohio land survey system. Samuel avoided land deals east of the Great Miami River. The surveys completed under many different systems created confusion, bringing with it scrutiny by judges dealing with the deeds. This land, with the church and parsonage, he smoothly dealt with and had no problem gaining the property deed. The church now owned one-half section of land, free and clear, because of his knowledge and dubious dealings.

Someone had recently opened the church windows. An oiled-wood smell emanated from a huge pulpit and a walnut baptismal font at the church front. Keeping with the Reformed church standard, there were no statues, paintings, or other hints of the Holy Triune.

A slender, gray-haired man dressed in all black, except for a white shirt under his vest, entered from the front of the church. An area to their left had a door, hinged in brass, with a nameplate attached: The Reverend Abner Hayman. The lanky man smiled as he approached. "Mrs. Hayman, Reverend," he nodded to Samuel, "I'm Alexander Schroeder, at your service." He bowed slightly at the waist. "Welcome."

"Come, Mary," Samuel said, "let's tour your new living quarters while Alexander shows Abner his office and the heating system." He guided Mary by her elbow to an inconspicuous exit leading to the parsonage.

Mary said, "I—"

"Mrs. Hayman," Alexander softly spoke, "I promise to make the church tour brief." He thinly smiled at Carnes.

Chapter 24

Fall came late. The first killing freeze settled in New Westville in mid-November. The brilliant forest colors of October rapidly faded with the heavy frost coating, and subsequently created a prolific leaf drop. For Abner Hayman, it made no difference. The new church, Mary's pregnancy, and establishing a ministry circuit occupied every moment.

He stoked the wood stove in the living room and the cooking stove in the kitchen. Mary slept late this morning as they had talked well into the night. They discussed possible baby names, preparation for winter, their available funds to buy food and clothing, and Abner's circuit into Darke County near New Madison.

Perplexed by Abner's going so far north, Mary held her tongue; she didn't challenge him, feeling he would take her wrong. Chirt wanted him to reach out to the people in her area. Mary felt that Abner might mistake her concern as jealousy.

His south circuit went to Campbellstown, nearly as distant as to the Kreulfs' farm near New Madison. The congregation, in slightly over a month, grew more than twenty percent. The word of Abner's preaching brought new members each Sunday.

A soft rap at the door interrupted their conversation and cook stove preparation.

"Reverend Hayman," Alexander called. He stood with his wife, bundled against the cold morning, holding a small carton of eggs and a package of salt pork. "May we come in?"

"Certainly, please do." Abner stepped back and took the eggs and pork from Alexander. "Thank you." He closed the door and placed the meat and eggs in the food preparation area. "Let me take your coat, Nettie."

Alexander shrugged out of his wool jacket and finished feeding wood to the cook stove. He looked up as Mary came from the bedroom. In the time since the Haymans arrived in New Westville, Alex realized she held the family strength. This, he knew, attracted Samuel to her, for Carnes liked his women beautiful and strong, much like Chirt Kreulfs. "Good morning, Mrs. Hayman."

"Good morning, Alexander. Nettie, it's good to see you again. Thank you for the edibles." Mary moved the eggs close to the stove and handed the salt pork to Abner. "Abner please cut some strips."

Nettie moved next to Mary and put an arm around her shoulder. "Please, let me do this while you visit." Mary started to protest. "No, don't argue with me." She smiled nicely and edged Mary to the side.

Alexander held a chair for Mary and waited for Abner to take a seat. "Nettie, you need help with anything?"

Nettie shook her head. She placed several thick pork slabs in the cast-iron fry pan and set four cups on the small table beside the stove. Wisps of steam rose from the spout of the fire-blackened pot, her only movement—except for a small thump of a barely noticeable egg-cracking—occurred when she dropped an egg into the ground coffee.

"Mary ... Nettie told me the good news," Alexander said.

Mary grinned. "June is when we think the little one arrives."

"Do you have a name for the child?" Nettie asked as she poured the egg-coffee mixture into the boiling pot. She moved the pot to the side of the stovetop to slow the boil.

"If it's a boy, we'll name him, John Edmund," Abner said.

"And if a girl, we will name her ... Mercy Ann," Mary added.

"I like both names," Alexander said, "Mercy Ann Hayman is wonderful and John Edmund Hayman fits his lineage."

The draft from the open door momentarily cooled the room. Nettie carried a small pot of cold water to the stove and added a small ladle of water to the boiled coffee. "Good," she said, watching the lump of grounds begin to settle. Her hands moved swiftly to the sizzling pan of pork. She added eight eggs and sprinkled on ground salt and pepper.

Alexander stood, "You're making excellent progress with the house, Mary."

"Thank you, it's a pleasure to live in a fine structure. My life's much easier. God blessed us."

Abner took the eating utensils from Alexander and placed them on small mats. Nettie had made the mats in her loom as a welcome for Mary. The rugs adorning the floors and throughout came from Nettie and Alexander.

"I feel like a queen," Mary said.

"Good," Alexander replied, "and well you should, taking such good care of the minister."

A small woven basket with a white cloth appeared in the center of the table. "Biscuits to go with the pork and eggs, and the coffee beckons us," Nettie said. "Alex, please pour and I'll join you after I fetch some butter."

"Alexander, you married a fine woman," Abner said. "Where did you meet her?"

As Alexander sat he said, "Right here, in New Westville."

Nettie sat and said to Abner, "Please grace us with a prayer, Reverend."

They folded their hands and bowed their heads. The savory aroma of the breakfast drifted over the oak table placed at the room center.

Abner began. "Father, we thank you for the safe night, and for the pleasant morning light. For providing wonderful rest and food and loving care that makes the day so fair. Help us to do what we should, to be kind to others and be good, in all we do, and in all we say, to grow more loving every day. Dear Lord, we thank you for blessing us with such a fine couple who joins us in delivering your Word. Amen."

"Lovely, Pastor Hayman," Nettie said, "thank you."

"You're most welcome." Abner turned to Alexander and asked, "You come from where, Alexander?"

Alexander wiped his mouth on the cloth. "I come from New Jersey and Nettie comes from Kentucky." He took Nettie's hand and held it for a moment. "We met at the dry goods store in New Westville where I clerked."

"When I first met Alex I never thought I'd marry him." She sliced a small piece of fried salt pork and dabbed it in the soft egg yolk. "After running errands for many of the elderly in the town, I came to know Alex. He always exuded confidence with his sales talk, but most importantly he's honest."

"You must know Samuel well," Mary said. "Where did you meet him?"

"After I dropped out of the seminary," Abner's stunned look made Alexander pause, "yes, Pastor Hayman, I attended two years of the Seminary, from where you graduated."

"What happened, if I may be so bold?" Mary asked.

"The administration falsely accused me of philandering with one of the instructor's wives," he said and breathed deeply, slowly letting out the air. "They asked me to drop my enrollment with the agreement that I never reveal the pastor's wife's name. Why pick on me? Somehow they found out I was the only student who knew of the affair."

Abner placed a hand on Alexander's shoulder. "You're saying false accusations; you didn't challenge them?"

"I did," Alexander quickly answered, "but they meant to make me the sacrificial lamb."

"You needn't continue, Alexander," Mary sympathetically offered.

"It's best you know." He turned back to Abner. "The main player involved in the affair," he sighed, "your mentoring instructor, Abner. Samuel Carnes came to help me."

"How?" Abner asked.

"Samuel's father is a huge contributor to the German Reformed church, although I don't think he ever attended. Somehow he knew the instructor and didn't hold the man's honesty in high esteem."

"You're saying my mentoring pastor was a dishonest person?" Abner queried.

"Bluntly, yes."

"I guess that explains his early retirement." Abner shook his head in disbelief.

"To move the story along, Samuel's father came to my rescue. He met with the seminary board and demanded the resignation of your mentor or he would disclose him as the philanderer. You see ... Reverend Bach played a game with his wife and me and set us up to cover his shames."

"How did Samuel's father find out?" Abner asked.

"I'll never know. I asked Samuel and his answer was," he paused to think, "*It's best to not know.*"

"Alexander, what did you do after dropping out of the seminary?" Mary asked.

"I traveled to Baltimore looking for work. I heard jobs abounded on the waterfront." He sipped his coffee. "I worked the docks for a year and that's where I met Samuel."

Nettie said, "And the rest is history." She rose and gathered the dishes. Mary started to rise to help, but Nettie put up a hand to stop her.

"Samuel worked in Washington as an aide to a senator from Pennsylvania," he said and noticed Abner wanted to ask a question, "I don't know which one. What I know, is Samuel's father kept track of me and put Samuel in touch to help with the public land office. That's what brought me here."

"But you worked as a clerk when Nettie met you." Mary looked perplexed.

Abner sat quietly, watching the man's expressions.

"As Nettie said, I'm an honest man. I had difficulty with the conduct of selling congressional lands."

"Dishonesty takes place?" Abner asked.

"Perhaps yes … perhaps no, I didn't like the fact the government sold the Indian's lands, again and again, to pay off the war debts. It's twisted, Pastor Hayman, and a further discussion will take time away from our morning together."

Nettie turned from her cleanup chores. "After we married, Samuel offered to help and assigned us to assist with the church and help you."

Chapter 25

Winter proved mild in western Ohio, which of late had been a rarity. Several times Abner and Alexander held service away from the New Westville church. Both men worked in harmony on the treks to the north where crazy Chris spewed venom about Abner and his assistant; in fact, Chris targeted all ministers. Chirt ignored her father, as did the near-area settlers, seeking to bolster their religious learning.

The southern treks proved less fruitful than the soirees into Darke County. Ministers of other denominations south and east of New Westville held tight to their congregations not wanting to lose their parish members to the German Reformed pastor. A small cluster of German immigrants moving into the south area kept Abner and Alexander hopeful they could maintain the southern route and make contact with newcomers.

Swamp areas to the north receded under the relentless onslaught of settlers clearing the land, their efforts slowly succeeding in planting the land to crops. Reverend Hayman and Alexander, as they traveled toward New Madison, took notice of the agricultural progress.

The frigid day found both men bundled against the cold in ankle length wool coats; a heavy blanket lay across their laps. Draped over the horse, the bright-blue woolen blanket appeared antithetical to the all-black of the pastor and his assistant. The horse's breath rose in frosty bursts as they followed the frozen roadbed through cleared land.

Abner slowed the horse when they approached a small drainage ditch. "Alex, will this work make the land more productive?" He looked over the land and brought the horse to a halt before trying to cross the small plank bridge. He handed the reins to Alex.

"Pastor, the earliest settlers tried to make the land suitable for crops, to no avail." He gently snapped the reins against the horse's rump. "Those earlier settlers didn't use the land draining technique developed by crazy Chris.

"Samuel mentioned the trees Chris wanted for good lumber suffered from bark-stripping porcupines. The critters ate the tender bark from the old man's best walnut trees."

"What happens to those trees?" Abner asked as Alex eased the horse over the planks.

"Growth above the gnawed point becomes deformed or dies. Chris figured he could do the same as the quill-covered animal, so he set out to do the same to the smaller trees over the acreages difficult to clear. He found, in time, the trees die and the land became suitable for crops or for adding to his walnut forest. Through his observations and perseverance, Chris Kreulfs overcame the marshes. His use of the iron plow helped remove the old stumps, which Chris burned after girdling the tree.

"The sly old man used all his senses to conquer the land. His keen sight helped him discover the lay of the land." Abner frowned at that piece of information. "Chris told me he noticed the trees he let stand for capturing or preventing snowdrifts helped him visually calculate water flow and drainage during spring melt."

"Slow down and stop," Abner said. "You mentioned all his senses."

"Chris used all his senses, like smell and sight," Alex went on as Abner admired the flat land Kreulfs developed into cropland, "to figure which plants to eliminate … or to use for medicinal and food purposes. All of these native vegetation uses he learned from his wife, which she had learned from her mother and other tribal members."

"The crazy man is not so crazy after all."

Alex chuckled. "Watch yourself with him, Pastor." He urged the horse forward after checking his pocket watch. "With these revelations, he developed his land by channeling furrows of increasing depth towards the nearest natural drainage. Where he had no choice but to leave the marshes he took advantage of the wildlife for feeding his people, including the wayward

Indians he came to know.

"Crazy Chris also preserved a marshy area located deep within one of his heavily timbered acres. He gave up tries at clearing that forest and marshland. Chirt said she watched her ornery father disappear into that forest land one fall after crop harvest, armed with freshly picked and sun-dried berries she had harvested from the previous year."

They made excellent time to the log cabin where Chirt arranged for them to meet with people wanting to meet the pastor and his assistant. On a small rise above the farm, they watched the chimney smoke curl skyward in the cold, still atmosphere.

"Not until she was older did she understand that her crazy father distilled some of his grains in the forest and flavored them with the berries. It was the money he earned from the sale of the grain alcohol that paid for Chirt's schooling."

"God works his will in many ways," Abner cheerfully stated as they approached the cabin.

Chirt met them the moment they stopped at the hitch rail. She pushed the wool robe hood off her head and beamed a radiant smile when she saw them. "Head to the barn where the horse can have some warmth and oats."

Alex reined the horse to his right and stopped at the barn door. Abner stepped down, opened the door, and felt the warmth rush from the cozy area. They quickly unhitched the horse, pulled the blanket off, and stabled the mare for the time they would be inside.

Chirt stood at the barn door. She watched the pastor kindly pat the fine mare as he supplied oats, providing extra energy for the return trip. Alex and Abner then turned the buggy in the heated barn so they could hitch the mare and quickly be on their way to New Madison for the evening stay.

Alex shook Chirt's hand and gave her a gentle hug. "You're so kind to arrange this with the Friedrich Bach family."

"Thank you, Alex." She smiled at Abner who held out his hand. "They're looking forward to meeting you and Reverend Hayman. Follow me," she took Abner's hand, shook it, and pulled him into a hug. She kept hold of his hand and led him toward the cabin.

Inside the main living area sat Mr. Bach, his wife Anna, three small children—two girls and a boy—and a large, black dog. Two women sat near the fireplace, one being Chirt's mother, the other a shriveled, bright-eyed old woman.

"Mother, you know the two gentlemen." The woman nodded. "This is Abigail Muenster, from southwest of New Madison. Abigail has five boys and three girls all married with children of their own."

Abner walked over to Abigail and introduced himself and Alex. "Mrs. Muenster, thank you for coming."

"I wanted to meet the minister I done heard so much about." She grinned, exposing a smile with no front teeth. "My young'uns wanted a report on you so they know if to invite you to their houses."

Chirt laughed and said, "And they do have full houses. How many grandchildren do you have, Abigail?"

"Thirty-five and one on the way," the shriveled little woman proudly responded.

Chirt took Abner by the hand once again and led him to three elderly men sitting around the wood stove. One smoked a pipe that had a hand-carved look. The other men, sat with their gnarled hands wrapped around a cup of strong-brewed tea, suspiciously eyeing him.

"The pipe man is Thomas Gerdes, the old man with the bigger cup is Malthus Krast, and the third gentleman in suspenders is Joseph Harder, my father's best worker."

The old man winked at her and glanced at her hand tightly clasped in the minister's and said, "If he weren't married, I'd say you would be trying ..."

Chirt smiled. "God gives me power through him, Joe." She released Abner's hand so he could shake hands with each man.

After all the pleasantries concluded, Abner led off with a prayer and launched into learning about each person and their families. He and Alex spent the best part of two hours listening to everyone, learning they all settled in the area south of New Madison after purchasing government land.

Thomas asked, "Aren't you going to preach to us about going to hell if we don't believe in your way?"

"Thomas," Abner said, "I came here at the invite of Chirt and Mr. and Mrs. Bach." He noticed the couple sit straighter when he acknowledged them.

"Their time is precious, as is yours."

"So, you ain't gonna preach to us and ask for money?" Joe said.

Alex snorted. "You sound just like Chris."

"Alex, most of the ministers come in here and preach the high and mighty while there are many who suffer."

"Please explain, Joseph," Abner said.

The pungent smoke from Thomas' pipe stung Abner's nose as it floated in the room air. He sniffed and lightly coughed.

"Not a smoker, Reverend?" Thomas laughed.

"No, Thomas, I'm not."

"What we want to know," he looked at the other two men and around the room, "is why you really came?"

"Fair enough, Thomas," Abner said, "and I will honestly answer that I do this when I first come into someone's home. "I want to know you so I can properly minister to each and every one of you with God's word." Abner turned to Mr. Krast. "Malthus, what did you expect? Be honest with me."

The old man thought a moment and replied, "Chirt told us about ya. It sounded too good. Bein' of a curious nature, I wanted to meet you to see what my first impression might be."

"And …? Abner urged him to continue.

"Too short of time, but maybe she's right. I'll wait 'til the Missus meets you, and we both hear you preach in your church."

"Well, you ain't what Chris said," Joe jumped in with an energetic voice and a chuckle.

Alex broke in, "Time to be on our way, Reverend Hayman."

"End the meetin' with a prayer please," Abigail said.

"I'll be happy to, Abigail." Abner took her arthritic hands, looked straight into her eyes, and said a quiet prayer for her family and the families of each person in the room. He shook each person's hand on the way out.

"Abner, you're genuine, and they know it, but watch yourself, for Chirt has a strong attraction toward you. Just words of caution."

"God gives her strength," Abner said. He finished hitching the mare.

"And the devil tempts," Alex said, and took the reins, heading the buggy toward New Madison.

Chapter 26

It had been three months since Alex accompanied Abner to New Madison. The spring months proved difficult to travel in Preble and Darke Counties, thus they remained at New Westville, completing needed tasks around the church and parsonage.

Nettie sent Alex to the small general store to buy supplies for the school they planned to open in the fall. Her studies at the Hartford Female Seminary in Connecticut qualified Nettie to become the head teacher at the school. She had trust from congregation members the children's education would rival any school in the state. The only objection came from the elderly males concerned that any woman educated under the tutelage of Catharine Beecher might disrupt their households.

While Alex rode the short distance into New Westville, Nettie saddled her horse and traveled to the parsonage to check on Mary. Educated with many other strong-willed women, Nettie convinced Mary to help teach. Their plan evolved while their husbands, over the past eight months, traveled the Reformed Church ministerial routes. The mile to the Hayman house became an easy ride, even in the semi-sloppy road conditions. Two buggies passed Nettie on the way. A hearty wave from the woman seated comfortably by her man communicated she had gained the woman's respect. Nettie's reputation as an upstanding citizen of the county precipitously rose over the short time she lived in the area. The marriage to Alexander didn't hurt, for most people respected him for his work with Samuel Carnes, and later for the local dry goods store.

The leaves of spring, with a light-green blush, adorned the stately trees in the forest behind the parsonage. Nettie dismounted by the barn, unsaddled the horse, and led it to an empty stall. At the back of the barn Abner stood, staring out the open, upper half of the door.

"Abner, hello," she softly said.

He slowly turned and looked at her. He didn't utter a word and turned back to stare out the door.

Nettie walked to him and put her hand on his shoulder. "Are you alright, Abner?"

He shook his head.

Nettie looked at the wet hair near the collar. "Abner, please talk to me. What's wrong?"

He shifted so his profile became backlit by the mid-morning sun. Sweat poured off his face as if he'd been running.

"Abner, please talk to me."

"I'm in pain, Nettie. I came out here so I wouldn't concern Mary. Fetch a doctor. I have to know what is wrong, so Mary doesn't catch whatever I have."

Nettie asked, "Where does it hurt, Abner?" He pointed to his abdominal area. "Can you walk?"

He nodded.

"Come with me." She led him to a recently cleaned stall full of freshly placed straw. "Were you cleaning here when you fell ill?" She watched her friend and pastor nod. "Lie down."

Abner winced as he knelt and nearly collapsed on the straw. "Get a horse blanket, Nettie." She grabbed the blanket and a towel off a stall rail. With a deft hand, Nettie wiped his face and unfolded the blanket to cover him. "Does Mary know you're ill?"

He groaned and responded, "No. I mentioned to her I felt somewhat feverish and I wanted to come out here to work up a sweat to maybe flush it out of my system."

"Oh, Abner, you stubborn German, that wasn't smart." She stood, found a saddle blanket, and rolled it into a small pillow. "I'm going to fetch Mary."

He started to protest and winced.

"I'll be right back."

Within a minute the two women returned. Mary, in her seventh month of pregnancy, rushed to the barn entrance.

"Don't come near," Abner said, "I worry it might be contagious."

Mary stood at the barn door, feeling helpless.

"Abner, I'm going home," Nettie said. "Alex must be back from the general store. He can bring the doctor."

"I'm staying right here, Abner," Mary said as she watched Nettie saddle her horse and gallop down the lane to the road. Mary felt the cool of the spring morning. "Abner, I'll be right back."

He heard her talking to herself when she returned. "Mary, are you okay?" He waited for her answer.

"I and the baby are doing fine, Abner. Please rest."

"I'll try to sleep until the doctor and Alexander arrive." He sank deeper into the straw and pulled the blanket tight to his body. The musty odor of horse and old manure from the stall floor mingled with the new straw smell.

Mary brought her Bible and read the first fifty-one verses from the Gospel of John. Her soft melodic voice and the rhythmic cadence continued until she finally heard his deep-sleep breathing. She kept on reading until the pounding hoof beats and the rattling carriage came closer to the barn.

Mary rose from her stall and slid back the large barn door. Alex jumped down from his horse and trotted to her.

"How is he, Mary?"

"Asleep, Alex," she said while watching a rangy, bespectacled man lift a black case from the rear of his buggy. "Do you know this doctor?"

"I do, Mary, and he's very good." Alex turned to the man and said. "Doctor Sidney Grossman, this is … Mrs. Mary Hayman."

He looked at her and asked, "Is it the seventh month of your pregnancy, Mrs. Hayman?"

Mary nodded.

"Tell me about your husband's symptoms before he came to the barn."

"Abner appeared healthy last evening. On rising this morning, he ate a light breakfast and an hour later said he felt feverish and wanted to work out here to sweat out what he felt might be a cold."

"Has Reverend Hayman been out and about in the county?"

"No, he's remained at home with Alex, working on the church building and sermons for the coming months. Why?"

"There's concern about cholera in Darke County and an outbreak epidemic similar to what England experienced."

Mary blanched at the news. "Oh dear ... this is terrible news."

"Alex, you and the Haymans practice excellent hygiene so I'm not too concerned that we have the same problem, but we must be very careful." He walked to the stall where he heard Abner moving about in the straw. Alex and Mary started to follow. "Don't come with me," he said.

Abner looked up when the doctor entered the stall. His sallow features punctuated his illness; sweat rolled off his face.

"I'm Doctor Grossman, Reverend." He placed the small bag beside Abner and opened the latch. "I'm going to ask you some questions about your travels and who you've seen in the last forty-eight hours. From the answers, I might be able to determine the cause of your difficulty."

Doctor Grossman took Abner's pulse, gauged his temperature by touch, examined his eyes, palpated his abdomen, and then launched into questions. As Abner answered, Sidney jotted notes in a small black notebook. After a moment of deep thought, he said, "Reverend, I don't think you have the same illness that plagues Eaton and parts of our county. What I think ... is you have loose bowels from something other than cholera which is occurring mostly in the southern part of the county." He paused and continued, "I don't want you to come near your wife because of her pregnancy." He stood and called for Alexander. "Mrs. Hayman, please stay where you are. I'm concerned the Reverend might pass on what he has and that could cause problems for your unborn."

Alex asked, "Is this what I heard about at the general store?"

"Yes, I believe it is, for Pastor came in contact with one of the families who reside in the township to the south and all had the runs, but they recovered in two to three days."

"Will Nettie be affected?" Alex looked troubled.

"Possibly, so keep a close eye on her. The best we can do is to make sure you eat properly and drink boiled water. It should pass in two days and if Nettie isn't ill by then she can help Mrs. Hayman. I'll send a woman who's immune. She can care for the Reverend and Mary."

"And holding church services on Sunday?" Abner asked.

"No, it's best to cancel. People gathered in buildings seemingly increases the illness and the same is true in crowded households. The church might add to this problem and we don't need an epidemic in New Westville and the surrounding area."

Abner flinched when he thought how his son and wife became so sick with the strangling disease. "Alex, might you make a sign and pass the word there will be no church services this week?"

"I can do that, Abner."

Chapter 27

Crops in northern Preble and southern Darke counties broke the soil earlier than usual in May. The atmosphere held hope for a bountiful year, hope for better times after the intestinal flu and cholera outbreak. This scourge came to Preble County because of increased travel through and immigration into the area, cholera being most prevalent in Eaton.

The new rocking cradle sat in the parsonage bedroom. A special blanket covered the Hayman daughter, Mercy Ann. The little girl was the pride of the pastor and his wife. Each passing day small dimples became the trait that characterized the healthy infant. Abner doted on his young daughter and spent an hour each morning with her, unlike his son born in Mercersburg.

Nettie and Mary set in motion their plan to begin a school. It started with opening the church to young girls, teaching reading and writing, simple arithmetic, geography, and Bible study. The class began in the church on Sunday afternoons with Nettie teaching math, geography, and sharing Biblical teaching duties with Mary. Both women enjoyed reading and writing, thus splitting time on the subjects.

Other times for education were open by special arrangement. Compensation for these classes came from labor to improve the church and grounds, parsonage, and barn.

Older girls whose mothers and fathers died of cholera outbreak attended classes during the week. To solve the housing problem, the young girls stayed in homes of the elderly to help with daily chores. For the young women, Nettie taught midwifery, which did not sit favorably with the older doctors in the area.

The school did not interfere with Abner's efforts to preach and draw more parishioners to the German Reformed church, now crowded on Sundays. To stay out of the way of Mary and Nettie, he and Alex plotted a summer strategy to spend more time afield in the south region. The people on the south loop took an immediate liking to Alexander. Abner decided to engage the church elders, of that area, with more Bible study under the tutelage of Alex. Visits and sermons by Abner came on the third Wednesday in the month.

The north loop became Abner's exclusive territory. A large log cabin formerly owned by an elderly couple became the site for his mid-week sermons and Bible study. Chirt, when she had time, helped arrange for the afternoon and evening sessions, usually on a Thursday. The inroads to the people of northern Preble and southern Darke Counties came about because Abner visited their homes on Tuesdays and Thursdays. He spent time helping with chores and educating the children. He taught reading, writing, and math, all after completing the chores and Bible lessons.

Fridays became a special time for Abner as he spent the early morning learning about the land and people where he stayed for the night. It proved a way to serve their spiritual needs. Many times, he returned with new plants for the large parsonage garden. Alex took notice and followed Abner's approach of bringing back plants from the areas near Eaton.

By late July, Abner became a school observer on Mondays, the school had successfully taken hold at the church. He watched with pride the attention given to the special-needs children, and especially the depth of midwifery lessons taught by Nettie. The new frame building being readied for the winter education session, a short distance from the church, provided a welcome sight.

The summer turned hot and dry, and concern for the crops developed. The marshy areas on his northern loop began to evaporate, exposing non-vegetated soil, and the area farmers took advantage by draining other land to produce fresh vegetables for the stores in New Madison and New Paris.

Chris Kreulfs increased his wealth during the drought period. He sold his services developing drainage canals for Darke County farmers wanting more land for grain production.

Before returning to New Westville, Abner decided to visit with Chirt for a few minutes. She had been absent the past month from the church and his meetings around New Madison. The Kreulfs' log cabin was simple and in need of repair, neglect of daily care quite obvious. This trip Abner did not drive the buggy but chose to ride the mare. He loved the spirited horse that occasionally pleasured him with a fast ride. Abner enjoyed the quiet run along the county roads with the wind surging through his thick hair.

Abner dismounted and tied the mare in the shade of a large hickory tree. His nose wrinkled at an overpowering stench. A pile of rotting vegetation and manure emitted the nauseating smell. He slowly made his way to the cabin door. The entire scene bothered him. He hadn't visited the Kreulfs' homestead since first coming to Darke County.

The first rap on the cabin door brought no response. Abner loudly knocked a second time. "Mrs. Kreulfs," he called while peering off to his right. A noise came from the barn. The bruised and battered woman stumbled through the door, her hair hung in greasy strands over a dirty cloth wrapped around her forehead. He ran to her.

The distinct odor of urine came from her faded and stained dress. She looked up at him, one eye was swollen shut and the other red streaked. She clutched a bottle tightly in her right hand; she lifted it slowly to her lips and took a long drink.

"The bastard, the dirty bastard, he beat me again," she said and again tilted the bottle to her mouth, drinking freely, some of the liquid trickling down her dirt-streaked chin. Mrs. Kreulfs stared at Abner over the bottle. "What you want, preacher man?" Again, she tilted the bottle to her mouth and gulped the liquid. A loud belch roared from her fetid-smelling mouth.

Abner stepped back and gathered himself. "I stopped to check on you."

The old woman drunkenly grinned at him. She looked at the empty bottle and tossed it toward the small ditch running downslope from the barn. It landed in a muddy spot, disturbing the flies buzzing around an unidentifiable animal carcass. "What's the matter preacher, never seen a drunk Injun woman, huh?"

"I—"

"You high-and-mighty Bible spewing men …" Vomit flew from her

100

mouth. The stomach contents splattered over his legs and boots. She groaned and wiped her mouth on her dress sleeve. A foul odor filled the surrounding air.

"Where's Chirt?" he commanded.

The booming voice startled her. She stepped back and carefully eyed him. The tall man deserved her respect, but lately, her so-called husband had tainted her view of all preachers.

He waited while she looked him up and down. "Is Chirt safe?" he finally asked.

She nodded and pointed to the west.

"Where is she?"

The woman began to wail. Then she blurted out, "The girl gathers plants and berries."

"Where is she?" he again asked. "I need better direction."

She teetered and he reached to help her. She shook him off. "Stay away, devil man."

He grabbed her as she was about to pass out. The sound and smell of loose bowels caused him to step to the side while he supported her. "Dear God, you need help." Abner steered her into the barn and settled her onto a straw pile near a battered stall.

Susanna Kreulfs stared up at him. "Thank you. Chirt's somewhere near the big marsh. You'll find her there. She loves that meadow. If not there she will be … at the small forest beyond." Susanna passed out.

Before leaving her, he found an old pile of rags, rolled up his sleeves, located the water pump, wetted the rags, and returned to wipe her face and clean her hands. The slovenly smell made him gag. It took ten minutes and three wet rags to clean her. All the while he quietly recited prayers, for Chirt and her battered mother.

At the pump, he found an old soap bar and washed his hands and face. He cleaned himself of the trip grime and Susanna's vomit that splattered his lower legs and boots. While washing, Abner wondered at Chirt's well-being. At a sunny spot near his mare, he raised his face and arms skyward, feeling the breeze and sunshine warming and drying his head and hands. Tears trickled down his tanned face.

Before stepping into the stirrup, he leaned against the saddle and stared at the ramshackle farmstead. "God ... help this woman." He gathered the reins, swung easily into the saddle, and mumbled, "I'll return to help."

He trotted along the road, sitting easily in the saddle. Crops browning from the heat and lack of rain covered the gently rolling land. What promised to be a rich production year, slowly turned to near failure. He thought a good rain might save some crops, but only God could help. Abner urged his mare along and over a slight knoll.

In front of him lay a vast prairie with a marsh in the center of the grass and flower-filled field. Yellow-flowered plants dominated, interspersed with lavender and purple blooms. The dry grass warned of conditions that a prairie fire might happen if a lightning storm occurred. He reined to a halt, stood in the stirrups, and scanned the peaceful acres left undisturbed by the sod-breaking settlers.

Chapter 28

Dust rose from the roadbed as he urged the mare through the countryside, wondering if he correctly heard Susanna's words of Chirt's whereabouts. The land started gently falling to the west. A dry drainage channel across the road meant the beginning of a small stream somewhere ahead. There was more rolling land straight away. From his visits, he learned the creek to the west, the Whitewater would yield more forested land with a steeper slope.

To his right, he spotted a forest stand of oak, beech, hickory, walnut, and ash trees. In a small ravine to the west, a horse grazed on the grass at the forest edge. The old horse tethered to a small stump looked up as Abner approached. A small four-wheel wagon backed into a downslope allowed for easy loading without lifting. The old nag went back to grazing as Abner dismounted from his mare and hitched her to the wagon sideboard. He found a small, worn footpath leading into the heavily treed slope. A small stream trickled toward Whitewater Creek. He shed his vest and tucked it into a saddlebag with his Bible.

About three hundred feet up the path; he heard a steady, expressive voice. The woman's chanting didn't sound like Chirt. He waited as the chanting stopped and then began again. It faded deeper in the forest and nearer the clear, bubbling stream. Abner left the path, working his way, through underbrush tangle, toward the wailing voice.

A sharp rise created a swirling action in the water current. The wailing came from no more than thirty feet in front of him. He parted the small tree branch overhanging the water. "Oh my God, Chirt," he gasped.

She stood facing a limestone outcrop that created a small waterfall. The cool water flowed over red welts that crisscrossed her bare back. Whimpering sounds came from deep in Chirt's throat. At the sound of his voice, she turned to face him, covering her breasts. Her lower lip, split and swollen, sagged to her chin. Purple-black bruises marred both of her normally expressive eyes. Blood oozed from a cut over her left eyebrow.

Abner rushed to her, splashing through the water coursing toward Whitewater Creek. He took her in his arms and tightly held her to his chest. A violent shudder racked her body.

"Who did this to you, Chirt?"

She mumbled into his chest, "That devil-loving bastard. Chris found me and demanded to know what I wanted from God." She pushed away from him and stared at his face. "Abner … I … don't want to go back to the farm." Her voice rasped as she spoke.

He lightly titled her face up and looked at her neck. Bruises marred both sides. "Did he try to choke you?"

She took his hand from her chin, kissed the palm, and looked up at him. "He stank of whiskey and sweat … Chris tried to …"

Abner eyed her torn top sagging from her waist. "Let me help you." He lifted the tattered top so she could slip her arms into the sleeve remnants. I'll take you to a doctor in New Westville." Gripping her shoulders, he gently turned her and pulled the garment up and over her arms and welted back. "I'm going to fasten the remaining ties." He felt her shiver.

"Abner," Chirt turned and placed her arms around him. "Thank you. Thank you."

He stroked her wet hair and cradled her in his arms. "Can you walk out?"

"I can." She stepped away from him. "What brought you here?"

"Your mother, Chris beat her too."

Chirt's head dropped and she sighed heavily. "My father needs to die."

"Chirt, try to forgive the man."

"No, Abner, I cannot forgive for what he does to my mother, her people, and what he has tried to do to me, an only daughter."

Chapter 29

Nettie helped Chirt into a small room off the large open learning area in the new school building. This room, intended for Nettie and Mary as work and study space, could serve as a place for Chirt to stay. Being late Friday afternoon, men working on the building had returned to their farms, or to New Westville.

The draw curtain quietly closed and Chirt shrugged out of her soiled, torn dress. The doctor had applied a topical treatment to her small cuts and bruises and bandaged the cut near her eye so the edges would better heal together. Nettie gave her a soft cotton dress and Mary supplied stockings and a shawl. Alex had stopped earlier and supplied Chirt with a comfortable pair of shoes and boots for everyday use.

Tears rolled down Chirt's cheeks and dripped onto the hardwood floor. "Nettie, how will I repay you and Mary for all your kindness?"

"Not to worry, dear," Nettie said with a grin, "we have a plan to put you to work."

"How?" Chirt asked. She turned and Nettie loosely fastened the back of the new dress.

"School begins after harvest. We're not a public school as the Ohio politicians envisioned. We, Mary and I, decided to introduce a strong Christian teaching with our reading and writing education. We want you to teach the Indian use of herbs and native plants and their spiritual ways."

Chirt turned and tightly hugged Nettie. "But what of my father, he does not like the church? The people don't call him crazy Chris for nothing."

"We'll deal with him—"

The deep voice of Samuel Carnes interrupted their conversation. "Chirt, are you in there?"

The curtain flew back and Samuel Carnes stood tall and powerful, looking in the small room's entrance. He studied both women and spoke in a commanding voice, "Tell me what's going on, Nettie."

Nettie puffed up like a bantam hen. "Simply stated: Chris beat his wife and daughter."

The anger in Samuel's face made Chirt cringe. She wanted to say something, but remained quiet.

"I suggest you take a moment to talk with Pastor Hayman before you go off half-cocked, Samuel." Nettie knew Samuel well enough to share her feelings with this man. "This is not a new issue with Chris and Susanna. Am I right, Chirt?"

Chirt meekly nodded.

Samuel stared at Nettie, opened his mouth to say something, abruptly stopped, whirled around, and stomped away.

The church altar reflected the sun when Samuel threw open the doors. "Abner Hayman, I wish to speak with you," he bellowed. The boot stomps broke the peaceful silence. Samuel stopped before the altar, staring at the closed door to Abner's study. The doors quietly closing behind him caught his attention.

Alexander stood tall at the back of the church. He said nothing, did nothing but stand and eye Samuel.

"So?" Samuel said to Alexander.

"So, is that all you have to say to me, Samuel." Alexander stiffly walked toward his mentor. "I'll not be a part of what is in your head, Samuel." He stopped immediately before his former boss and tutor. "You come back from your journey, find a former lover in dire straits, and become filled with thoughts of revenge. I know you, Samuel, you will avenge. Leave the Haymans out of this. Leave Nettie and me out of this."

The surprised look and silence allowed Alexander to continue with his tirade of feelings. "For so long ... you have taken advantage of those around you. I knew this when I signed on with you. Sure, you have brought me good fortune, but is it the devil's fortune?"

"I—" Samuel began.

"Allow me to finish, Samuel," Alex interrupted. He pointed to a front pew where they could sit and talk. "Before we continue … in a civil manner, I want to know how you knew about Chirt's beating."

"I have taught you well," Samuel said with a smug look. "You're even better than I imagined at assimilating a dilemma."

"Don't try to divert me, Samuel."

"Much better, I must say." Samuel crossed his legs. "The doctor who treated her told me." He noticed Alexander's chagrin. "I have my contacts that keep me informed, and they receive good pay for keeping me current on happenings in and around New Westville."

"I know I'll not keep you from doing as you want; that is, revenge for Chirt. But what I want is for you to keep the Haymans from harm, brought about by your thoughtless actions. And stay away from Nettie, for she succeeds in fulfilling her dream … with God's help."

"Granted, Alexander, I like you and your wife and the Haymans more than you know—"

"Stop right there, Samuel." The angry expression and the tone of Alexander's voice made Samuel stay silent. "You have designs on the pastor's wife and don't deny it."

Samuel smugly shook his head.

The gesture enraged Alexander. "Samuel, deny it, deny it here in the house of worship. Deny it before God."

"No, damn you, Alexander. I am a man of principle—"

"Come now, Samuel, you're a man who will do anything to win in any arena. You created a facade with the church and the promises to the Haymans, all to gain Mary's favor."

"No," Samuel boomed. His voice echoed in the empty church. "No, that is not true."

"You tried the same with Nettie, Samuel," Alexander snorted. "You are like a bull elk in rut." Alexander folded his hands and sat quietly.

Samuel sat staring at the pulpit. After a minute, he said, "Why do you think that, Alexander?"

"Nettie is a highly intelligent woman, Samuel. She knew there was an attraction between the two of you, but she understood the underlying implications if she did not resist your charm and … power."

A deep sigh came from Samuel. "You're right, Alexander, and Nettie is right. I have a deep desire for Mary."

"No, you don't. Samuel, all you want to do is conquer another woman like a piece of land to sell, with no emotion. Don't you understand? Mary will never fail her God or Abner. She will not denigrate her character even if she desires you, and I don't think she does."

Samuel stood. "Alexander, I hope we can remain friends. I will do what needs doing with Chris Kreulfs. He's a scourge on humanity and the land." He held out his hand.

"I cannot excuse what you are about to do, Samuel." He ignored Samuel's attempted handshake of peace.

"So be it, Alexander, I love you like a brother." He noted Alexander's skeptical expression. "Take care of the Haymans. I'm right to do what I know is necessary."

The church door quietly closed. Alexander turned to the front and said with an upraised face, "God help us, for we are all sinners."

Chapter 30

Nearly two months had passed since Chirt came to the Brethren Reformed Church School. The two women, Mary and Nettie, tutored and prepared her to work with the infants up to two years. Mercy's care became a pleasant surprise. The little tyke stole her heart with the wonderful and the constant smiles when Chirt held her. Mercy appeared most happy when Chirt carried her close to her bosom in a small sling fashioned with deer-hide straps, enabling Chirt to move about with the other children. Mercy's coos and gurgles created smiles in the other children and they begged Chirt to let them hold the Hayman's child.

Word of the fine church school spread throughout the Preble County townships. Subjects taught by Nettie and Mary, plus the native studies developed and presented by Chirt, steeply increased enrollment. The three women collectively decided to cap the number of children attending their classes.

"Have you ever seen such an uproarious room?" Alexander said with a smile. He watched the groups of children throughout the large learning room.

It neared noon on the frigid Friday before Christmas. Chirt prepared a large pot of stew made from fresh elk that Alexander harvested from the Kreulfs' farm the previous Monday. The animal cured in the barn a few days before the Christmas celebration. After the school event, the children would spend a week at home with their families.

The entire learning center, decorated with biblical passages and chalk drawings, lined the halls and hung from the ceiling. Each child worked in a group, telling what they covered in the previous three months. The groups contained students of varying ages. Community members selected from New Westville and the surrounding area graded each learning group. Nettie and Mary designed the criteria and provided examples and answers for judging the students. This helped the volunteers manage the group presentations and relieve the pressures of not knowing how to evaluate a difficult presentation or production.

The two-day evaluations conducted by Nettie, Mary, Chirt, Abner, and Alexander followed the volunteers who judged student work. The students moved through the Friday morning without a hitch. Promptly at noon the students and volunteers gathered for a prayer conducted by Reverend Hayman before sitting down to a meal prepared by volunteers. After the meal, a Christmas pageant, led by the older students, celebrated the birth of Christ. Costumes sewn by the girls and props designed and built by the boys sat at the front of the learning center. The play, written and directed by the students lasted nearly ninety minutes. At the end of the play, the students cleaned the large room and gathered their homework assignments before their parents took them home.

When the final family departed, Abner and the group moved to the church for a private service of thanks to God. As Abner said the final words for the day, a pounding on the church doors broke the calm.

"Reverend Hayman," Zebulon Hartman frantically called as he burst into the church, "you're needed at the Kreulfs' farm."

Chirt jumped up. "Zeb, what's wrong?" A panicked expression covered her face.

Zebulon said, "It's your mother, Chirt." The boy of fourteen sniffed and wiped his eyes. "Father says she's nearly dead."

"Abner, I'll hitch the mare to the buggy. Chirt, get dressed in warm clothes and you travel with us." Alexander turned to his wife. "Nettie, get the sheriff." He spoke to Zeb, "Did your father find Mrs. Kreulfs?"

"Yeah," the boy swallowed hard, "he did."

"You were with him?" Abner asked.

The boy nodded.

"We knew Chirt were down here teachin' the children. Mom sent Dad and me with baked goods for Susanna." He started to turn pale and sat on a bench. "Jest the thought of her makes me sick."

Mary looked toward Chirt's room. "What did you see?" Mary asked as she sat down next to the boy.

He dropped his head and tears fell on his woolen pants. Mary put her arm around his shoulders.

"Somebody beat her, bad." He gulped in air. "Her face …" His body shook as the tears flowed.

Chapter 31

The road to the Kreulfs' Farm remained frozen. The trip took no longer than normal, even slowing for the ice-covered puddles. Alexander expertly handled the reins and allowed the mare to avoid irritating ruts in the road. Abner and Chirt remained silent for the near hour trip. A heavy sigh came from Chirt as they neared the farm.

A stooped man stood outside the cabin, periodically clapping his hands to keep them warm. When he exhaled, frosty puffs formed in the cold air. Beside him, a young man in his early twenties leaned against the door jam. At the sound of the approaching buggy, the two men moved to greet them.

The moment the horse came to a standstill the older Hartman son, Daniel, grasped the bridle to steady the mare. Abner and Alexander stepped down and waited by the cabin door. Walter Hartman held out his hand to help Chirt from the buggy. Daniel led the mare out of the cold, north wind into the barn.

"Tell us what you found … and know," Abner said.

"We—Daniel, me, and Zeb—was bringin' food for Susanna. When no one answered, we went in," he gulped, "we found her next to the fireplace." His grizzled face scrunched for a moment. "Daniel, you tell em."

Daniel rejoined the group after putting up the horse and checking the buggy. "The smell of death hit me as I leaned down. She had her clothes ripped and torn; her moccasins kicked to the side." He paused when he looked at Chirt. "I'm sorry, Chirt."

"I want to go in … now," Chirt commanded.

"Are you sure?" Alexander asked.

She nodded, took a deep breath, and reached to open the door. "Help me, dear God. Abner," she took his hand, "please come with me."

He responded by taking her hand as she opened the heavy door. A damp chill hit both as they stepped inside. Susanna lay sprawled on the dirt floor in front of the flameless fireplace.

Chirt sobbed. "Oh ... dear God ... Abner, hold me."

Alexander moved to the body. He knelt beside Susanna and eyed her from the top of her battered head to her bruised lower limbs. He looked up at Abner and shook his head, his facial expression full of sadness.

Abner whispered to Chirt, "Is there a place we can sit in the barn?" He felt her nod against his chest. "Let's go there until the sheriff arrives." Holding her at arm's length, he put his hands softly on either side of her face. "Are you going to be okay?"

Tears flowed from her dark eyes. She nodded and looked up at him. "The devil has been here, and his name is Chris." She breathed deeply, turned, and walked past Daniel Hartman into the cold air.

The reek of horse manure, urine, and rotting straw filled the barn. Abner climbed into the haymow and found prairie-hay bale remnants loosely tied with hemp twine. He wearily tossed them down to Walter and Daniel who had followed Chirt and Abner to the barn in the chill of the late afternoon.

Alexander found a dozen old bricks tossed behind the barn, loaded several on a dilapidated cart, and moved them to a spot in the barn where they could safely build a fire pit. He stacked the bricks where he wanted the wood unloaded.

While the other men gathered dry wood to burn and heat the barn, Walter and Abner moved the bales a safe distance from the pit area to prevent a fire. From an empty stall near the rear of the barn, Chirt gathered horse blankets not encrusted with waste or crawling with pests.

The entire exercise took less than thirty minutes and ten minutes later warmth filled the barn. Even Abner's mare seemed to enjoy the break from the cold. A feedbag full of oats hung from the post for her. The only sounds came from the horse's grain crunching and the crackling fire.

Abner broke the silence by asking for a moment remembering Susanna before his prayer. "Dear God, giver of life, please watch over Susanna's soul. Keep her in your heavenly light and protect her from all evil until the second coming, and the day of judgment. Amen."

Everybody responded with a soft Amen.

"Chirt," Abner said, "do you know your mother's wishes for burial or …?"

She looked at each of the men. "Susanna probably would want to tell each one of you thank you for caring about her, and me. She told me not long ago that she wished to be buried with her Miami tribal ancestors."

"Chirt, do you know where?" Alexander asked.

"Somewhere in Indiana … I think it's recorded in her Bible."

Walter Hartman spoke up, "Chirt, the boys and me can haul her body to wherever you want."

"Thank you," Chirt responded, "that's kind of you." She noticed Daniel seemed uncomfortable with the vow. "Daniel, do you want to say something?"

"Yep, I do." He fidgeted for a few seconds. "Your mamma was one of the kindest women I done knew. She taught me lots about trapping and hunting. I'd like to be the one to dig her grave or however she wants to rest before going to meet her spiritual leader."

Abner stared at the boy. "Daniel, did she talk to you about her spirituality?"

Daniel shrugged. "She did mention that her spiritual upbringing and the Catholic faith did not differ much." He cleared his throat. "I don't much unnerstand all of it, but I do know she felt comfortable with both."

Alexander said, "Daniel, help gather wood to keep the fire burning until Zeb and the sheriff arrive." Walter stood to help them.

When all three left the barn, Chirt said, "Reverend Hayman, would you bury Mother?"

"Chirt, I'm honored to be the pastor for her burial."

She rose from her seat and softly kissed him on the lips. "Thank you, Reverend." Her eyes, misted with pain, begged him to respond. When he did not move, she said, "Hold me, Abner."

Abner took her in his arms and rocked her. He waved at the three men waiting at the barn door to enter. He began humming a hymn.

Chapter 32

The Hartman family cleared the cabin and set it on fire after Chirt pleaded for them to do so. While the cabin smoldered, Chirt cleansed her mother in the barn next to the fire pit. She dressed and wrapped Susanna in her favorite clothes and blanket for the burial. Reverend Hayman and Walter Hartman then delivered Susanna's remains to the resting ground in Indiana. Chirt's anger and pain finally began to subside on the return trip to Ohio.

When Walter's wife asked about the burial, he talked about the service that involved both Christian and Miami spiritual ceremonies. Walter made a point to let her know several French missionaries and Frenchmen attended the burial, which he found rather interesting. Mr. Hartman cut off further conversation about Chirt and Abner when he mentioned their parting ways near New Madison.

Abner returned to New Westville after the Preble County Sheriff re-examined the death site. Six months after the Sheriff's final investigation, Abner spent the winter in New Westville except for one week. During that time, he unsuccessfully tried to establish a church with its own pastor on the northern route while preaching in homes and working evenings in New Madison, preparing Biblical teachings. After Easter season, he joined Alexander on the southern route, meeting new congregation members and baptizing the newborn children and adults. Every home where he spent time with the families he heard high praises for Alexander.

On the trip, back, Abner encouraged Alexander to take classes at Miami University in Oxford. Alexander remained silent for the balance of the trip until they neared New Westville. He admired the church buildings and grounds he and Nettie so lovingly tended. His difficult decision became clear when he learned that Abner would be a father again in September.

Planting season rapidly descended on the Haymans and Schroeders after the mild winter. Mary cared for her two children, Mercy—now past two—and their son, John Edmund, now eight months. Both children kept Mary, Abner, Nettie, and Alexander busy. The Hayman children displayed high energy and an inquisitiveness beyond what the parents and godparents expected.

After their evening meal and a prayer, Alexander and Nettie sat under cover of the large hickory tree near their modest home, enjoying the mild, late May evening. The sunlight filtered through the greening leaves, casting swaying shadows at their feet. The intermittent wind gusts carried the smell of newly turned sod. Tomorrow Alex and Nettie would begin the garden planting, which served needy church members and their families.

Nettie sighed. "It surely is one of the finest spring evenings we've had in the past two years." She looked toward Alexander sitting quietly reading the last edition for the college year of the *Literary Register* he brought back from Miami University. "Alex, is everything okay?"

He looked up from the student publication, smiled, and went back to his reading.

She sat staring off at the large garden where she would spend many forthcoming hours with the students attending the church school summer session. With Alexander's help, she would teach the young women, who came from motherless homes, how to garden and the care for the household.

"Alex—"

"Yes, Nettie," he broke in, folded the paper and placed it on his lap, "what is it?"

A thoughtful expression took over her features before she spoke. "Has anyone seen, Chirt?"

He turned toward her. "I don't know. Abner hasn't spoken of her on our trips together. Why do you ask?"

"While you've been attending classes at the University, Abner seems withdrawn."

"Withdrawn?"

"Yes, from us and the church."

"Give me an example, Nettie."

She hesitated and then spoke. "I'll summarize. When Abner returned from Susanna's burial, he seemed ... distant, but over the summer and after John Edmund's birth he changed."

"What do you mean ... changed?"

"The Reverend seemed more like his old self. Then he took a run up north to minister to a family northeast of New Paris after the Christmas season, and when you had returned to classes." She stopped to gather herself. "A rider came hurrying in, carrying a message. The Reverend wanted us to know it would be a few days before he came back to New Westville. And that was all it said."

"So," Alexander said, "you're thinking what?"

"It's been eighteen months since Chirt's mother died. No one has seen Chirt since the funeral in Indiana. If she has returned to the New Madison area do you think ... something's going on between Abner and Chirt?"

A solemn moment passed and he responded, "I'm not the one to judge."

Chapter 33

Abner waited patiently while Chirt walked over the ground where the cabin once stood. It began as an innocent relationship when she first appeared at the home of the rural New Paris family. At first, he thought it an apparition that day, but she floated from under the leafless oak tree and stood in the doorway.

This woman tore at his heart. She didn't walk, she glided, her posture straight—a proud trait from her Indian heritage passed on by Susanna. The intelligence she possessed inspired him when he visited with the people, in southern Darke and northern Preble Counties, seeking religious and spiritual help.

He stepped down from the buggy and quietly walked to where she stood. The wash of sunlight reflected from her black hair. Abner slipped his arms around her waist and held her tightly. They stood without moving, the wind stirring the leaves piled against a charred log.

"Come back to the church, Chirt."

She turned in his arms, looked up at him, and softly kissed him. "I love you, Abner."

He felt a mix of emotions pass over him. A response would not come.

"Abner, born into sin is what you preach and that we easily fall into sin, but ... God forgives." She kissed him once again. "We have sinned. We have broken a vow to each other this should not and would not happen. It did. All we can do is what you preach, and what I believe."

He held her, felt her tremble, and tilted her chin so he could look into her eyes. "You are right, we did sin, and we can ask forgiveness." Abner kissed her, longingly. "Chirt, I love you."

"But we cannot, and must not destroy the path God has set for … us."

"Then you'll return to New Westville?"

"I will, Abner. We've made a mistake, but our Lord, and Savior, points us in a direction we must follow."

"Then we'll have your belongings packed and sent to New Westville and the church. You can again be with your family."

"Abner, I think it best I not stay at the school, but with the Schroeder family, if they'll allow me, or I can live in New Westville. The room at the school deserves better use." She stepped back from him and smiled. "I love your daughter, Abner. She's a wonder and I want to see your son again."

It took most of the morning to pack her belongings and say goodbye. The family Chirt stayed with over the past eighteen months presented her with a new blanket. The children began to cry and Chirt leaned down and gave each a hug. They clung to her, not wanting to let go.

Abner felt sadness for the children, but her return was a blessing for the German Reformed Church. He stood watching the moment play out. Chirt had endured bad luck of living with a father who became a drunk and wife beater. Her kindness and intellect played well with the children whose lives she touched, including his daughter Mercy.

"Tell me about John Edmund," Chirt said as they traveled south.

He drew a deep breath, smelling the surrounding cool countryside air mingling with the oiled buggy leather. He grinned and said, "John, like Mercy, has an innate curiosity." He gently slapped the reins against the mare's rump, encouraging her up the stream bank. "He's beginning to explore more every day. His eyes are changing color, away from the blue like Mercy's. He's more dark-skinned, not fair like Mary."

"Stop the buggy, Abner." They were on an isolated stretch of the road headed toward New Westville. When he reined in the mare, she encircled him with her arms and kissed him. "I want you to know I'll follow you wherever you go. I'll be faithful to God and to your family." A sob erupted from her throat. "Abner … God has brought us together for a reason, just like you and the Shroeders. There are great days ahead for you, Mary, Alexander, and Nettie. I'll faithfully serve God."

Chapter 34

Every Sunday began with Abner welcoming the congregation in the Lord's name. He followed the standard liturgy: a call to worship, confession, hymn, scripture reading, sermon, offering, hymn, and the benediction. As the congregation leader, Abner made a point to ask for food and labor to help the needy around the New Westville area and maintain the church and grounds. This reminder statement came after the hymn and before the benediction and he included it in his German service on every third Sunday evening attended mostly by the older settlers.

This fine, early November Sunday brought many members to the service. A full church, fervent singing, and prayer resounded from the beams holding the sturdy walls of the rural New Westville Reformed Church. After the benediction and doxology, Abner spied the church elders huddled behind the last pew talking quietly with Samuel Carnes.

Abner stood at the church entrance bidding a good week ahead for those who stopped. Before the last of the members finished talking to Abner, Samuel walked to his minister and said, "Reverend Hayman, we'd like to speak with you and Alexander."

"It will be a few minutes, Samuel." A family visited with Mary and Nettie about their children's progress in the fall school sessions while they waited for Abner to finish speaking with Samuel. "Meet me outside the office and we can visit."

Samuel nodded and pointed to the church front where Alexander gathered slips of paper and coins from the offerings. He and the elders walked along the side aisle, all of them wearing serious faces.

It took ten minutes for Abner to complete the discussions with the two congregation members who remained. The lengthy discussion came from the young couple considering marriage. Their lighthearted banter brought a proper ending to Abner's Sunday service.

"Mary," Abner said, "do you have any idea why Samuel and the elders are so serious?"

"No," she looked past Abner to where Alexander talked with the five men. "They're members from the northern area of our congregation." She looked around for Mercy and John. "Chirt must have escorted the children home while we visited. I must look after them."

Abner approached the men talking with Alexander. "What can I do for you?" Several children raced through the pews and then outside. Abner shook his head and pointed to the church office.

After they settled into the chairs, Samuel began. "The Sheriff from Darke County stopped me yesterday on my way through Greenville. Chirt's father is in custody." The elders shifted uncomfortably.

"Samuel, you appear distressed. Why?"

"Chris Kreulfs is pointing the finger at me for the death of Chirt's mother and he claims I tried to make it look like he did the killing."

"There's more?" Abner asked.

"Yes, the crazy old man claims you and Chirt collaborated with me, while you carried on an illicit affair with her."

Alexander sat quietly behind the men hanging on every word. He watched Abner's expression when Samuel stopped talking.

Silence filled the room. Finally, Abner spoke. "Is all this coming from the Sheriff?"

"Yes," Samuel said.

The elder from the farm south of the Kreulfs' land spoke up. "Reverend Hayman, we're concerned with the rumors that will come from Chris' claims."

"One more question," Abner said, "why now, why did Chris show up all of a sudden?"

"He did not show up," Samuel said. "The Sheriff arrested Chris after he got into a skirmish with a farmer north of Greenville."

Alexander moved to the vacant chair by Abner, sat, and asked, "Clarify about the confrontation with the farmer and why the Sheriff became involved."

Samuel looked to the elders. They nodded for him to proceed. "The Sheriff arrested Chris for beating the farmer and his son. He also burned down their barn."

"So, he's being himself," Alexander offered. "What's the concern?"

"He wants Reverend Hayman to be brought before the court. He has asked the Sheriff to arrest you, me, and Chirt for Susanna's murder."

"And …?" Abner said.

"The Sheriff plans not to arrest us, but asks we testify at the trial to send Chris to jail for a long, long time."

The second church elder spoke up. "Reverend Hayman, we're concerned how this will affect all of us. We know you're innocent and Samuel too. But Chris has a person who will testify he didn't kill Susanna."

"Do you know who?" Alexander jumped in with his question. The man shook his head. "Samuel, do you know?"

"No, Alex, but I can find out," Samuel said.

The first elder spoke up. "We'll help put this to rest and see that Chris gets his due."

"When's the trial scheduled?" Alex asked.

"Chris' trial begins next week." Samuel looked at Abner.

"Samuel, can you find the witness in that short time?" Abner asked.

"I can."

"Then with my blessing find him or her. I'll talk to Chirt and we'll be prepared for Mr. Kreulfs' false claims." Abner looked to each one of the elders. "God is with us, gentlemen. We will let Mr. Kreulfs hang himself." He rose and shook hands with each man.

Alexander shook hands with each and, with Samuel, walked them to the church door.

"Samuel, we must talk," Abner said when Carnes returned.

"I'll come back after the noon meal in New Westville. I'm dining with the Preble County Sheriff. "I think I can get the needed information."

Alexander returned. "Samuel, at one time you had an affair with Chirt;

this is common knowledge of those in northern Preble County. If this trial comes about it's the devil's dance before it's all over."

Samuel grinned at Alexander. "You believe the rumors?"

"Samuel, you cannot claim the affair to be a rumor. Too many of these people saw you with her in your fancy buggy."

"You're correct, Alexander." He sighed. "Chris is crazy like a fox. He knows Chirt has a love for the Reverend, especially after Abner brought her here after the beating Chris and her mother."

"Why in the world would Chris want to beat her to death? I know anger can drive a person to do meaningless acts, but ..." Abner shrugged.

"Tell him, Samuel." Alexander's stern expression and cool voice shocked Abner.

"Susanna bought the land from me and placed it all in Chirt's name. It's complicated."

"Let's hear it," Abner firmly said.

Samuel hesitated. "Chirt is not Chris' daughter." He eyed Abner for a reaction, being none, he continued. "Chirt's father, a Frenchman, lived among the tribe for many years. He fathered several children with his many women. Since Susanna was part Indian, she legally couldn't buy the land, but there being a legal loophole Chirt became eligible. It appeared she could do so if Chris claimed to be the father."

"Then you sold the land for money that Susanna had saved doing work in the area for the new residents." Alexander shook his head.

"I did."

"Why?" Abner sighed.

"Because I wanted Chirt," Samuel said. "You know her beauty and intellect. I did become involved with her and struck the deal. It turned sour when old Chris swilled too much of his own alcohol after Chirt met you, Reverend."

"Enough," Alexander said. "Samuel, this mess must go away. You have the means to do so. Will you, do it?"

"Yes, but I want to know if there's something going on with Chirt and the Reverend that will create havoc in the church."

Abner stood straight and strongly answered, "No. Chirt had feelings for me, and we straightened that out before I brought her back to the church and our families." He gave Samuel a disgusted look. "And I want to know if you will stay away from my wife?"

Samuel paled. "Reverend, you only think you know that I desire Mary?"

"Let me answer that, Abner," Alexander shot back at Samuel. "You're famous for wanting fine women like you want deer and elk trophies. Mary's a fine woman who suffered the loss of a child and nearly lost her husband. She too wondered about Chirt and Abner, as did Nettie. I've seen Abner's work help so many people. I will not let Chris hurt his family and the church."

"But—"

"Stop Samuel, I've known you for a long time. Don't think only of yourself this time. Help Abner and Chirt out of this mess. If you bring harm to this church ... I will see to it that you will not sell land or have any more dealings in Ohio."

"And how would you do that, Alex?"

Abner waited quietly.

"I know how you have sold, bought, and resold the land. How you came about owning all the freight and stage lines." Alexander's face became solemn-looking. "Need I bring out more before the good Reverend?"

"I'll take care of this mess, Alexander. I pledge this to you and Abner and it will go away." He turned to walk out and stopped. "I promise, Abner, I will not tread on your family or hurt any of you, especially Mary." He walked out without saying another word or making a sound.

Chapter 35

Snow fell lightly across the Preble County northern prairie lands the week after Samuel Carnes walked out of the church. Alexander and Abner had explained to Chirt that Chris leveled accusations about Samuel, Abner, and her wanting to kill Susanna for the land.

Samuel fulfilled his promise to Abner and Alex that he would protect the three of them and the church. He found Chris Kreulfs' witness. Chris convinced the person he, Chris, would inherit the land if set free. If this came about, Chris planned to sell the land, giving one-half of the profits to the witness for testifying.

Chris' witness did not show for the trial and left Chris feeling the noose around his neck, after receiving a visit from the Carnes lawyer. Chris subsequently convinced the jury to put Chirt on the stand, suggesting they would understand what really happened. He stated his daughter wanted the land free and clear, leaving him without any means of making a living when he went free. The jurors agreed Chirt should take the stand. The judge stated that the jury's decision of guilty as charged would stand unless Chirt's testimony made him declare a mistrial.

Samuel offered use of his coach to transport Chirt to Greenville for her testimony. The snow slowed their travel, which allowed them time to discuss the part she needed to play to ensure the jury made the correct decision of guilty, with the death penalty. They did not want to see the jury overturn that decision.

With Chirt's fear Chris might go free, she knew the testimony must be airtight. The lawyer Samuel used for all of his western Ohio dealings traveled with them. This man knew his law, both civil and criminal. When issues arose, the lawyer found loopholes and easily disposed of them, leaving no problems for the Carnes holdings and actions.

The stagecoach trip took about four hours under good conditions, but with snow covering the main road and causing some problems at the stage stations, it took nearly six hours. They arrived thirty minutes before the scheduled time for Chirt to take the stand. As they entered the courthouse the Sheriff stopped them.

"Mr. Carnes," the Sheriff said, "Chris Kreulfs escaped from my deputy and is on the run."

"How ... what the devil happened?" Samuel asked.

"When the deputy brought Chris from the cell an armed and masked man stopped my deputy, freed Chris, and they fled. The deputy and I think they're heading for Michigan Territory or seeking you and the others."

"Sheriff," Samuel sputtered, "this is ridiculous."

"Calm yourself, Samuel," his lawyer said, "I'll sit down with the Sheriff and map out a strategy to make sure you, Chirt, and the others are safe from this convicted killer." Samuel's lawyer turned to the Sheriff. "Is there a place my clients can wait while we work through this?"

The Sheriff nodded, slipped on his coat, and led Samuel and Chirt to a small tavern. A group of men sat around a wood stove, used to warm the room, while the owner prepared food at another stove. Two men nodded at Samuel.

It took the lawyer less than an hour to convince the Sheriff to send three armed deputies in search of Chris Kreulfs. They would carry wanted dead or alive posters that listed a bounty of one-thousand dollars for Kreulfs' capture. The lawyer added that if the Sheriff and the deputies caught and returned Chris to Greenville they would personally receive the reward and a bonus, providing the capture or death occurred within five days. On the return trip to New Westville, the lawyer explained the agreement and he expected Chris not to be returned alive.

Samuel asked, "Chirt, does this bother you?"

To the lawyer, Chirt said, "I feel you did right. Chris is an evil man and doesn't deserve to live."

The lawyer shook her hand and said, "It's over, Chirt."

"No." She looked at Samuel and said, "You're not to bring any harm to my friends and their families. Also, I want the land deeded to Walter Hartman. Finally, dedicate part of the acreage for school land with the stipulation of hiring a teacher."

Samuel said, "Done."

The lawyer nodded and confirmed the deeded land per Chirt's wishes in the name of Walter Hartman.

Seventy-two hours after Samuel left for New Westville the Sheriff delivered the message: Chris Kreulfs' dead body arrived at the courthouse in the possession of his deputies.

The Carnes' lawyer the next day asked no questions and he paid, as promised.

Chapter 36

Mary received word from her father's lawyer that Hilmar had taken ill, and would likely be homebound for the rest of his life. It took Abner a short time to find adequate funds for Mary's stagecoach trip to Philadelphia. Alexander helped by quietly talking to the church members, taking up a collection to support the round-trip cost. Nettie took up discreet collections from the parents of the school children enrolled over the past year. Finally, Walter Hartman, through his generosity, stepped in and bought the round-trip ticket and asked the school use the funds collected by Abner, Alexander, and Nettie.

Dove and meadowlark calls punctuated the spring morning while cardinals flitted from tree to tree, protecting their territories. It was difficult for Mary to part with her family. Mercy celebrated her fifth birthday that day and didn't want her mother to leave. Little John tugged at her dress and did not want to let go when the stagecoach arrived to begin her long journey.

"Don't worry, Mary," Nettie said, "Chirt and I'll take good care of the children." Alexander held John while Mercy sat on Abner's shoulders watching the horse exchange.

"New driver, aren't you?" Mary asked.

"Yes ma'am, I came on last year," he said as he helped her into the coach.

Mary nodded at the woman seated on the far side. The stage door closed behind her and the driver immediately climbed to his seat.

"Mommy," John cried. "I want you to come back."

Mary heard Alexander consoling her son. She slid to the rectangular opening and felt her heart sink when she saw her son's red face. "Alex, bring him here, please."

"One minute more, Mrs. Hayman," the assistant driver said.

Alexander lifted John to his shoulders so he could be face-to-face with Mary.

"John, I'm coming back. You're a big boy and you must take care of Father and Alex, okay?"

John sniffed. "Okay, Mama. I'll be good while you're gone." He leaned over and she kissed his cheek. "Thank you, Mama."

"I love you, John." Alex stepped back and the stagecoach lurched forward.

A mile down the road the older woman smiled and said, "Did I hear our driver say ... Hayman?"

"Yes. I'm Mary Hayman, Abner Hayman's wife."

"Winifred Clark, I'm on my way to Cincinnati from Greenville."

"Pleased to meet you, I'm going to Philadelphia."

"Chirtlain Kreulfs assists you and pastor?"

Mary smiled a small smile. "She does."

"I presume you know ... Samuel Carnes?" Winifred said. A distasteful smirk played at the corners of her lips.

"We do, and have known him for some time."

Winifred sat straight and began to say something and stopped.

The children were distraught as the stagecoach transported Mary and Winifred from sight. Chirt had been in the New Westville station and noticed the upset children. She took Mercy from Abner. "Miss Mercy, are you ready to help?"

Mercy nodded. "We're going to read?"

"Yes, and then we're going to weed."

"Aw, do we have to?" Mercy pouted.

"Do you want the garden plants to die?"

"No, but ..."

"Come we'll ride together." Chirt led Mercy to her small buggy. She stopped at the cry of John's voice and turned. He ran toward her. She looked up at Abner and he nodded approval. "Careful, Mercy," Chirt giggled as the girl launched herself into the buggy. John jumped into Chirt's open arms. She kissed and hugged him. "I don't want you wiggling around, John."

He grinned and nodded.

"Mercy, John can sit between us."

"Yes, Chirt," Mercy answered and slid her brother to the middle.

Chirt waved as she urged the horse away from the station.

Nettie turned to Abner. "Your children love that girl."

Abner smiled and nodded.

"C'mon, Nettie, we can pick up some dry goods in town and I think you might have books at the store." Alexander held out his arm.

"My, my, Alexander, why do you approach so gallantly?"

Alex just grinned.

Nettie turned to Abner and said, "Wipe the smile off your face, Reverend."

Abner laughed. "Will I see both of you this evening?"

"You will," Alex offered. "I promised John I would take him to the pond beyond the woods."

Nettie watched Abner climb into his buggy and set a quickened pace for his mare to catch up to Chirt and the children. "Alex—"

"No, Nettie, I know at one time we wondered about Chirt and Abner, but now I believe they are past that questionable time. Chirt has her goals and she'll reach them without interfering in Mary and Abner's life."

"Sorry, Alex, I'm not sure, but I hope you're correct."

"The children make the difference."

"Let's hope. Chirt becomes lovelier each month. She has the expressive power locked up for now, but ..."

He watched Abner's buggy disappear around the small bend, heading for the parsonage. "With any hint of infidelity, I'll trim Reverend Hayman's ears back."

"Alex, you wouldn't," Nettie said with a smile.

"I would, because he has a wonderful family, and ..."

"And ...?" Nettie urged him to answer.

"I want Chirt." He roared with laughter at the look on her face and immediately took her in his arms and kissed her.

Chapter 37

Enough late season snow fell to make it possible for Alexander to treat John Hayman to a sleigh ride. Alex had tapped four trees and found the sugar maple stand in the forest south of the church showed good sap flow. Mary's father had worsened shortly before Christmas and she remained in Philadelphia over the winter months. In her absence, Chirt, Nettie, and Alexander helped Abner with his children. John sat ready for the sleigh ride, his small legs covered by a wool blanket. Nettie wanted to go with Chirt and Alexander but had to prepare lessons for winter students' writing and Bible classes.

The bells tied to the harness and sleigh softly echoed over snow-covered highlands of western Preble County. John sat mesmerized by the sparkling snow and the animals scurrying about in the sun-filled roadside.

"Chirt, Chirt," John yelled, "what's that red animal?"

"That's a fox." She grinned at Alex.

"Are there lots of them?"

Chirt thought for a moment. "Not many, but they like to hide … there might be more than we know."

"Why?" John asked.

"They don't like humans."

"Humans?" John frowned.

"That's us, John. We're humans."

"Why don't they like us? I'm nice."

"They protect themselves by running away and hiding."

He still held a troubled look. "But we don't want to hurt them, do we?"

"John, some people trap them for their fur." His small face looked puzzled. "People use the fur for clothing like we use wool off the sheep."

"Oh ..."

"John, you ask good questions." Alex smiled down at him. "Keep on asking and you'll learn what's around you. That will be good." He slowed to cross over a small bridge before entering the maple forest.

"Oh, what's the big animal?" A tan, furry critter scurried in front of the mare.

"That," Alexander said, "is a woodchuck."

"A what?" John watched the animal disappear into the wooded acres.

Chirt chuckled. "It's also called a groundhog."

"Like the pigs Alex raises?"

"No, not like them, it probably gets its name from being fat, like a hog. Before winter sets in they get fat and then go to sleep all winter under the ground until it starts to get warm," Chirt said.

"Whew, John, you're full of questions today," Alex said.

John nodded and smiled at him. "I like to be outside, so many animals and plants to see."

"Stay that way," Alex said.

Alex stopped the sleigh near the large maples he had tapped. Chirt jumped from the sleigh, lifted John out, and walked him to a tree with a tap. "John, God made these wonderful plants to help us. You like the cookies Nettie makes?"

"Yeah!" John answered and clapped his hands.

"Nettie takes the maple sugar ... the sweet stuff and adds it to her cookies."

Alex joined them. He carried a tap and two buckets with him. "John, the tree has sugar stored in what we call roots. They grow below where we stand."

"Below?" John looked up at this tall man.

"Under the ground," Alex scuffed the snow away with his boot. "The roots send sugar water up the tree," he said, pointing to branches above John's head. "The sap goes from below us up to the branches ... and the buds use the sugar to grow and make leaves."

John stared at him. "We steal the food from the tree?"

Chirt laughed. "There's plenty for the tree and it gladly shares with us if we don't put too many holes in it."

Alex began to tap the large maple and John cried out, "Don't hurt the tree!"

"This won't, John," Alex reassured the small boy. "We don't put more than two or three in a tree this size. It will heal like your scratches."

John thought about what Alex said, then nodded.

Alex turned to Chirt. "Do all children ask questions like this?"

"Only John and Mercy ask so many questions—"

"Does God make the sugar for the tree?" John interrupted.

"Great question." Chirt picked him up and hugged him. "Let's help Alex tap another tree, shall we?"

John vigorously nodded, "And Nettie can make cookies for us."

"Mr. John, she can," Alex said.

"Does Papa know how to do all this?"

Alex looked at the little Hayman boy. "He does."

"Why isn't Papa here with us?"

Chapter 38

Abner and Samuel sat quietly in the sanctuary. The sunny day might have helped them past some issues, but this one had gnawed at Abner since the day Chris returned to Greenville, dead. Light spilled through the east windows, leaving the women's pews glowing in the soft sunlight. The pulpit with a large, open Bible stood before them, presenting a solemn presence to the discussion.

"I can't deny that I wanted to see the man dead for what he did to Susanna and Chirt," Abner said, "God help me for not forgiving as I should."

"God forgives," Samuel said, "isn't that what you preach?"

"It is, Samuel, but He sees and knows all."

Samuel frowned. "What do you mean?"

"I've always wondered how you singled me out of all the ministers residing in Pennsylvania." Abner stared at Samuel. "What made you come after me for your grand plan, whatever that might be?"

Samuel sat, not sure how to respond.

"Samuel, did you want me to come here so you could remove Chris Kreulfs and get the deed to the land?"

"Come now, Abner, you know better than that," he said, barely above a whisper.

"What was it? You found an inexperienced young minister, wanting his own congregation—?"

"Don't flatter yourself, Abner. I could have chosen many a minister to do what you are doing." He stopped and turned his eyes on Abner. "You're playing God, Abner. Stop…"

"Then what's your grand plan, Samuel ... what do you want?"

"I want nothing more than to see this state grow and the country to expand beyond the Mississippi. I want to be a major player in how it takes place." Samuel stood. "Is that so bad?"

"Not if done honestly. Have you always done that?"

"No." Samuel grinned at Abner's shocked expression. "What do you expect? Did you expect denial? Abner, wake up. There are people willing to take control of this country's direction, strictly for personal gain.

"I for one will do everything in my power, and in God's power, to see this country becomes a world player and power." He stared at Abner. "What's wrong with that?"

Abner instinctively stood. "Samuel, you're intelligent, you own land beyond what most people would ever hope for. Your fingers are on the transportation pulse of this country." Abner paused to catch his breath. "What's with you? Samuel, you've had women at your call. You have wealth, power, and you serve God in the way you think is best, even though misunderstood by us mortals. Yet you want something ... or lack something. What is it Samuel?"

Samuel looked to the front of the church and turned back to Abner. "I lack what you have."

Abner did not respond.

"Say something, Abner."

Abner only looked at this man, a man envied by so many.

"Abner ... I'm alone."

"Explain, Samuel."

"All I have is materialistic holdings. I have no wife, no children, no self-respect ..."

"What do you lack?" Abner quietly said.

"I ... don't know," Samuel said and folded his hands.

"Samuel, what do you lack?"

Samuel shook his head.

"Come on, what is it? You know ... don't you?" Abner placed his hands upon Samuel's shoulders. "What is it?" Abner demanded.

"I lack ... God."

Abner removed his hands from the man's shoulders. "How do you correct that?"

"Abner, I can't join in communion because I'm not baptized nor confirmed in your faith or for that matter any faith."

"How can you change that?"

"Will you baptize me, Abner?"

"Yes."

"Is confirmation in the Reformed Faith needed?" Samuel looked lost.

"It is. What can we do to fix that?" Abner asked.

"I don't know."

Abner held out his hand. "We shall study together for your confirmation."

"Abner, you're perceptive, it's why I did not want someone else."

"And," Abner sternly looked at Samuel, "you wanted or still want my wife."

Samuel looked at Abner's outstretched hand. "How did you know?"

Abner smiled and turned toward the front. "Let's begin with the baptism."

Chapter 39

Mary felt her spirits rise when the church came into sight. The school building had a new wing and the parsonage and barn bore new paint. Her children followed Chirt in the garden, pulling weeds, and laughing at John's clumsiness as he walked down the growing rows of corn. At the sound of the approaching buggy, the children looked away from the work and fun.

Mercy first recognized her mother. "Mama," the small girl called out, "Mama, I love you."

Chirt stood and scooped up John who had fallen while running down the row of carrots. She put him on her shoulders and trotted behind Mercy to meet the buggy.

Alexander heard the children and hustled to the church door. He smiled and rapidly strode toward the buggy where the driver dismounted and held the reins. Alex helped Mary from the buggy, gave her a hug, and stepped back.

Chirt stooped and released a wiggling John from her shoulders.

Mary dropped to her knees and held out her arms. Her two children clambered into the open arms, sobbing with happiness. "Oh my, you two have grown."

John placed his head on her shoulder and sobbed. "You came back, Mama, like you promised."

Mary tousled his hair and lavished kisses on her son.

Mercy pouted, "Mama, don't you love me?"

Mary looked at the little girl. "Come here, please." She pulled Mercy to her bosom and whispered, "I missed you more than you know."

Nettie came to the schoolhouse door and watched the display of affection. Slowly she inched her way beside Alexander and Chirt. "A wonderful sight it is." She took Alex's hand in hers and squeezed.

Mary looked around the acreage. "Where's Abner?"

Alex answered, "He's with Samuel. It's a day to be proud of your husband, Mary."

She looked at Chirt and Nettie. "How ... he's not here to greet me?"

Nettie asked, "Did you tell Abner when you would arrive?"

A sheepish look crossed Mary's face. "No, I wanted it to be a surprise."

No response came from her friends.

The buggy driver cleared his throat. "Mrs. Hayman, where would you like your luggage?"

Alex stepped forward and said, "We can put the luggage by the parsonage door."

Mary composed herself. "What's the special occasion for Abner?"

"Mary," Chirt said, "Abner is conducting several confirmations, which includes Samuel Carnes."

Mary said, "Miracles do happen."

Alex shook the buggy driver's hand and thanked him for safely delivering Mrs. Hayman.

Mercy and John stood next to Chirt and Nettie and eyed their mother. "Come with me, children," Mary said.

She took each by a hand and walked to her luggage. "I have something special for both of you. You didn't know your grandfather, but he wanted you both to have a present from him."

"Where is Grandfather?" Mercy asked.

"He is with Jesus." Mary opened the larger bag and pulled out two separate packages. For Mercy, Grandfather Schmidt sent a doll, and for John a little, stuffed bison.

The children stood with large eyes and took the gift from their mother and from a man they never met.

"Thank you," Mercy shyly said.

John stared at the small stuffed buffalo and tears trickled down his face.

He stepped to his mother and hugged her leg. "I love you, Mama, and Grandfather, too."

Nettie took one bag and Alex the other. "Mary, let me finish with my class assignments and we can catch up on your life over the past year."

Chirt led the children back to the garden to finish their chores.

Mary walked into the house, so familiar with the stove, table, cupboards, and the chairs where Abner and she spent many hours talking about their lives and their future. "It's so clean. Who's responsible?"

"Your children and husband took care of the house," Nettie replied. She hugged Mary. "I'll return … shortly."

"Abner should be back in two hours," Alexander said. "You want your bags in the bedroom, Mary?"

"Yes, thank you." She turned a circle, taking in their living quarters beyond the kitchen. The pictures Mercy and John had drawn of her hung on the walls.

Alex returned to find her standing with her hands folded. She looked up at him. "Alex, you've been so kind to my husband and children. How do I repay you?"

"You have."

She gave him a puzzled look.

"You came back. Welcome home."

"Oh, Alex, I missed all of you."

"Mary, take a moment and unpack while I prepare a light meal for all and a treat for the children, and your homecoming.

"Alexander, I …"

"I planned for this moment. It won't take long to prepare the meal." He pulled her into his arms. "God's with you, Mary. You're radiant, like an angel."

Alex walked out and Mary immediately sat at the table. She folded her hands and quietly gave thanks to God. It took a moment to gather strength to stand and walk to the bedroom to unpack her belongings.

A half-hour later the children charged into the house. "Mama, see what I found," John said. He held out a large caterpillar.

"It's beautiful." Mary peered at the striped organism.

Chirt entered the house with a small bucket and cheesecloth in her hand. She watched John and his mother examining the caterpillar. When Mary looked up, Chirt said, "John and I are going to feed it and see what happens."

Mary smiled at her and said, "You're always coming up with great ideas."

She looked at her daughter, busy printing on a slate board. "Mercy, you're busy."

"I drew another picture for you." She handed her mother the slate board with the name Mary neatly printed below the angel.

Mary sat beside Mercy and held her. "I love you."

"Don't leave, ever again," Mercy pleaded.

"I won't," Mary wiped the tears from her daughter's cheeks.

Chapter 40

Life for the Hayman family, after Mary's return, settled into a comfortable pattern. The church and school attendance held steady for three years, even in the financial crisis facing the country. With the help of Alex, Nettie, and Chirt, their children grew mentally and physically. Mercy and John attended the church school with all the other children, learning to socially interact, compete, and share.

"Nettie," Chirt whispered, "watch the two boys at the end of their work desk." She moved her head with a slight tilt.

Nettie moved only her eyes to take in the two older boys Chirt wanted her to follow. A grin rapidly came and faded. "So, they've noticed, too."

Chirt nodded. "Little Mercy Hayman blooms." The two boys drew her attention when they suddenly tossed a dried locust seed at Mercy. "Gentlemen, please behave," Chirt cautioned.

Mercy leaned over and plucked the locust seed from the floor. She examined it and put it on the puncheon top next to her geography book. The small girl next to her picked up the seed and passed it along the smooth-faced plank to the next girl. When the seed reached the last girl, the boys sat with their shoulders hunched around their heads.

Connie held the bean up to her face and squinted at the brownish seed. "Oh my, there are letters on it." She moved it closer to her eyes. "Hmm, G-U-S." She looked at August Toepfer, a twelve-year-old from New Westville. "Did you lose this, Gus?"

A quiet giggling began and turned to raucous laughter as Connie sauntered toward the blushing boy. When she stopped by his side she took his hand and gently deposited the seed in the palm. Connie turned and proudly walked back to her place at the end of the long study plank.

An eight-year-old boy said, "Can I see the seed, Gus? Does it really have your name on it?"

August grimaced and shook his head.

Not to be outdone, Mercy rose and crossed the room to stand by August. She took his hand, smiled sweetly, and said, "Gus, you are so sweet to share. Do you think Isaac has a seed with his name on it?" All the boys broke out laughing, and the girls clapped for Mercy.

"Enough fun, students," Nettie said, "we have one more week of classes and then the exams." She went to the front of the room and began reading a poem recently written by Henry Wadsworth Longfellow. When finished, she asked, "Was Longfellow's portrayal of the blacksmith positive or negative?" She stopped and looked around the room at the girls on one side and the boys on the other. "Get back with your assigned study group and discuss." She walked between the benches, stopped, and turned to August. "Gus' group will be first up after you have agreed on the answer."

"Gee, thanks, August," one of his group members said.

The students didn't notice Alexander slip through the side door and approach Chirt, while Nettie circled among the study groups. Chirt's expression showed shock and quickly cleared to a neutral look. Her gaze fixed on a small girl sitting beside John Hayman.

"I'll get her, Alex," she whispered. Chirt excused herself when she interrupted the group and asked Callie Weber to come with her. The girl, eight years of age, gathered her books and followed. John knew something happened as he watched Anna follow Chirt.

Abner met Alexander and Callie at the church front and climbed into the buggy. The Preble County Sheriff sat comfortably in the saddle while Abner eased himself next to Callie; the Sheriff turned his horse and galloped ahead. Alexander followed, heading toward New Westville.

Callie tugged at Abner's sleeve. "Reverend, what's wrong?"

Abner looked at the tiny face peering up at him. "Callie, there's concern for your father. The Sheriff came to get all of us." Tears welled in Callie's eyes. "Your mother's okay and she wanted us to bring you right away."

Callie turned to Alexander. "Mr. Schroeder, I'm scared."

"I know, Callie. We'll be at your farm before long." He moved his hand to her shoulder and gently patted it.

The Weber family consisted of Callie, her mother, Lucinda, and father Hans. Callie, being a close friend with John, spent many hours with the Hayman family on Sunday afternoons. She and her parents faithfully served the church and Hans took his turn as a deacon, joining with Alexander to establish the church building and grounds. His financial advice and insight allowed the church to be debt free within five years. Since the 1839 crisis, Hans' health declined, mentally and physically.

Lucinda moved to New Paris, Ohio from Kentucky, and met Hans only months after arriving. They took their marriage vows from Abner, his first ceremony he performed after arriving. The birth of Callie occurred two years later, and Alexander stood as her godfather at the baptism conducted by Abner.

The white frame home sat on a small knoll off the road east of New Westville. A red-painted barn and an aged smokehouse sat a short distance to the rear of the house. Hans loved flowers, and he and Lucinda planted many gardens along the approach to the stately home.

A Preble County Deputy stood next to the barn door, his horse tied to a hitch loop attached to the large structure. A funeral coach parked between the barn and smokehouse presented an ominous scene, causing Callie to begin weeping.

"It's Daddy, Alexander?" Callie sobbed and buried her face in his jacket.

Alex wrapped his arms around the trembling girl. He held her tight and stared at the bonnet lying on the buggy seat. They huddled together as Abner took the reins, urging the wary mare forward.

Sheriff HW Guthrie dismounted, held up his hand—signaling he wanted time with Lucinda—and entered the house. Fifteen minutes passed before he came out with her on his arm, and led her to Abner's buggy.

"Callie," Lucinda said, "Hans died this morning." Her red-rimmed eyes turned to Sheriff Guthrie and she asked, "Can we see him now?"

Guthrie said, "I want to look around before you come in, Lucinda."

Lucinda nodded and said, "Whatever you need to do, Sheriff." Callie kept her head buried against her mother's neck, intermittently sobbing. "Abner, Alexander, thank you for bringing Callie. We'll need to arrange the funeral. I have his burial clothes laid out. Can we do it soon?" She looked to Abner.

"Yes, Lucinda, we can. Do you want to have Hans buried in the New Westville grounds?"

"Please." She looked to the barn where Sheriff Guthrie waved for her to come inside.

Chapter 41

Three days after the funeral, on an overcast, gray day, Sheriff Guthrie made an unannounced stop at the Reformed Church. He sent his deputy to fetch Lucinda and Callie, who had not returned to school. The Tuesday exam events at the adjacent school made his stop low key. HW Guthrie had a niece attending the church school and she told him about the tests. He decided exam week was the best time to stop, for the students would pay him little attention. As the newly elected Sheriff the past year, he knew he must quickly get on top of this potentially criminal situation. His predecessor left behind a reputation for shady action or no action on the suspicious cases, one being Chris Kreulfs death.

Abner and Alexander spent the morning finishing paths to the new men's and women's privies and covering the area with the old waste pits. They turned from the wash pump when the Sheriff headed his horse up the lane, dismounted, and casually led it by the reins.

"Good day, Reverend Hayman, Mr. Schroeder. Looks like it might rain come evening."

"What brings you up this way, Sheriff?" Alexander asked.

"Need to visit with both of you and Mrs. Weber 'bout Mr. Weber and his death."

"Is something wrong, Sheriff?" Abner said.

"There're some questions that need answers." He swiveled slightly to look at the parsonage and the school. "I sent my deputy to fetch Mrs. Weber. There's some evidence we came across the day Hans died."

Alexander stared at the Sheriff. "Are you saying someone killed him?"

"Not what I said, Mr. Schroeder, I'm following up on some inconsistencies … might be something … might be nothing." The Sheriff's mouth twitched like he smiled.

The three turned at the sound of a horse-and-buggy.

"My deputy returns with Mrs. Weber and Callie." He spoke directly to Abner, "Can we use the church or the house, Reverend Hayman?" He smiled. "I don't think the school or barn is suitable."

"The house is best, Sheriff."

"Thanks, Reverend. Mr. Schroeder, please attend with us, as you might find this interesting."

The deputy steered the buggy to the house at the signal of the Sheriff.

Callie held out her arms to Alexander. He lifted her and carried her to the school building. "Callie, are you ready to come back to school?"

She nodded.

Near the door to the school, he put her down. "We'll get you settled for your exams, okay?"

"Thank you, Godfather."

John came running out the door and hugged Callie. He took her hand and led her into the schoolhouse.

Nettie stood in the doorway with Alexander. "What's going on, Alex?"

"I'm about to find out. It's something to do with Hans Weber's death."

"It wasn't suicide?" Nettie said.

"I'll talk to you later." Alex walked to the parsonage full of pride and confidence.

Abner sat at the table with Lucinda and the Sheriff. Alexander took the vacant chair next to Lucinda and said nothing until the simple pleasantries ended.

The Sheriff turned so he could speak directly to Alexander. "Mr. Schroeder, you have previously worked for Mr. Samuel Carnes?"

Alexander nodded.

"Please tell me in what capacity you served Mr. Carnes."

Alexander told Sheriff Guthrie what he explained to Abner when they first began working with each other. He continued by saying, "Reverend Hayman can corroborate this. Also, the proprietor of the dry goods store in

New Westville can vouch for my work and how I served Samuel."

"Reverend," the Sheriff said to Abner, "do you agree with Mr. Schroeder's work description?"

"Yes, Sheriff Guthrie, I do and do so vehemently." Abner seriously eyed the Sheriff. "And I'll add that he served Samuel like he serves God and the church."

Lucinda asked, "Why do you question Alexander and Reverend Hayman?"

"Lucinda, I sat down with my deputy to close out the case when he handed me a note, an anonymous note, he received from someone that the suicide may not be what happened." Sheriff Guthrie quietly said, "Lucinda, I know this is difficult, but I want you to go back over that morning before you found Hans."

Alexander took the hand she held out. "Hans took the day off after working late at the bank the night before." She sighed and her eyes wandered, seeing nothing, as she recalled that morning. "He decided to take Callie to school early. The Carson girls' parents usually took Callie to school and—"

"Can anyone verify this?" Sheriff Guthrie said.

"Chirt can," Alexander said.

"Thank you, Alex," Lucinda answered. A small frown knit her brow. "Funny, now that I think about it I didn't notice his return. In fact, I'm not sure when he came back. I assumed he went directly to the barn to ready for the afternoon because we planned to do some work in the flower gardens. Hans wanted to do some work on meat in the smokehouse before the day ended."

"You say he had some meat in preparation?" The Sheriff asked.

"Yes, Hans had purchased a half hog and wanted to smoke the ham. He preferred to do his own ...," Lucinda said.

"You did not store the ham before that morning?" Sheriff Guthrie said.

"No," Lucinda answered. "Why?"

"Did Hans take a ham to someone that morning?"

"No," Lucinda said.

"Are you sure?" The Sheriff shifted slightly to look at Alexander.

"Absolutely, Hans and I talked about the excellence of the meat. He wanted to have the hams available for guests he expected in the next few weeks…"

"He didn't seem out of sorts … suicidal?" Sheriff Guthrie probed.

"He had problems, bank problems, but didn't feel they were insurmountable." Lucinda dabbed at the tears beginning to flow.

"Reverend Hayman," the Sheriff said, "can you vouch for Mr. Schroeder's whereabouts the morning Mr. Weber died?"

"I can," Abner replied, "and he worked here from daybreak until dusk that day except for the time he spent at Weber's farm."

Lucinda asked, "Do you think Hans didn't commit suicide … by his own hanging?"

"I do." The Sheriff sat for a minute waiting for some telltale sign of one or more of the three. None came. "Who or why we might never know."

Alexander asked, "Do you think Samuel Carnes might have been behind this perplexing death?"

The Sheriff did not respond, He stood and said, "Thank you for your time." He turned to his deputy and said, "Please escort Mrs. Weber home." He walked out.

Chapter 42

Sheriff Guthrie never returned to the parsonage or to the area. Samuel Carnes had disappeared shortly after the death of Hans Weber. The Hayman children, now maturing into adulthood, stood by their father and mother at every church event. This included the marriage of Lucinda Weber to a hotel owner in New Paris. Rumors floated around Preble County that she scorned Samuel shortly after he returned from a business trip to Washington. The day she wed, Samuel Carnes appeared on the streets of Eaton, Ohio in a drunken state. The word throughout the county left the impression Samuel fled to the western frontier.

An unscrupulous land agent replaced Samuel, creating havoc with the entire public lands ownership, which in turn complicated the entire banking scene in Preble County. An outgoing, handsome banker replaced Hans Weber and faithfully attended the New Westville Reformed Church. His attendance at all worship services attracted attention because he spent time conversing with Mary. The banker set many hearts aflutter shortly after his arrival because of his status as a grass widower. Ty Bishop came to New Westville with his ten-year-old daughter Maria, and both became enamored with Mary Hayman through their school and the church work.

"Alexander?" Nettie sat quietly knitting a shawl for one the needy children, "I'm concerned about Mary."

"Yes?"

"Mr. Bishop, our banker friend, distracts Mary from her teaching."

"So?" Alexander sighed.

"Do you think …?"

"Nettie, if I remember correctly, we had the same conversation about Abner and Chirt's relationship. Remember?"

"I do, Alex. What does this have to do with my present … concern?"

"It should not be our concern," he answered.

"It is … if it affects our school children."

Alex placed his newspaper on his lap and stared at Nettie. "I understand your concern, but has she failed them over the past year?"

Nettie pursed her lips and said, "No, but—"

"No, Nettie, what Mary does is between her and Abner, and God. We have no right to meddle in the affairs of others, without due cause."

Nettie crossed her eyes at him and went back to knitting.

A buggy passing by their home broke the chilled silence. They watched the driver, Mr. Bishop, merrily chatting with his passenger on the calm, humid spring evening. As they passed the Schroeder farm the woman turned away. A stunned Alexander stared at the disappearing buggy and passengers for nearly a minute.

"Need I say more, Alex?"

"Nettie, there are many women who dress like Mary."

"Don't deny it, Alexander, you knew the woman …"

They sat quietly. Alex sat deep in thought finally said, "It's none of our business, Nettie, and I reiterate if the affair doesn't affect the children."

"That doesn't make it right … what Mary might be doing." Nettie took Alexander's hand said, "I'm going to talk to her tomorrow after school."

Nettie tossed and turned the night through, weighing how she would approach Mary about her concerns with the banker relationship. The best way she finally settled on had to be the concern about the declining enrollment in the face of the precarious economy.

The buggy sat in front of their home, but with no Alexander. He had hitched the horse for her and tied it up. She looked around and found him sitting on his horse in the shade of an old elm tree.

"Alex, what's wrong?"

"Nothing, I felt it best to ride alone for you're going to talk to Mary after classes. Am I correct?"

"Yes, you are. Thank you for your thoughtfulness."

"I'll ride ahead."

Nettie smiled. "Thank you again."

He reined the horse toward the east, whipping it into a full gallop the moment he came to the main road.

Nettie took her time driving the buggy to the school, thoughts rolling over and over how and what to say to Mary. When she arrived at the school she put up the horse and buggy for the day. Chirt, as usual, entertained Mercy and John before the other students arrived. They were moving about observing the early morning wildlife.

"Chirt," Nettie said, "…what are the critters telling you and the children?"

John Hayman quickly responded, "They're disturbed about something."

Nettie frowned at him and said, "John, how so?"

"It's like they know something bad is about to happen. They're eating more, flitting about … not in their normal habits."

Chirt patted John on the head. "He's always right, Nettie. I have to agree about the animals, especially the birds. Something's changing."

"Well, Mr. Naturalist, you keep an eye out and an ear open in case something drastically changes."

John beamed with excitement. "I will, Nettie." He liked her calling him a naturalist.

Through the day the children fidgeted more than usual. They had problems with their attention span, and the three women worked hard at keeping the children on task. Most of the male students had dropped out of school for the farm year. Only the youngest boys and the older ones who did not live on a farm remained in class.

The afternoon turned hot and humid on a mid-May Day. John kept peering out the single window to the west. He felt something, but couldn't explain it to his friends or the women. At three o'clock he raised his hand to ask permission to use the privy. When he walked out of the school he looked to the southwest—his jaw dropped. A large cloud boiled upward above the school and church. Sunlight reflected off the towering upper layer and at the bottom of the huge formation, a greenish blackness sent chills down his spine. Despite his awe, and wanting to watch, he hurried to the privy.

After he finished and dashed through the small swinging door he stood frozen on the path halfway to the school building. The clouds, like out of control clock hands, spun in a counterclockwise direction. The sickening green color made him shudder. Suddenly, a funnel-shaped cloud dropping from the blackness rapidly began to descend to the ground. He rushed into the school and yelled at Chirt. "The birds and animals have all gone quiet. A cloud shaped like a cone twists toward us."

All three women had experienced whirlwinds and twisters over the past two years but from afar. Chirt first called to the children to stay together and to lock arms. Nettie called for them to follow her. Mary called out, "Do what we've taught and stay together." They all locked arms and followed Nettie.

Abner and Alex ran to the children and women, helping guide them to a deep hollow to the east of the school at the forest edge. The lingering student who broke away and needed urging along belonged to Mary and Abner. John wanted to see the powerful clouds and experience what they had studied in science class, a violent twister.

Abner grabbed John's arm and dragged him into the deep ravine. The roar deafened the children, the deepening low air pressure sucked litter from the forest. The small children's cries were lost in the roaring winds tossing small trees high into the atmosphere.

The rain accompanying the powerful storm subsided with the passing of the gigantic, twisting cloud. Not until the rumbling noise quieted did Abner and Alex allow the women and children to climb out of the ravine. What the two men saw made them gasp. The barn, with the horses inside, stood fully intact, but the twister destroyed the church and school. The forest to the west and behind the church received the brunt of the storm, uprooting and leveling nearly all the trees. They stared at a nightmare of destruction beyond imagination.

Within an hour the parents came on horses and in buggies. Fear masked their faces and immediate relief washed over them when they found their children safe. Four children's parents did not come; they lived near New Westville and included Maria's father.

The residents of New Westville poured out of town, following the path of destruction to help at the church and school. When they arrived, they found the pastor and his family with no place to live. Housing was arranged that evening for the pastor and his family and the homeless children. The parsonage loss left Mary in a shocked state. Chirt and Nettie helped bolster her hopes for the future with a new school and home.

Two weeks after the New Westville twister, two families adopted the four homeless children at a special church ceremony held outside the Hayman's barn. A month later, with the church attendance declining, Abner realized that rebuilding the church and school would not happen.

Chapter 43

This trip reminded John of his feelings when he rode along on a buggy trip to the northern Preble County marshlands. The exhilaration of seeing the new country for the first time imprinted in his mind a want, the want to learn more about his new surroundings. The Preble and Darke County lands differed from those around New Westville—many plants and birds he hadn't seen before. On those special trips, he had most enjoyed the blackbirds; one with a vivid yellow head, another with bright red-feathered wing bands.

The hustle and bustle of the city amazed John. People moved about from one of the many stores to another. Teams of oxen, horses, and mules pulled wagons laden with goods, supplying those stores. The steamboats, with their horns blasting, sailed every direction.

He had become confused when his father told him they must leave the New Westville area and find a new life. When he asked his mother, she reassured him they would find land with plenty of room to roam and build a new home and school. She said they would travel to Cincinnati and ride a big boat on the Ohio River, taking them to another large river called the Mississippi, and to a land called Illinois. This confused John, but he compensated by viewing the trip as a way to fill his mind with a new adventure. Mercy clung to his mother while they explored the big city.

After walking the streets and browsing the stores, John and Mercy felt their legs tiring. They soundly slept that night in a cramped hotel room next to the Shroeders and Chirt.

At dawn, the next morning they rose from deep sleep refreshed and ready to sail on the big steamboat. A deacon from their church came to the hotel front and transported them to the wharf where their steamboat docked, ready for travel on the Ohio River to the Mississippi.

While his father and mother settled on the upper deck with Chirt, Jon and Mercy explored the big boat fore and aft. As the boat traveled downriver, the land rose from the big river to the areas of forests and towns, the latter where people stood waving from the shores. Below them on the deck, just above the flowing water, men milled about, taking account of the cargo loaded and unloaded at each stop. John noticed that the black men worked the lower deck. He wondered about the different color and why so few white men did the heavy work.

At lunch, Mercy and John sat with Chirt. Their parents and the Shroeders sat across from one another and Chirt sat across from the two Hayman children.

"John," Chirt said, "something's bothering you?"

He slid his plate to the side and burped. "You make a better meal."

"The food bothers you?"

"No. I'm wondering about the black men doing most of the work loading and unloading the boats." He shrugged.

"I don't understand what you mean?" Chirt frowned.

"Why don't more white people move the heavy loads on and off?"

Mercy said, "Why, Chirt? The black men all work hard and the white men stand around and tell them what to do."

Chirt said, "They're slaves."

"Slaves?" John said.

"White people or white companies pay them little money to do the work. It saves money for the company." She eyed the children to make sure they understood what she said, although she knew John would ask if he didn't.

"Why all black men, why not others, like brown or red men?"

Chirt smiled at him. "John, you amaze me."

He tilted his head forth and back. "What?"

"John, some people believe those of color other than white, aren't as good as them." She watched his reaction.

"But ... Papa preaches that we are all God's people. Does that mean we aren't? I don't understand."

Chirt looked to Abner. "Help me out, Reverend Hayman."

"John," Abner said to his son, "for a long time, people have grown up with the idea colored people are to do the hard work."

John sat quietly with a knit brow and a perplexed look on his face. "Papa, I still wonder how God allows this?"

Alexander laughed. "Pastor Hayman, I do believe you have a son who is going to question many of the difficult social and political decisions or actions. Good luck."

Mary moved beside her son. "Is that right, John? Probably not? God looks on all of us as his children, regardless of color or the way we believe."

Abner's head turned toward his wife, peered at her, and shook his head.

"Father does not agree with me, John. But that came about long ago and the church we preach for has the idea other religions are not teaching God's ways according to the Bible."

Nettie began to laugh when she looked at John's face. "John, if you keep wrinkling your nose you'll begin to look like the bat in the barn back at New Westville."

"Oh no, Nettie, I don't want my brother to look like that." Mercy laughed and punched John's shoulder.

"C'mon children," Chirt said, "let's take a walk and I'll try to delve into Johns deep questions."

"Where'll we go?" Mercy asked.

"I think I can talk one of the nicely dressed men to take us up where the man steers the boat along the river."

Ten minutes later, John forgot about the slave questions for he sat in the captain's chair at the large wheel. The captain found it difficult to refuse Chirt's request for a mate to show them all areas of the steamboat.

Two hours later John fell asleep in Chirt's arms. She carried him to the Hayman berth and tucked him in as the reddish-orange sun set on the western horizon.

Chapter 44

Seven days later they boarded a Mississippi steamboat sailing from St. Louis to Galena, Illinois. John still wondered at the difference in the way people treated one another. Many steamboats docked in the muggy air of a town, where the two large rivers joined, and took on passengers and freight. The beginning of the western frontier Abner called it. John had no idea what he meant but wanted to find it in the years to come. At this small town, appearing in want of washing away, they boarded a large steamboat taking on wood for the boilers. The boat slowly backed from the moorage and began an upstream push toward what his father said would begin a new life for them.

It wasn't long before the family experienced the teeming city of St Louis. The town approached a population of thirty thousand people in the early 1840s. The Haymans and Shroeders wandered the streets near their hotel but did not wander far with an increased number of ruffians plying the back alleys around the near-river expanse. The next morning, they caught a more elaborate Steamboat for the same price.

A familiar voice called Abner's name. He looked up at the second deck and found Judith and Richard Thomas frantically waving at him. A small boy, about the same age as Mercy, stood beside them.

"Mary, look," Abner said and pointed to the far end of the upper deck.

Mary squinted into the rising sun and shaded her eyes. "It's Judith and Richard."

They hurried to the upper deck and greeted the Thomas family with hugs and handshakes. The young boy grinned at Mercy while she hugged his mother. John stood back with the Shroeders, watching his parents react to the couple and their young boy, Alfred.

"Where's your room?" Richard asked.

Abner gave him the number for the lower deck.

"Richard," Judith said, "we can't have them down there with the riffraff."

Mary frowned at her. "What do you mean?"

Judith laughed. "You would need only one night to understand. But we'll not have you put to that test." She waved a cabin attendant over and quietly talked with him. She turned and said, "You'll move to the upper deck for the rest of your trip to Keokuk."

Richard looked at John. "And you are?"

"I'm John Edmund Hayman, sir."

"John, you certainly are proper. Reverend Hayman has taught you well."

The large steamboat's paddlewheel slowly began to spin and the boat eased into the Mississippi. John hurried to the ornate rail so he could watch the other steamboats arriving and leaving St Louis.

Mercy stood beside him. "Do you like them, John?"

"The boats?"

"The Thomas people, silly," Mercy said. She watched people on shore waving goodbye to friends or relatives on board.

"Oh, they seem okay, why?"

"I don't know ... they seem to like that man that came to see Father so many times."

"The big, tall man with the fancy clothes, named Samuel?" John felt the boat shudder as the captain stopped, reversed the paddle wheel, and moved into the river current to take an upstream heading. Mercy didn't notice the boat movement while waiting for his answer. "They're friendly with Mom and Dad, so it's okay with me."

Mercy huffed and said, "Well, the boy seems a bit ... uppity."

John paid no attention to Mercy who always liked to make something out of nothing. He watched her stomp off and turned back to admiring the scenery of the Mississippi shoreline. Every few minutes a flatboat or another Steamboat cruised by, heading downriver. His curiosity got the most of him when several boats seemingly attached to one another floated past.

He hurried to Alexander and asked, "What're all those boats carrying?"

Alexander shrugged. "I don't know John, but let's ask someone able to explain." Alexander took John's hand and led him to the upper deck where a man leaning on the rail watched the flatboats drifting south. "Sir, my young companion would like to know what all these boats headed south are carrying?"

The man smiled and answered, "They're loaded with lead mined upriver ... near Dubuque, Iowa."

"What's lead?" John asked.

The man grinned. "It's taken from the earth and made into bars used for pewter, pipes, weights, paint, and of course, ammunition for firearms."

"What's pewter?" John said.

"Aha, you have an inquisitive son." Alexander ignored the son reference. "My boy, companies use pewter to make dishes and other items of everyday use." He looked at Alexander. "The boy asks good questions. He'll go far."

Alexander smiled at the elderly man. "He does ask good questions, and I can't answer most. Thank you."

"My pleasure," the man said and shook hands with Alexander and John. They moved on.

"I don't mean to ask so many questions, Alexander." John innocently looked up at the man he admired.

"John, keep asking, for it will serve you well."

"Look, what's the big bird wading along the shore?"

"That I can answer, it's a great blue heron."

John, over the past two years, soaked in his surroundings, amazing his parents with the innocent thirst for knowledge. Alexander had taken John on rides through the south circuit several times before the twister destroyed the church and school and ruined the parsonage. The boy learned from all adults, especially his parents. From Alex, he learned tree and plant names. Chirt taught him about the uses of the plants he collected when riding with Alex, and he made notes of all this in his prized writing book.

As they walked, Alexander reflected on the fact Mercy didn't like John traveling with him and Abner on their ministry routes. But she finally realized Chirt became more attentive to her needs and wants when John wandered along on the circuits with his father and Alex.

With John gone, closeness developed between Chirt and Mercy. That bond made it easy to say yes when Mary asked Chirt to travel west with them, helping with the children and starting another church school.

Nettie and Alex, spared from the tornado devastation, wondered about moving to Cincinnati. When Abner asked for them to come to Illinois, they silently thanked God. His kindness of wanting them to join in establishing a new church and school in Hancock County, south of a town named Carthage, left them openly weeping.

John stared at the backwaters along the Mississippi. "Alexander, there are marshes like … near New Madison. Father taught me about the plants that like water and the birds that live there," he paused, "… the grasses and cattails and bulrushes and—"

He abruptly stopped to watch two fishermen haul in a catfish with a mouth opening the size of a man's head. John pointed, unable to speak because of his excitement.

"What's John so worked up about?" Abner said as he approached.

Alexander grinned. "I've never seen the likes of these catfish. It could feed all of us, including your Thomas friends."

"Speaking of them, they want us to join them for the evening meal, at their pleasure."

Chapter 45

Chirt agreed to join them after occupying the children with study assignments. Judith asked if Alfred might join with Chirt and the Hayman children, and Chirt enthusiastically welcomed him so Alfred could share stories about his life. She would learn more about the Thomas family from the boy than all the rhetoric Richard Thomas might spout.

Most people were cooking their meals, but not Richard and Judith as a cook attended to their dinner with fresh vegetables brought aboard during a wood-fuel restock. The upper deck teemed with individuals, mostly men, gambling, dancing with damsels, and drinking whiskey. Abner watched this indulgent behavior unfold as the evening progressed. Judith, Nettie, and Mary caught many a wandering eye as the men moved about for their meals and to stop to convey their good wishes to the travelers.

Richard sat next to Alex, carrying most of the conversation while the women chatted equally among themselves. Abner watched Judith, who unlike her husband, listened to Nettie and Mary. She caught Abner eyeing her during the evening and heaped smiles his way. Mary finally excused herself to check on Mercy and John. Nettie became involved in a discussion with Alex and Richard, which left Abner to fend when Judith rose and sat next to him.

"Abner," Judith slurred his name, "I understand you're settling in Carthage or near there."

"We are."

"Why?" Judith leaned so close he could smell the alcohol on her breath.

"It's a long story; the short one is the Lord blessed us with a visitor shortly before the twister wiped out the church and school. He wanted to know if we might offer the Lord's services in the Carthage area." Judith listened politely. "When our difficulty arose, we heard from one of his relatives shortly after and he asked us to come to Illinois."

"Abner," Judith said, "you're aware Samuel Carnes plies the Mississippi River as a drunk and scoundrel?"

"What? Samuel's working around where we intend to settle?"

"Noooo, Abner, Samuel moves about to avoid the law." She looked for a glass to pour more whiskey, found one, and filled it half full. "Abner, would you like some?" She held the bronze-colored fluid in front of him.

He politely shook his head.

"Ummmm, good," Judith said and licked her lips of a drop about to escape. "Samuel came to the river about four years ago. He started a business with transportation and it failed along with his other businesses, which I don't pretend to understand. I don't think he ever recovered from it because he had always succeeded. Failure never became a part of his vocabulary ... until then." She sipped and eyed him.

Abner asked, "Judith, do you know where I can find him?"

"No, but Richard might."

Mary returned, a large smile covering her face. "I think John's overwhelming the other children with his facts and readings. Chirt laughed the entire time I spent with them."

"Not our son," Abner chuckled. He stood to hold the chair as Mary took her seat.

"You two are getting along?" Mary asked of Judith.

"We are," Judith turned to Abner and then back to Mary, "I'm telling stories about Samuel Carnes."

The look crossing Mary's face caught Alexander and Nettie's attention. "Mary, you look like you've seen a ghost," Nettie stated.

"Hearing his name so surprised me because I thought we'd never see or hear of him again." Mary asked, "He works in Illinois?"

Judith loudly laughed. Heads turned at the next table to wonder at the frivolity. "Samuel Carnes, as I told Abner, runs from the law. His businesses left him destitute, and he's a scoundrel taking advantage of unaware folk who move to the Illinois and Iowa cities and countryside."

"Imagine that," Nettie said.

"Nettie ..." Alexander cautioned.

"He's still a swashbuckler," Richard said, "and many a woman is willing to take him in until they learn of his deception."

"Does he look the same?" Mary asked.

"Mary," Judith said, "kinda skinny, but oh my." She raised her eyebrows and said, "Probably more handsome with his rugged, lean look and a beard ... when clean and trimmed."

"And when he's not drunk and unkempt," Richard offered.

Alex asked, "What's he do to earn money?"

Richard blurted out, "Gambles with wealthy widows' money, escorts them to fine hotels, and steals hearts of the young and innocent women."

"No different from the past," Nettie offered.

Judith sat down her drink and said, "I do think he's unhappy ... and something else is wrong with him."

"What?" Abner asked.

"Sometimes I think ... he's losing his mind." Judith picked up her drink and finished it in two swallows.

Chapter 46

John diligently worked on his reading lessons in the candlelight of the old log cabin at the edge of Carthage. His study time, since leaving the Mississippi River and settling in Hancock County, revolved around reading, writing, math, and geography. His best lessons and education came not from the books, but from the trips around the county with his father, Alexander, and Chirt.

Abner spent more quality time with John over the past year. They both found an increasing love for the prairie in the central part of the county. Of course, Abner continued his staunch Bible teachings every trip. John admired his father's ability to quote scripture to fit every occasion. But something made John wonder at his father's fervent distaste for people of the Catholic and Mormon beliefs. Before coming to Hancock County, John very seldom heard his father speak with a vile tongue about the rites and rituals attached to other beliefs. On the northern route from Carthage, Abner steered clear of Nauvoo, the community established by the Mormons who fled Missouri. Of late, when questioned about the Mormons, he brought in scripture to make a case for his growing tirades against it and the people.

The trips with Alexander and Chirt proved to put John more in touch with his love for nature. Alexander, when working the western townships of Hancock County, made every effort to expand John's knowledge of fishing and hunting. They spent time on the big river with some of the new congregation members, catching fish and watching the eagles move from their nests, gathering food for their young. The smaller streams proved to be a haven for Alexander and John. They often took trips to the Mississippi tributaries to fish, explore, and gather berries for eating and drying.

Chirt took John to the east county areas where she taught him how to find the edible plants such as the berries he and Alexander harvested on the west county trips. Also, she passed along her cunning for hunting and trapping, which she learned from her mother, Susanna, and relatives living with the Miami tribe. John and Chirt would quietly sit in the zone where the prairie faded to the forest, then move to spots within the forested areas, watching wildlife. The quality with which Chirt mimicked the bird whistles made John eager to become as adept. His favorite bird songs he practiced daily, such as the cardinal; Carolina house and marsh wrens; and the eastern and western meadowlarks. The black-capped chickadee songs dominated his newfound hobby.

It was a cool, fall day when John, Alexander, and Chirt drifted south in the Hayman buggy in search of new bird sightings. Alex and Chirt made it a game, which John enjoyed when the three traveled together. Coming over a rise, they suddenly came on a healthy marsh surrounded by grass, cattails, and bulrushes. Open water toward the marsh center reflected the clouded, blue-gray sky. Alexander reined the horse to a stop atop the next small rise. A dozen small ducks sailed over, bound for a water landing. After warily circling, they cupped their wings and prepared to land in the middle. They smoothly settled into a small cluster on the marsh water. A sudden blur came at them from an odd cattail grouping near the gently rippling shoreline. The birds rose skyward in the face of danger, but two of three closely grouped suddenly dropped, followed by a loud firearm crack. Two men rose from the cattail grouping and splashed their way to the downed ducks. The dog bounced around their legs and stopped when one man put up his hand, leaned over with the duck, and allowed it to sniff at the small, plump bird.

"John, that's duck hunting at its finest," Alexander said. "Would you like to learn?"

"What kind of guns do they use?" John looked up at his mentor.

"My guess is a fowling piece that uses small lead shot and has a percussion or cap lock. That's why we did not see a flash of powder."

"Why don't we find their horses or buggy and wait for them. We can ask about the hunt," Chirt said, "and they might suggest a gun John could start with and use in the future."

The two men walked with their dog to the horses tethered to small willow saplings at the far marsh edge. "Howdy, folks," the graying man said, "what can I do for you?" The glance toward Chirt made Alexander take notice.

"We're studying the area for a new church and happened on your waterfowl hunting." Alexander climbed down from the buggy, held out his hand, and introduced himself. The man took it and again looked at Chirt and let his eyes drift to John. "The minister's son is a devout outdoor enthusiast," Alexander continued. "We wanted your advice on fowling pieces for him."

"So, you'd like to do some hunting, eh?" the gent said as he let go of Alexander's hand and stepped to the buggy.

John nodded.

"What you want to hunt, boy?" The man spit tobacco juice in the grasses at his feet. The buggy horse turned its head at the sound of the stranger's voice.

"Like you, I want to shoot some ducks," John said.

"Anything else you'd like to hunt, young man?"

John looked at Alexander. He got a nod to go ahead. "I'd like to hunt turkey and most of all, some quail."

The old gent laughed. "No deer?"

"No sir," John quickly replied.

"Why?"

"Too big for me to handle," John said, giving him an honest look.

The well-dressed hunter stood watching the give and take between John and his guide. Finally, he said, "Gentlemen and ma'am, I'm Sidney Albrecht, an avid hunter on vacation from the state of Maryland." He stepped forward and shook hands with Alexander and John. "Ma'am, you are …?"

"Chirtlain Kreulfs, Sir," she quickly said.

"Are you a hunter?" Sidney said.

"Not with a fowling piece, but by other methods."

"What does that mean?" the guide asked.

"That means I must know the habits of the animals I hunt and harvest them without a fowling piece." Chirt smiled.

"You mean by hand or by the bow?" The guide turned and peered at Alexander, who had moved up behind him. "Mr. Schroeder, I'll provide a piece of advice for your young man." Alex nodded and moved to where they could comfortably converse. "First use a percussion lock and second get him to fire a gun that will not knock him on the seat of his pants."

"Sound advice, sir," Alexander said. "Do you know of a person who might carry guns that John can test fire?"

The guide grinned. "You are looking at him. Fact is … I'll take the boy hunting if you come back in a week."

"What's the cost?" Alex said.

"Only that the boy buys his gun or guns from me."

"Fair enough," Alexander said, "I'll bring John down next week. What day's best?"

"I've got a couple of young men want to hunt ducks and quail on Wednesday next." He looked at John. "You want to do that, mister?"

"Yes, sir, thank you, sir," John said and grinned ear-to-ear.

Chapter 47

The following week shaped John Hayman's future. The old guide taught John how to hunt and gave him lessons with duck calling, which Chirt never completely mastered. Over the fall and winter days when not too much snow impeded travel, Alexander dropped John off each week with the guide and continued on his way ministering to those in need.

Not to be outdone, Abner found a family to help John with trapping skills. The winter season proved the prime time for good pelts and meat, especially with the plentiful rabbit population. The family taught John how to locate, harvest, skin, clean, and preserve the pelts.

"John," George Alderman said, "you wanna hunt bigger animals than rabbits?"

"Yeah, I suppose." John hesitated. "I don't know if I could handle the bigger animals, Mr. Alderman."

George slapped John on the back. "Don't worry 'bout that, I and the sons will show you how to hunt the bigger animals and to shoot. Once you learn you can help cut up the critters and get them on the packhorses for the trip back to the house."

"Come along, John," Abner said.

George held up a hand. "I got a suggestion, Reverend Hayman. Why don't you leave John with us for the next three days, and we'll bring him back to Carthage? We have to come in for some supplies so it won't be any trouble." George laughed when he saw John's beaming face.

"That's mighty kind, George," Abner said. "But John needs to be in school—"

"Reverend, your boy ... he don't need book learnin' as far as I can tell. What he needs is to know the way critters live and how he can survive if it ever be necessary."

"Father, please ..." John pleaded with folded hands in front of his chest.

"Fair enough, George. I'll leave John with you for three days. But to keep Mary from worrying, I must tell her before I work the west county." Abner shook hands with George and asked Mrs. Alderman, "Is this fine with you, Grace?"

Grace Alderman grinned at her minister. "Reverend Hayman, my youngest can learn from your son. They're in need of some book learnin', even if George don't think so."

Abner said, "John, you behave and help with the chores."

John nodded. A young boy about the same age as John motioned to hurry along. The two tore out of the cabin and ran a beeline to the barn where a dog was about to birth puppies.

George walked with Abner to the buggy and took the small satchel with a change of clothes for John, plus an extra wool coat, and pair of boots. Reverend, don't you worry about your boy, we'll make sure he stays safe."

Abner had told Mary the trip needed two overnight stays. He wanted her to know the change in plans. Besides, Chirt and Nettie took Mercy to Quincy for a week long winter trip while Alexander spent time on his southern ministerial route. He could spend a quiet evening with his wife.

A chill settled on him near the cabin. The sun hung low in the west, an orange orb, creating little heat on this winter day. He reined the horse in at the closed barn door. The quiet whinny from inside shocked him. Abner reached for an oil lamp and lit it. A weathered stallion stood in the usually empty stall.

A frown creased his brow. He mulled over the situation while he cared for his horse and backed the buggy into the barn. After feeding the horse and checking over the hard-ridden stallion, he quietly walked to the cabin.

A light burned in their bedroom. Little light reflected from the main living and dining area. Abner felt like a voyeur as he crept toward the oilcloth-covered bedroom window. He waited in the chill, listening for sounds. When he started to turn away, after hearing nothing, the first sound surprised him. The familiar voice stopped him. Samuel Carnes. A painful squeeze enveloped his heart.

Abner raced to the cabin door, threw it open, and stormed to the bedroom. His mouth fell open at the sight in front of him. It sickened him and he turned, rushing back to the barn. He threw a saddle on the mare and galloped down the road toward God only knew where.

Chapter 48

Wind sighing through the window woke Abner. He groaned and rolled to his side and looked around. The bed belonged to Alexander and Nettie. A bottle of wine used for the church communion sat on the floor. His head throbbed from overindulging. He stumbled from the bed and reeled into the large living area. A Bible lay open on the table. He searched the storage cabinets for something to eat. The sound of a horse outside caught his attention. Abner swung open the door and found his mare tethered to a tree near the cabin.

"God, forgive me."

After putting up his horse and finding bread and a cold slab of ham, he built a stove fire, heated water, and steeped tea. Abner sat quietly staring at the Bible. He opened it to Joshua 1:9 and loudly read, "Have not I commanded thee? Be strong and of a good courage; be not afraid, neither be thou dismayed: for the LORD thy God is with thee whithersoever thou goest."

His fingers flipped the pages to Luke 6:37. Again he read to the vacant cabin, "Judge not, and ye shall not be judged: condemn not, and ye shall not be condemned: forgive, and ye shall be forgiven."

Abner closed the Bible and rose. He added more wood to the stove and stood near it until the heat made him sweat. The pan of water sitting above the fire began to steam. Abner removed it and poured in fresh, cool water. A small cabinet holding bathing materials sat to the side of the stove and next to a slotted-floor area. From the lowest storage area, he plucked a sponge and soap bar, stripped naked and scrubbed, wanting to wash away all his sin. The alcohol began to seep from his sweating pores. After soaping his entire body, he rinsed and dried in front of the stove.

For an hour, he sat naked at the table reading the Bible. After completing the readings, he donned his clothes and left the cabin as he found it, to the best of his recollection. Abner decided his next action.

She heard hoofbeats approaching the cabin. Mary peered out the small window toward the barn where the horse sounds disappeared. Within minutes Abner came from the barn and stiffly approached the cabin. Before he could open the door, she flung it open and stood in the doorway. He marched past her and stood by the stove warming his hands.

"Abner … do not turn your back on me."

He stood in front of the stove vigorously rubbing his hands. A shiver pulsed down his body.

"Abner," Mary quietly said, "do you hear me?"

He stopped rubbing his hands and his head dropped to his chest. His hands fell to his side. Still, he did not face her.

"Husband," Mary walked directly behind him, "it is not what you think." Still, he did not turn. She quoted: "Either how canst thou say to thy brother, Brother, let me pull out the mote that is in thine eye: when thou thyself beholdest not the beam that is in thine own eye? Thou hypocrite cast out first the beam out of thine own eye, and then shalt thou see clearly to pull out the mote that is in thy brother's eye."

He turned slowly and looked directly at her. "Luke 6:42." He took her hands and watched tears fill her eyes. She smelled of soap and natural plant oils. "God forgive me."

"Abner, allow me to explain." She felt him squeeze her hands. "Come sit while we have tea and biscuits." Mary took his coat and led him to the table where she earlier sat eating and reading.

He sat and folded his hand and stared at the plate in front of him. The biscuits cast small, warm-air swirls from the surface. He didn't say a word.

"Abner, look at me," Mary said as she sat across from him. "Would you like some maple sugar in your tea?"

He shook his head.

The soothing tea fragrance filtered between them, acting as a salve. A moment of silence passed before Abner looked up. He sipped at the hot tea and over the cup rim said, "I will listen if you want to share."

"I want," Mary said. "But first, I have to know John's whereabouts."

"Mary, he's safe. The Alderman's invited him to stay and learn about the outdoors. You should have seen him when an Alderman boy his age told him of their dog about to have puppies."

Chapter 49

Noon sun filtered through the small south-facing window. The crackle of burning wood broke the silence. Abner returned to the table with a pan of fried potatoes, eggs, and a slab of salt pork. He put the pan on the black slate square and poured more tea.

"What made him come here?" He sat and served the food.

Mary toyed with the potatoes. "He feared for his life."

"From what or who, I should ask?"

"I think it's the Preble County Sheriff. Remember that Hans Weber served as an important figure and deacon for the church and how his health went downhill after the economic slump?"

Abner nodded.

"Rumors in the church circles claim Mrs. Weber became romantically linked to Samuel." Mary took a bite of her biscuit. A look crossed her face as though something popped into her head. "Abner, the tie could be the money for the church and Hans' wife."

"What? I'm not clear about what you're suggesting."

"I think the Sheriff found evidence that Samuel became involved with Mrs. Weber and that Hans knew about it." She stopped to put the right words in place. "Samuel could have been using Hans to pass questionable funds to the church and his businesses. With the economic downturn taking its toll, Hans likely wanted to call in money from Samuel."

"That's pretty dramatic."

Mary paused to take a bite of pork. "The Sheriff in Ohio felt Hans Weber's death could have been murder."

"You think Samuel killed Hans?"

"Yes. He or someone he hired."

"Mary," Abner said, "that's a strong accusation."

"I know, but it fits the pattern with Chris Kreulfs' death."

"That I cannot argue," Abner ate a forkful of potatoes, "but what else might cause his problems?"

"He rambled on like he lost his thoughts. He seemed ... rather crazed."

"Did he say anything about his businesses?"

Mary said, "Yes. That's what set him off. I asked about the stages and railroad involvement and he started to rant."

Abner sat up straight and looked directly at his wife. "Explain to me what I saw."

"You saw me toweling a freshly bathed man desperately in need of clean body and clean clothes." Her icy look made him shrink back. "God help you, Abner, I explained it no longer than two hours ago." The muscle at her jawline tightened. "I found Samuel in the barn, drunk, filthy, and talking wildly. I cared for his horse, got him to the cabin, bathed him, laundered his clothes, and sent him on his way."

"The look on your face it ..."

"Oh, dear God, Abner," Mary took his hands in hers, "I felt so happy I could help a man who helped us many times."

"Through our marriage, you've never had another man?"

"How do I answer? You will not believe, or you want to place sin on my shoulders; I will not allow that." She watched the redness of his cheeks brighten. "Don't be angry, Abner. We have two beautiful children, three loving friends, and a new place to continue our lives." She breathed deeply and released a heavy sigh.

"Do you want to ask me if I strayed?"

"No."

He sputtered, "Aren't you curious?"

"No," Mary abruptly said. "I love you, Abner, isn't that enough?"

He sat quietly in thought.

"Our son is a bright and handsome young boy, like his father. Our daughter ... have you looked at her lately, Abner? She matures with grace and beauty. If you haven't noticed, you should, because all the boys are taking notice."

"You're right. Mercy and John are growing so fast it worries me."

"They are good children. You should watch John while you lead a congregation or minister to those in need on your visits. He admires and loves you, and it shows. Take note on a Sunday in the new church."

"When it's completed and consecrated," he said, "I will dedicate the building to all the congregation members and my family."

"That will be wonderful, but what I need and the children need is your attention. Abner, I want you ..."

Chapter 50

The Alderman buggy arrived in front of the Hayman cabin on the edge of Carthage two days after Mary and Abner had their talk. John dove out of the buggy with a bow, quiver, and a tightly tied package. After picketing the horse, George Alderman stepped down and followed the energetic young boy. His admiration for the lad increased with each hour over the two-day stay. The entire Alderman family spent every waking hour educating and talking with John. The Alderman children treated him as family and after only two days they had a difficult time saying goodbye.

John placed the hunting gear against the cabin and clutched the package to his chest. He turned and motioned George to follow. "C'mon, Mr. Alderman, I want you to tell Mother and Father about our hunts, trapping, and meeting your Indian friend."

Before John opened the door, Mary stepped out and took him in her arms. She smiled at George. Abner stepped through the doorway and motioned George to come in and then put his arms around both John and Mary.

"John," George said, "show Reverend and Mary what you have in the package."

John broke free from his parents and opened the package. "It's meat from the deer. George … Mr. Alderman, he and his boys helped me shoot and skin a deer. His oldest son is tanning the hide for me." John handed the package to Mary and grabbed the bow. "Look what the Indian friend of Mr. Alderman gave me." He held out the bow for Abner and Mary's inspection.

"A mite big for you isn't it, John?" Abner said.

George laughed. "The boys decided to make a bow fit him, for now, and they'll bring it by in a few weeks. Got to find the right wood; wood that's properly aged and strung so John can draw it back. They'll give him lessons how to hunt with it."

"The Indians are friendly?" Mary asked.

George tilted his head and looked at her. "Mrs. Hayman, like every color there's good and bad. This one's a kind person." He elbowed John and continued. "Show her the bracelet he gave you. This means he's a good friend of the Illini."

John pulled a bear-claw bracelet from his coat pocket and handed it to his parents. "May I wear it at school when we start again?"

Abner smiled at his son. "Chirt and the Schroeders will like the present."

"Mother?" John said, looking at her with pleading eyes.

"You may." She handed the bracelet back to him.

"Sit for a spell, George," Abner pointed to a chair at the table. "We're fortunate to have coffee in a time when it's expensive."

"Coffee, that's great." George took off his coat and handed it to Mary. "Pastor, I wanted to let you know I've rounded up a coupla dozen men to start the church construction and it should be ready by mid-May. Won't be fancy, but it'll be functional."

"How did you come by land?" Abner said.

"Two new members who heard you and Alexander speak the Lord's Word want to provide two or three acres on their adjoining property. It's south and west of Carthage. If that meets your approval, we'll start. In fact, … there's a landowner meeting about finalizing the church raising and timing. We have to talk with local bank president, but I don't see a hitch with the last few years of good harvests and the sale of pork and beef to markets on each side of the county. We've been able to sell our pork to the steamboat people down in Quincy. That's helped keep us in good change and we can thank the Lord for the blessings by building a new church. The Sunday school teachers," he nodded his head to Mary, "are so good we want our children to continue with that fine education."

"I don't know how to thank you, George," Abner said.

"Best way to thank us is to stick around and keep preaching the word that you both do so well." He cleared his throat. "Of course, we need you to help keep our families' safe from the preacher, Joseph Smith and his followers. You know about them folk, Reverend?"

"I do and I will learn more."

"Thanks, Pastor. We, people, know the Reformed preachers know all about the Catholics." The right side of his mouth twitched. "I don't mean to be blasphemous, but …"

"George, when we form the church and get agreement from all, establish the church boards, and elect the elders and deacons we can take care of your and other member's concerns."

Chapter 51

Spring of 1844 turned into a glorious time for John. Snowfall did not deter his search for wild game in the woods or the edge areas between prairie and forest. The days when he wandered more than five miles from the town, Chirt or Alexander would be with him. After John completed his new bow lessons and how to make arrows for the small and large game, he found this method of hunting more and more to his liking. Guns were okay, but he liked the bow hunts, as he must understand the animal habits, food tendencies, and bedding areas to bring home the food he sought for the family.

Over the winter John trapped rabbits for the hide and food. The most enjoyable part of his trips to the grassy areas became scouting the area for prime rabbit habitat, sitting quietly watching, and placing his box traps and snares. He didn't like the iron-jaw traps. The jaws seemed cruel, but he knew the use determined success or failure of some settlers' lives.

Rabbits he learned, from the Alderman boys, like to frequent the land between farmland and forest. The time to hunt for the best meat and pelts came after the first freeze and lasted through the winter months. Following this advice, he rarely found a sluggish or weak rabbit. If he did, he left it for the predators, mainly fox and bobcats, although others like the skunk, coyote, hawks, and owls preyed on them.

For his last birthday, John received three writing instruments and three notebooks, ranging from small to large. The small one he designed a cover with tanned deer hide, which Alexander helped him form. Today, Alexander planned a treat by riding with John to the Mississippi River where the small town of Warsaw nestled along the eastern bluffs. There the two could hunt deer and turkey as the habitat proved more favorable than the prairie land around Carthage.

Mary rose before dawn and helped John prepare for the day. Mercy, old enough to prepare breakfast, fried thinly sliced potatoes in a cast iron skillet greased with lard from the diced pork chunks. John helped his mother by collecting two buckets of water from the well outside the cabin. Abner left the previous afternoon for a circuit around the northern townships, planning his return to the services on Sunday.

"John," Mary said, "do you have all your gear and extra clothes packed in case you get wet?"

He nodded, not responding because potatoes filled his mouth.

"John," Mercy peered at her brother, "you eat like the pigs."

"C'mon, sister," he said, "I got to get goin' because Alexander will soon be here."

"That's no excuse to eat and grunt like the hogs." Mercy wrinkled her nose.

He shrugged.

"Didn't we forget something?" Mary said.

Her children put down their eating utensils, folded their hands, and began their silent breakfast prayers. A buggy arriving outside the cabin ended John's prayer. He leaped up and dashed to the door. When he opened it, Nettie grabbed him and gave him a hug and a kiss on the forehead.

"You're getting so big, and you look more like your father every day."

Alexander stood behind Nettie waiting for the spontaneous greeting to end. He waved at Mary and smiled at Mercy. "John, is the horse ready?"

"Nope, I gotta get her saddled and tie on the saddlebags."

Alexander found a small mare for John and a saddle with easily adjustable stirrups so he could grow into it. "Hustle up, we need to be on our way for its two hours over to Warsaw and the river."

He quickly moved his soiled plate to the washbasin, poured in hot water, and scrubbed it clean.

"I'll finish that," Mercy said.

A grin crossed his face. "What will I owe you?"

"Tail feathers from the turkey you harvest." She smiled sweetly.

"Deal," he said as he slipped into his coat and dashed out.

"Sit for a spell while I clean up," Mary said to Nettie and Alexander.

"I'll clean up, Mother," Mercy said. She rose to take the plates and utensils to the washbasin. "Alexander, Nettie, would you like some tea?"

"Perfect," Nettie said.

"Alexander," Mary said, "when do you think you'll return?"

He gave it some thought and said, "Most likely before the sun sets, that's if I can get John away from the river and the woods. You know how he loves to see something new."

Mercy giggled. "Brother John, he can be a pain."

"And you are always the perfect angel, daughter?"

"Yes, Mother." Mercy stifled a laugh. She brought Nettie and Alexander their tea and warmed her mother's.

"Alex, will the church be ready for Easter services?" Mary said.

"Aye, if the weather stays like this we'll finally sit in pews rather than chairs all squashed beside one another. I think—"

John's rush through the door interrupted him. "Alex, I'm almost ready."

Alex chuckled and said, "I'll finish my tea first, young man."

John hurried into the bedroom and returned with his archery gear and his packed saddlebags. On his return he grinned at Alexander and ran out to his tethered horse.

They all sat listening to him talking to his mare and whistling back to the cardinal that perched outside the cabin every morning.

"He's crazy," Mercy said, "but I love him anyway."

"Crazy, like a small fox," Nettie said, "and he's as lovable."

Alex turned his attention back to Mary. "There's talk of building a schoolhouse by the church."

Both Mary and Nettie leaned toward him. Nettie said, "Alexander, you said nothing of this before."

"No. With good reason, for I only found out when I passed the banker on our way here."

"That's wonderful," Mary said, "How long to build it?"

The school and parsonage will be finished by fall." Alex smiled at her.

"Did I hear you say a parsonage?" Mary beamed at Alex.

"You did. The banker mentioned he began arrangements to have all the wood for the church, school, and parsonage transported from the sawmill next week." He swallowed the last of his tea. "Mary, we need you and Abner to pray for good weather."

"We'll do that, Alexander."

"C'mon, let's go, Alexander," John yelled from outside the cabin.

Alexander rose and walked to Mercy. He gave her a strong hug. "You take care of these two, Mercy."

"I will, Alexander." She kissed him on the cheek.

"Mercy, you leave my husband alone."

"I'll try ... but he is so handsome and lovable," Mercy said with a grin.

Mary shook her head.

Chapter 52

A cloudless morning greeted John and Alexander for their ride to Warsaw and the Mississippi River. Long shadows stretched in front of them. They both sat easy in the saddle, enjoying the light breezes, which turned the prairie into an undulating grassy sea. Central Hancock County, mostly in native grassland, had not attracted many settlers who found easier farming in the townships east and west of Carthage.

As the morning brightened, Alex and John alternated speed-walking and trotting the horses along the road to Warsaw. Normally, Alexander followed a fixed route to visit families wishing his service, or simply to talk. Today, he didn't follow his usual route. Instead, Alex rode over new roads, until he came to the divide between the streams flowing northeast to the Mississippi and the other stream flowing southeast to Bear Creek. This familiarized him with lesser traveled roads and where they might hunt on the return trip.

Cabins and a sprinkling of frame homes dotted the landscape the closer they came to Warsaw. Formerly the site of a fort, Warsaw housed more people than the county seat of Carthage. The smell of the river drifted up from the bottomlands signaling they neared the winding watercourse.

The sun cast a welcoming light on the hilltop. They dismounted and led the horses to the edge of the unique area. The professor in the class Alexander attended while in Ohio mentioned some of the areas along the Mississippi, this being one of them. The soil, deeply laden with sand, presented an entirely different landscape than lay behind them because the glacier had stopped at Warsaw. The land above the floodplain became scoured by the glacial retreat and presently lay covered by wind-blown silt.

"John, what're you thinking?"

John looked around, taking in the entire area. "It's so different than the country we came through."

"Do you see any trees you know?"

John peered down the slope to the river bottom. "Looks like oak and hickory trees. I don't know the grasses and the other plants where I stand."

"You'll learn them this fall and next spring. Chirt and I are taking our classes to the prairies and the drainages like we crossed." John's wide-open eyes and the grin made Alexander chuckle. "You like that?"

"Oh yes, I can hardly wait."

"You don't have to. We're going to start learning as we hunt. Picket the horses with these." Alex withdrew two stakes and rope and handed them to John. "Hold these and I'll grab the mallet. He walked around the horse and took out the sturdy tool. Taking the reins, he walked—followed by John and his mare—to a soil area where the stakes would remain secured.

After attaching the reins, they started down the slopes from a small opening. It became difficult to walk the drainage, except when they moved horizontally along the face of the bluffs. They found a good stand of hickory and sat, waiting for the prey to pass by.

After an hour John became antsy. "You sure anything lives here?" John asked.

"Be patient, John."

They sat for another thirty minutes. Suddenly, a loud gobble came from directly in front of where they sat. "John," Alex whispered, "did Chirt teach you the gobbler's calls?"

He nodded and shivered with excitement. "Should I try?"

"You must bring him close. The bow will not penetrate the heavy feather layers if he is too far off."

John started to call and found his mouth too dry to make a sound.

"Here," Alex said, "and handed John a small deer-hide canteen.

After calming himself and washing his mouth he started to gobble like Chirt taught him. He waited.

Alexander quietly said, "Be patient."

A loud gobbling to their right startled them.

John set off a hen call and got a gobble back, this time closer.

It took only a few minutes and John finally saw the gobbler no more than ten yards in front. He lifted the bow, pulled an arrow from the quiver, nocked it, and slowly drew back. He waited for the turkey to present a good shot and, let go.

Alexander clapped loudly. "You're going to make a great hunter, John."

He didn't charge out to bring back the fowl; instead, John said a silent prayer and turned to Alexander. "Thank you and I thank God."

They hiked to the river and gutted the bird. After washing the cavity, Alex salted the inside and wrapped it in a loose mesh fabric. "This should keep the meat safe until we get back to Carthage, providing we keep to the shade while we eat in Warsaw."

The climb back up the drainage challenged both, but John's excitement with the adventure kept him from noticing his own exhaustion until they reached the top of the bluff.

Alexander slipped the tom into another mesh bag to hang off the saddle. "Hungry?" Alex asked.

John nodded.

They had to travel south and backtrack northeast to drop into the valley where Warsaw had sprung up along the river. A tavern sat off the bank no more than twenty yards. A large oak shaded the hitch rail, providing a cool spot for the horses and John's turkey. Before tying the horses, they watered them at a large trough.

"Herr Schroeder," the rotund barkeep greeted Alexander.

"Mr. Schultz," Alex responded while removing his wide-brimmed hat. "Meet my hunting companion, John Hayman."

August Schultz stuck out his hand and said, "John, welcome to the Fort Tavern."

"Mr. Schultz, this is an interesting place."

August laughed. "Why do you say that, John?"

"It's all the antlers hanging on the wall. Did you shoot all of them?"

August grinned. "Nah, I tell people where there is a good hunt and they bring the antlers to me."

"Why do you call this the Fort Tavern?"

"You ask many questions for a young man. That's good. You'll learn, my boy, keep asking."

"What's good to eat?"

August roared with laughter.

Alexander said, "You've made a friend, John."

"John, we have fresh caught fish or pork. And the tavern name comes from the fort, Fort Johnson, which once stood on this land. Before you ask, it burned down and the government rebuilt another north of here."

"Thank you," John said. "Alexander, what do you want?"

"I always have fish when August says it's fresh."

John and Alexander ordered fish and fried potatoes. They talked about the sandy hills where they hunted. During their talk three men entered and sat at a corner table. One man talked loud and held his hand up to one ear. The other two loudly responded to him, and when the talk turned to the Mormons, Alex glanced over at them.

August came from the kitchen with their food. He glanced at the three men. "Enjoy, gentlemen." He gave John a pat on the back and walked to the table with the loud talker. Two other men came in and sat at a table a fair distance from the threesome. After taking the order from the three loud-talking men, he moved to the newcomers and talked with them for a few minutes before taking their orders.

"How's the fish, John?" August asked.

"Very good, thank you."

"Alex, he's polite too." He slapped John on the back and scurried into the kitchen where his wife prepared the food.

Over his nearly cleaned plate, John quietly asked, "Who're those men? They sound like they are mad at the Mormons."

"The loud one is old Tom Sharp. He doesn't like the Mormons and he makes it known through his newspaper." Alexander motioned to August they wanted to leave.

"Alex, can I go around and look at the antlers?"

"Sure, but don't linger, we need to be on our way so we can stop at places I want to show you."

"What … what you gonna show me?"

"Be patient," Alexander said, "you'll enjoy it more when we get there."

John started at the far end of the unique bar and took in all the large antlers along the west wall. He stopped to study the large elk antlers near the table with the loud, brash men. He overheard their conversation about the cursed Mormons and a need to stop the scourge of Joseph Smith on the county. As he walked by the table one of the men looked up and smiled. John tipped the brim of his hat and kept walking.

The other man, not so hard-of-hearing whispered, "That the Carthage minister's kid?"

"What makes you ask?" the other man said while the big man scribbled notes, concentrating on his writing.

"He's with the fella over there."

A slight nod of the man's head caught John's attention. He looked that direction to notice Alexander talking to the two who avoided the threesome.

Alexander looked at John approaching. "You ready to go, John?"

John nodded and slipped past Alex to look at two more deer antlers. He overheard one of the men ask, "He the Reverend's boy?"

"Yes," Alex said.

"He gonna be a minister like his dad?"

"I think God has other plans for John."

Chapter 53

The time at the Fort Tavern and the months after, in 1844, shaped John's attitudes and behavior for many years to come. The trip back to Carthage from Warsaw taught him more than hunting. It begged his understanding of words like persecution. John decided this word fit how the whites felt about and treated different colored people.

John began the month of May hunting and fishing with the Aldermens until the middle of the month. The last week, on a Monday, they appeared, at the Hayman cabin, with a wagon full of wood and building tools.

"John," yelled the oldest Alderman son, "come out, we have to help with the church building."

Abner laughed at his son. "Don't look so shocked, John. You need to learn how to do this, for one day you may need the skills."

The seven miles to the church passed rapidly as the boys chattered like crows. Nearly two dozen men worked at the site unloading lumber and materials. Several trees remained standing to form a pleasant shaded nook for the building. Someone had earlier marked the area for the footings and placed the beams next to the layout.

Alexander stood off to the side while the oxen-pulled wagon carried the footing ballast and huge timbers on which the church walls would rest. He waved for John to join him.

"John, you know what this is?"

John snorted, "It's a shovel, Alexander."

"And what do you do with a shovel?"

John chuckled. "You dig ... and I suppose that's what I'm going to do."

"You're a smart boy." Alexander led him to the southwest corner for the new building and he showed John how to dig the footing trench. Eagerly, John joined in and immediately stopped at Alexander's direction. "Put on gloves, boy."

By noon, all thirty men and boys completed the foundation trenching and ballasting. Three wagon loads of food and water arrived with lunch. An hour later the men and boys—the youngest running errands—measured cut and laid out the four walls for fastening to the footing timbers. Late in the afternoon the walls stood joined.

"It's beautiful," Alexander said. "Tomorrow we put up the beams for the roof. You like to climb?" He smiled at John.

"I'll try anything once," John said.

"I know John, I know." He steered John toward his buggy, and they rode back to Carthage discussing the news coming from Nauvoo and Warsaw. The sound of meadowlarks floated on a northerly spring wind. Smoke from chimneys in Carthage drifted over the road and mingled with the smell of newly cut roadside grass.

"Why do people want to argue about their personal belief? What's all this about? I don't understand all the anger." John's face became shrouded in frustration.

"Talk to your parents tonight. They can help you try to understand."

"Try ..."

"I don't understand it, nor do I like it. I try to stay away from the bickering and whining." Alexander shrugged.

Alexander stopped the buggy at the Hayman cabin and watched Mary open the door and call for John.

"Thanks, John. You did great work today. The fun begins tomorrow."

"Bye, Alexander. What time tomorrow?"

"Daybreak," Alex said as John hopped from the buggy.

His gloves stuffed in the belt behind his back and dirt coating his lower legs, he hoofed it to the cabin where Mary waited. "I'm sorry, we were a bit late because we needed to finish framing the last wall of the church."

She smiled at her son. "Wash up, supper's ready."

Mercy sat talking to Abner over a glass of water and the Bible. They watched John drag himself to the bedroom and return with his underclothing showing sweat and grime.

"Yuck," Mercy said.

"You look tired, John. I rigged a washing site under the oak tree. There's water in a pail hanging from the lowest limb. You can tip it with a gentle tug on the rope. Scrub all over." Abner returned to his visit with Mercy.

After all the sweat and grime of digging and hauling timber and tools, the water felt good. He reflected on the past month and one-half as he dried with a cloth Mary supplied.

When he got settled for the meal, Mercy said the prayer and they ate in silence until almost finished. John put his fork down and asked, "Father, why all the arguing by Mr. Sharp and Prophet Smith?"

Mary glanced at Abner and stood to clean the table. Mercy helped. Abner nodded. "John," Mary said, "Mercy asked the same question. Give us a moment to clear the table and clean the dinnerware."

Ten minutes later the four sat at the table in flickering. Other lit candles cast dark shadows on the cabin walls and the smell of melted wax filled the room. Abner said a silent prayer and looked up to find his children staring at him.

"It's a difficult subject to understand," he began, "for Mr. Sharp comes from a Methodist background and Mr. Smith from a vision." He paused to study the children's faces. "Let me put it another way, there's a disagreement between the two men on many subjects. The two main points are religion and politics."

"But why, aren't people the same even if they are of different color or religion or politics?" Mercy asked. She looked at John who vigorously nodded in agreement.

"Mercy, many teachings of the church I represent are not necessarily good. I chose to follow the doctrines the leaders set forth."

"Even if they're … wrong?" John said.

"John, sometimes we make mistakes. I take the doctrines into consideration by putting them aside if it's fairer for our followers." He eyed John. "Let me give you an example. I think people of our faith should not condemn others for what they believe. If they are put in a bad light by others we should help them."

"Father, should we protect Mr. Sharp and Mr. Smith from each other according to God's word?" Mercy asked.

"Excellent question, Mercy," he answered, and noticed the gentle smile on Mary's lips. "We serve God by teaching peace and love through his son Jesus Christ."

John sat thoughtfully. "I heard nasty talk from some of the men helping build the church."

"Like what, John?" Mary said.

"They said Prophet Smith ought to hang, or somebody should shoot him." John sat sadly in his chair.

"Not good," Abner said. "We should do everything in our power to not let this disagreement end in violence."

"But what can we alone do?" Mercy asked.

"We don't do it alone," Abner said. "As the minister, I can lead our members, as Christ did with his disciples."

"You'll preach about it in church and meetings?" John said.

"Yes, as soon as the men finish the church and I begin again on my ministry circuits. Our followers in the Reformed faith must follow the Ten Commandments."

Chapter 54

June proved a tumultuous time for Carthage, Illinois, and for John Hayman. The church was completed and consecrated by the last day in May, finally providing the growing congregation a place to worship that they could call their own. The first Sunday, June 2nd, Abner caught many of the open-minded members, including Abner's family, Chirt, and the Schroeders, by surprise. The sermon normally followed the Reformed liturgy, but this Sunday Abner ended his sermon with a rousing discourse about the blasphemous Mormon, Joseph Smith. Several members gasped at the vehemence and fiery nature of his pompous delivery.

John stared at his mother. The longer his father advocated the Reformed approach and demeaned the Mormon faith the more his mother fidgeted. He felt for her as she never talked badly about anyone or any religion as long as John could remember. John found Chirt and Nettie three rows behind his mother. The slight shaking of their heads told him they could not believe what they heard. His gaze shifted to Alexander seated behind the church elders. Alexander's rigid posture meant he had engrossed himself in deep thought.

After church, several members from near Nauvoo stopped to congratulate Abner on his fine sermon. The rumors circulating in Carthage abounded with accusations that Joseph Smith had bilked many of his followers, taking such drastic steps as banning the newspaper. The talk included his support of polygamy and ousting followers who disagreed with him. John sat quietly in the rear pew listening and thinking about what he heard. Could it all be true? John thought back to the man in Warsaw. Perhaps his father knew more than anyone else because he traveled the north ministry circuit.

"John," Alexander said as he sat beside the boy, "we're all surprised by the fiery delivery your father made." He could feel John stiffen under his hand. "Don't fret."

"Alexander, Father has always preached that we should try to understand and listen to others about their beliefs. He said we should follow the peaceful ways of the Lord." John gave Alexander an angry look. "I'm confused."

"Talk to him, John. He might be willing to talk about it."

"Thank you."

Mary, Mercy, Nettie, and Chirt didn't wait to leave the church until last. They left without saying a word to Abner. Several women lingered, including the woman John noticed smiling during his father's tirade. This woman caught John's attention because her husband died the last year and Abner conducted the funeral service. They had no children and now she lived alone. Being the last in line meant she could speak freely to her pastor.

John slumped low in the rear pew and watched. It turned painful for him as his father held the woman's hands in his, and talked softly. Tears filled the woman's eyes and she leaned into him. Abner held her tightly. John felt sick when the woman kissed his father on the lips and Abner responded. His sick feeling turned to anger, because his father preached against polygamy. Abner had ignored some of the Ten Commandments.

John skipped lunch, changed clothes, and took to the prairie. He saddled his pony, tied on the saddlebags, and headed east to the next township where several open marshes held waterfowl and provided a place for shorebirds migrating north. The entire afternoon he sat, watching the habits of various species of male and female ducks and noting the incessant dabbling and skittering about by the shorebirds. These moments always brought peace of mind, which he needed after questioning his father and God.

His tethered horse nickered, breaking his thoughts. The small horse raised its head from grazing and peered to the west. Within minutes John heard rapidly approaching hoofbeats. He stood, watching Chirt slow her animal to a walk.

"John," Chirt greeted and dismounted. The split reins dropped to the ground. She walked to John and pulled him into her arms.

"I love you, Chirt."

I love you too, John." She stood back and studied his face. "You're upset with your father's sermon this morning?"

"Yes. I don't understand him all these years, preaching about loving your neighbor and then doing what he did today." He paused in thought. "How did you know where to find me?"

"C'mon, John, you're a smart person."

"Alexander?"

"Yes." Chirt motioned him to sit. She sat beside him and said, "Is there something else you want to tell me?"

He folded his arms across his uplifted knees and rested his forehead and stared down at the flattened grasses.

"Is it about the woman up north?"

His head popped off his forearms, fire in his eyes. "Blast him! He does not follow what he preaches and teaches." John turned back to the marsh.

"John, look at me." She waited until he turned his head. "Sometimes we cannot overcome temptation. What we do wrong can hurt others, but we must forgive. We can't always forget, but we can forgive."

"I thought only God forgives."

"That's the supreme forgiveness. For now, God looks down on us. He teaches us to be kind, merciful, and to forgive the wrongdoers through Jesus."

"How do know and understand all this?"

She smiled at him. "I am older and more experienced. Someday you will say the same to your children."

Chapter 55

For the next two weeks, Abner hammered at the rumored incidents happening in and around Nauvoo. His sermons and passages he chose to fit the time and circumstances of the rift in the Mormon followers.

The third Sunday after Abner completed the service, John noticed one of the men he saw in Warsaw with Thomas Sharp stop to talk to Abner. The conversation turned serious for several minutes. The man flushed, clamped his jaw, and stomped away. The following week Abner took Alexander's south ministry circuit and when he left he seemed on edge, stating he wouldn't return until late Friday.

Alexander, not on his normal schedule, watched the state militia in Carthage become active. Days later the governor personally came to town, threatening to bring in more troops unless the Mormons surrendered. Joseph Smith and his brother, and several other Mormons came in peacefully. Hyrum and Joseph Smith and another Mormon member remained under guard at the Carthage jail, the others going free.

On Saturday, the son of a congregation member scurried out of Carthage to tell Reverend Hayman a mob of men milled in the streets of Carthage, decrying that Joseph Smith must immediately go or die. The boy, after calming down, relayed that his father and other members of the Reformed Church wanted someone to intervene because the state militia had not returned from Nauvoo.

"John, hitch the horse to the buggy. I need to go into town to help."

"Can I go?"

"No, stay here, I'll take care of this." Within five minutes Abner whipped the horse toward town.

John rode bareback not more than three minutes behind Abner. On arriving in Carthage, he saw men circling the jail, shouting and cursing at the imprisoned Smiths. He did not see his father. John dismounted and led his horse out of sight and looked for his father. For the next thirty minutes, John stayed back watching the angry crowd continue to shout at the Smiths. Suddenly, a dozen men dashed from the angry mob and stormed the jail steps. Shots rang out at the upstairs jail door. A minute later someone appeared at the second-story window. Gunshots popped loudly and the man toppled from the window to the ground. Several men moved toward the body and the loud cry rose in the air "The False Prophet is dead." Another man yelled, "Behead false Prophet Smith."

John frantically looked for his father, hoping he would emerge and help. Finally, he spotted Abner huddled in the shadows, leaning against a building, his arms wrapped around his chest, watching the frenzy unfold.

A lean, tall figure appeared. "Go home all of you. You've done an evil deed outside the law. Go home."

John gasped, "Alexander ..."

The following summer Carthage settled back to a sleepy community, the carnage not forgotten, but for now buried. Like John, many of the boys worked the summer either in town shops or in the country helping with farm work. John found a job with the new dry goods store, working with Alexander. The word of a war in Nauvoo persisted in 1846 and ended when the Mormons fled from Nauvoo.

The Hayman children grew weary of their father's demanding nature and wish to control their lives, which neither wanted. They asked to enroll in the public school established in St. Mary's Township. Mary had difficulty with the children's request and wanted to say no. When news came that the teacher at the public school asked Alexander to help at the school, teaching the older students, she knew the answer.

This led to an uncomfortable break between Abner and Alexander but solidified Alex's relationship with Mercy and John. In the fall of 1848 the three rode together to the public school, Mercy was excited to find new friends and know she would have a diploma in two years. John spent as much time outdoors as in. He wanted to know the winter habits of the animals in St. Mary's Township so he could write a paper for his science studies. Alexander proved as successful with teaching as he had with his associate ministry.

Alex found a family in the village of St. Mary's without children. They gladly housed Mercy and John, finding them to be studious, polite, and caring children. The Byrnes, Bridgette and Timothy, arrived in Hancock County in 1830, became the proud parents of two girls, and lost both to cholera at the ages of two and four. Mercy filled the void of their two girls and John the void of their not having a son. The Catholic religion came into question only once when Abner came to visit.

In Mercy's final year of school, Abner planned a trip to the Byrnes' home. He wanted to make sure they were not influencing his children with Catholic teachings. Alexander accompanied Abner to the Brynes' home on a Sunday after his service. It had been two months since Mercy and John last came to Carthage and the Reformed Church. The buggy ride from Carthage took fewer than three hours on a good day. Alexander handled the reins while Abner studied the proposed changes to the liturgy coming from the diocese.

"Abner, I want to make it clear," he said as he reined the horse east toward St Mary's, "no belittling of the Catholic religion."

Abner looked up and stared hard at his close friend. "Speak as you wish, Alexander."

"This man and wife are kind and caring people. Their religion makes no difference to your children."

"But—"

"No, Abner," Alex harshly said, "Mercy and John are safe and healthy. Do not spoil it for them because of your zeal for the Reformed faith."

Abner remained quiet for two miles and finally spoke, "I will control myself." He gazed at the land transitioning from prairie to moderate forest cover along the stream drainages. A deer bolted in front of the horse, making it shy toward a primitive drainage ditch.

Alexander took control of the frightened horse and coaxed it away from the deep drop. "If you try to move the conversation to religion I'll take you on like I did this horse."

Abner chuckled. "I've forgotten your strength. Your strength of believing and doing endears my respect and love for you."

"One final statement for you, Reverend Hayman," Alex said.

Abner took heed because of Alex's tone.

"Mary told me she is pregnant once again." He sighed. "How do I say this? If you don't stop bedding the widow up north, I will take you to the woods and beat you within an inch of your life."

"Alex, I'm not bedding that woman."

"Horse manure, Abner, you can't control yourself. You and Samuel Carnes always want a woman or women in your life. Your son saw you several years ago."

"He lies."

"No, Abner he does not, for I too saw you. If you do not change your ways, you'll lose both of them."

Abner snorted a reply, "I'll have many more children."

"Maybe, Abner, maybe, but don't count on it."

Chapter 56

Mercy impressed her teacher the first year in the public school. Last year she assisted him, teaching the incoming students reading and writing. Several of the older boys took a liking to her and escorted her to dances and township spelling bees. The last month of her schooling she met a man who dazzled her with his knowledge and charm. The man lived in Quincy and encouraged her to seek a job in the city after her graduation.

John made a point to talk to her about becoming involved. "Mercy, I'm not one to interfere in your business … but you're getting a little silly over this Quincy man."

"You're right, John. Stay out of my business."

He started to say what he wanted and stopped. The look on her face left him shocked.

"John, Abner controlled my life for years, you're not going to do the same, understand?"

Using their father's first name shocked him so he couldn't answer. He nodded and went back to his studies.

Mary, Chirt, the Schroeders, and Abner attended her graduation from the public school. Immediately after the Byrnes' served lunch in honor of her finishing school, Mercy's teacher arrived with a buggy and stowed her bags in the back for her journey to Quincy to seek employment. He told Abner and Mary he found an interview—at Mercy's request for help to find a teaching job—at a new grade school.

As the dust settled behind the teacher's buggy, Abner said, "God bless you, daughter." He turned and walked to the buggy. Mary shrugged and followed. With Mary beside him, Abner switched the horse to a trot and pointed the buggy west.

Timothy Byrnes asked, "Alexander, will you stay on at the school?"

"Yes, until John graduates and then he and I will move to Jacksonville to attend college."

"What will you study, Alexander?" Bridgette asked.

"Education, Mrs. Byrnes, I want to hold a degree for teaching so I can work at the school of my choice."

"Please explain," Timothy said.

"I will not stay in Hancock County. I'm not negative about this school or the area; I simply need a degree to become a teacher in Iowa."

John looked at him and said, "Alexander, where in Iowa?"

"I want to teach in Keokuk, or somewhere upstream, near the Des Moines River."

Alex's genuine smile always pleased John. He felt the honesty of it, not so with the grimace his father made, thinking it a preacher smile.

"Nettie and I've been talking, John. We want you to join us for a time, get your feet under you. After we graduate, you can go with us to Iowa and stay with us or live nearby." The look on John's face almost broke his heart. "Let's go fishing and do some bird watching along Bear Creek. No need to answer now."

"I would like the trip to Bear Creek, Alexander."

The Byrnes couple shook their hands, asked Nettie to stay, and said to John the evening meal would be ready when he and Alexander returned.

The teacher did not return the next fall; therefore, the board hired Alexander. In turn, he asked John to help his classmates. Alex got approval before asking John, telling the board they both would leave the school in two years.

The days of summer, after Mercy rode away with her teacher, went too fast. Bridgette and Timothy showed their appreciation for John by presenting him with a special daypack. The daypack contained a dictionary and other work of Webster.

"Bridgette," John said, "where did you get Webster's works?"

"Timothy and I, when we found out you would help teach the township children, decided you should have them." She gave John a hug. "Nettie helped find them."

"There's a catch," Timothy said, "you must sit with us in the evenings after you finish your studies and help us learn, using Mr. Webster's books."

Bridgette added, "We want you to share your bird and animal knowledge with us before you leave."

John stood, not knowing what to say or how to react. Finally, he did as Alexander would do, smile, and share a loving hug with both.

The fall brought a new parsonage for Abner and Mary and a schoolhouse—though small—for Nettie and Mary. Nettie and Alex found a small cabin east of Bentley so both would live closer to their work. A new barn became a reality for the Byrnes family when Alexander and John taught town children construction methods. John loved this teaching, for the children learned arithmetic, the need for accuracy, and a skill.

During the fall John and Alexander fulfilled the curriculum of reading, writing, arithmetic, and geography. The thirst for more knowledge enveloped John. He yearned to explore beyond the boundaries of Illinois.

Before the students left to do farm work, or return to jobs in town serving farmers, Alex decided the older students should teach some of the lessons. They found it helped the students retain what they studied. Over the Christmas break, John stayed with Bridgette and Timothy, except for a few days to visit his parents and his new sister, Amanda. The birth took a toll on his mother and she appeared frail on Christmas day, so he accompanied her to the church service, his first since teaching for the public school.

The next summer followed the same pattern and John felt comfortable with the routine. He did shorten his field observations, but not much. Chirt visited every two weeks until the grain harvest, spending time in the field with him. She shared her knowledge of Indian rituals and their appreciation for nature.

Classes started the first Monday in November and ran to seven days before Christmas. The first Monday after the New Year, classes resumed and ended after the second week of April. In March, Alex and John prepared for their last lessons, before moving to Jacksonville to attend college. They planned to work over the summer before starting in the fall, but the professors at Illinois College—recognizing the unique opportunity for accelerated education—urged Alex and John to work on classes over the summer.

His decision came in a burst of words. "Alexander, I'll study hard and join you and Nettie in Iowa." The two proudly rode together on their newly purchased horses, one a young boy—rapidly maturing into a man—the other, a man who gained a son.

Chapter 57

The killing of Prophet Smith and the doubt that John's father didn't believe what he preached, faded with time. Thanks to Alexander, John felt better days lay ahead. The choice of Iowa didn't come down to what, but whom. Alexander and Nettie received an offer from a Fairfield, Iowa school to teach and nurture the community's children.

John helped Alexander and Nettie move with the belief he might assist at the school. To his dismay, he found the world could be cruel no matter where he lived. He discovered his father's reputation—good and bad—had traveled far and wide, deterring a start anew teaching in southeastern Iowa.

Fairfield grew rapidly in the time John lived with Nettie and Alexander. To pay for his room and board he first worked maintaining the home and barn they bought from an elderly couple who returned to Ohio. That first summer he broke ground for a garden, planting a myriad of vegetables. He helped Alexander repair the old log barn and add an area, which he could call his own. They combed the countryside for a wood-burning stove to heat the room and part of the barn. It took the better part of the first summer to find suitable logs for sale and to locate a farmer willing to let them cut trees and pile the logs for construction and fuel. By late October the three settled into a routine, Nettie and Alexander teaching in ungraded and graded schools, respectively.

The break came for John when the farmer where they obtained the wood mentioned John's hard work and pleasant manner. The dry goods and farm-and-home store owner had two employees abruptly leave for the goldfields and he sought immediate help.

John met with the owner and the other two employees the first week in November. The proprietor cared little about Abner's reputation. He needed a hardworking man to work with his customers. The logging and farm work with Alexander toughened John and he immediately handled the feed store tasks with little difficulty. This job helped John because he found areas where, in his spare time, he could hunt, fish, observe, and keep a record of the animals and plants.

The next year the dry goods store lost the employee who handled the inventory and cash, some of which turned up missing. That man quietly resigned. Being an honest person, John became the prime employee to replace him. With his background, personality, and zeal to succeed, John became the rising star in the dry goods shop. The owner made a deal with John to entice him to stay: a raise in pay and time off to study Jefferson and the surrounding counties.

In June of 1855, a man stopped at the store to replace his well-worn boots. He struck up a conversation with John about his travels in the Nebraska Territory. The talk turned from the Indians and their removal from reservations, to the rolling land most people ignored. The traveler's description awakened John's curiosity and his desire to move on to a new life in an unsettled area.

That evening, sitting in the shade of the elm tree outside the barn, Alexander and he discussed the reality of John's move. Alexander closely watched John as he described the land as the stranger had.

"John, what attracts you to the area?"

John pondered the question. "It's the marshes he talked about, and the plants and the wild game."

"How about the people," he whittled at a block of wood, "did he mention people?"

"No, he said the area had few people, in fact, he only met three people on his north-south travel between the Mormon and Oregon trails."

"Do you know what the man did while on his journey?"

John shook his head.

Alexander offered, "I've talked to student's parents who have relatives that traveled the Oregon Trail. No one wanders off the Trail for fear of the disgruntled Indians in that area."

"But they're on reservations and in villages," John quickly responded.

"True, but bitterness surely exists with the loss of their … land."

"But they signed a treaty and moved to reservations."

"John, remember what we explored in our school teaching and our learning at the college."

"I'm sorry. In my enthusiasm … to explore … I'm ignoring what I know … and should realize." His chest rose and fell with a heavy sigh. "I have to go. Something pulls me west. I don't know what or …"

"Then go. Start the life you wish." Alexander looked at the young man he loved. "Do you believe in God?"

John flinched. His eyes misted. "I don't know, Alex, I don't."

The Settling

John Burroughs, American Essayist and Naturalist, 1837-1921

"If I were to name the three most precious resources of life, I should say books, friends, and nature; and the greatest of these, at least the most constant and always at hand, is nature."

Chapter 58

From the moment John made his final decision he never looked back. The time had arrived to make his own way, and he left with the blessing of Alexander, Nettie, his mother, and Mercy. He spent a pleasant night with his mother, Mercy, and small sister, Amanda, at the parsonage south of Carthage.

Abner did not come to see, nor to wish his son well. He had decided two days before to conduct a ministry tour around Hancock County. Did it bother John? No. The respect for his father, the Reverend Hayman, he lost many years before.

John enjoyed the prairie isolation along the Iowa upland divides, although it slowed his travel. He kept his mare at a walking gait for most of his travel, occasionally trotting her on the gentler ground. His desire to record new observations and the concern for his packhorses dictated the trip's pace. The grasses and flowering plants along the roads and trails swayed in the southwesterly wind, encouraging his dismounts to study the plants and insects. While he studied, the horses had time to rest and graze in the lush vegetation. At times, he would walk and lead his horses for miles before stepping back into the saddle. He dropped into the stream valleys only to water the animals and sit in the cool shade, noting the birds and small animals seeking water.

The two packhorses carried all of John's belongings, which included his bow in a handmade scabbard and an old quiver with arrows. He neatly packed the camping gear, ammunition, and tools. The older and largest horse carried most of the gear. He had to thank Alexander for all the knowledge he gained when they packed and moved from Illinois to Iowa. He felt blessed.

The Colt hunting rifle he tucked in a saddle scabbard, butt forward and level with the saddle horn. The pistol, a present from the Schroeders, he hooked on his belt, positioned for comfort while in the saddle and for a quick cross-draw. Before the beginning of his journey, John practiced firing guns from the saddle and positions near the horses, ensuring they would not bolt from the firearm noise.

Early on, with Alexander and Chirt, he learned that on long horseback treks the animals must rest after six or seven days. On the ride across southern Iowa, he alternated riding and repacking loads among the horses, even though the oldest could easily carry the pack for three consecutive days. He stayed in towns and used a livery the first three nights. John had calculated and knew how much money he could spare for this part of the trip.

The travel across southern Iowa took fourteen days. The three counties directly west of Jefferson he traversed with few difficulties. On his arrival in Montgomery County, he found few good roads. The streams in the county flowed southwest to join the Missouri River according to a crude map drawn by a man returning from the western goldfields. The old miner suggested a flat divide that would take John southwest through Fremont County to the Nebraska City ferry crossing.

John carried little cash with him for he asked Alexander to send his meager earnings on a steamboat sailing up the Missouri River to Nebraska City. The trail proved little challenge and on entering Fremont County he dropped off the divide to a decent road leading to Sidney, a community of three hundred plus people. John, unfamiliar with the road, didn't know that several scoundrels used it, seeking to rob innocent travelers. As he neared Sidney, John for the first time felt the gnawing presence of danger, not from wolves, but a more forbidding predator.

At a stream, not far from the town, he dismounted and led the horses to a backwater area. Over the years the meandering channel had dropped sediment on the slow-flowing side, forming a decent flat. John walked the horses down a gentle slope to the site so his animals could rest and drink. The three horses stood side-by-side as they drank the slightly turbid water.

Suddenly, the oldest raised its head and snorted. John quickly moved alongside the large animal and waited, watching the stallion's nostril flares. The ears perked up and the eyes moved to a clump of willows. From within the crowded saplings, he detected movement and sunlight glint. He eased his rifle from the scabbard and waited. A rifle barrel protruded from the willows and slowly moved to and fro.

"Come out," John yelled. The barrel rapidly slid back into the branches. "Come out now or I'll shoot." No answer and the willows remained motionless. "You shoot one of my horses and I'll make you pay."

"Don't shoot," said a high-pitched voice. "I wanted to see what you be doin' at the stream."

"And I believe you like I believe the devil. Toss out your rifle and step out where I can see you."

A man in his mid years—filthy and bearded—stood, tossed his rifle from the saplings, and stepped out with his hands high. "You won't shoot an unarmed man—"

"I should …" John motioned him to step further away from the gun.

"Please, don't shoot."

"What do you want?" John asked.

"I need money to buy food."

"You wanted to rob me and steal my horses?"

"No, sir," the man swallowed hard, "I just need money; I were gonna ask you to help."

"Nope," John said, "I don't believe you. As I'm a good person, I'll let you go, but not with your rifle."

"You gonna steal my gun?"

"No, I'm going to take it into town and give it to the sheriff. You can collect it from him and go on about your business."

"Cain't you leave it on the roadside?"

John shook his head. "I'm going to let you go. You try to rob me again I'll track you down and see to it you serve jail time."

"Cain't I put my hands down?"

John laughed. "Not until we get to your horse."

Through squinted eyes, the man scanned the rim of the stream bank.

"My horse …" he pointed with his raised right hand, "… is up there."

"Good, let's walk up there and I'll see you on your way."

John stepped into the stirrup, steadily pointing the gun at the man's sunken gut. He slowly swung into the saddle and motioned the man up the sloping bank.

The man looked back at his rifle. "You gonna leave my gun?"

"No." John quickly slid from the saddle, grabbed the rifle, and remounted.

An old horse, with mud-crusted legs, raised its head on their approach.

"You got a gun stashed on that poor animal?"

"No, sir. I ain't lie-en."

"Better not or you won't live to see tomorrow." John dismounted and walked to the horse, its ribs showing through the hide. After searching the saddlebags and walking around the animal, John motioned for the man to mount. "Remember, you bother me again—"

"No, sir, I won't." The man slapped the horse's rump and headed north, away from Sidney.

It took a little time to stop at the sheriff's office and drop off the rifle. While there he asked about a good road or trail to the Nebraska City ferry.

The sheriff said, "Sorry 'bout the bad experience. You're lucky; many strangers lose their money and possessions up there."

"Sheriff," John said, "what's the best route to the Nebraska City ferry?"

The sheriff drew a map for John and marked a place to camp in the bluffs. "The ferry stopped running because of high water on the Missouri, and it'll be two or three days until you can cross that muddy flow."

Chapter 59

From a bluff ridge, John looked over the flat Missouri River floodplain. Pale-blue haze blanketed small patches of cropland and prairie. A joyful smile formed on his tanned face, which quickly faded. Thoughts flashed across his subconscious, *what if the land ahead does not turn out like the old man described? What if it isn't what I expect?*

The negative musing quickly disappeared when he heard the restless horses. He turned back and scampered down the small knoll. If the ferry didn't run for two more days he would camp, hunt, write, and organize his plan for survival in the new country. The sun warmed him as he removed the packs from the horses and set up camp. A small spring formed a trickle leading toward the valley. He led the horses to the clear water, took the time to let them drink their fill, and led them back to a grassy flat. His bedroll lay under a large oak, providing a comfortable shelter.

A few old trees along the small stream would supply dry wood to build a fire. After chopping what he needed, John went in search of new plants and animals. He tucked his small notebook in the deer-hide vest he made while in Fairfield. John wandered the hilly area above the valley, making notes and taking the time to breathe in the new smells surrounding him, finally ending back atop the small knoll overlooking the valley.

Below him all three horses lay in the grassy area, resting after their fourteen-day trip. The panorama below and in front of him flooded John with sadness. When would he see his mother and Mercy or Nettie and Alexander? He cared for them, loved them, but still the same pull to a place somewhere beyond the wide river lured him from his past. His father? Ha. The setting sun and the blue haze felt like a spiritual calling … maybe? He turned back for his camp.

Two days later, John loaded all his possessions on the horses and dropped into the valley. He began to mull over his reaction to the robber. It surprised him how calm he had remained. The coldness of his action bothered him—no fear, no hesitation. Would he have shot the man? Yes.

Several cabins appeared on the flat horizon as he neared Eastport. Tan and gold grain patches dotted the countryside near the farms. Wheat stubble, with a few scattered shocks, abutted the dirt road. He waved at several children working pigs in a pen. Their mother watched him urge his horses toward the ferry, and then she went back to her garden work.

Grain wagons, handcarts, and buggies—waiting for the ferry—filled the tiny community's one street. John dismounted and led his animals to the back of the line. Three well-spaced water troughs sat along the street and in front of the two stores and a tavern. After watering the horses, he checked the pack and cinched it tighter on the stallion.

He looked down to find a small girl, holding on a floppy bonnet on her head, peering up at him. She returned his smile with a big grin. A woman called out and she took off toward the front of the line. Cheering signaled the ferry's approach. John casually strode toward the river and watched as the flatboat captain began yelling for riders and wagons to get off. The size of the flatboat, the river flow, and the number waiting to cross to Nebraska City meant a long wait.

When he returned to his place in line a two-seat buggy had stopped behind his animals. A man and woman chatted, not paying him attention. He sat on his haunches at the edge of the street, knowing he had to wait a long time at Eastport than planned.

"Sir," the buggy driver said, "where're you headed?"

"West," John answered.

The well-dressed man, a neatly trimmed beard covering his chin, said, "Come sit with us." He pointed to the small rear seat.

"Much obliged." He took off his floppy-brimmed hat and the dark-brown hair cascaded onto his shoulders. "Ma'am," John politely said. "Thank you, sir." He easily stepped into the buggy.

"I'm Hiram and my wife Maggie."

"John, John Hayman." He took Hiram's extended hand.

"Are you headed for the mountains?" Maggie asked.

"No, I don't rightly know, yet. I'm looking for a place to settle." John liked her polite manner for it reminded him of his mother. "I might stop and begin my new life not far from Nebraska City."

"Not much west except grass … and some Indians who keep people from settling." He noticed John didn't seem surprised. "You know about the area?"

"Only what a passerby told me when I worked in eastern Iowa. It seemed like it might be a place I'd like to live … rather unique." John noted the look on the man's face. "What do you wonder?"

"Your speech, it's very good … educated. You've had to school beyond the average citizen."

John nodded. "I graduated from Illinois College two years past."

"What degree?" Hiram asked.

"Teaching," John said, "I hoped to teach in Fairfield, Iowa, but it didn't work out."

"Hiram, perhaps he could teach in Nebraska City and—"

John interrupted, "Excuse me ma'am, but I plan to keep moving as soon as we get across the river." he looked to Hiram. "Sir, what's your profession?"

"I'm retired military, a degree from back east."

Their conversation stopped when they heard the rude cursing, spewing from the ferry captain's mouth. The hunched and swarthy captain waved them forward; he kicked at John's horses on his walk back toward the river.

Hiram turned to find the kindly look on John's face had turned to anger. "Don't mind him, he's always like that. In fact, he beat a passenger last week when they got into an argument about the price to cross the river."

John's facial muscles slowly relaxed. "Has he hurt others?"

Maggie nodded. "He has a bad reputation, but he's the closest to us. Many people go back and forth between Iowa and Nebraska at this point."

The captain returned, stopped at John's horses, and said, "Git these nags movin'."

John leaped out of the buggy and charged toward him.

"These yours?" he punched the mare with a filthy finger.

"Yes," John said through clenched teeth.

The captain nastily quoted the ferry price and held out his hand.

John pulled a small bag from his vest and paid the quarrelsome man.

"Hiram," the captain said, "you paid me for a round-trip?"

"I did," Hiram answered. "How much longer do we have to wait?"

"Coupla hours, I'd guess," the captain said and headed back to the river. As he passed by John, he coughed and spit.

John smirked at the nasty gesture.

Hiram waved for John to rejoin them. "Don't let him upset you," Hiram said as John again climbed into the buggy. "He goads people into fights. Be careful, he's stronger than he looks; he beat the daylights out of a man about your age last year."

For the next two hours, the couple talked and walked with John on the street of Eastport. The line began to move. John shook hands and motioned Hiram to move ahead of him. Hiram nodded and urged his horse down the dirt street toward the ferry. John walked behind, leading his horses. Two wagons and several horseback riders waited behind him. The gruff captain stopped in front them and said, "No more room." He stomped back to the boarding planks.

As John started to lead his horses onto the ferry, the captain abruptly held up his hand. He eyed John's biggest packhorse and looked at the last space on his flatboat. "Mighty big animal you got there, sonny."

"So—" John said

"Gotta charge you more," he said, coughed, and spit at the horse's rear hooves.

John flinched. He looked up at Hiram who lightly shook his head.

"Another fifty cents, boy," the captain said. "And another twenty-five for the nasty look you gave me."

John paid him and led his animals onto the ferry.

"Cast off," the captain yelled at a man on shore.

The trip across the strong Missouri River flow drew John's attention away from the captain. He stood at the rail watching Iowa recede in the

216

distance. He walked to Hiram and said, "You say this is a common trip for you?"

"Yes, I work in Sidney, and Maggie accompanies me once a month."

"It's a pleasant ride, except for the captain."

"Watch him on your way off the ferry, John," Maggie said.

"Yes ma'am, thank you. I will." John turned back to watch a steamboat moving downstream. His thoughts floated back to the trip on the Mississippi. Those large steamboats carried passengers in luxury compared to this method of transportation. John had seen flatboats on the Ohio and Mississippi, but he never experienced the gruffness of a businessman, on water or land, like this operator.

They neared the shore and men working the sweeps and oars guided them into the dock area by the ferry house. "One question before we dock, Hiram. Is the operator of the ferry the owner?"

"Not on your life. The owner and his sons normally manage the ferry, but for the last three months this disgusting man stepped in for them." Hiram frowned at John. "Why do you ask?"

"Mainly curious is all. They have someone else to take his place?"

"Yes, but he took ill and won't be back until next month."

"Thank you," John said and looked at Maggie. "And thank you, ma'am, for the conversation. If I come back this way may I contact, you?"

"You may," Maggie said.

Chapter 60

Last on and last off the ferry, John knew he would not make the distance he planned for his first day in the Nebraska Territory. He watched Maggie heartily waving as they rolled off the flatboat. The obnoxious captain snorted at John as he led the horses over the landing planks.

The captain reached out and grabbed John's arm when he stepped on the road leading away from the river. "Hey, boy, you owe me another fifty cents."

John, normally a calm person, flared and slapped away the fist that moved to grip his vest.

"You're a smart horses rear, I'm gonna make you pay for tha—"

He never finished the sentence. John hit the man squarely on the chin with a left uppercut. The captain stumbled back and fell on his backside. He rubbed his chin, and before he said another word, John pulled the ferryman to his feet. He punched the nasty captain in the midsection and landed another uppercut. "That's my payment, with a tip."

Several people watching the action cheered, hoping John would continue to pummel the man. Silence followed when John swung into the saddle and trotted up the road toward the town.

He fumed while he waited for the wheelwright to finish a wheel repair and fit it with a better metal band and bolts. His day had not begun like he wanted, but Alexander's favorite two words echoed from his memory: *Be patient.*

John had stopped at the steamboat-landing house to collect his money that Alexander sent. He wanted to buy a wagon for his travel into Nebraska

Territory. Over the last year, he trained the two older horses to pull a fully loaded wagon. Today he found a wagon and harnesses for sale sitting outside the wheelwrights building. Both looked in good repair, though not exactly what he sought. His savings over the two years working in Fairfield easily allowed for the purchase.

From all his questions he asked travelers, heading east through Iowa, he learned of scarce wood and water if he did not follow the main trails. On the road out of Nebraska City, he bought salt, ammunition for his percussion cap guns, a barrel for holding water, and food supplies. Now, with his wagon full, he followed the main trail to the west and northwest along the high ground.

He covered the gently rolling land with ease. Two migrant trails, one to the north carried the Mormons westward, and to his south, the Oregon Trail moved others to the far west. A trail, not well known, carried emigrants across eastern Nebraska Territory through the grasslands north of the Platte River, where it followed along the south shore to Fort Kearny. John used the crude map to locate a little-used trail into to the marsh country. For the remaining days of his journey, he wanted solitude.

The first evening he camped on a divide that drained the high ground to the south and north. From this prominence, he could view the vast prairie to the west. As the sun sank slowly toward the horizon, bird songs in the dry air sounded the coming evening. There had been little rain at the site where he chose to stop and ponder the next day of travel. He stood in front of the wagon seat, breathing in the grassland smells lazily drifting in the dying wind.

The small drainage to the south offered a low spot to rest and wait for sunrise the next day. John guided the horses down the meager slope and stepped out of the wagon near a fire pit not more than two or three days old. While John looked for something to build a small fire, the horses began grazing. He cursed himself for not adequately planning. Along the roads and trails in Iowa he had plenty of readily available wood, but here ... nothing. He erred by not purchasing firewood in Nebraska City. Tonight, he would begin eating more of the dried berries and meat he packed in Fairfield.

After unpacking his bedroll, he unhitched the horses from the wagon and untied the saddle horse. He tethered each horse with a rope so they could graze at will without becoming entangled. He watered his horses along the stream draining from the northwest shortly after leaving Nebraska City. Another concern loomed: John worried about the lack of water in these grassy lands. He made a mental note to water the horses often where he found a spring or a stream.

He drank sparingly from his water pouch and did not touch the water keg fixed securely to the wagon sideboard. From under the wagon seat, he removed the food pack and stowed it next to his bedroll. John nibbled at his dried food, hoping to find the game to harvest and cook over a fire, if he found the wood. The thought of the last two days drifted into his conscience as he gazed at the yellow-red sky fading to pale blue. A brilliant star winked at him from above in the dark-blue sky to the east. The moon appeared like a scythe blade ready to harvest the grasses.

His reaction to the robber and the flatboat captain surprised him, especially the pummeling he gave the captain. The anger left him with some concern because he never before experienced this ire. Alexander had warned him, and trained him, to deal with these battles. John now felt a calm confidence that he could deal with scoundrels.

Before he nodded off he mulled over the conversation with Chirt, talking in a haltingly quiet voice about the beatings she suffered from her stepfather. John now understood violence of meeting and dealing with people looking to harm others, but …

The movement from the horses and the brightening sky woke John after a restless night. He peered into the pale-blue sky, listening to the grassland birds awakening the prairie with boisterous songs. A hawk soared above, seeking prey. John sat up, stretched, and washed his mouth with a swallow of water. His movement created a flurry of activity around his pack. Several small rodents disappeared into the undisturbed grasses ringing the flattened area created by his bedroll and pack.

"John, you've learned another lesson from this vast land." The horses stared at him at the sound of his voice, the mare quietly nickered. "Yes, I'll brush you and your pals and we can be on our way."

The mice did little damage, other than creating a hole in one pouch trying to reach the dried berries. John took the time to repair the small opening, repack his gear, and hitch the horses to the wagon tongue. He climbed onto the rough wooden seat and urged the horses up the slope to the ridge top. An hour later John arrived at a level divide, taking him southwest on grass-covered land. A northeast flowing stream meandered off to his right. Sparse shrub stands and a few scraggly trees dotted the stream banks.

After cutting a few limbs and finding dried wood near the stream, he secured enough fuel for a fire in the coming evenings. While riding out of the valley, he came on a flock of birds, each the size of a chicken. They scattered by twos and threes, seemingly unafraid of his presence. John jumped from the wagon seat, wrapped the reins around the brake handle, pulled the rifle from the scabbard below the seat, and trotted off after the birds. Ten minutes passed and he returned to the campsite. He examined the two harvested birds before he gutted and skinned them. Even though slightly paler color than the birds he shot in Illinois, John knew he bagged his first prairie chickens in the Nebraska Territory. The Hancock County prairie held isolated populations of the birds where they once abounded. The memory of Illinois and Carthage seemed far behind and began to fade in his mind's eye.

The second night of camping went better than the first. The horses lazily grazed on the slopes of the gentle land, their only uneasiness came with the flies that persisted in pestering them. This time John, through better attention to detail, built a small, relatively deep fire pit to prevent a prairie fire.

Over the flame, he skewered the prairie chicken breasts to a spit made from green wood; he heated water for cleaning his hands and face. The green and some dried wood pieces served their purpose for this night and he felt better about his second day. Thinking more clearly, he realized he must locate a business to buy supplies, likely south along the Oregon Trail. His concern lessened and he enjoyed the setting sun and the sounds of the birds settling into the prairie. Before the light dimmed he took his dried foods and hung them on a y-shaped pole stuck in the ground next to the saddle he used as a headrest. The horses seemed more at ease resting in the knee-high grass.

Chapter 61

Day three began peacefully. John moved about checking the wagon for damage from the constant prairie jolting. West and slightly south of his overnight camp he came on a stream bathed in a haze bluer than that over the Missouri. The stream valley carried more water than those he followed the last two days. He took this opportunity, after fording the stream, to gather more wood from the sparsely treed land. A small drainage rose to the west and he followed it until it disappeared into a flat expanse of prairie unlike any he ever saw. From horizon-to-horizon, except from where he came, the grasses dominated and swayed in the prairie wind. John uttered, "Will it ever end?" Ft. Kearny, he knew, lay somewhere ahead.

Slight rises existed here and there, but they were few. On one rise he topped, he spooked an antelope herd. "See that," he said to the horses, "not deer, but the fastest animal on the prairie." The saddle mare snorted. "Don't be afraid, they're our friends."

The flat land made traveling easy and it became easier when he discovered a trail leading due west. John felt he could readily travel the same distance as the sum of the last two days without tiring the horses or himself. As he had done in Iowa, he lightened the load by walking with the horses along the narrow trail. Besides big bluestem, John spotted new grasses, which he hoped to soon come to know. After several minutes gathering grass samples, examining the flowering plants, and those going to seed, he climbed aboard, wondering what lay ahead.

An ocean of grass grew unbroken. At midafternoon, the first marsh appeared as the old miner described: grass, grass, grass, and suddenly before you the strange pockets filled with cattails, bulrush, and some with open water. At one of the larger marshes, John stopped, stood on the wagon seat and felt a strange sensation envelop him. He breathed deeply and wept openly. If someone saw him they would have questioned his sanity. "This is the place we settle." All three horses' ears pricked up because the tone in his voice registered differently. The animals, with whom he had spent so many hours over the past two weeks, seemingly knew they would rest.

He would not forget, this early September day, a land of no trees with shallow basins surrounded by grassy slopes and dotted with flowering plants of lavender and gold. Here he knew he would eventually build a brick or frame house, sitting on the upslope west of the large wetland, teeming with waterfowl, and other life. He knew he would die, overlooking this marsh.

John circled to the north around the huge body of water. The land above this peaceful pocket abounded with grasses, enough to feed his horses and nourish some cattle, but where could he buy some? Again, he found his planning woefully lacking; he knew he must adjust, and quickly.

He had no fear, just a curiosity, of how he would go about building a place to call his own. No desire to move further west niggled at him. The peaceful site fit him; he lacked only a house to make this his permanent settling.

The reeds and a reed hut would do him for the remaining summer and early fall months, but for the winter he needed a lasting shelter. The slope facing southeast would work for a dugout built into the hill. He studied the site and found the area for the sturdy beams: roof beams and door and window frames on the southeast-facing slope. All the learning in college, and working with Alexander, he could now put to personal use. Tomorrow he would build a reed hut and search south for a place where he could buy added supplies to survive through the winter. The next day he would start the demanding task of breaking the sod and removing earth to form the dugout.

His long legs carried him upslope to the top. The open water of the large marsh rippled in the late summer southerly breeze. On the calm water areas, ducks glided about, some with a second hatch of young trailing in single file behind a parent. John removed his hat, ran fingers through his long hair and quietly said, "Will the little ones will survive to migrate south?"

From his perch atop the northwest rise, John estimated the elevation above the marsh at twenty feet. The spot where he stood would lend itself to forming a dugout with a roof. He could cut the sides into the small hill, leaving a back wall of earth. Only a small area at the rear would need sod bricks or an earth plug.

He would soon need to ride south to find the Oregon Trail. Timbered streams must flow south of where he stood, feeding the river the Oregon Trail paralleled. John hoped for a stream with enough trees to yield logs to face the dugout and erect a gabled sod roof.

The sun dipped low on the horizon casting a golden glow on the land to the east. He jogged down the slope, untied the youngest mare, and led her to the edge of the marsh. She snorted and shied at the movement in the grass. A squirrel-like animal darted through tall grass surrounding the moist area dominated by arrowhead plant, cattails, and rushes. This animal looked like a tree squirrel except it did not have distinctive ears like the squirrels, back east, that lived in the trees. The color of this grass-dwelling squirrel matched the surrounding vegetation, which John figured protected it from the hawks and eagles soaring above. He grabbed the halter rope and swung onto the mare's back. The horse trotted forward at John's urging and they moved around the entire marsh. As he rode along the marsh edge, John decided he would set corner markers on the land and lay claim to it. Most people would not want this marsh and surrounding land, but John saw something different. What he wondered: Would the marsh financially help in hard times, if needed?

After finishing his ride around the wetland, he made markers for his land claim, an area he estimated at four hundred acres. Eighty acres would work for good crop production, the remaining dedicated to cattle grazing. For the next few hours, he marked the dugout area with stakes fashioned from the wood he collected on the blue haze river. Finished, and satisfied, with the dugout area for his living quarters and another for a barn, he rode the older mare around the marsh, stopping to mark the boundary.

Dusk settled on the land John called his own. He carefully led the horses to the place at marsh edge where he could water them without sinking to their bellies in wetland muck. The red-winged blackbirds chattered from their cattail perches, watching every move these new animals made as they drank from the small, open shoreline. John noticed the small hillock on the southeast side of the marsh and it aroused his interest. Study of the unique physical layout would have to wait for now. The horses needed care before dark and he wanted to eat something to fill the hollowness in his stomach.

With visions of his future home, fronted with a porch to sit and watch the birds, he fell asleep. The strange-sounding "quork" caught his attention; he focused on the black-crowned night herons at the marsh edge. A small smile stretched across his lips. John reclined on the bedroll and fell asleep to the bullfrog calls echoing over the smooth, open marsh water.

Chapter 62

After moving his packs and equipment to the deep grasses along the marsh, he circled the acres. The grass disturbance, left by his moving around, probably would go unnoticed by most people passing through. Even his boundary markers didn't appear out of place.

The cool of the September morning created a thin, translucent fog layer over the water. As the sun inched above the horizon the quiet began to disappear with the sounds of arguing yellow-headed and red-winged blackbirds. A buzz of insects increased with the warming daylight. Through the dissipating fog, ducks appeared—trailed by small V-shaped trails that lazily broke the smooth, sparkling water. A pair of muskrats busily worked at repairing their house of cattails.

With his mare tied to the back of the wagon loaded with a saw, axes, and ropes he set a southerly heading. John tucked his compass in his vest pocket and snapped the reins against the horses' rumps. Two miles south he came on a large flock of prairie chickens. His spirits rose as he knew food for the short term could be had. Thirty minutes later he had crossed two dry drainages and veered east, following the upland ridge between two mostly dry streambeds. He could smell the water and hear the gentle stream trickle not far away. The dry streambed to his right gradually sloped toward a heavily green-grassed gully. John eased the wagon toward the spring. The wheels bumped and thumped against the dry slope until he came to sedges and water-loving plants. The marshes he so often visited in Illinois had a different odor. The mare and stallion wanted to drink of the fresh trickle, but John held them back until he could inspect the area.

They were not alone; the buzz startled him and the horses. A rattlesnake sought the cooler grasses as the day warmed and the rodents stirred in the lush vegetation. He pulled the rifle from under the seat and waited for the snake to again buzz its warning. The mare tied to the end of the wagon snorted, signaling danger. She stood frozen, staring at the ground near the right rear wheel. Her nostrils quivered and her neck bowed. John shushed at her and talked quietly as he climbed over the seat and into the wagon bed. The mare snorted again and her eyes stared at a spot about ten feet from the wheel rim. From the wagon, he gently untied and led her to the opposite side; he draped the rope over the wagon sideboard. She would stay quiet when he fired the gun, if necessary.

Inching back to the opposite side, he scanned the area where the mare spotted the snake. Again, a rattle, but this time it came from upslope away from the wagon. Then he spied it, an adult, not like the timber rattlers he previously faced, but the color much lighter and the bands more like blotches edged with black, rather than white edging. It quickly disappeared up the hill.

He led the mare back to her original spot and retied the rope to the wagon. Following the green vegetation east, he finally came to a clear flowing spot with a gravel bottom. This small oasis offered a respite from the snake encounter. He sat for a moment and listened before he climbed down to lead the team to the waterhole. An hour passed before he finished exploring downstream. He turned back west, checked his compass heading, and reined the team south.

Along this route he made several detours around marshes, noticing the internal drainage. All the water ran off the land into an area that reminded him of washbasins. They ranged in size and depth, some bearing a large, open water body and others nothing more than a shallow vegetative expanse. As abruptly as the marshes appeared, they disappeared. He followed a new stream flowing south, carrying slightly more water than the last stream where he had sought a water supply. John stopped and scanned the land below where trees lined a large stream. Deer bolted across the small valley to a hill on the opposite side and stopped. Their ear size much larger than the deer the Alderman boys shot in Hancock County.

Drifting quietly toward him from the southwest direction, faint dust clouds drew his focus. It had to be the wagons and people traveling the Oregon Trail alongside the river slowly rising toward Ft. Kearny. John decided against traveling beyond this spot. He had found the trees he needed. John would camp here as long as it took him to fell the number of trees he needed for beams and supports to construct the dugout roof and front.

It took him an hour to fell the first tree. The larger trees he could harvest the next day. The twelve-foot long wagon allowed an overhang of two feet without creating a weight distribution problem. Upstream he found two trees suited for the long roof support and two that would work for the crossbeams at the gable ends. He calculated that seven small trees, after splitting, would make enough rafters to support the sod.

From a small limb, he fashioned a pole, and from a string ball he cut and waxed several feet of line. To the line end, he attached hooks fashioned from thin, sturdy wire. John turned over a rotted log and began digging bait worms from the moist soil. He explored the stream, found a good spot, and jammed the pole into the stream bank and returned to set up camp.

The fading light and his low energy level halted his limb work on the first log. He set all the timber tools aside, built a fire pit, and with the green wood from the limbs built a spit, hoping for food from the stream. John leaned back against the wagon wheel, watching the fire turn to embers. He moved the glowing chunks around dry-wood pieces and relaxed. Small birds flew up and down the stream, skimming insects. John nodded off and woke with a start nearly an hour later. He stood, stretched, and wandered to the stream where he planted the pole.

The taut line moved back and forth in the slow current; he knew he had a catch. He slowly retrieved a sleek catfish of nearly two feet. The gutting and skinning took a few minutes and within the next half hour, he sat eating fresh fish taken from the spit. Before turning in he gathered an armload of dry twigs and branches for a morning fire. The thicker branches he turned into poles to plant in the stream bank, hoping for a bountiful catch. His three horses had already bedded down for the night when he returned from setting the fishing poles. Sleep came rapidly.

The youngest mare quietly nickered and stood watching John's still body. She moved closer and nickered again. He raised his head and sleepily stared at her. Her head dropped close to his face and he scratched her forehead. His laugh, when she head-bumped him, disturbed the other two. A frog croaked and a coyote yipped in the northern distance. He rose from his bedroll and stretched. With the dried wood, he gathered last evening, he started a fire and hoped to fry a whiskered catfish, if overnight he made a bank-pole catch.

John checked each of the eight poles and found half with catfish ranging from twelve to thirty inches. The smaller one he took back to camp for the breakfast fry and the others he left on the line in the cool water. To go with the fish, he peeled and fried a potato. This had to be the morning he gave himself a treat. Nettie gave him a tin of coffee as a going away present, so he boiled a small pot, enjoying the familiar smell rising from the spout.

The stallion snorted and stared uphill. Staring down at them, a large deer with an antler rack so large it made John whistle softly. The moment the large buck disappeared, John stood and walked over to his stallion. He rubbed the big horse's neck and quietly praised him. The animal stood proud, like a young man after his first successful deer hunt.

The morning started cool in the valley. John waited until the sun drenched the few trees with soft, gold light before he began timber work for the day ahead. He spent time cleaning his cooking utensils with scouring rush, sharpening the knives, and tightening wagon bolts, as needed. An hour after the sun rose he began the work of felling one of the two big oak trees for splitting and hauling onto the wagon. The stallion would do the heavy work; John knew this animal would be up to the task. The second oak tree proved more difficult to fell because of thick heartwood.

The other two trees proved no challenge so John used his energy to split them before dark descended on his small camp. He sat back and admired his day's work: two large trees for splitting, two smaller trees that had been split, and bundles of limbs for multiple uses in construction and fuel for the dugout.

With his fish, he prepared a slab of pork, sliced and fried a potato, and warmed the remaining coffee. He did use tobacco, but had yet to acquire a desire to continue. An image of Chirt and Alexander smoking their pipes, after the hunts together, floated before his eyes.

He finished his meal, carried the tin plate and utensils to the stream and washed them. An idea crossed his mind; he went in search of a deep pool to bathe and wash clothes. Nearly a half mile downstream he found a deep area where he could stand and wash. In fifteen minutes, he cleaned his clothes and body, walked out of the cool water, and hung his pants, socks and shirt on a tree limb high enough to gather the wind to hasten drying. Mary, his mother, always said: "Cleanliness is next to Godliness."

Nightfall appeared in the eastern sky. John decided to carry the semi-wet clothes to the wagon sideboards and finish drying them. The horses, full of curiosity at his undressed nature, stared at him. He chuckled and began to give each one a quick brushing.

Tomorrow he planned to split the large logs, load them, and stack the remaining wood pieces on top. If he completed all this, John would leave the following morning for the trek back to the Hayman marsh.

He lost track of the weekday, but he didn't care. Here he had freedom to work and do as he pleased before winter set in and turn the prairie to a frozen land of brown grass and white drifts. For now, he enjoyed every moment of the newfound land and its offerings.

Chapter 63

Gray sky and a cool wind welcomed him for the day trip back to his claimed land. To lighten the wagon load he saddled the mare and rode ahead of the horses hitched to the wagon. For a brief moment, he didn't know if they could pull out of the stream valley to the flat land ahead. John decided to tie a rope to the wagon center just above the tongue and loop it around the saddle horn, using a three-horse pull rather than two. The trip took less time than he thought.

A surprise waited for him. On the small knoll, directly in the center of the outline, he marked for his dugout sat a man dressed in buckskin. His horse and a mule stood in the center of the area where John wanted the dugout for his animals. John slowed his approach, caressed the rifle scabbard, and touched the holstered pistol.

The man stood, pistol and rifle resting against the pack at his feet. He remained motionless, arms crossed over his chest. Behind him, gray clouds floated south. The wind played at the stained hat brim and tattered buckskin fringes.

John dismounted, tied the mare to the wagon, and walked up the slope. "Sir," John said, "what do you want?"

The man grinned, showing tobacco-stained, yellowing teeth. "You got a name?"

"John … John Hayman."

"Good name. I'm Morris McFarland, Jack of all trades, master of none." He cackled. "I do work at Ft. Kearny helping keep up the old buildings and put up new ones." He looked John up and down. "You lay claim to this here land, boy."

"I have—"

"Yep, I done noticed your markers." He looked past John to the marsh. "I spotted yer hidin' place for yer supplies and stuff." He looked back to John. "Ya gotta do better, John Hayman."

"Yes, I do."

Morris shifted his gaze to the loaded wagon. "You gonna start on the dugout tomorrow?"

"I plan to do so."

"John Hayman, you want some help?" He didn't wait for John to answer. "I'm your man."

"And how do I pay you? I have little money for your work."

"You'll owe me a place to bunk if need be, when passin' through this lonely country each year. Gets a might tough some springs with late blizzards. Your land is about the right spot for me to rest." He gave John a toothy grin. "What ya got to say, John Hayman?"

John held out his hand and said, "Deal." Morris had a viselike grip. The buckskin clothing and this man's shabbiness belied his strength. "Then let's start." John turned and marched down the hill to the wagon and unhitched the horses.

"I'm gonna start a fire and cook you a meal that'll make you stronger." Morris took a bundle of dry wood from the wagon and began to scratch out an outline for a fire pit. "You got some spades or shovels hidden down there?"

"I do." John led the horses to their grazing area.

"Mind if I let my mule graze with your critters?" Morris waited.

John gave him a thoughtful look. "That mule's good-natured?"

"Yep, and it'll do a day's work … though it can get stubborn as a mule." Morris' laugh resonated over the marsh and triggered a din of blackbird chatter. He left the pack on the flat ground and walked the mule to John's horses. The smell from his body startled the mares, but the stallion stood his ground. "Mighty touchy mares you got, John Hayman. The stallion will make a good stud horse. That why ya got him?"

"I did." John watched Morris as he introduced the mule to the mares and make friends with the stallion. "You want a colt out of them, Morris?"

"That'd be good pay for my work. Thank you, John."

"What, no Hayman?"

Morris grinned and meandered down to the marsh to fetch a spade and shovel. He yelled over his shoulder. "John, you unload the easy pieces of timber and I'll hep ya after supper, deal?"

"Deal," John said and began moving the wood near where the dugout would take shape. He paid little attention to Morris while he unloaded the timber and his tools. The sun dipped below the horizon through the broken gray clouds while they labored to finish as much work as they could before dark.

Morris groaned and stretched his back. "John, I'll start us a fire and do the cookin' while you set out the lines so we can dig tomorrow. It's gonna take a goodly time to cut through the sod."

John staked the dugout as envisioned, which ran fourteen feet long, ten feet wide, and with six to seven-foot-high walls. The gabled roof would slope approximately two feet. The animal dugout turned out almost square with an adequate height for him and the animals to stand comfortably.

The smoke drifting over the rise, to where John worked, smelled good. He wondered what Morris cooked that could have such a mouthwatering effect. When he finished, Morris looked up at him and motioned him to come eat. "You're making me hungry, Morris. What is it?"

"You gonna eat natures finest … from these here parts of the country. An old Injun woman taught me how to make it."

"You're not gonna tell me, are you?"

Morris shook his head. "I want you to tell me if you think it's any good, and then I'll tell ya the secret."

The hind legs Morris served reminded John of rabbit but didn't have the shape to be from any rabbit he'd eaten. The chopped meat mixed with a vegetable ladled over biscuits had a strange, delightful taste. "Morris," John said, "c'mon, what's in this meal?"

"Muskrat and cattail, and don' you go puking it up."

A grin slowly crossed over John's face. "Why would I?"

"Most people don't think a critter like these swimmers makes good food.

Let me tell you they have saved my life in this harsh land more than once."

"To be truthful," John hesitated, "I expect I will be glad for this creature."

Morris nodded. "The cattails I fix many ways, so I expect you to pay close attention when I'm cooking." He took a wet rag and wiped his plate. "After we stow all this we can talk some." He twitched the corner of his mouth. "I'll give you another treat in the mornin'."

"One more item before we bed down," John said. "I want to dig a well. You know how?"

Morris laughed. "C'mon, John Hayman, I'm the best well digger around."

As he looked around, John said, "And the only one."

Chapter 64

It took them three weeks to remove the earth for the dugout and set the timbers. They didn't do it alone because Morris' friends wandering the marsh country stopped to help. Some men stayed for as little as a few hours, and two stayed until they completed the jobs, cutting sod blocks and shaping stone for the well. John and Morris used tents and the large reed huts to house themselves and the visitors while digging and building.

A few Pawnee and Oto rode through searching the isolated land for game. Morris said, "Buffalo no longer roam the land between the marshes except an occasional small herd. The Pawnee and Oto know about the antelope, muskrat, ducks, and geese." Morris and his cronies waved at them. "We trust them ... sure as the sky's blue they trust us ... I hope."

Morris' crony, who hauled in the limestone from the salty creek area near the Platte, said, "John, the Indians will return. They come into the marshland in November, hunting the waterfowl. Might not hunt this one since you're here, but they'll use other nearby marshes."

The two men who stayed placed the well stone smoothed the dugout walls and improved the living space and well depth during that time. They helped John fashion a bed, table, and benches from oak pieces left over after forming and cutting the beams. John fit the bed frame with a reed mat and covered it with cloth and wrappings stuffed with cattail fluff.

With both dugouts completed on the hillside above the marsh, Morris said, "Time for us to move on." His two friends nodded. "But I'll be back in ... I'd say ... 'bout ten days." John hoped he might stay for the winter, teaching him the needed skills to survive in this new land. He thoroughly enjoyed the man's company and knowledge; he would miss him.

During the time when Morris traveled east, John traveled north toward the Platte River. The trip, cut short by his discovery, ended at a river draining to the east probably to the river with the heavy blue haze he crossed weeks before. Here he found more trees, still sparse in number. His curiosity rose about how these tree seeds came to this site. He didn't ponder long and felled two hackberries, an elm, and a cottonwood. From the elm and cottonwood, he planned to erect a corral for his three horses and hopefully a foal in the spring.

A shallow crossing made it easy to maneuver the wagon across the river. His horses pulled the load with few problems if he did not overtax them. He decided to rest them for the night. John picketed each and prepared food he carried. For dessert, he snacked on wild berries found along the river, complementing the dried ones he packed. The cool November weather felt good.

Under the buffalo blanket—that Morris gave him—he rested comfortably. The stars dotted the skies by the hundreds, shining brightly with no moonlight to obscure them. A pack of coyotes yipped as they circled their prey. He dozed and then woke when the coyotes called from nearby.

A snort from the stallion broke his light sleep. With the sudden silence, John knew the coyotes had killed whatever they chased or something had interrupted their hunt. The older mare snorted. John felt that same surge of danger he experienced near Sidney, Iowa and quickly rolled under the wagon, the buffalo blanket now out of reach. His teeth began to chatter from the cool night air. He sucked in cold air to clear his sleep-dazed brain and calm his nerves.

A movement along a small terrace ridge caught his attention. Two bodies silently crawled toward his disheveled buffalo robe. His breathing slowed and the right thumb silently cocked the rifle hammer. A loud snort came from the stallion as he raised his head. The crawlers stopped and waited for the horse to quiet.

Morris told him about the Pawnee and Oto and their habits. He warned John about the Sioux, always at war with the Pawnee, and the dislike for most white men. John waited, a voice in his head said, "Be patient, John."

He caught the nod from one of the Indians, and they inched forward. The stallion stood like a statue, making no sound. The two men came to their knees, checked the horses, and the land behind them. A tomahawk rose above the bigger man's head as he sprang toward the buffalo blanket. John did not hesitate, these two wanted him dead. He squeezed the trigger and the gun angrily roared.

The one in John's sights screamed and flew backward with the impact. The other froze, dropped his tomahawk, and cried out, "*Hee ya, hee ya.*" And in English, he uttered, "Nooooo." His head shook back and forth as he backed up, almost tripping over his dead companion. The Indian watched John crawl from under the wagon.

John stood and motioned for the young brave to move back. He did not want to shoot again. The Indian took advantage of John's hesitation and charged, knocking the rifle from John's grip. They rolled on the sod, grunting and cursing each other in their languages. The Sioux rolled John to his back and straddled him. His left hand squeezed tight on John's throat and his right arm rose, with the tomahawk in his clenched fist, for the kill.

From under the Indian, John had one chance; he bucked hard. The move tossed the youth off balance. From his holster, John grabbed his pistol, pushed hard, and rolled away. Both men scrambled to their feet. "No," John yelled at the Sioux. The pistol roared. The young man's blood gushed from his mouth as he fell toward John's feet.

A scream echoed in the cool atmosphere. It took a few seconds to realize it came from him. A violent shiver shook his body, and he broke into a sweat. He fell to his knees, wondering why.

Standing from his kneeling position, he felt a nauseating pulse rise in his throat. A vile taste made him gag. He turned away from the dead bodies and emptied his stomach contents on the turf. The sweat poured off his face as he stared at the dead humans.

"Why, God? I ask you why?" John looked to the heavens. He had not uttered God's name aloud since his college days.

Chapter 65

Braying broke the late afternoon calm. John moved from the dugout to check who approached with a noisy mule. He touched the two tomahawks hanging above the door as he stepped out. The hat brim obscured the man's face. John knew it had to be Morris by his dress and the cantankerous mule. He leaned back against the door frame and waited. A long round object protruded from a heavily loaded pack in the two-wheel cart harnessed to the tired mule.

Morris' disgusted, harsh voice carried toward the marsh. Both man and animal appeared angry with each other. John understood the mule's problem for it pulled the cart loaded with a small stove tied securely to the sideboards. The long, round object had to be the stovepipe.

"Well, just don't stand there grinning," Morris said as he came up the slope. "Help me get this stove unloaded and set up. We'll both be a lot happier."

John helped untie the stove and carry it into the dugout. The burning candles provided extra light, casting soft shadows against the packed and smoothed walls as they lugged the stove to the middle of the dugout room. They set the stove slightly off center of the roof peak, allowing for the stovepipe to pass the main beam.

Morris pulled over a bench to stand on and began punching a hole in the woven, marsh-grass mat. "Get your tail outside and cut through the sod from above so I can get the stovepipe properly set."

John followed the order, and in thirty minutes Morris completed installing the cast-iron stove. "Morris, how—"

"Don't ask." Morris frowned at his friend. "The less you know ... the better." He looked around. "You been busy: more benches, chairs, and ... whoa, what have we here?" He stared at the tomahawks above the door, fastened in an X-shape. "Sioux—how—where did you get these?"

John paled.

"That bad was it, John Hayman?"

"Yes." John's voice croaked. "I ..."

"No one likes to kill another man, leastways that's how I believe," Morris softly said. "They come here?"

"No. I went north to scout the area for wood. At night, they snuck up on me—or tried—and I got the drop because the stallion warned me."

"You're learning, John Hayman." Morris slapped John on the back and walked outside. He came back with small pieces of wood, which he quickly started by firing the cattail fluff he stuffed around the kindling.

John watched as his friend checked the stovepipe for leaks and then trotted out the door and onto the roof. Morris hollered down to John, "Get me some fresh sod pieces so I can seal the roof around the pipe."

John gathered the sod. "Is this enough?"

"I didn't want the whole prairie," Morris said with a chuckle. "Let's get the gear off my horse and bed my critters down for the night. And don't ask where I got the horse."

After the meal John prepared, they talked for two hours. From his pack, Morris brought out a lamp and a supply of oil. "Better than all the candles smokin' up the house, don't ya think?"

"How much do I owe?" John said.

"Not a dime, I got this with the stove."

"You gonna tell me how you got all this?"

Morris shook his head. "More important you talk to me about killin' the Sioux. You ain't said a word about it."

"It was a nightmare, Morris." John stared at the oil lamp Morris filled. "I got sick and didn't sleep for several days." He looked up at his friend. "You ever killed a man?"

Morris nodded. "Yes, a white man, but he deserved it, just like the Indians sneaking up on you. They meant to kill you and take all you own."

John didn't speak.

"It'll take a long while for this to go away. Do you understand?"

"I think so." John breathed deeply. "Right or wrong, I did what I did."

A reed mat lay on the floor across from John's bed frame. "I'm so glad to see you … will you stay for a time?"

As Morris unrolled his blanket he looked to John. "You're a young man … you got many good years ahead … but a lot of learnin' to do beyond the book knowledge."

"Such as …?"

"Gettin' a good night's sleep and to prepare for the comin' winter months." Morris removed his boots and crawled under the blanket. "Like makin' sure ya got enough wood laid up for the winter and bundles of dried marsh plants in case the wood runs low." Morris groaned, "Damned mule."

Within minutes both men began to snore.

For the next two weeks, John and Morris roamed the creek areas to the south and north, gathering hardwood, hauling it back to the dugouts, and cutting it to stove lengths. They lined the well with more limestone and sod and greased the hoist gears. Morris added a rope to the bucket frame as a safety precaution, in case the gears froze or failed. John fashioned a well cover to keep animals from falling in and fouling the water.

"Been around enough people that got cholera; I suspect that might come from bad water. You probably need not worry, but it's best that you've taken precautions."

John grinned. "You are not as you appear, Morris. You're an amazing man."

Morris smiled, nodded, and packed his pipe for an evening smoke.

Chapter 66

Early next morning the sound of waterfowl woke the two men. The quacking, honking, and pummeling of air became thunderous. The birds rose into the sky ahead of the gray scudding clouds racing in from the northwest. A small skiff of snow covered the landscape, uninterrupted until the mottled land met the cloudy, gray sky.

"Gotta haul in a load of wood," Morris said. "We'll eat breakfast and then bundle up to harvest some of them cattails before they freeze solid."

"What'll we do with them?" John asked and yawned.

"You're gonna learn how to make flour from the plant and then I'm gonna teach ya to bake these cakes."

Morris prepared breakfast cakes made with cattail and hickory-nut flour. He had packed dehydrated maple sugar and added it to boiling water to make a thick syrup. The man always came prepared. He had arranged for one of his cronies to haul in more stone for lining the well. Another friend brought posts fashioned from a tree he called the hedge apple monster, for the wood dulled his axes and saws within an hour of chopping and cutting. They all ate breakfast together and tightened their bond with John before they left.

They faded from sight into the now brown and white of the marsh country. John said, "Morris, you married?"

He roared with laughter. "Why? You wanna marry me?"

John shook his head and laughed. "I'm curious how you learned to cook. The other work I know you learned by doing."

"Young man, I got me a Pawnee woman and three ornery boys."

"No daughters?"

Morris thought a moment. "Not that I know of …"

"What does that mean?"

"John, when I first came to the Territory I found an Oto woman. She and I lived in one of the lodges up near the mouth of the Platte."

"Oh …" John stared at him.

"I notice you got a Bible. Are ya religious?"

"I don't know …"

"What does that mean?"

John cleared his throat and said, "Long story and isn't worth talking about."

Morris let the subject drop. "It can get a mite lonely out here, John. I hope you're prepared for it." He pulled a pipe from his vest and packed it tightly with fine tobacco shreds, stuck a twig into the stove door slot until it burned brightly, drew it out, and held the flame above the pipe bowl. "When you're snowed in this tobacco helps pass the time. And believe me, you're the only living creature stirring except for your horses and wild critters lookin' for winter food."

"We put up plenty of grass bundles," John said, "and your friend from southeast of here brought me a good supply of grain."

"What you see out there now ain't what you'll see come a couple of months. The drifts can get arse high." He studied John's face. "Boy, the winters can be dangerous, especially in this marsh country. The problem is the land when covered in snow, all looks the same. It's easy to lose your way and freeze to death mighty fast."

"You talk like it happened to you or a friend."

"John," he sucked on his pipe, "I'm still here, but a friend died south of here about three years past when a mean winter storm blew in. I finally found him after a Pawnee said a horse he hadn't seen before roamed the marshland."

"The Pawnee didn't capture the horse?"

Morris said, "Didn't ask, didn't care, I just wanted to know where he spotted the horse." He sighed. "Found my friend three days later, frozen to death at the edge of a large marsh south and a bit west of here."

"The storms blow in that fast?"

"They do," Morris puffed the pipe, "they can catch you on the open prairie within minutes; that is, if you don't know how to read the skies."

"You teach me this before you leave?"

"I plan to be with you for another week and make sure all's good around here." He pulled a small box from his saddlebags. "Here you be, John. I figured you musta had a birthday sometime." He grinned and held out the hand-fashioned box covered with birch tree bark.

John slowly untied the thin leather strap. A corncob pipe nestled on a bed of dried corn silk. "I don't know what to say, Morris."

"How about thank you, and pass the tobacco."

"Thank you, and pass the tobacco." John held out his hand and took the sack of brown shreds from Morris.

"Go easy, if you ain't smoked before you might feel kinda light-headed and sickly." He puffed his pipe and tamped the bowl with his index finger. "I can tell you ain't been a smoker."

John packed the pipe half-full and put a flame to the first of his future habit. He coughed. "This'll take getting used to ..."

"It will, John, but it will help ya pass the winter days you're out here with nothing but your animals and tobacco."

Chapter 67

Morris's words rang in his head: "It gets a mite lonely out here when you're miles and miles from any living being." November probably fooled John about the prairie. In Illinois, he experienced snowfall—in late November and early December—deep enough for the sleigh runners to glide smoothly along the country roads. Trees on the east and west sides of Hancock County provided landscape relief. They restored horizons that often blended with the gray sky. Here, John had no trees to help with horizon definition except for the bright winter blue that always heightened his spirits.

The loss of knowing what day and month bothered him. Last night's blizzard left him dazed and disheartened. The horses needed care and John did not let them down. The rope he secured to guide him, from the dugout to the animal shelter and back, lay under a blanket of snow, the white cover seemingly extending to the end of the Earth. Over the past hour, a north-raging wind howled like a wounded wolf. He knew that sound, for he had to ward them off the first week after the turn of the year.

Candles and the oil lamp burned quietly in the warmth of the dugout. John sat on the bench staring at the stove that held a steaming pot of water. Luckily, he had used good sense and stacked dried wood in the corner, the only problem being the mice skittering in and out of openings between the logs. A squeak drew his attention to the pile. A small mouse sat on its haunches nibbling on a crumb it gathered from under the table. The tiny critter stopped chewing, and with its dark eyes stared at him. John quietly watched the furry mouse with a coat of bright-brown above, white below—including the feet—and a sharply bicolored tail, like the body colors.

The little creature went back to nibbling, ignoring John until he moved. With lightning speed, it disappeared into the woodpile. This small moment changed John's entire mood. He pulled the corn cob pipe from the wool coat-pocket. After packing a full bowl and drawing the smoke deep into his lungs, he rose to fetch his pencil and a small notebook. The faint sound of pencil on paper drew the curious mouse back to inspect the new noise.

"Come to see what goes on, eh?" John noticed the animal jerk at the sound of his voice. "Yes, I too realized that I make no sound in this underground habitat." The mouse's nose twitched as if it wanted to talk. A small squeak and it began to groom its long, white whiskers. John reacted by reaching to his face and felt the long growth covering his face.

"You trying to tell me something?" he said to the mouse and went back to drawing a picture. Below the drawing, he made notes on the mouse color, size, and movements. The pipe smoke lazily drifted throughout the primitive, yet homey dwelling. A rectangle with seven boxes in a row, arranged in seven columns filled the next page. John recorded a guess at what day and month and entered the time from his pocket watch that he bought before leaving Fairfield. The page following the calendar he sketched a diagram of the dugout with his meager belongings platted on the floor plan.

Gently he closed the notebook. He'd been too busy since arriving in the marshlands to even consider thinking about his natural surroundings. John stood and stretched. He knocked the pipe bowl against his hand and let the ashes drop to the dirt floor. From a wood box, he withdrew the Bible he so many times studied in school and at home. The image of his father preaching before a crowded church floated from his deep memory. He sat and stared at the worn cover. He pushed it aside, turned and moved to his bed. The wind had slightly subsided and the burning oak smell faded.

Sleep overtook him for the better part of the morning. He awoke and shook off the lethargy, realizing the wind sounded muffled. The dugout warmth remained even though the fire had died. John decided to check on the horses and after dressing in his warmest outer clothes opened the heavy door. Panic nearly overtook him. Before him a solid wall of snow. The words of advice from Morris: "John, make sure you have a shovel inside during the winter … on the outside one near the door. It can get rough if the heavens dump on you."

Now wide awake, he spun around looking for the shovel. Nothing. He swore at himself and sucked in a deep breath. How could he do something so stupid? The snowdrift, so solidly packed, put a greater fear in him than the Sioux skirmish.

A small sound behind him made him turn. The little mouse dashed across the room and behind the open door. John eased the door shut, his mind racing over digging out with his hands. He looked down at the mouse skittering toward the woodpile, back to the log where little critter normally sat. John looked back at the closed door and the window covering. There stood the shovel propped behind the window drapery that almost extended to the floor.

Shakily, he sat at the table and reached for the Bible. Flipping through the pages he found what he sought: Job 12:7-10 - *But ask the animals, and they will teach you, or the birds of the air, and they will tell you; or speak to the earth, and it will teach you, or let the fish of the sea inform you. Which of all these does not know that the hand of the LORD has done this? In his hand is the life of every creature and the breath of all mankind.*

Chapter 68

From the dugout roof, John watched the spring migration of ducks and geese pouring into the basin. The past months he twice had burrowed his way out to feed the horses and provide them with some company. He smiled at the thought of a young foal soon to romp on this prairie. The past week the sun brightly reflected off the snow, rapidly melting the hip-deep layer circling the marsh. The water and ice in the basin below shimmered in the midday sun. John, for the first time in the last three weeks, could see the prairie greening beneath the matted grasses.

The area around the stovepipe needed a grass trim and new sod pieces. He had tired of his procrastination and placing a bucket near the stove to catch the drops before they splattered on the packed-earth floor. A movement to his left caught him by surprise. A small herd of antelope wandered over the slight slope to the north and lifted their heads to catch the scent of the grassland around them. With the north wind to their rumps, they did not catch his scent, which had become rather potent. Antelope had the best vision of all the prairie game, and this chance to harvest one may not happen again for months. After the Indian incident, he never went anywhere, even to his rooftop, without his rifle and pistol.

The antelope herd worked their way into the basin and turned east toward an open strip along the marsh. John, to better judge the distance, raised the rifle to his shoulder. He wanted to shoot a female but knew one less female meant one or two fewer offspring. John flattened himself on his stomach and waited. *Be patient.*

The young bucks in the herd drifted away from the females and mixed back after an hour. A single buck eyed the horses next to the dugout and moved cautiously toward them. John, still flat on his belly, waited until a good side shot presented itself. The moment the pronghorn turned to check the herd, he pulled the trigger. The animal bucked, raced fifty yards up the slope and dropped to the snow-covered sod. The herd had fled at the rifle shot sound and disappeared within seconds.

John slid from the roof and trotted to the youngest mare. He led her into the dugout, grabbed a rope, slid a halter on her head, and saddled her. As soon as they cleared the entrance he smoothly swung into the seat, urging her down the slope. He dismounted, hooked the rope around the horns, moved back into the saddle, and wrapped the rope around the horn.

Near the edge of the marsh, he field-dressed the antelope and left the remains for the coyotes and wolves. He used the snow to remove blood from his hands, dried them on a cloth hanging from his belt, and remounted. After pulling the carcass to the animal shelter, John used the same techniques the Alderman boys taught him to preserve the deer meat. The carcass hung by the head until cooled, then he rubbed salt into the meat until the blood no longer oozed from the muscle.

Over the next two weeks, John harvested ducks and geese and a month later he helped himself to some of the duck eggs for a fried treat. The spring days in late March and early April left him in awe of the massive waterfowl migration. He had no previous experience rivaling the sight of thousands of ducks and geese blackening the skies, their deafening calls, and the wings hammering the air.

He ate his fill of ducks and geese before they rode the rising thermals created by a warm southerly wind. Not far behind the massive waterfowl exodus, small shorebirds arrived by the thousands, settling in for an energy-gathering stopover. The marsh sounds had quieted except for the remaining ducks and geese nesting and raising their young and the unrivaled sounds of the boisterous blackbirds.

In his notebook, he marked off what he guessed as the first week in May. His work outside the dugout took shape: a small corral for his horses and a trough filled with water from the hand-dug well. The mare bearing the foal swelled in size and John wondered if she would deliver twins. The day after he placed the last corral section, his mare delivered the foal without any complications. John watched as she became a mother for the first time. The foal took all her attention, done lovingly and firmly.

The mare needed no help in raising her offspring and a week later John allowed the stallion back with the foal and the other mare. After he put the stallion in the corral the comedy started. The big male would snort and rear as the foal, with increasing strength each day, playfully romped around him.

What bothered John most—his friend had not appeared as promised. Morris, before heading back to Ft. Kearny, told John he would return in late spring. The lack of Morris' company had a profound effect. John moped about his dugout and spent time wondering about, and fearing for, his friend.

Chapter 69

It had been two months since John spotted anyone traveling through the marshlands. August heat settled in, the humidity prevented the complete desiccation of the prairie lands surrounding his dugout. He hadn't ventured far from his claimed land; at least, what he felt as his claimed land. John didn't know how or where to go to register the land, for he was not aware of a public land office in the territory if one existed. He'd moved the stakes several times over the last year to claim more land surrounding the marsh.

John hoped he could claim this valuable resource for his hunting and studying pleasure. The new spring had brought the shorebirds. The frogs began their deafening breeding chorus in his wetland and the smaller surrounding ones. Over the summer he reverted to his studies, hoping and waiting for Morris to show before winter.

All summer he watched his foal grow into a fine specimen. The wetland flourished with increasing numbers of birds, amphibians, and dragonflies. At times, he felt alone in this prairie and marsh country, but he loved it and the feeling would rapidly disappear, for he lived with the land and watched how it thrived.

He sat at the marsh edge sketching the dragonflies, not hearing the riders approaching from the south. They quietly rode in using the cattails and rushes to their advantage. Both riders wore bandanas over their faces and held pistols aimed at his chest. The two men motioned for him to stand.

In a muffled voice, the rider sitting on a mustang said, "We want your money and horses."

John shook his head.

The second rider laughed. "You have no choice, boy. Give us your mare and the foal. You gotta have money inside that dungeon you call home."

John sneered at the two men. "You think I'm afraid?"

"Sonny, you should fear us, for we'll kill you and take everything, not just what we demand."

"Kid," the second rider said, "I don't see any reason for you not to give us what we want. You'll lose everything and gain nothin'. My pardner ain't in the arguing mood and you sure the hell ain't got any bargaining power."

"We don't want any killin' hangin' over our heads," the first rider said, "so do as we ask."

"Why?" John said.

"Tie the smart mouth," said the red kerchief man as he held out a short rope for his partner, "and make sure he can't get loose."

The second rider grabbed the rope and dismounted. "Turn face down, kid. Hands behind your back and raise your legs."

John reluctantly rolled over. Within minutes he was securely tied with his legs bent back and bound to his arms and wrists.

"Kid, you're gonna die out here. Before anybody finds you, the wolves will have you for a meal. Thanks for the mare and foal." He cackled as they headed their horses toward the dugout.

The men hurried to the corral and haltered the mare. They ransacked his dugout, presumably looking for money.

"No whiskey, no money, only a damn Bible," rider two said.

"C'mon, let's get outta here." They spurred their horses, leading the mare and foal from the marshland.

Buzzing insects and an occasional bullfrog croak broke the quiet that descended on the marsh as evening approached. John struggled with the rope and finally realized it would do no good. His anger subsided to a cold calm. His only hope came from the cordgrass. The sharp edges might saw through the strands; that is, if he could survive the coyote and wolf attacks during the night.

The full moon, bathing the marsh in a wash of white light, deterred the wolves from attacking. If they sensed his helplessness they might prey on him in this bright light, but the dark of night coming shortly before dawn might be why they waited. The coyotes would glean the remains if the wolves left anything of his body. John buried the thoughts and continued to work the rope against the sharp cordgrass blades. He learned the hard way about the saw-like edges while thatching the dugout roofs.

He could hear the stallion and young mare in the corral bumping and uneasily moving about. They sensed something wrong, and wouldn't settle down. Their restlessness discouraged the few wolves that threatened to close in and nip at John. Each advance brought a loud snort and a scream from the stallion, discouraging the wolves. When the full moon set, John knew he couldn't fall asleep, for the wolf pack would surely move in for a kill when he became still.

At dawn, the muscular aches and cramps became so horrific he didn't think he could remain conscious. The marsh awakened with birdcalls and the muskrats chirping and whining, which kept him from dozing. As the blood-colored sun rose over the eastern horizon, exhaustion and sleep overtook him.

A sudden jerk on the rope woke him with a start. He peered at a huge knifepoint floating before his blurred vision.

Chapter 70

Her withered and wrinkled skin never looked so good. An old Indian woman held the knife, much smaller now than it first appeared. She signaled him to turn to his belly. He did not argue with her and felt a tug on the rope. When the rope fell away from his legs and wrists he turned over, sat, and nodded to her. Where had she come from? What brought her here? He survived the night and now he had would survive, period.

She croaked the words, "*Quel est votre nom?*"

He knew the French word for name. John replied, "*Je ne parle pas français.*" John had two years of college French, but he knew it would not be good to try to speak with her in that language. He pointed at himself and said his name, "John Hayman. *Pouvez-vous parler allemand?*" He wanted to know if she might speak German.

She grinned at him, a toothless grin, and shook her head. "*Non.*"

One last attempt, hoping this would work. "*La langue des signes?*"

She nodded and pointed up and spread her arms. "*Ciel* … sky."

He stood and rubbed his wrists. His legs trembled; he quickly sat before collapsing.

The old woman gave him a worried look and in sign language tried to mime her concern.

It took him a minute to interpret what she meant, realizing she cared and wanted to know if he needed help to stand. "*Non.*" He shook his head. "No." John slowly came to his knees, waited, and inched his way to a standing position, still wobbly. This time he felt stronger as the blood circulated into his legs.

The top of her head came only to his chest. He pointed at his chest and said, "John Hayman," and pointed to her and asked, "*Quel est votre nom?*"

The stooped woman, smelling of smoke replied, "*Vieille femme de l'herbe.*" She grinned at him because of his puzzled look. In sign language, she mimed out her name. From his reaction, she knew he didn't understand some of the words. She tried again and watched his handsome, bearded face light up.

He again pointed at his chest and said, "*Homme* ... man." Then he pointed to her and spoke, "*Femme* ... woman." She nodded. John continued by saying, "*l'herbe* ... plant." She shook her head and stroked the grasses next to her feet. "Aha, *l'herbe* ... grass. But ... *Vieille?*" He shrugged.

The little woman hobbled about and pointed to her wrinkled skin.

He blurted out, "Old ... Old Woman of the Grass."

She slowly nodded her head and pointed toward his dugout.

John wondered if she could speak English but chose not to do so, for whatever reason.

The next two months she helped John better understand his natural surroundings, which endeared her to him. The loss of the mare and foal still hurt, but he would go in search of another mare to bear a new foal. The old woman's arrival helped him in many ways, most importantly the means to survive by using all the natural surroundings, especially the plants.

She wouldn't allow him to cook what they caught from the marsh and uplands. Her knack for cooking prairie chickens with the native plants such as the wild onion, or "*osidiwa,*" pleased his palate. Many of the plants she used to cook and flavor the meats originated with the Pawnee or Omaha Tribes.

Woman of the Grass used dried leaves from the abundant upland species that she, the Omaha, and Ponca called "*te-huntonhi*" to brew tea. This name translated to English as the buffalo bellow plant as it dominated during the Buffalo rutting season. This lead-colored plant with purple flowers, found among the grasses, yielded a flavorful yellowish tea.

The other plant for brewing tea, she first gathered the dried leaves from the stems and placed them in a deer-hide bag. Then Woman of the Grass cut the stems and showed him how to make a broom. She immediately gave him the new broom to sweep the dugout floor. When she wanted him to clean, she uttered the Pawnee name, *"kiha piliwus hawastat,"* meaning broomweed.

At her direction, John dug many plant roots with a spade. Woman of the Grass stood and watched, periodically uttering pleasantries for her not having to dig as in the past. Her slightly hunched back cast a shadow on him as he knelt to clean the clinging soil from the roots. They hauled their harvest back to the dugout where they processed and stored the roots for the coming winter. They tried to mouse-proof the food by hanging them from the thatched roof and beams supporting the sod roof. In the wetlands, he dug plants she called by the Pawnee names of: *"its"* and the *"kisu-sit."* In the drier or uplands, he recovered roots the Pawnee named: *"pilahatus"* and the plant with the feathery, lavender flowers on a spike called the *"kahtsu-dawidu."*

Where they could find them, they dined on the fruits of wild plum, chokecherry, and the wild rose fruit called rosehips. The prairie birds such as the prairie chickens and sharp-tailed grouse loved the rosehips. The meals always ended with the berries or the squeezed juice.

As they learned to communicate, John's life became fully enriched. He felt the spiritual nature of the marshland life and knew it would never leave him. When the time came, John wanted to die and have his remains placed in the soil to nourish the flowering plants and the grasses overlooking the marsh.

Chapter 71

Winter with the old woman sharing his dugout helped him better pass the time. Woman of the Grass taught him simple Pawnee, Oto, Omaha, and Ponca words and he shared common English words with her, but he felt she already knew most of them. Together they spoke broken French and laughed at each other's errors using the language. They talked through many frigid nights until the morning sunlight filtered through the draped window.

With spring warming the days, they sat together on the roof enjoying the vast waterfowl return to the open marsh waters.

"John … you want … learn more?" said the old stooped woman.

"Grass Woman, I do." He looked down at her scratching the reddish-brown skin, weathered by time and the elements. "What now?"

"You must learn the good medicine the plants have to offer." she pointed south toward the creek with much sand.

"Why not north … toward the Flat-Water River, you said offers so much?"

"Not the time yet, white man." She slapped his arm and pointed to the giant Canada geese floating toward the water. "It's time to shoot one of those for tonight's meal, yes?"

"Yes." He rolled off the roof and waited for her to slide down. She floated into his arms, light as a feather.

The previous night Grass Woman told him of the difficult move to the reservation along the Nebraska-Kansas territory border. Being a tribe that depended on their earth lodges and raising crops they did not fit the so-called stereotype of the nomadic Sioux tribes. They'd had a good relationship with the Pawnee, Omaha, and Ponca, but the Sioux—what could she say—they took advantage of their fellow Indian tribes. Woman of the Grass hated the reservation life for it confined her and the tribe from the spring and fall game hunts. The Buffalo now lived west of the marshland she and John trekked over each day in search of medicinal plants. The Pawnee had been free to farm and hunt at will. Now, the pressure remained high to cede their land to the white man and live in a village along the Loup River.

Woman of the Grass lamented that her brothers and sisters would go the way of the Oto Tribe. Her wish included regaining the previous ground, but she knew this would not be realistic in the far-reaching future. She came to love this young white man, who so loved the marshland she once freely roamed. Her influence with the Ponca, Omaha, Pawnee, and Missouri Tribes went beyond the bounds of the marsh country. The respect for her plant knowledge and the benefits gained by all tribes from that understanding placed her in special tribal honor. Even Sioux tribes respected her expertise and paid their respect when they met her on the prairie.

The one plant she showed John had a lasting effect on him. The purple rays surrounding the flower head made it stand out in the grassy cover. He had learned to identify it from the emerging to drying stage. One particular healthy plant she found not far from the dugout made her stop. "John, come here."

He minded her like a grandson and quickly obeyed her request. "What do you wish, wise woman?"

"The plant you stand on is a valuable medicinal plant for many tribal generations." She watched him shuffle to the side. "The one you trampled on … dig the root and peel off the outer layer."

He did as she asked and waited.

"It looks good?" She asked.

He nodded.

"Then take a very small bite. Tell me what you taste and feel.' She waited for his reaction.

"Sweet, somewhat and it …" He felt his tongue numb, "It dulls my mouth."

"Good. Spit it out and your mouth will feel better by sunset." She smiled and led him by the hand through the uplands. "Many of the plants I show you the past fall that we use for food also helps with many ailments. Remember them, for they could save you or a friend's life."

After walking for two hours they descended to the marsh edge. "Woman, you have not shared many wetland plants with me. Why?"

"I have never found the need to explore these plants. Many are grasses in these wet areas. The life here is special to the birds and their feeding needs. There's a balance needed for these water bodies to remain healthy." She pointed to the arrowhead plant, the rushes, the cattails, and to the animals using them for food and cover. "The cattails and reeds you know how to use. I do not want to waste time, for my living years become short."

After her lessons on the natural plants, she taught him to grow the crops that helped the Oto survive when the hunts did not prove successful. She came to this marsh carrying seeds of melons, squash, and corn. By late spring the garden flourished under her watchful eye and strong guidance. John had grown a garden where rains occurred more often, thus he used water from the well and rainwater collection directly from the roof runoff. She liked this man's intuitive mind to use what nature provided and how they could improve on these gifts.

The hot August evening left both John and Woman of the Grass lazing beside the marsh edge. He discovered the big green frogs loved to eat the bright-colored insects flitting and skittering about in the grass-filled habitat. John wondered what would happen if he rigged a fishing line with a bright piece of cloth. He ran back to the dugout, fetched string, one of his poles, and baited a hook with a tiny, brightly-colored cloth remnant. Woman of the Grass watched him run to the marsh edge, plop down, and begin twitching the pole. A minute later his voice echoed across the marsh; he held up a squirming frog and grinned.

"John?"

"Woman we can eat this critter if we run out of other food." They dined on the legs until fall when the frogs burrowed deep. The waste they buried in the garden area.

Chapter 72

Three horsemen rode in from the northeast, trotted to the marsh edge, and stopped to survey the land and the dugouts to the west. John pulled the monocular off the oak stand near the door and raised it to his shooting eye. "What have we here?"

Woman of the Grass rose from her rocker and stood by his side. She squinted, holding her hand over her eyes. A small grunt came from deep in her throat. Her other hand came up and he placed the monocular in the palm. Her quickened breathing suggested she did not like what she saw. "Trouble," she mumbled.

The word use caught him by surprise. "What, you said … trouble?" He looked down at her.

She peered up at him and tilted her head, a tiny smirk on her lips.

"Why… trouble?" he asked.

"Sioux … will want something from us. They do not come into this country unless they want something." She handed the monocular back to him. "They came for buffalo when the herds wandered this land, but now … they come with the devil."

"Woman, you know of the devil?"

"Remember, I lived with the French and their priests when they came to our land. Their beliefs … they taught and wanted us to believe.

"The riders are young. They will want food and water. We must be careful they do not try to take more, which they might want to do when they see me dressed as a Pawnee."

He watched the three Sioux rein their horses toward the dugouts. The stallion and mare snorted and raised their heads as the riders cautiously closed the distance between them and the corral. Halfway up the slope they halted their ponies and stared at John leaning against the door frame, smoking his corncob pipe. The oldest of the three slid off and said something to the other two. They stayed mounted as he led his horse forward. He walked with pride and stopped ten yards in front of the dugout, surveying the layout of the immediate surroundings. He started to say something and stopped.

From behind John, Woman of the Grass stepped through the door, now dressed in different clothes. She said a few words and the young Sioux shook his head. With more force, she said words that caused his facial expression to go hard. Abruptly Woman of the Grass said in English, "Sioux warrior you will not bother us or I will lay a curse on your shoulders."

John's frown deepened as he watched the Sioux lad puff up his chest and answer her in broken English. "Old woman I do not fear you and the white man. I come in peace … you show hate for your brothers." He spat on the ground. "You … you like him …"

She stepped forward, raised her gnarled hand, and pointed a finger at him. "You come to take our horses and food."

His eyes opened wide at her words "No," the lad burst out.

"Do not speak untruths, Sioux boy. I know what evil is in your heart and your friends sitting on their ponies with the devil. I know, for I am the Old Woman of the Grass."

When she said her name, he stepped back. A small nod indicated he knew of her. "We come only for food and water."

"This is John's home. Only he can grant you permission for water and to give what meager food he can share." She turned to John and said, "Your turn." A sneaky smile quickly came and went.

"Tell your friends they can water the horses at the trough. You and the others can draw water from the well to drink. Woman of the Grass will pack a day's food supply and you will leave us."

The Sioux nodded he understood and led his horse to the trough where the stallion watched. He waved for his companions to come and water their horses and motioned for them to drink from the well.

John had both rifle and pistol within easy reach in case they changed their minds. A soft sound came from behind John. Woman of the Grass handed him his bow and quiver. The youngest Sioux eyed John as he shouldered the quiver and propped the bow against the door frame.

The woman returned with a small bag of food and gave it to John. He picked up the bow and an arrow with his free hand and walked to the three boys. "Food," he said handed the sack to the smallest of the three and stepped back. The Sioux looked past John, his jaw muscles twitched, and the emotion of fear floated across his face. "She will not place a curse on you. Leave us in peace."

They finished watering the horses and quickly mounted. The smallest held the food up and nodded. They galloped by the dugout and over the ridge.

John turned to Woman and said, "You could speak good English all along."

She smiled.

"Why didn't you speak it when you found me ... and cut the rope?"

"You did not ask if I could speak your language, John." She smiled and patted his arm.

Chapter 73

She fell asleep in her chair, lightly snoring. John placed a blanket over her lap and softly patted her hunched back. He returned to his place at the table, which always held an open book and notes from his marsh observations. Woman of the Grass continued to take more and more naps over the three years they had been together. In winter, she slept in the dugout, coming in when the temperature at night remained below freezing. Summers, she preferred to sleep in a reed hut situated between the two dugouts.

Few people had traveled past the dugouts during the four years after he decided to stay. Last year, a literate and hardened man stopped on his way to Ft. Kearny. The man, named A. Troester, claimed to be a preacher. He rode a frisky horse and led a pack mule with the same temperament. Reverend Troester did not quote any Biblical passages when he learned John came from a German Reformed background. As he sat at the table wondering about the old woman's health, John's thoughts drifted back to last year.

Troester spent considerable time with Woman of the Grass, talking of Indian spirituality. She explained in sign and Indian languages (Oto, Pawnee, and Lakota) her history. It took time as John had to interpret for both. He would smile inwardly when she talked in Pawnee language of her feelings about Reverend A. Troester. John tempered the interpretation with his English explanation the best he could. At times, he could not stifle his laugh and had to explain away the humorous moments during a serious discussion.

Before Reverend Troester left for the Fort, he and John discussed the events occurring east of the Missouri. "First," John said, "I need to ask what the year, month, and day might be."

The man stared at him. "How long have you lived here?"

John laughed as he flipped open his notebook. "Best I can figure," he said while adding up the months, "… is going on four or five years."

Troester's mouth twitched like he couldn't believe what he heard. "Five years you guess. What year did you come here?"

"Eighteen hundred and fifty-five … fall of that year."

"You kept a good calendar, John. The year is 1860, the fifteenth of May."

The notebook pages rustled in the dugout as John turned the pages to his current calendar. "I learned to judge the seasons and months from her teachings." He looked over at the sleeping companion. "She's a great teacher," he looked at the crude calendar sketch, "I'm only off a week and two days. Can you tell me what day of the week?"

"Yes. I left Omaha on Monday, so this is my fourteenth day out so … it's a Monday." He leaned back in his chair. "You get away from here?"

"No."

"How do you live and eat?" His face revealed he didn't believe John. "Don't you miss people and the camaraderie?"

"You speak well Reverend." John looked at the good cloth which A. Troester dressed. "We have everything I need right here. I and Woman of the Grass subsist off the land."

"No money, you've no hankering for a young woman and family?"

"Money no, there's not a need. A woman perhaps, but I believe that will happen when it happens." John noticed a nearly imperceptible change when the Reverend found money did not exist in their humble house.

"I'll be leaving tomorrow, John."

"While the Woman sleeps, let me show you the marsh and why I do not leave."

They sat near the wet meadow watching the muskrats busily repairing their reed houses in the open water. Ducks and geese that stayed on for the summer broke the water calm as they paddled near the water plants lining the aquatic basin and dabbled in the shallows.

"You know the names of all the plants and animals?"

263

John shook his head. "I don't, but I hope to find a person with the knowledge to educate me. That's why I keep notes, so I can talk with that person and he ... or she ... can fill in the names. Until then I use the Woman of the Grass' words."

"What'll you do when she dies? She's ... what ... in her eighties?"

"I don't know. Does that answer both questions?" They sat quietly, John's reply hanging before them. "I live day-to-day, Reverend. The time will come when I have to deal with what you ask, but for now, I live for the moment, for there's much to learn."

The remaining time A. Troester stayed, John learned of unrest with the slavery issues and the debate by politicians about the need for a national rail system, which would likely cut across the Nebraska Territory. The Reverend brought up the Pawnee village north of the Platte. There was the word of unrest within the young tribal members—because of their lost land and changing life.

"One place you should visit is the Oregon Trail," Reverend Troester said, "it's used by stagecoach lines and the pony express."

A rattling cough snapped John back to the present. Over the past months, Woman of the Grass showed signs of increasing consumption. When he tried to talk to her about it, she frowned and waved him off. Nonetheless, he had a festering concern for her. The question from the Reverend, if he was a minister, about her dying, had put the thought firmly in the forefront. He rested his forehead in his hands and slipped into prayer.

"Who do you pray for, John?"

"You, Woman, you have me worried."

"John ... worry does no one any good. I am old and my days are short. So, finish your prayer, to your God or ..."

He stood as a wracking cough shook her small, thin body. She raised her hand and stopped him. "John, do not treat me like a child ... or an old woman. Be patient, John."

He nodded.

"We must go to the marsh and have a few more lessons about the life there. We can sit and both enjoy this wonder created for our pleasure and its life-giving quality."

He stepped back, as she feebly stood, and asked, "Where do you want to spend time by the marsh?"

"You know ... the small point that extends into the marsh?"

"Yes, we will go there and talk."

"We will, John. And we will experience the spring wonders of the small flying critters and the frogs that feed on them. We will see the duck nests and the squirrel that comes to fill its belly with the eggs and young ducklings."

They rode together on the big stallion to the point of land fringed with arrowhead, bulrushes, and new cattails. He picketed the horse at the edge of the wetland and they slowly walked to a spot where they could look from the point over the open water. Along the short walk she pointed to the water-loving plants with vibrant white flowers.

At the end of the point Woman of the Grass squatted and heaved a long sigh and sat back. "I cannot walk like I once did." She coughed and closed her eyes. "Learn to listen to the marsh sounds, John. They will give you important information that might save your life."

He looked down at her and held out his hand. She took it and with the other hand invited him to sit next to her. He sat so he would not obstruct her view. For the next hour, they watched the wildlife and talked about the plants the animals used for food and for cover.

Long-legged insects skittered about on the marsh water, their feet set in tiny dimples that kept them afloat on the water top. Other small bugs floated and whirled about on the surface. A four-winged insect darted from cattail to cattail, making a stop at a wide-leafed plant that John wanted to know more about.

"John ... John ...?"

He turned to look at her. The color of her skin now a dark gray, her breathing so shallow his heart sank. He became frightened.

"John ... my son ..."

She slumped against him. He wrapped his arms around her and felt life leaving her. His tears began to flow as he put her head on his lap and kissed her cheek. "Woman of the Grass, I love you, and you forever will live in my heart. We'll someday meet again at another marsh, another life."

John buried her above the marsh where the sunrise danced on the horizon. He cried tears all the time he dug the grave. In the late afternoon of fall, a glorious blanket of gold sunlight would cover this spot. The one large stone left by the water well he used for a headstone.

Through the summer months, he worked the garden and harvested the crops for immediate use and to store for winter. What John enjoyed most came from what he learned from her about his surrounding environment: the animals for food and clothing and the plants for food and medicinal uses. The one plant she grew, she obtained seeds from the northern tribes in the Nebraska Territory, that plant: tobacco. She taught him to use the leaves and the dried and ground, green seed capsule, which she prized for her smoke after a fine meal.

By chance, they had come on a small isolated buffalo herd on the rolling land northwest of the dugouts the last year they spent together. Woman of the Grass figured the buffalo roamed the area between the *Kickatus* (John understood the word came from the Pawnee for Flat Water) and the *Maa-ozhi-ke* (Pawnee for a river full of cottonwoods). She transferred the English meaning to him by signing. He shot a young calf and they field dressed the animal while she danced with delight. They took the heart, liver, kidneys, and the dressed animal back to the dugout and processed the meat and hide for food and clothing, respectively. That night they feasted on buffalo tongue and liver. At the meals end, she brought out the ground tobacco seeds for the first time. That night he became hooked on buffalo meat and the tobacco of her ancestors.

Each night for the first month after her death he sat by the headstone, smoking the green seed tobacco. He continued to honor her grave with prairie flowers or a bundle of wetland plants.

On a golden September evening, he sat silently by her grave and stared into the setting sun. Three wagons, trailing several heads of horses and cattle, appeared on the rise. When John recognized the man in the lead wagon he openly wept.

The Murder

Matthew 5:21 (KJV)

*Ye have heard that it was said of them of old time, Thou
shalt not kill; and whosoever shall kill shall be in danger of the judgment:*

Chapter 74

As the shadows crept across the marsh and slowly blanketed Woman of the Grass' grave, John asked, "Why so long to return?"

Morris decided to tell John about his problems at the Fort. He puffed the freshly lit pipe. After a pensive moment, he said, "Bad fortune."

"You want to explain?" John asked.

"The Fort commander had to take on a new lieutenant sent from Washington. After several months of taking his badgering, I exploded, kicked his rear, and wound up in trouble."

"What do you mean … trouble?" John stared at his friend.

"That, my friend, means they threw my arse in jail."

John gazed at the distant prairie blur under the darkening horizon. "You ran into trouble, gave them the truth … which they didn't like … and they put you away."

"Yes, and confiscated all my worldly belongings … threw my wife and sons out to fend for themselves."

"And …?"

Morris watched the nighthawk gliding above the grass searching for a resting spot before continuing its journey south. "They could've cared less about me and my family. They kicked me off the Fort land, ignoring the fact my Pawnee family would help me survive. We, the wife and boys, spent the next year in the Pawnee village by the Loup River."

"You returned to the Fort?"

Morris looked at him in amazement and chuckled. "John, I returned at their request and they welcomed me with open arms."

"Why ...?"

"I had kept peace with the Pawnee and they didn't realize it until a few belligerent braves tore into outlying areas near the Fort. The captain told me they'd made a mistake, and they sent the bungling fool back to Washington."

"Your hard work and dedication paid off from the looks of all the equipment you brought."

Morris shook his head. "John, I survive by being crafty, like the fox that roams the prairie. I gathered these goods from the people headed west. The farming and building tools came from one man who led a group of travelers. While at the Fort stopover, he said his wife abandoned him." Morris watched his boys wrestling with the buffalo hides to cover the teepee poles. "He claimed she ran, not wanting to assume responsibility for their young-un and him." He stopped and hollered for the boys to help their mother. "I learned from some of the travelers in his group that he kicked her off the trail for another woman. So, I confronted him."

"What'd he say?"

"He knew better than to lie. The bastard asked what I wanted to keep quiet." Morris grinned. "I got most of that heavy farming equipment." He pointed to the plow and harrow.

"What of his wife?" John asked.

"Best guess ... she abandoned the train straight south of here."

"She's wandering out here ... alone?" John sucked in the fresh night air and slowly exhaled.

Morris squinted at the horizon. Below it darkness nearly consumed the marshland. "When do we ride?"

"We ...?" John asked.

"Yes. John, she's probably dead, but I know you ... and you'll set off to find her. You cannot do that alone. There's native unrest within splinter groups of Pawnee and Sioux. The boys and I can help find her."

They saddled at daybreak, John on the stallion and Morris and his oldest two sons on mustangs. They rode south to where Morris figured the woman escaped the trail. The two boys, Morris, and John galloped south skirting several small marshes on the trek.

"The boys learned to track from scouts at the fort; they eagerly want to use their skill," Morris said as they slowed to cross the sandy river. "We'll ride on to the Trail; from there we'll work the grasslands rising north from the river valley."

It took the better part of the afternoon until the middle son called out from a far stream bank leading up from the small sandy stream. "Morris," Little Feather said, "we have a woman's shoe. Tracks lead north toward the marshes, five or six days old." He rapidly rode to the top of the watershed terrace. "Another shoe," he called out and galloped over the rise.

"Follow him," Morris said, slapping his mustang's rump. The other boy continued to search for more signs in case this wasn't the woman they sought.

It took Little Feather until the horizon turned a pale yellow and red before he and the other boy found her. The slender lad slid off his mount and pulled her from the edge of the small slough. "Nearly dead," he said, looking at the woman's swollen face and tattered and shredded clothing.

Morris dismounted, gently placed his hand over her heart, and said, "She breathes ... and her heart beats strong. We'll take her to your dugout where Evening Star can help."

The boy nodded and with John's help draped her over his mustang. The boy swung onto Morris' horse, behind his father, and they trotted toward John's dugout.

"John, hurry ahead," Morris hollered, "tell Evening Star we need her help with a battered woman."

Chapter 75

Evening Star smiled at John while he helped with the plant preparations. "Woman of the Grass taught you well, John Hayman." She began preparation of a paste made from spindly, few-flowered plants scattered throughout the grasslands.

John, over the past years, collected dry leaves to make a fine powder from the lead-colored leaves of a shrub-like plant. From a spoon, he gently blew the powder into her open wounds. Woman of the Grass treated him in the same manner when he suffered deep scrapes after his stallion took a notion to buck him off on a hot, late-summer day. Scabs rapidly formed where she treated his scratches and scrapes with the healing talc.

A gasp erupted from Evening Star when she lowered the woman's frayed and torn dress. John glanced at the unconscious woman's bare breasts covered with long welts and bruises and weeping circular burns. He felt the bile rise in his throat.

"You be sick, John?"

John gently shook his head.

"The white man did her much harm. We will take care of her ... make her well," she said. "Fetch swellings from the dry *pahatu* plants. We char and crush them to heal the seeping sores."

Before leaving to gather the spherical swellings, caused by insects damaging the wild rose stems, he asked, "What do we feed the woman?"

"Do not worry, John, I take care of her. You must help heal her mind. Can you do that?"

An upturn of the left side of his mouth answered her question. "I can ...

and will."

"She's a fine woman, strong of body ... but her mind will hurt for many moons." Evening Star returned to treating the woman's injuries with her gentle touch.

The rising sun bathed the marsh, the pink roses beckoning him near the wet edges. It took an hour to collect the insect galls from the stems. When he walked into the open door of the dugout he heard a quiet chanting. The singsong lyrics warmed him, for he had heard the same from Woman of the Grass.

"What do you chant?" John asked.

Evening Star looked up at him. "I ask the spirits to bless this woman and heal her with nature's medicine." She held out her hand for the galls and stared at them. "Our land will change, John Hayman, and... perhaps... not for the best."

He watched Evening Star char the swollen pieces of the rose stem.

"John, as soon as these cool ... grind them and then I will make a paste."

After they finished, she applied the poultice to a soft piece of deerskin and covered the woman's chest. Evening Star then wrapped the hide in place, fastened with flat strips of cloth tied in front. After treating the wounds, they gently moved the woman to a clean, soft bed of goose down Woman of the Grass made for John.

They moved outside into the sunshine. Evening Star hugged John. "You are a kind man."

"I'm not—"

She placed a finger on his lips. "John, you think you know yourself, but I sense your concern for the woman. Sometime we will visit about your past as Morris has shared little with me. You're a caring man." She kissed him on the cheek. "It is time for me to prepare the meals for the day. George will bring the food for the woman when the sun is high." She looked at his puzzled face. "What is it, John?"

"George?"

A smile broke across her face. The dark eyes sparkled. "Yes, Morris insisted we not use native names for all the boys. George looked so much like a white boy we decided to name him after President Washington."

"George is the youngest?"

She nodded as he helped her hitch the horse to the wagon. He assisted her as she climbed into the wagon. "John, see ... you are a kind man. My men would not have helped me with the horse and onto the wagon seat."

He watched her as the wagon swayed and bumped over the small rise to the southwest, headed to the land where her husband and boys toiled to make their home.

The stallion snorted and John turned to look what drew the horse's attention. Two men with hats pulled low on their heads had stopped to look across the marsh toward the dugout. They shifted in their saddles while they looked around and behind them. The bigger of the two stood in the stirrups and peered at the small walking trail John had worn around the marsh to Woman of the Grass' grave. Each man, leading a packhorse, slowly urged their horse forward, descended to the worn path, and rode toward the dugout.

Concerned with all the horses bearing rifle scabbards, John stepped into the dugout, strapped on the holstered pistol, and cradled the Colt rifle in the crook of his right arm. As the men rapidly neared the dugout he leaned against the door frame. They reined to a halt when they saw he held a rifle and briefly began talking back and forth. He could not understand what they said, except the last word came loud and clear over the marsh edge.

"Hello," John replied.

The smaller man handed his packhorse rope to the other and eased forward. The rifle butt rose above his saddle for easy access. A pistol, butt forward, sat high on the man's left hip.

John's stallion nervously pawed the ground; he tensed as the man kicked the horse into a trot and rode directly at him. "Close enough."

The man quickly reined to a stop and sat steady in the saddle. "I'm a surveyor, mister."

"A surveyor?" John asked. He looked at the other man sitting quietly on his horse, hands resting on the saddle horn. "What can I do for you?"

"Can I approach and step down?"

"You may."

The surveyor flinched with the proper language use. "Thank you." He dismounted and glanced at the stallion warily watching him. "The big horse acts like a watchdog."

"He does," John said.

The small man slowly unbuckled his pistol and hung it on his saddle horn. He sidled up to John. "My name's Luther. You got a handle?"

"John," he replied and shifted his weight so he could reach his pistol, if necessary.

Luther held out his hand and said, "Glad to meet you, John. I'm heading up a team of men assigned to survey the area." He shook John's hand. "We're workin' the area to the east of the sixth principal meridian. You know what that is?"

John shook his head.

"A survey of the 40th degree of latitude east to west from the Missouri River is complete—that's south of here—and separates the Kansas and Nebraska territories. There's been concern about the problems with the natives west of here so we surveyed north and south along the Sixth Principal Meridian." He noticed how John intently listened and continued, "I will lead the team to work the areas west of the sixth meridian and we're armed because some natives east of here gave us problems."

John asked, "Which tribe?"

"We aren't sure … we think Pawnee, but some Sioux prowl the area." He looked to the southwest. "Saw the Indian woman headed that way," he motioned with his head, "your woman?"

"Nope," John simply offered.

"How long you been here?"

"Been here since 1855," he watched the other man step out of the saddle.

"You marked your boundaries. You gonna have to pay the government for the land. You're aware of that?"

"Yep," John said.

Luther looked at his partner, standing by the pack animals. "My assistant's losing his patience. I need to get goin'. We'll be back next year, probably in late summer." He turned, mounted up, and trotted back to his partner.

Chapter 76

John squatted alongside a small rodent trail in the mid-grass prairie near the marsh. He wanted to capture and compare the small rodents that he found near the marsh and in the upland area. To understand the difference between these unique critters he needed several specimens. The ones near the marsh had brownish-black upperparts and a gray abdomen. In contrast, the similar upland rodents had a buffy abdomen.

With his concentration on the animals, he lost track of his surroundings. A hand lightly gripped his shoulder and he jumped up, drawing his pistol. The frail figure jerked back at his violent reaction. John stared at the woman who had not spoken since she arrived a month ago. Her wounds had healed nicely, but—as Evening Star stated—her mind had not.

"J-J-J-John, what are y-y-y-you doing?"

The words, though stuttered, rang melodiously on his senses. He holstered his pistol and took her hand. "I want to find a small … I think … mouse."

"Y-y-you want to catch a mouse?" she chuckled, "w-w-why?"

He nodded and had her squat beside him. "See how they leave little trails through the grass?"

She put her hand on his while he pried away grass from the tiny runway.

"Those that live by the marsh look like the ones up there," he said and pointed to the grassy upland. "Except the bellies of the ones down here are gray, not a buff-colored like the same-looking critter up there."

"You a-a-are a crazy p-p-person, John," she said with an ornery laugh.

"I am. Welcome to the speaking world." He lightly touched her lips and then to his ears. "It is good to hear you talk."

"But ... I s-s-s-stutter b-b-badly."

John looked into her kind eyes. "You have suffered ... it will take time to heal, like your wounds."

"W-w-who is the woman that c-c-comes every d-d-d-day to feed and care for me?" She frowned, searching for the right words. "I d-d-do n-n-not know her name."

"Her name is Evening Star."

"Why d-d-does sh-e-e-e care about me?" the woman asked.

"It's who she is," John said.

"She's wonderful, do y-y-you l-l-love her?"

He looked at her small hands gripping his callused palms. "She belongs to another man. They live over there." He motioned with a turn of his head.

"How l-l-long have I b-b-b-been here?"

"A few days longer than a month," John answered.

"You saw me?" she touched her chest as she talked. "I-I-I am-m-m-m embarrassed." A flush painted her pale cheeks and descended to where she pointed.

"Not to worry ..."

"You h-h-hesitate, w-w-why?" she asked.

"I don't know your name."

"Nor I," she said, "I am t-t-trying to find me in m-m-my mind." A tear trickled down her cheek and dropped onto the dress Evening Star had sewn for her.

"You will; it takes time to recover from your misfortunes."

"Can you t-t-tell me w-w-what h-h-happened?"

He thought for a moment. "You lost your way from the wagons along the trail that goes to Oregon." He didn't know how far to delve, so he stopped.

She shook her head and moaned. "Oh dear, I'm s-s-so c-c-confused."

"Don't worry," he hesitated, "you will be safe ... here ... with me."

The woman dropped his hands and put her arms around him. A tremble rippled over her body. "T-t-t-thank y-y-you, John Hayman."

"You're welcome ... Maggie." He surprised himself with that name.

"I like the name … it's my real name?" she said with a hopeful tone.

"For now, yes."

She hugged him tighter. "You're a k-k-kind, handsome m-man, John."

"Someone told me that."

"W-w-who?" Maggie asked.

"Evening Star," he quietly said.

Maggie stepped back from him and sighed. "She w-w-would know." Again, she took one of his hands and asked, "Will y-y-you take me b-b-back to my bed, John? I-I-I'm tired."

They walked together to the dugout in the fading November light. Her hand slipped into his.

Chapter 77

Wheat Morris and he planted in the fall had begun a vigorous growth. The winter snows, although light, protected the small plants from the unusually cold January temperatures. John and Maggie easily shared time together as she continued to improve. Her help with the horses and the cows made him feel like the land belonged to them. The marsh held a special fascination for both and they spent many winter hours bundled against the cold, watching how the animals survived.

The familiar sounds of March descended on the marsh. Maggie opened the dugout door and gasped. The geese filling the sky sent a chill down her spine. "John, look."

He rose from the table where he sat studying his journal notes. His arm slipped over her shoulder. "It's an amazing sight." She responded by slipping an arm around his waist. "The migration's just beginning. The display lasts until mid to late April."

"You love it here, John?"

"I do. There's something unique about the area. I like the Mississippi and Ohio Rivers, but this display of water, plants, and wildlife always raises my spirits." The open water continued to fill with waterfowl. "Woman of the Grass' spirit floats over the marsh. She sat many days watching the spring display. Her heart longed for this country. The reservation life pained her. I know she wanted me to find a nice woman."

"Evening Star and you ... I have to thank for saving my life. Morris and the boys are wonderful. They're so helpful ... and knowledgeable." She looked up at him. "I would like to have boys like them, especially George."

Tears filled her eyes. "I no longer stutter, but I … I still speak with … hesitation."

"Maggie you've improved beyond belief since Little Feather and Morris brought you here. Evening Star said she could help you heal physically, but I must help you with healing your heart and mind. I hope—"

"John, say no more. You've helped more than you will ever know. I love this land, the sod house … and you. I want to have a son just like you."

After the wheat harvest, Maggie and John became husband and wife in a marriage ceremony orchestrated by Evening Star. In John's dwelling, Maggie waited in a deer-hide dress sewn and beaded by a Pawnee woman in the village by the Loup River. When the time came, Morris called for Maggie to come from the sod house wrapped in a blanket with only her eyes showing. John, in the Pawnee tradition, wrapped a blanket around her. They spoke, thus taking the first step to marriage. Evening Star pointed for Maggie to return to the sod house where she sat at the rear with a cushion near her. John entered his home and sat next to her. She rose and filled a bowl with buffalo stew, returned, shared the food, and when they finished the ceremony ended. John and Maggie invited the McFarland family into their home.

"Where's Hawk?" Maggie asked.

"He will join us … soon … or at least he had better show soon." Morris grunted when Evening Star elbowed him. "To complete the ceremony, we will finish our meal and …"

A deep voice outside the sod house called out, "I, Hawk, son of Evening Star and Morris McFarland, ask the married couple to come outside."

His brothers, George and Little Feather, helped Maggie and John from the cushions and escorted them from the sod dugout.

"Oh, dear me," Maggie gasped. A horse blanketed in the bead colors Evening Star used for the dress, stood quietly beside Hawk's horse. She looked at Evening Star and smiled. "Thank you, thank you with all my heart."

Little Feather brought John's stallion saddled only with a blanket. "You will take the wife on a ride with her Pawnee gift."

John helped Maggie onto the horse that Hawk held steady.

"The mare's gentle," Hawk said, "well trained by my cousin." He handed her the reins and stepped back.

John stepped into the Little Feather's waiting folded hands—held out to boost John onto the big stallion's back.

"We will return to our home," Morris said, "while you ride." He stepped back and watched Mr. and Mrs. Hayman walk the horses for a few yards until they began a trot toward the marsh.

Maggie and John stopped on the rise across from their sod dugout. They quietly sat, watching the McFarland family until they disappeared.

He held out his hand. She took it. "Welcome to the Hayman Marsh, Maggie Hayman."

Chapter 78

Voices in the distance echoed across the marsh as the sun rose, brightening the cloudless sky. Maggie and John peered from the east-facing window, watching the men silhouetted on the ridge, laboring with poles and chains. The other men moved over the land with various paraphernalia: tripods, levels, and staffs.

Shortly after the marriage ceremony, Morris McFarland and John Hayman built corrals on the opposite sides of their separate marshes. The increase in cattle and horse numbers necessitated rotating the grazing to maintain good grass. Also, fences held the animals on land they wanted to claim, keeping out squatters. The marshes did not prove valuable for farming, but offered food through wild game harvest and use of various plants for food and shelter.

The men working the land with the survey equipment stopped to watch as John trotted up on the stallion. They noticed the rifle and pistol positioned within easy reach, suggesting he expected problems in this isolated area. Luther, the lead surveyor, tipped his hat back so John could see his face.

John reined to a halt and leaned over in the saddle to shake hands. "You're back just like you said."

"John, how are you?"

"I'm doing well, thanks. I wanted to see all the activity."

"Let me get the team working and we can sit a spell to talk." Luther gathered the men and pointed to the marshland. Notable discussion took place about the long fence. After several minutes of pointing and checking what the fence surrounded, Luther returned to John. He signaled the young man tending the wagon to bring two portable seats.

"We had to discuss how to deal with your fence. From our calculations, you'll straddle two different sections when the township survey is completed and—" He stopped abruptly. "Do you know what is going on?"

"I only know you are surveying the land; I don't understand your concern with my claim."

"John, there's talk of a new law to encourage homesteading. It will allow new settlers to come in and lay claim to land for a low cost. All they must do is build something on the land and prove they're using and improving the acres. You've been on this land how long?"

"More than half-dozen years," John said, "and put up the markers on the land to the east about two years ago."

"I wondered about the markers over east," Luther said, keeping an eye on one of the crew. "It's better farmin' land than the marsh location." He looked at the wetland. "When we get the township markers I can have the crew shoot some lines and give you the legal boundaries."

"Then what?" John said.

"There's a public land office in Nebraska City. A law passed in '41 gives rights to early settlers to claim the land as theirs, and at a decent price." Luther thought a moment. "I can get a land warrant for the other acres by using the military buying plan."

"I don't understand." John looked troubled. "Is it okay to do that?"

"Best not to ask too many questions, John," Luther replied, "it is bein' done and the big wigs back east have been doin' it for years. Tomorrow I'll get you the paperwork to claim the land. The boss over in Nebraska City is open to helping you early settlers who've worked hard to live out here." He held out his hand. John shook it and started to say something. "Don't ask questions; enjoy your homestead, okay? You're a good man and I want to help." Luther shook John's hand, slapped him on the back, turned, and walked away.

John heard Luther swearing under his breath at the man he'd been eyeing. The sunlight bathed the marsh as Maggie stood in the dugout doorway, a hand shading her eyes. A sense of well-being crept over him, erasing any doubts about settling in this land.

He swung onto the stallion and trotted back to his dugout. After putting the big stud in the corral near the animal dugout, he sidled back to Maggie, noticing the broad smile on her face. "I love your smile, Mrs. Hayman."

"Thank you, Mr. Hayman. I'm smiling because my husband is such a good horseman." She stood on her tiptoes and warmly kissed him "You look so pleased. Tell me what you talked about with the man."

"He told me to file our land claim in an office in Nebraska City." The stallion nickered and shook his head. "I think our stallion likes what the surveyor said."

"When are you going to Nebraska City?"

John pulled her close. "We ... we'll leave in two or three days."

"We'll go in the wagon?"

"Yes," John replied.

"Drive slow," Maggie said with a glint in her gray eyes.

Chapter 79

Between the time John and Maggie had their first child, Calvin, and the last, Henry, they amassed nearly three sections of land between the two major tributaries flowing to the Big Blue River. They used the major portion of their land for grazing cattle, tilling the upland acres for wheat, oats, some corn, and in the summer, produced food in their large garden for the people passing through to Oregon. During the early years, the Haymans teamed with the McFarland family to supply goods, horses, and meat to the stage and pony express stops along the Oregon Trail. The most lucrative and successful business came from the horses sold to Fort Kearny.

The sons helped their fathers with the cattle and crops. Evening Star and Maggie kept the men in clothes and sold the extra to travelers. Several years they subsisted on the food gathered by hunting for antelope and Hawk, who loved to hunt buffalo, brought home more than the families could consume, so they sold some extra meat to the Fort and stage stations. They lived off the land as Woman of the Grass had taught John. The native plants with a tolerance of dry weather still provided them with food and medicine, the latter rarely needed.

Two years after Calvin entered the marsh country as a healthy child the times for Maggie and John became exciting, and at times terrifying. In late 1864 a band of marauding Pawnees inflicted damage on their land. These belligerent young men did not like the surveyors marking the land for the hordes of settlers claiming prime acres in their former hunting grounds. The activity drove out the buffalo, the antelope became rare, and the grasses disappeared under the plow for the white man's crops, which the Indians knew could not survive the dry years.

On a late September evening John, Maggie, and Calvin rode to the marsh ridge east of the dugout to determine the land capability for handling the existing livestock. A dry, southwest wind carried ominous signs. The restlessness of the marsh animals and his horses did not bode well. Little moisture combined with the unusual warmth concerned John. Normally he would dismount and spend time at Woman of the Grass' grave.

"John, what's wrong? You're as skittish as the red-winged blackbirds."

He turned to her, her natural smile gone, replaced by a frightened, ashen look. The small boy sat between the saddle horn and his wife's leather riding pants, looking up at his father. "Something bothers all of us except for Calvin." John watched the small patch of water for signs of activity. None. "The animals sense something." He stood in the stirrups, straining to understand the huge cloud rising in the west. He cried aloud, "It's a grass fire." The biting smell suddenly assaulted their noses and the ferocious, roaring sound pounded their eardrums, Calvin began to cough and cry.

"John, we must get back to the dugout."

"No time." At that moment fire pillars twisted and danced over the west rise.

Maggie gasped and tears streamed down her cheeks. He handed her his kerchief. Over the sound from hell, he yelled, "Wrap it over your nose and mouth." John took Calvin from her saddle and sat him so his little tear-streaked cheeks faced into his clothing. "Head for the marsh," he screamed over the howling storm of burning grass.

Maggie kicked the horse's flanks and bent into its neck. Sod exploded from under the hooves as it raced toward the rushes and cattails, tossing out the fluff from the fall seed spikes.

John followed, keeping the stallion on the heels of the sorrel mare. It took only a minute to reach the marsh edge. He stepped out of the saddle with Calvin tightly clutched to his chest. Maggie sat in the saddle transfixed on the menacing firestorm. With all his strength, he tugged at both horses' reins and led them into the muck toward the open water. He could barely hear the frantic screams his wife made at the fire and smoke.

"Maggie, get off the horse … get off. Pull it down, can you do that?" She sat frozen, a maniacal mask covered on her face. "Come on, Maggie," he yelled, "Calvin needs you." The boy's name snapped her out of the trance.

Maggie slid into the water and took Calvin from him. He pointed to lie down and he pulled the stallion and mare into deeper water. "Maggie, crawl down here." He took Calvin as soon as she came within arm's reach and quickly dunked him, making sure he thoroughly soaked the boy. She followed suit and soaked herself. He handed Calvin back to her and pulled the horses to the deeper water so only their heads showed. They did not fight him.

With a sudden wind change, the fire shifted to the northeast at a blistering speed. John turned to watch the fire burn the prairie nearly bare as it swallowed up the dead and dying vegetation. Damp soil and water at the marsh edge, angrily spit and steamed, arguing with the range fire. Within two minutes the fire devoured the upland plants, scorched the marsh, and roared out of sight.

"What started the fire, John?"

The answer to her question came over the horizon. At least twenty Indians stopped and watched the fire spew its anger, destroying all in its path. They held up charred surveyor posts and tortured surveying tools. The lead Indian held up a lance with a scalp dangling from its point and freely waving in the fire-generated wind.

John shook his fist at them and pointed to the Woman of the Grass' grave. His cry echoed over the marsh and bounced off the ridge, "You will choke on Woman of the Grass' revenge."

"White man," an older Indian yelled back, "Woman of the Grass lies where?"

John pointed to her gravestone behind him.

"We meant no harm to her spirit ... or you." The band members listened as he told them what was said in the white man's language. The translation caused several of the younger braves to stare at the grave area. The leader, holding the spear, reined his horse north and galloped away, glancing back at the Woman of the Grass' headstone.

Chapter 80

Trade along the Oregon Trail waned because of the Indian attacks. Several people lost their lives, and others traveling along the Trail stopped only at trading posts. Nuckolls County settlers abandoned the area when the Indians killed several families near the Little Blue River. All this time the Hayman and McFarland families escaped the long shadow of darkness afflicting the area. The story of John and the Woman of the Grass echoed through the different Tribes roaming and terrorizing the whites along the Little Blue tributaries. They avoided the marshland because of the rumors that she cast demon spells on anyone who bothered the two families.

The change came rapidly in the area around 1870 with troops stationed, southeast of Fort Kearny to protect settlers moving into Fillmore County and returning to Trail stops along the Little Blue. Life again settled into a routine for John and Morris. Profits soared with the influx of people into the State of Nebraska, established in 1867, commensurate with the railroad completion along the Platte River. Some people arriving by rail began their own destruction: land speculation,

The mild dry years, alternating with wet cycles that persisted over the area in the late 1860s and the early 1870s, created a predatory land claim fiasco. Settlers who earlier squatted and those filing Homestead Act claims did not know how to farm this semi-arid country and left in the face of crop failure during the dry years. They sold their land to the wealthy and fled west.

John and Morris survived, for they lived with the land, taking advantage of the wealthy predators. In the early 1870s, the two men established a working relationship with the Burlington and Missouri Railroad businessmen. In the wet springs of 1869 and 1870, they made good money guiding hunting parties to the marshes. No hunting laws existed, but the two men kept an eye to good conservation practices ensuring the wildfowl and animal population would sustain themselves.

In 1870 John became the father to another son, Joseph. Morris' youngest boy, George, came to live with the Haymans to help with daily chores and keep the two Hayman boys in tow while Maggie worked in the gardens, at the stove, and at the outdoor fire pit. George closely resembled his white father, but possessed his mother's traits of patience and understanding, which he needed with the energetic Calvin.

John continued to make journal notes about the marshes. His writings took on a textbook quality. George learned from John to read and write and, in exchange, John learned Pawnee language and customs from the mild-mannered boy. Of all the customs, John came to love the sacred bundle. Evening Star owned one and taught George and Maggie about the Sacred Bundle importance to the Pawnee, for they contained the tools related to planting and harvesting ceremonies. Only Pawnee males could use or open the bundle and apply it to the proper ceremony. The Pawnee believed an improper opening spelled disaster.

The summer of 1873 began with the plans for Evening Star, Little Feather, and Hawk to join with relatives to hunt the buffalo near the Republican River in Southwest Nebraska. The buffalo hunt had been part of the rites of the Pawnee and they heavily relied on the massive animal for their survival.

Morris rode in on a hot July afternoon to camp with the Haymans while his wife and two sons took part in the hunt. While living at the Fort, the buffalo hunts became a yearly custom of the McFarlands. Little Feather and Hawk loved the hunting excitement. The Pawnee suffered crop failure, numerous diseases, and malnutrition, since confinement to the Loup River village. Thus, this one hunt became important for the tribe's survival.

"John, where's George?"

John watched Morris dismount and start unsaddling his horse. "He's taken the boys for a ride to the large marsh to the south."

Morris turned the horse into the corral with the other horses. He made sure the gate hitch fell in place before walking with John to the dugout. "Calvin's what ... ten?"

"In Calvin's words ... I'm eleven." John answered.

Maggie met them at the door. "Want some sumac tea, Morris?"

He nodded and exclaimed, "You are more beautiful every day. I hope John appreciates his fine wife." Her soft laugh and broad smile welcomed him.

They sat in the cool dugout talking of the hunt. "When will they return?" Maggie asked.

"Evening Star said most likely late August before they return to the village with the buffalo hides and meat." Morris pulled a pipe from his large shirt pocket, packed it with tobacco from John's canister, and lit it with a match retrieved from a box near the stove. "How's George doing?"

John and Maggie waited, not knowing how to tell Morris his son had found someone as important as the boys. John noticed Morris' frown when they hesitated. "Morris, we believe George has taken a liking to the young daughter of our neighbor to the east."

Before Morris said anything, he leaned back and let his eyes roam over the dugout interior. "You keep a proper home, Maggie." He puffed on the pipe and tamped the bowl with his thumb. "How well you know the family?"

"Casually," John replied.

"They know George is half-Indian?"

Maggie said, "I don't think so, George has never said anything about it. Why?"

Morris heaved a sigh. "Don't fit well with some people, especially when they find out a person's a half-breed. And they'll find out." He picked up the teacup and saluted Maggie. "Mighty fine brew, where'd you learn to make such good tea?"

Her index finger moved from her cup and pointed at John. The crinkles around her eyes deepened as her lips formed the familiar smile.

"What brings you over, Morris?" John said and stood to pour more tea.

"I'm on my way back to Nebraska City and I'll stay over a few days in Lincoln." He stopped as he heard his son directing the Hayman boys to care for the horses. "I'll go to the Pawnee Village from Lincoln on my return and help Evening Star and the boys bring back buffalo meat and hides from the hunt."

George came into the dugout with the boys in tow. "Father, what are you doing here?"

Morris stared at the handsome young man standing before him. "That's mighty proper, boy."

George laughed. "I'm taking lessons from John for proper use of the English language."

"I gotta get you back on the McFarland farm," he said and winked at John. He smiled and said, "I'm real proud of you, George."

Chapter 81

George McFarland quietly sat among the grasses at the marsh edge. He and John watched the small rodents, weaving through the barely visible trails. A dry, cool breeze from the northwest settled in the area for the past two days. After the heat of early August, they thanked the spirits for the respite from the Nebraska heat.

"John, do you believe in the God and his beloved son, Jesus, my parents tell us about?"

"Do they teach you about another?"

George pointed to the hawk diving toward the grassland on the southeast ridge. Flapping wings beat on the grass where it plunged into the mass of green and golden blades reaching toward the sun. "Mother teaches the ways of the old Pawnee, the spirits of the land, water, and sky." He stood and applauded the hawk taking flight with a large snake clamped firmly in its talons. The ensuing moments changed George's life. He looked at a familiar horse slowly walking along the north rise; the rider's body slumped over the saddle horn, gripping a whiskey jug.

John and George dashed across the prairie, grasses whipping against their leggings. The horse startled by them suddenly veered and stopped. Morris toppled to the turf, the jug disappearing from his hand into the bunchgrass surrounding the horse's lower legs.

Morris came to his knees, rocked side to side, and retched. Feebly he said, "Damn Sioux," and passed out.

"George, help me drape him over the saddle." John grabbed his friend by the shoulders and leaned Morris against his chest. Together they hoisted Morris over the saddle and led the tired horse to the corral.

Calvin came from the dugout with a book in hand and stared at the drunken Morris. "Dad, George, how can I help?"

"Fetch a bucket of water from the well," John said.

Joseph, clutching his mother's dress, stood in the doorway, his eyes fixed on this normally upright neighbor. "Is Mr. McFarland sick?"

"Very sick," George said to his little friend. "Morris took in too much firewater, which he's not used to."

Calvin, struggling with the bucket in two hands, plunked the three-quarters full container in front of his father.

"Thank you," John said, "step away from Morris." With a single motion, John lifted and poured the water on Morris' head.

The cool water shocked Morris awake. "What the dickens," he sputtered and stared at John, "why'd you do that?"

"To wake you and get you sober so we can figure why you're so drunk."

Morris sat up, the land spinning in front of him, and mumbled once again, "Damn Sioux."

Maggie came from the dugout with a wet rag and a dry towel. "Morris, let me wash your face."

He turned to her and nodded. "Thank you." Morris took the dry towel and wiped his face before saying, "She's dead; they're all dead." A sob shook his body.

After the evening meal, Morris sobered enough to make sense. They all sat in front of the dugout quietly watching clouds drift southeast into the darkening sky. A coyote dashed across the ridge in pursuit of an unseen rabbit.

"Over three hundred Pawnee went to the hunting grounds along the river that drains to Kansas. They had a successful hunt, but it all ended when a thousand Sioux massacred them on their return trip to the village. The last count maybe seventy Pawnee died, including Evening Star, Little Feather, and Hawk."

George placed his arm over Morris' shoulder. "Father," his voice broke, "they died doing what they loved and needed to do; it is better to die that way rather than from some white man's dreaded disease."

"What are you going to do?" Maggie asked.

"I don't know. I need time to heal."

"Father, I'll go with you." George stood to stretch and take some water from the refilled bucket. He handed Morris the ladle, "Drink, it will speed the recovery from the whiskey."

"How do you know this?" Morris took the water ladle from his son and drank.

"I learned this from the family to the east. Their father drinks too much … nearly all the time." George took the ladle from Morris and placed it on the bucket.

"You stay and help with the boys. I need to be alone. I'll heal." He shook his head. He picked at the dry grasses between his feet.

Coyotes began to yip and howl with the sun now well past setting and the marsh melting into the darkness. Suddenly they went quiet, capturing the prey they hunted.

Chapter 82

Late August changed rapidly from hot, searing days to torrential downpours, creating flash floods and filling the rainwater basins. After the skies cleared the muskrats turned to rebuilding and repairing their push-ups and feeding platforms. Many waterfowl species moved to shallower marshes in the acres surrounding the Hayman marsh. The adaptations of the creatures fascinated John; his naturalist enthusiasm carried over to George and Calvin. The two learned to keep records, just as John did, without him showing them how. Into the winter the weather turned dry and many of the non-migratory species returned to the large marsh, which offered better conditions than the semipermanent and seasonal marshes in the surrounding area.

The garden became the favorite place for Maggie and Joseph because the insects interested all, except for ones that mysteriously appeared in small numbers in August of 1873. When she first noticed these different grasshoppers, she drew John's attention to them. They watched as the insects busily deposited their eggs in the upland areas for six to eight weeks.

Maggie gave birth to the third son, Henry, in November and the clan gathered about her every day over the winter. Calvin, George, John, and even little Joseph handled all the chores because Maggie had a difficult time with the birth. She improved each week with the care extended by her sons, husband, and George, who seemed more like a Hayman than a McFarland. With her strength nearly recovered in the spring of 1874 she trekked to the marsh with the boys and John. They sat, appreciating the wildlife that survived the dry, mild winter. In May, she helped her men—as she called them—plant crops with Henry secured on her back on a board or bundled in furs.

John and Morris loaded the wagon with flour, freshly slaughtered beef, and clothing sewn by Maggie and Joseph. They drove north on an early September morning under a cloudless sky to deliver the wagon full of goods to the new rail line extending across northern Fillmore County. The Burlington and Missouri Railroad provided the two men with a diversion from Evening Star's death and the loss of Little Feather and Hawk. Morris continued healing, and he came often to see George and enjoy the Hayman boys growing into sturdy lads.

The assignment George got from Morris and John kept Calvin and Joseph busy. They had to repair the stones surrounding the well, mend the corral fence outside the animal dugout, and turn the garden where the plants died off. While Calvin worked the garden, he noticed the numerous grasshoppers. He dropped his spade and stooped to peer at the different type of grasshopper depositing eggs in the fallowed sod where spring crops stood. "Hey, George, come here—see what I found"

George shoved his spade in the sod and trotted to Calvin. A frown creased his brow. "Those all eggs?"

"Yep, these hoppers lay a whole lotta eggs. Gonna be a ton of them when they hatch in the spring."

"How do you know when they hatch?" George asked.

"I asked Dad and he spends a lotta time reading; he has a college education in science."

"No one mentioned your dad went to a college. That's impressive."

"Dad told me my grandpa's a minister."

"Really, no wonder you and Joe are so smart."

"Not any smarter than you. Evening Star and your brothers taught you a lot about how to live."

Maggie finished her inside cleaning where Calvin and Joseph slept. Henry sat in a small swing rigged from a ceiling beam, gumming a small piece of pemmican. After stacking the wood alongside the heating stove, that also acted as a cook stove, she pulled Henry from the swing and slipped a pair of moccasins on his small feet. Henry learned to stand and walk early and his curiosity had a tendency to get him into trouble or to wander off. As she stepped from the dugout to check on the three boys a swirling cloud on the east upland beyond the marsh caught her attention. She gasped at the sight.

George looked up and asked, "What's wrong, Maggie?"

"Look over yonder." She pointed east. "What are those?"

All three boys stared at the swarming mass. Calvin lifted his head topped with a mop of black hair. "I think they're what I read about in the Bible, Mother. They're called locusts in the Book of Exodus."

"And in the second Book of Chronicles," Joseph said.

Henry waved his pemmican at George and cooed.

George looked at the small boy holding out his arms and lifted him out of the seat and onto his shoulders. "See ... Henry, those are insects, and your brothers are educating me. But you and I like to play in the grass and explore the marsh waters." He grinned at Calvin and Joseph. "They like to read and write ... me ... I like to hunt and spear fish in the marsh."

Henry bounced up and down and pointed at the marshland area where few grasshoppers existed. Calvin swept him off George's shoulders and tossed him skyward.

"Little brother, I bet George is thinking about riding east to check on the sodbusters ... several miles that way."

George turned to him. A smile pulled his thin lips tight. "How'd you know?"

Calvin cleared his throat. "George, it ain't a secret; you're like a coyote on the prowl. When you see the sodbuster's daughters, especially the oldest, you go all funny."

George's dark eyes flashed a twinkle. "Think I'll saddle my horse and ride east to see how far the insect swarm takes me."

"Bet you get far enough east to spend time with the Logan girl," Calvin teased.

Maggie came from the dugout with a small sack of food. "Pemmican and bread for you ... be careful, George."

"I will." He filled his water bag and with a lively step moved to the corral. He saddled his horse and noticed the older Hayman boys chuckling about something. "What's so funny?"

"I wonder if you'll get back before dark," Calvin said.

George swung into the saddle, guided the horse out of the corral, and closed the gate. "I'll be back before the sun disappears behind the west ridge, I promise." He motioned to the upland above the dugouts with his hand.

"You'd better be back by then, George… or John and Morris will make you pay," Maggie said. She watched as he galloped up the ridge and disappeared, the insect swarm rose a minute after his passing from sight.

"You know Pa Logan doesn't like Indian mixed people," Calvin said. "He lost family down south when the Pawnee and Sioux killed along the Trail."

The first sign of dust to the north indicated someone approached the Hayman farm riding on more than horses. Henry sat by his mother in a small deer-hide swing John had constructed from willow limbs. Maggie brushed the hoppers from him when they popped up on his arms and legs. He would squeal with delight at the tickling and then scream when they nipped at his small limbs.

Dead hoppers, or what her sons called locusts, littered the area around her reed-woven chair. She watched her youngest son nod off and the drool land on his tummy. It became apparent she would have no more children, but she clung to a thin hope for several daughters. Maggie looked back at the rising dust and at the two men sitting tall on the wagon seat. The rattling wagon woke Henry, and he looked up at Maggie with a smile. "Dear little Henry, your father returns."

Compared to some farmers who came to the area in droves after the Homestead Act in 1862, Morris and John fared well. The distinct advantage came with understanding how to live with the land and not try to conquer it. The crops planted over the year consisted of wheat, oats, and barley. These crops did not demand the water corn needed for survival and good production. The two men wanted to raise corn, but the land they lived on better supported other crops and they made more from raising beef, carefully haying the uplands, and acting as guides for wealthy hunters wanting to bag game from the marshes.

After unhitching the horses and caring for them, they pushed the wagon to the reed hut, which remained part of the Hayman life. This simple hut housed Morris during his stays, which became more frequent.

Maggie said, "Good trip?"

"Excellent," John responded. Henry looked up at his father with sleepy blue eyes and held out his arms. "Dad-da, hold me."

Maggie gave Morris a hug and a peck on the cheek. "Are you hungry, Morris?" He nodded. "John?" He nodded and kissed Maggie on the lips. Henry wiggled into his mother's arms. The warm day triggered the grassland essence of aromatic prairie plants. From the marsh, the flapping of wings and quacks resonated up the slope to the dugout.

"Where're the boys?" John asked.

"Joseph and Calvin are inside. George went east, the boys said, to visit with the Logan gal."

"Damn," Morris said, "he's taken a likin' to that gal Shelly."

"What's wrong with that, Morris?" John asked.

Morris gave him a smirk. "John you're too innocent. Some people hate the breeds."

"Breeds, I don't understand?" John sighed.

"Not all white," Morris said with gritted teeth, "that's why Hawk and Little Feather liked the Pawnee village; still full Indian, although some Indians didn't like them boys any better than the whites." He pulled a pipe from his vest pocket, loaded it with tobacco, and lit the shredded leaves. When he finished lighting it, he carefully disposed of the match.

Small white clouds floated in from the northwest and a slight breeze turned to a cool wind. "When's George coming back?" John asked Maggie.

"He said before the sunset." Maggie slid Henry to her hip. "He wanted to find how far the grasshopper—the boys called them locusts—moved east or wherever."

"Locusts?" John asked.

"Yes, that's what they said. They've been studying your Bible, John."

Inside the dugout, Joseph and Calvin sat at the long table reading in an alternating pattern. "Your turn and then we discuss what we think it means," Joseph said.

Calvin stared at him. "You read to me the passage: *Ye have heard that it was aid of them of old time, Thou shalt not kill; and whosoever shall kill shall be in danger of the judgment.* Is that correct?"

Joseph nodded. "What do you think?"

"He whosoever kills, shall be judged by God in the final judgment, as predicted, even though the killer may be deemed innocent here on Earth," Calvin quoted.

Morris raised his eyebrows and stared at the two boys. "Who teaches you these passages?"

"We learned from Maggie and notes Dad made in his Bible. Want to see?" Joseph asked.

"I'll pass," Morris said.

"When did George say he would return?" John again asked with a hint of concern evident in his voice.

"Before sunset," Calvin replied.

Chapter 83

With the full moon lighting the marshland, Morris set out to find his son, for George hadn't appeared with the setting sun. After Morris' watch swept past midnight, he paced in front of the reed-thatched hut. At one o'clock he quietly saddled his horse and led it from the corral. As he turned to step into the stirrup, John emerged from the dugout.

"What do you think you're doing, Morris?"

"I'm going to find my only son left on this prairie. What're you doin' fully dressed?

John moved through the corral gate, placed a halter on the big, aging stallion, and plopped a saddle on the horse's back. Two black-crowned night herons swooped overhead, sailing into the big marsh to feed. "Morris, those birds taught my son's how to catch the big, green frogs—you know the fried legs you so enjoy." John tried to relieve some of the tenenesses in Morris.

The two trotted from the dugout area and south around the marsh. A full moon lit the bowl where the open water had evaporated to half its normal size. They didn't talk until they reined to a halt near Woman of the Grass' grave.

A splashing at the edge of the open water meant a prey probably died and the predator would survive another day. "Life and death, that's what the world's all about," Morris said and stood in the stirrups, scanning the eastern horizon. "I feel him calling, John."

"Which way?" John asked.

Morris pointed southeast. "Hurry, but I feel we're too late."

They rode for two hours around the big marshes east of the Hayman land.

The moon began to set, they lost good light, and the search became futile until the dawn. After dismounting they sat above a nearly dry seasonal wetland. The horses stayed in place with the dropped reins, which they learned early, during their breaking.

"That old stallion's still giving good service?"

John laughed and said, "Probably better than most men."

"How many colts you got outta him?"

John sat in the short grasses overlooking the marsh, thinking. "I'd say about ten or twelve."

Morris squatted beside John. "We've been together many a year. What say we start a store up north along the rail line? We can cut out the middleman and provide better for our boys." He tipped his hat back and scanned the dark environment around them.

"You make good sense, Morris."

"When we find George, we can take him back and talk with him, Maggie, and your boys." Morris sat back and held out his hand. They shook hands and agreed to pursue the business.

The men quietly sat for an hour listening to the frogs, herons, and coyotes. John stood, took the saddle off his stallion and placed it so he could comfortably recline to catch sleep until daybreak. Morris followed suit, internally pining for his remaining son.

At daybreak, both men jerked awake when the stallion snorted and nickered. A horse stood in the distant southeast horizon, a dirty yellow sky presented an ominous sign. The gray clouds hovered above the open sky like a cruel cap. The wind turned north, causing Morris to shiver. "I'm scared stiff, John. That's George's horse, right?" John nodded. "Somethin's wrong, somethin' bad happened to my last boy." The last words caught in his throat.

They saddled their horses and gently eased onto their backs. Even slowly approaching George's horse, it still backed away, eyes full of fear. It snorted at them and shook its head. "Whoa," John calmly said. He slowly moved the stallion forward while he softly talked to George's horse. "Whoa, you're gonna be okay." As he leaned down to catch a rein, he noticed blood on the horse's side. He plucked the other rein and moved back into a sitting position on the stallion. Blood sheen slicked the saddle. "Morris, start circling the wetland to the north. I'm going to find a place to picket the horse and I'll ride over to the small wetland to the southeast." He figured they were two miles from the Logan farm. An old willow, bare of leaves, provided a picketing post. John dropped to the ground, patted the horse, talking in a calm voice.

He stood with George's horse for several minutes then led the stallion along the edge of the small marsh looking for hoof prints. The sky, overcast with flat gray clouds, foreshadowed the cold weather to come. Morris reined up next to John and dismounted. Each man scanned the horizon and back to where they stood. The mare picketed below raised its head and whinnied. A woman rode toward them over the small rise.

"The Logan gal," Morris said.

They sat, keeping a tight rein on their animals as Shelly galloped toward them. When she stopped, they noticed her red-rimmed eyes.

"Thank God you showed." She looked over to George's horse. "I tried to catch it last night after it wandered onto the farm. It ran away and I couldn't follow for Pop got mad and made me come back home."

"Did George come to see you last evening?" Morris asked.

"Yes, we rode around the farm and he stopped to check on some hoppers. We spent all that time together until dusk settled on us."

"Shelly, you know Mr. Hayman?" Morris asked.

She nodded shyly. "Not well, but we've met."

John asked, "Did you go back to the farm after he left the area where you said goodbye?"

She answered, "Yes."

How long after did the horse come back to the farm?" John watched Shelly's face wrinkled with thought.

"I'd say about two hours. He headed off in that direction." She pointed north. "Has something happened to George?"

"I'm afraid so." John turned to look at Morris whose face looked like weathered salt block. "I found blood on the saddle and horse's front flank."

The Trial

Amos 5:24 (KJV)

But let judgment run down like waters,
and righteousness as a mighty stream.

Chapter 84

On the ride to the Fillmore County Courthouse John reminisced with Morris, his recollection of Illinois and Iowa had rapidly faded into the distant past, until now. Southeast of their dugouts the countryside gently turned to rolling cropland, incised by small drainages flowing toward Turkey Creek.

They had passed the area where Shelly had led them to several small basins so she and George could be alone. They had found his body in a stand of cattails ringing a small marsh almost devoid of water. John had ridden hard to Geneva to report the death to County Sheriff Alan Bentley.

"Most of the crops around here the locusts destroyed. I'm wondering why not the other plants?" Morris talked softly, still in mild shock over the total loss of his family. "One summer we had a small scourge of hoppers that preferred the succulent crops. Why …?"

Morris reined up and looked off toward the small community of Geneva. He shifted in the saddle and grinned at John. "We've come a long way, John." Tears welled in his eyes. "I need to say this… and don't deny what I say."

John started to talk and abruptly stopped. The old stallion stood quietly, as if he knew that John needed to pay attention to what Morris wanted and had to say. The air around them rustled the grasses along the rough road. The grassland smell returned to a normal freshness; the birds and microbes had gleaned the locust carcasses from the land. The honks of migrating geese filled the air, periodically interrupted by lowing cattle grazing on the semi-devastated pastureland.

Morris wiped the moisture from his eyes. "George loved you and Maggie. Many times, he talked of you like a father. He was different from his brothers. Hawk, he had the nomadic Indian blood. Little Feather, he had his mother's love for the Indian culture. But George, he had the love of the marshlands ... like you." He straightened his shoulders and groaned. "You talk with big words; George loved to use those words when he visited us at our farm. I know you learned them from your parents and in school. I hoped George would eventually become educated like you."

The stallion shifted and John shifted with him, sitting steady in the saddle. He turned so he could directly speak to Morris. The man's leathery face reminded him of his friend Alexander. "Morris, my heart bleeds for you. Every day I silently thank you for all you have done for me, Maggie, and my boys. You loved and cared for Evening Star and your boys; you have my admiration for persevering through these difficult times." He reached out and touched Morris on the shoulder. "It's time we take care of this trial, and put away the person or persons who killed George."

"Thanks, John. It'll be difficult being alone."

"You will not be alone, for Calvin will work your land with you and Joseph will be available at your call. You ... we can overcome and we will do so." They shook hands and reined their horses toward Geneva to meet with the Sheriff at the courthouse.

The Sheriff pointed to the two chairs across from his desk. Alan Bentley came to Geneva from Omaha, his reputation preceding him. The strapping young man stood erect until John and Morris sat. After they sat, he eased into his chair and eyed both men. "I think we have three men involved in your son's death, Mr. McFarland."

Morris leaned forward. "What do you mean, you think?"

John placed his hand on Morris' shoulder and drew him back.

"The men we have under suspicion drifted into town about two weeks before your son died." Sheriff Bentley glanced down at his large hands gently resting on the desktop. "Sir, we lack the gun that killed your boy. What we have is evidence from the hoof prints around the marsh. The only problem is ... who pulled the trigger."

John asked, "Why would these men come under suspicion?

"The three came up from Kansas and have a … dislike for white people with Indian blood."

"Sheriff," Morris blurted out, "how would these men know George had Indian blood if they're strangers to the area?"

"That puzzles me, sir." He paused, being careful about what he wanted to say. "The only suggestion I can offer, someone pointed to your son as being of mixed blood."

"You have any suspicions of the person or persons who told these men about George's heritage?" John watched Sheriff Bentley lean back in his chair, an air of confidence on his face.

"I do." He lit a small cigar retrieved from his middle desk drawer.

Chapter 85

The trial began one month, to the day, after Morris and John met with Sheriff Bentley. Two of the men remained in the county jail awaiting trial in front of twelve men, which consisted of four Geneva residents and the rest from the surrounding countryside. The county building housed the courtroom on the main floor across from the county offices. The adjacent jail building housed the prisoners. The month being January, the weather ran the normal cold and windy with temperatures rising and falling daily between highs in the forties and lows in the single digits.

Morris and John, called as witnesses, braved the early morning wind and occasional snow showers. The temperature hovered near twenty-seven degrees with the wind steadily blowing from the northeast at nearly twenty miles per hour. The two men huddled in the wagon seat covered by old wool blankets Morris found in Lincoln before the tragedy of losing his wife and two sons. The scarves wrapped around their faces protected all but their eyes, which both men dabbed at with their wool gloves. The horse, belonging to Morris, trotted at a good pace, not bothered by the cold and the snow flurries. Small vapor clouds formed above the horse's nostrils as it trotted over the hard road.

On arrival in Geneva, John guided the horse to the livery and instructed the stable hand to keep the horse covered and provide it with hay and oats. They walked to the town square and entered the courthouse to find the Sheriff waiting in front of the courtroom.

"Gentlemen," the Sheriff said, "we have a witness stating the two detainees had been at the same marsh where you found your son, but at a different time." He looked at Morris. "This changes the entire court proceeding and we might have to drop the charges. Our case, as we previously discussed, is under negotiation with the prisoner's lawyer as we speak." He led them to a small room across the hall from the courtroom where they could wait. "Make yourselves comfortable. It'll be an hour before we hold the trial, if at all.

"What the devil ... I don't understand this whole mess," Morris said.

John shook his head. "Someone ... we don't know who jumped in at the last moment... I wonder..."

They both quietly sat deep in thought. Finally, John said, "You once mentioned that Shelly's family didn't like *breeds*?"

"I might have. Why?"

"Maybe someone in the county who knows you and your family talked to the Logan clan about George. The witness might be a Logan." John studied Morris' face for some reaction. "Could it be Shelly?"

Morris' shocked reaction turned to pain. "Why would she do something like that? George often talked of her and how they enjoyed being together." His frown deepened. "What makes you think that?"

"The day Shelly led us to the wetlands made me wonder about her leading us around the countryside. I've been thinking about that day and how she eventually led us to the small marsh ... right to the body."

The lapse in conversation left the room quiet except for murmurs in a room beside them. Morris pulled his pipe and tobacco from his vest pockets and filled the bowl. A match appeared in his hand and he dragged it across a spot on the wooden table where others had done the same. He puffed at the flame directly above the pipe until a thick blue haze floated from his mouth. He blew out the match and dropped it in a spittoon next to the table leg. "She did seem kinda nervous."

Scuffling and shuffling feet next door caught their attention and the Sheriff abruptly appeared. "The jury's going in for the trial. The judge decided to let the jury hear the evidence and render the decision." He caught the look between John and Morris. "Chances are not too good we'll win this one. Sorry, but there's still hope ... you never know what will happen with juries."

The judge appeared after the room quieted and the jury filed in from a side entrance. The bailiff made the announcement and the judge, in a black, flowing robe, signaled for them to sit.

"Would the prosecution please call the first witness?" The judge looked at the local county attorney.

"The county calls Mr. John Hayman."

John stood tall and straight as he walked to the witness box to take the oath. It took only a few minutes to question him about his identity, location, and what happened on the day they found George. John explained, "We got concerned about George not returning to my farm, so Morris," he nodded toward his friend, "and I decided to ride to the Logan farm, for we knew Shelly and George often spent time together."

The attorney asked, "Did you discover his body on your own?"

"No sir, we met up with Shelly Logan before we got to her place."

"How did she seem that day?"

John looked to where Shelly sat with her father and one of her brothers. "She seemed upset, very upset."

"Did you wonder why?"

"We visited and I figured she became upset because of her concern about George's horse appearing on the farm and running off."

"Mr. McFarland with you that evening?"

John nodded.

"Please answer so the court has a verbal response to the question," the judge said.

"Yes, sir ... and yes."

"Did either you or Mr. McFarland remove your guns?" The attorney turned to face Morris.

"No," John answered.

"Did either of you fire your guns that day?"

"No, sir."

"Shelly had no gun that you noticed."

"No."

"That's all for Mr. Hayman, your honor." The attorney called Morris to the stand and went through the same questions. He varied the questions only slightly and changed the order. The attorney dismissed Morris and said, "Your honor, I call Shelly Logan to the stand."

The judge sat straight and uttered, "You sure you want to do this?"

The county attorney nodded and called her name. Shelly Logan unsteadily walked to the witness box and gingerly sat. "Shelly, you're what we call a hostile witness. That means you're a witness for the defense and would not normally testify until the defense calls you. Do you understand?"

Tears welled in the young woman's eyes; she nodded, and added, "He said you might do this."

"Who's he?"

"The men's attorney," she said, looking at the defense table.

"You heard the testimony of Mr. Hayman and Mr. McFarland?" She nodded.

The judge signaled to the court recorder to write a yes.

"Shelly, I'm going to be direct. Would either of these men kill George?"

"Objection!" the defense attorney yelled and stood, lividly staring at the county attorney.

"Overruled," the judge said, "Shelly, please answer."

"No ... Mr. McFarland loved George."

"And would Mr. Hayman have shot George?"

Shelly gasped and blurted out, "Dear God, no. George loved Mr. Hayman and always talked nothin' but good about him."

"Shelly, I have one final question; I want you to answer only yes or no." He stood for a moment and then asked, "Did your father and your brother, who is present here today, approve of your relationship with George?"

The defense attorney bolted out of his chair and raced toward the judge screaming, "Objection ... objection!"

The judge's face turned crimson. "Sit down," he emphatically stated, staring at the defense attorney. He let the disturbance pass for a moment and turned to Shelly. "Please answer yes or no, Shelly"

"No." Shelly wiped a tear from the corner of her eye.

"Thank you," the county attorney followed with, "no other witnesses."

"Thank you, Shelly, you may go back to your seat." He turned to the defense attorney. "Please call your witnesses."

The defense attorney, a swarthy looking man from Omaha, stood and approached the bench. "Your Honor, I have only one witness now that the prosecution called one of my witnesses. I call Mr. Harold Logan."

Harold Logan stood and marched to the stand, sitting down with a thump after being sworn in. He scowled at John and especially at Morris.

After taking Harold through the usual introduction, the defense attorney asked, "Mr. Logan, do you know the two men at the defense table."

"I do."

"In what capacity?"

Harold frowned at him and asked, "Whadda ya mean?"

"How did you come to know them?"

"Huh?" Harold's neck turned tight, the cords protruding from under his buttoned shirt.

"How did you meet them and did you make any deals with them?" The attorney turned to the men at the table. He turned back to his witness.

"I met them coupla months ago, I think." He chewed on the inside of his cheek. "I met 'em in at the livery the first time and only said hello. And asked where they came from."

"Where did you next meet these men?" the defense attorney asked.

"I met 'em at the tavern; I went to get me a bottle."

"Were you drinking ... or they?"

"Huh?"

"Were you drunk, or were they?"

Harold looked at him with surprise. "Nah, we talked, had a few shots, and played cards."

"Clarify what you mean by shots."

A laugh erupted from Harold. "Shots of whiskey, you never heard of that?" One of the jurors chuckled and stopped when the judge looked his way.

"You weren't good friends, I take it." The defense attorney grinned at the prosecution table members.

"Nah, we just played cards ..." Harold looked at Morris, then to the two men on trial. "Maybe they got mad when I won more than they did." He smacked the witness rail and laughed.

"That's all the questions for Mr. Logan."

The county attorney moved swiftly to the witness stand. "Mr. Logan, I have one question." He paused and turned to look at Shelly. "Did you ever tell Shelly you wanted her to no longer fraternize with George McFarland?"

"Huh," Harold frowned, "what the hell ya mean?"

The attorney said, "Sorry. Did you tell your daughter never to see George McFarland again?"

"Nah," Harold looked at his daughter, "not once."

"So, someone lies. That is all the questions I have." The county attorney returned to his table.

Harold stepped down and when he passed the defense attorney he winked. Several jurors shifted uncomfortably when they saw the wink.

"As you have no other witnesses—"

The defense attorney interrupted. "I have one more, Sheriff Alan Bentley."

Bentley's head shot up and his dark eyes burned like two hot coals.

The judge sighed and motioned Alan to approach. The bailiff swore in the Sheriff and motioned him to the stand.

"Sheriff, I'm dispensing with the background because we know you … and know you as an upstanding law enforcement official."

Bentley bit his lower lip and remained quiet.

"On what evidence did you base your arrest?" The defense attorney turned to the look at John and Morris.

"I gathered evidence at the scene, which included drawings of hoof prints from horses that had recently been in the area where Mr. Hayman and Mr. McFarland found the body."

"And what did you find?"

"One horse had an unusual crack in the shoe. The other had an interesting pattern of several missing shoe nails."

"What made you arrest these two men?"

"I stopped at the livery and asked the stable hands, and the farrier, if they had seen the unusual shoes."

"Had they?"

Sheriff Bentley said, "Yes."

"There are three men who run together, why not arrest all three?"

"No evidence he was in the area."

"One more question." A dramatic pause and the attorney said, "Do you have the murder weapon, and only answer yes or no."

Bentley stared at the attorney for two beats and said, "No."

"Thank you, Sheriff." He smirked and returned to his table.

The jury returned an hour later with a not guilty verdict.

Chapter 86

After the trial, life returned to normal for the Hayman clan and improved for Morris. The family joy came when Morris helped a widow on the bordering farm manage her crops and finances. Her husband died suddenly from a farm accident, and she had no time to deal with the everyday demands of such large holdings that her husband amassed.

Both he and the woman decided to live together until she found a place in Fairmont or Sutton to continue with her life. When Morris introduced Rachel Hobbs Whitlock to Maggie, John, and the Hayman boys, the youngest named Henry immediately stole her heart. Each Sunday the Haymans, Morris, and Rachel alternated church service at their homes. John did not take part in the readings and studies. He had yet to find the same feelings for the Christian faith.

Sunday mornings John trekked to the marshes, holding to his routine of collecting information on native plants and animals. Never did he pluck a rare plant from the soil where he found it. The common plants and variants he pressed and dried to store in his collections, which he protected from insects and rodents with metal cases that cost him dearly. But cost did not deter him for he used the income from easterners wanting to hunt the wetlands. Every Sunday he paid homage to Woman of the Grass and the spirits protecting her soul.

One episode that drew him closer to the God he once knew occurred when a storm raged onto the grasslands from the north on a March day in 1881. That day he lost his wife, Maggie. She did not die that he knew; Maggie simply disappeared during or after the storm. She had bundled warmly, but young Henry could not remember if she carried anything to provide for a long and arduous hike in such harsh weather.

The first clue she might be alive came the next month when John and Morris delivered salted pork and fresh-ground cornmeal to Grafton and Sutton.

"Mr. Hayman, the doc wants to see you as soon as possible," the boy helping unload said.

"You know what he wants?"

"Nope," he answered and continued with his task of unloading.

Morris said, "Rachel wants me to pick up some bolts of cloth from back east. I'll do that while you visit with the doc."

John walked to the doctor's office located on the second floor of a frame building a block north of the railroad. The office occupied half of the top floor, consisting of a reception area, two exam rooms, and an emergency room for nonlife-threatening accidents. The receptionist and a nurse helped the doctor during the weekdays.

"Good day, Mr. Hayman," the receptionist said. "The doctor is with a patient and should be with you shortly." She went back to her work after giving him a pleasant smile.

After a five-minute wait, "John, the doctor will see you in exam room two." The doctor's nurse pointed to the room and turned to the receptionist to check the schedule. A dark-haired woman came from exam room one. She caught his attention, for she reminded him of Chirt: tall, lean, and very attractive.

A smile lit her face when she noticed him. "Aren't you John Hayman?"

He paused at the exam room door. "I am."

She held out her hand. "I'm Hannah ... Hannah Abernathy. I've always wanted to meet the person I hear so much about. You have a reputation, you know."

Doctor James Smith popped out of exam room one and said, "John, come in here. The nurse can take the next patient to the other room." He waved at John with impatience.

John looked into Hannah's dark-brown eyes and melted. "Sounds like the doctor wants to speak," he said, "I hope we can talk sometime."

"We will," she said and walked from the exam area.

"John, you met Miss Abernathy, she's the new librarian ... and teacher at the grade school."

The fine perfume Hannah wore floated in the room, not overpowered by the medicinal smells. "I did and I'm impressed we have a new educator and librarian in Sutton." He watched the doctor pull a greenback from his hip pocket.

Doctor Smith handed it to John and pointed to the upper right corner with the name written above the pictured woman. In scribbled writing, a name stuck out: Maggie. "Turn it over. Look carefully at the word; I believe it says ... *help*."

John peered at the bill. "I know it's her."

"The man I treated said he got into a row with a scoundrel at the train station in Fairmont. The bill came from the man who cut him, but no woman was with him." Dr. Smith allowed John time to study the greenback. "I sent a telegraph message describing Maggie to a constable in Fairmont. Here's his reply."

John slowly opened the telegraph paper and studied it. "Oh ... God, help her if she's alive."

Chapter 87

His frame house melted into the countryside. John Hayman believed in creating the least disturbance in a natural area, keeping the land as natural as when he found it in 1855. The three sons grew into men; all his sons were educated in the Grafton Schools. His eldest son, Calvin, went on to the University in Lincoln to study business. Joseph, his second son, traveled east to study for the seminary and Henry … Ah yes, Henry.

Henry stayed with his father helping with the crops and learning from John. Both thirsted for knowledge and Hannah slaked that thirst as an educator and librarian. Henry adored Hannah, as John had Chirtlain. Knowing Hannah would care for his father, Henry left for the east coast.

The coming years found Henry immersed in his education where his grandfather started, Yale. From Yale, Henry attended school at Cornell and earned a degree in conservation and business. He yearned for the marshes of Nebraska and returned, after traveling the eastern shores of the United States.

The Hayman family would continue in Nebraska as Henry settled in Clay County near a large, semi-permanent marsh inherited from the Hayman & McFarland Land Company. He continued to help his father at the Hayman marsh and grasslands.

In 1899, after living a prosperous and fulfilling life, John died while sitting on the porch watching the marsh animals he enjoyed. The three boys gathered to bury John in the family graveyard directly across the marsh from the Woman of the Grass. After the burial, the three boys talked of why their father never returned to his roots in Illinois. Would they ever learn of their grandfather and grandmother? And their mother?

The Discovery

William Shakespeare (1564–1616), British dramatist, poet.

1st Stranger, in Timon of Athens, act 3, sc. 2, l. 86-7.

Men must learn now with pity to dispense,

For policy sits above conscience.

Waterfowl, waterfowl, they coat the sky, God's dappled canvas. A white pickup travels the south section line, a trail of dust billowing skyward and drifting into space to settle in the field sitting idle until the owner begins spring planting. The familiar decal makes it clear that it's the US Fish and Wildlife Service personnel. This morning the personnel look for ducks and geese dying, or have died, from fowl cholera. My olfactory memory of the 1970s outbreak remains: a nauseating smell of burned feathers and charred waterfowl carcasses.

A lanky, bearded man steps from the passenger side of the pickup and begins a methodical scan of the basin. He halts, slowly moves the binoculars back and forth, lowers it, and says something to the driver. After the pause, the binocular follows the scanning path he began. Fifteen minutes of observation and he allows the simple tool to dangle from his neck. A cup appears and a steam wisp rises from the fluid into the calm air where the man rests against the club cab. He turns to talk to the driver and looks to where I stand and waves. They know to expect me at this time of the year. The coffee drinker pumps his arm up and down three times, signaling three dead birds; these three dead birds died from innumerable possibilities.

These men always come back, don the breast waders, and collect the dead. Their mission: to inspect and ensure the cause of death—I hope—rules out cholera.

The vehicle continues along the section line and disappears after an hour of inspection. I glance down at my watch; I'm expecting the governor's aide or aides to meet me with the message about the marshes. Over the past decade, my patience with the bureaucracy shortens. The entire federal government has become bloated and, being the cynic, I have concluded all government growth breeds mediocrity.

I stand beside my pickup, becoming more impatient with each passing minute. To calm myself I grab my binoculars from the seat and scan the birds settling back on the marsh below me. As I pan past the northwest edge I spot a black SUV racing along the gravel road. The speed seems a bit careless for our roads in Fillmore County, but—what the heck—they are the government. I focus on the brand and grunt. It's a Cadillac Escalade SUV. As the vehicle comes closer, I note the state license plate. The number is '1' and I wonder … could it be?

I can see the sunglasses; these glasses her trademark. There's only one person … it's the Nebraska governor. I've not seen Sue Rademacher since our thirtieth high school reunion. Sue left Fillmore County to attend the University in Lincoln. She graduated with an MBA—high distinction—and went on to earn a law degree from Iowa University. I can forgive her for the latter.

The black Caddy slows and turns into the Hayman Cemetery. She pushes her sunglasses up and into her hair. The door flies open and she steps out. Sue drops her governor persona and walks toward me, holding out her arms. Always an impeccable dresser, she now looks as I remember her long ago in the spring chill: blue jeans and a flannel shirt.

"Who're you expecting?" she laughs as we hug. "You're as you always are, Chance: lean, mean, and standing in a gorgeous scene. She turns from my arms and watches the waterfowl display.

"And to what do I owe the honor of having the governor drive out to meet a lowly taxpayer idling away time in the sticks?" I smile and look at wisps of her auburn hair tousled by the breeze.

"These are not sticks; this is my … your home." She motions for me to climb into my pickup.

"Rather classless for the governor."

"Damn it, Chance, drop the bull and get in the damn pickup. We need to talk."

I ask, "Why not in the beauty you're driving."

"I'd be out of place with you in the Gov's toy." She reaches into the Escalade and pulls out a thermos and two cups. "Now get your fanny inside and let's enjoy a cuppa, joe."

We climb into my dusty pickup and wait to talk until Sue serves the coffee.

I sip and say, "Very good." she places the closed thermos between us. "The staff … made this?"

"Geez, what sandbur got up …" she sighs.

My grin makes her trail off. "I remember when we dated in high school and I came to your farm. You made the best damn coffee in the county."

"Thank you, that is nice. We did have a good time together. Too bad we went separate ways." She closely studies me. "I like the graying in your dark hair. You turned out to be quite handsome. Karin must have been proud to take your arm."

I look out the windshield at my wife's gravestone. "Karin. A highly intelligent woman … beauty and personality to match … like the lady sitting beside me."

"Chance, you embarrass me." A blush kisses her cheeks.

"I mean it, Sue. You're a great person and an excellent governor; that comes from a person not enamored with what's happening in this country." She starts to say something and I stop her. "I'm concerned about what's happening with agriculture, our water, and health."

She looks serious. "So am I." Her coffee finished, she offers more. While Sue pours, she says, "I need your help." With the thermos placed firmly on the floor, Sue continues. "The environmental agency director came to me with a discovery made by one of the department biologists. The information comes from the department files, an early wetlands study." My clenched jaw makes her pause. "What is it?"

"I'm not sure about your environmental agency. I see these marshes still disappearing under the guise of feeding the world. The big wetlands will survive, but the small ones—necessary to fit with the larger ones—deserve restoration and protection, at an accelerated pace."

"Always an impatient man, Mr. Hayman, and I see nothing changes."

"Thank you," I say. "Continue, Sue … uh … Governor."

"Don't be a bombastic ass." She smiles. "I come here because the discovery happens to affect what concerns you, at least with wetlands." She touches my arm. "If these infra-red photos prove the hypotheses accurate we might … and I stress might … restore many of the smaller wetlands about which you have concern. We now have better diagnostic tools to analyze wetlands covered by land leveling in the 1950s. We'll face a challenge, like scaling Mt. Everest, but we will persevere."

"What can I do to help?"

"Now … that's the Chance Hayman I know."

Afterword

Undertaking this historical novel, at times, almost overwhelmed me. Why? The reasons are many. There's a plethora of written work available for background, ensuring relevance of the material for the Hayman family saga and theme. Most disconcerting in the background work are conflicts among historians discussing the same issues and areas. But these historical conflicts made me better understand present conflicts that will become history.

When I started this saga, I wanted to begin in Iowa, but Abner (the enigma) drew me into a longer than planned journey. So, I let him take the reins because I needed him to shape "The Naturalists."

Little historical material exists on the natural resources of the Rainwater Basin area until the University developed the grassland mentality from such great men as Weaver and Clements. The Fillmore County area comes from my memory and studies when I worked for the Nebraska environmental agency. I became acutely aware, by 1980, of the need to join in the movement to bring focus to disappearing wetlands and the quality of those remaining. I met some dedicated and understanding people working very hard to save what we had in the 1970s and 1980s. To those—some living and some not—thank you for your hard and untiring work to preserve the wetlands.

You will find a bibliography of many documents easily attainable from the Internet. I did not list all sources because it would overwhelm the reader. Second, I left out some to tickle your curiosity and hope you want to delve into the novel theme, the wetlands, and our history.

C. G. Haberman

The Naturalists **List of Characters**

Alderman, George, Grace, and sons – Reformed Church members

Bentley, Alan – Fillmore County Sheriff

Bishop, Ty – Preble County banker

Byrnes, Bridgette and Timothy – St. Mary's residents who take in Mercy and John

Carnes, Samuel – Public lands broker and entrepreneur

Deirks, Calvin – Church elder

Deirks, Matthew, Luke, Esau – Calvin's sons

Grossman, Dr. Sidney – New Westville physician

Guthrie, HW – Preble County Sheriff

Hartman, Walter and sons – north Preble County residents

Hayman, Abner – John Hayman's father

Hayman, Aletha – Abner and Mary's daughter

Hayman, Jeremiah – Abner and Mary's son

Hayman, John Edmund – Abner and Mary's son

Hayman, Mercy Ann – Abner and Mary's daughter

Hayman, Mary Schmidt – John Hayman's mother

Heidt, Josiah – Senior Pastor of Abner's first congregation

Heidt, Rebecca – Josiah's wife

Heidt, Obadiah and Job – Josiah and Rebecca's sons

Hoester, Maggie – John's wife

Higgins, Robert (Dob) – Hotel employee

Holtz, Abby – congregation member and friend of the Haymans

Kranz, Carter – blacksmith

Kreulfs, Chris – North Preble County settler

Kreulfs, Chirtlain (Chirt) – Chris Kreulfs daughter

Kreulfs, Susanna – Chirt's mother

Logan, Harold – farmer east of the Hayman land

Logan, Shelly – Harold Logan's oldest daughter

Luther - Surveyor

McFarland, George – Youngest son of Morris McFarland

McFarland, Hawk – Middle son of Morris McFarland

McFarland, Little Feather – Oldest son of Morris McFarland

McFarland, Morris – Wandering frontiersman

Rademacher, Sue – Nebraska governor

Schmidt, Hilmar – Mary's father

Schneider, Abram – Carter Kranz woodworker employee

Schroeder, Alexander – deacon and friend of Samuel Carnes

Schroeder, Nettie – wife of Alexander

Evening Star – Morris McFarland's Pawnee wife

Thomas, Judith and Richard – Stagecoach passengers

Troester, A. – Roaming minister of question

Weber, Hans, Lucinda, & daughter Callie – New Westville banker and family

Whitlock, Rachel Hobbs – farm widow living next to Morris

Woman of the Grass – Oto tribe elder who walks away from the reservation

Carnes stagecoach and buggy drivers:

> Pennsylvania: Williams, Billy; Smith, Johnnie; Bachmeier, Theophilus
>
> Ohio: Cyrus and Zach
>
> Ohio: Last leg to New Westville: Lothrop, Darius and Means, Josh

Partial list of Background Research for the Naturalists (Vol. 1)

Allen, Joel A. History *American bison <u>Bison americanus</u>*. [Extracted from the ninth annual report of the survey, for the year 1875.] Retrieved from Google Play books, My Books file

Andreas, Alfred T. 1882 *History of the State of Nebraska* Online Edition Retrieved from http://www.kancoll.org/books/andreas_ne/hon_tabl.html

Bates, Samuel B. 1887 *History of FRANKLIN COUNTY, PENNSYLVANIA, containing 'a history of the county, its townships, towns, villages, schools, churches, industries, etc.; portraits of early settlers and predominant men; biographies; history or Pennsylvania; statistical and miscellaneous matter, etc., etc.* Retrieved from Google Play books, My Books file

Curley, Edwin A. 1875 *Nebraska its advantages, resources, and drawbacks. Illustrated.* Retrieved from Google Play books, My Books file

Cutler, J. 1812 *Topographical description of the state of Ohio, Indiana Territory, and Louisiana. Comprehending the Ohio and Mississippi rivers, and their principal tributary streams: -the face of the country, soils, waters, natural productions, animal, vegetable, and mineral; towns, villages, settlements and improvements: and a concise account of the Indian tribes west of the Mississippi. - To which is added, an interesting journal of Mr. Chas. le Raye, while a captive with the Sioux nation, on the waters of the Missouri river.* Retrieved from Google Play books, My Books file

Farritor, Shawn J. 2009 *End of Pawnee Starlight* Xlibris Corporation

Fillmore County Nebraska 1918 Soils Map Retrieved from http://soils.usda.gov/survey/online_surveys/nebraska/

Gilmore, Melvin R 1991 *Uses of Plants by the Indians of the Missouri River Region* / forward by Hugh Cutler; Illustrations by Bellamy Parks Jansen—Enlarged Edition. University of Nebraska Press

Gregg, Thomas 1880 *History of Hancock County, Illinois: Together with an Outline History of the State, and a digest of State Laws, Volume* Retrieved from Google Play books, My Books file

Herman, John 1834 Reformed Church in the United States. Ohio Synod Retrieved from Google Play books, My Books file

Herndon, Sarah R. 1902 D*ays on the Road Crossing the plains in 1865* Retrieved from Google Play books, My Books file

Herrick, Francis H. 1917 *Audubon the Naturalist A history of his life and time* Retrieved from Google Play books, M

Howe, Henry 1908 *Historical Collections of Ohio in two volumes An encyclopedia of the state: history both general and local, geography with descriptions of its counties, cities and villages, its agricultural manufacturing, mining and business development, sketches of eminent and interesting characters, etc., with notes of a tour over it in 1888 1865*1Retrieved from Google Play books, My Books file

Hulbert, Archer B. 1902 *Historic highways of America Vol. 2* Retrieved from Google Play books, My Books file

Hulbert, Archer B. 1906 *The Ohio River, A Course of Empire* Retrieved from Google Play books, My Books file

Iowa, Map of 1855 Published by E. Mendenhall Cincinnati, Ohio Retrieved from http://www.iowadot.gov/maps/msp/historical.html

Jeffords, Christine (Date unknown) *An essay "GET OFF MY LAND!" How Settlers Settled It, Claimed It and Fought Over It.* Retrieved from http://freepages.genealogy.rootsweb.ancestry.com/~poindexterfamily/ChristinesPages/Land1.html

Kindscher. Kelly 1987 *Edible Wild Plants of the Prairie An Ethnobotanical Guide* University Press of Kansas

Kindscher. Kelly 1992 *Medicinal Wild Plants of the Prairie an Ethnobotanical Guide* University Press of Kansas

Lowry R. E. 1915 *History of Preble County Ohio her people, industries and institutions.* Retrieved from Google Play books, My Books file

M'Cauley, I. H. 1878 *Franklin County, Pennsylvania. Prepared for the centennial celebration. Held at Chambersburg, Pa., July 4. 1876.* Retrieved from Google Play books, My Books file

Middleton G. A. T. 1902 *Surveying and surveying instruments* 2nd Ed. Retrieved from Google Play books, My Books file

Sacred Pawnee Bundle Retrieved from http://www.kshs.org/p/sacred-pawnee-bundle/10118

Sheldon, Addison Erwin. 1913 *History and Stories of Nebraska* The University Publishing Co. Retrieved from http://www.olden-times.com/oldtimenebraska/n-csnyder/nbstory/nbstory.html

Unknown 1880 *The history or Darke county, Ohio, containing A History of the County; its Cities, Towns, etc.; General and Local Statistics; Portraits of Early Settlers and Prominent Men; History of the Northwest Territory; History of Ohio; Map of Darke County; Constitution of the United States, Miscellaneous Matters, Etc., etc.* Retrieved from Google Play books, My Books file

Unknown 1881 *Fremont County, Iowa, containing a history of the county, its cities, towns, etc. a biographical directory of many of its leading citizens, war record of its volunteers in the late rebellion, general and local statistics, portraits of early settlers and prominent men, history of Iowa and the northwest, map of Fremont county, constitution of the state of Iowa, reminiscences, miscellaneous matters, etc.* Retrieved from Google Play books, My Books file

Unknown 1879 *The History of Lee County, Iowa, A Biographical Directory of Citizens, War Record of its Volunteers in the late Rebellion, General and Local Statistics, Portraits of Early Settlers and Prominent Men, History of the Northwest, History of Iowa, Map of Lee County, Constitution of the United States, Miscellaneous Matters.* Retrieved from Google Play books, My Books file

NOTE: All the Nebraska background studies used are too numerous to list here. Information for each part of *The Naturalists* can be gleaned from the Internet at: the Nebraska Historical Society, various libraries (such as the New York City Library), and the Universities in all the States mentioned in the novel. You can contact the author at his website if you desire further information about the Nebraska areas depicted in the novel.

Thank you for purchasing, and reading *The Naturalists, A Historical Novel of the Hayman Family.*

Read on for a brief excerpt from

The Naturalists
Volume 2

C. G Haberman

New Light

THURSDAY EVENING STARTED AS USUAL and would likely end as usual. I am well on my way to a tannin headache. A weakness of mine for a long time, red wine. I consume too much with a longtime friend, Ed Carpas, who meets me at the local pub where they serve meals that demand vintage wine from California's Sonoma Valley. Our evening dress consists of jeans and rolled up long-sleeved shirts. No ball caps.

Tonight, a heated discussion begins on the federal farm bill and it rapidly becomes clear we won't agree. We agree to disagree and move on to focus where we might do some good; that is, an honest candidate for the open Congressional seat.

Carl Joyce recently returned from Washington after resigning his long-held seat in the U.S. House of Representatives for the state's vast third district. We have yet to hear from him. Ed and I always enjoyed Carl's company in this old business with worn wood floors, dim light, and hushed voices.

"So," Ed says, with a faint smirk on his wine-stained lips, "we have two Democrats and umpteen Republicans wanting that seat. Who do you think should represent us?" The smirk fades and changes to a full-blown grin.

"There's only one choice ... my neighbor down the road."

"Come on," Ed grabs his teetering half-full wineglass, "he's nothing but a pain in the rear and wants nothing more than to go back to the pre-irrigation days. Towns and the counties surrounding us, and those all the way to the Colorado and Wyoming borders, will never elect him." Ed waves to the waitress for another bottle of red wine as he drains his glass. "He wouldn't survive the agricultural communities' onslaught. There'd be attacks by folk who remember the *Buffalo Commons* proposal, if that's what you call such irrationality."

My mind races over faded memory banks and screeches to a halt at that inane idea. Some *back-east* professors wanted to make a national, open-range bison park for the western third of Nebraska, plus all other prairie states from Mexico to Canada.

Ed finishes his thought. "That'd doom your neighbor."

I chuckle after I down the last swallow of wine. "My guess ... he'd piss off everyone, but it might evoke some good conversation. There'd be a buzz in the pubs and coffee shops across this district like never before." I slid my empty glass toward him.

"Yeah … and bring every dude with a 30.06 rifle to his campaign stops."

The red wine pleasantly sits on my tongue. "Okay, I give up. But we can't keep on like we are … or we'll see the land and crop prices drop. Mark my word that will bring more land-use abuse. And the remaining wetlands gone forever, unless …"

Ed stares past me and waves at someone entering the bar. "I can't argue with you on those points. We can start by working with the local state legislators. And you can run for the opening on the conservation district board."

A minute later I find out who roused Ed's wave. *The Rural County News* editor sidles over with another bottle of red wine. He's all we need to keep a semi-surly conversation going. Alan Hammerschmidt carries three menus with him to the dining area where Ed and I often feast on pasta. The editor does not keep with the current trend of staying in shape. He smokes, drinks, and carries an extra fifty pounds on his less than the six-foot frame.

"Gentlemen, nice spring evening. What's new with you two world-problem solvers?" Alan parks his ample body on the sturdiest chair.

"Oh sure, the editor fishes for a story," Ed replies.

Alan ignores the comment and peers at me over his sweat-stained glasses. "I want to know how you're doing with the save the planet approach? I hear the governor visited you a coupla weeks past."

I glance at my longtime friend; his straight face focuses on me. "There're no secrets in the rural Nebraska setting where I live, sheesh." Every three months the editor drops by to dine with the two of us. We discuss newsworthy items with Alan and he later develops stories to his liking. To his liking means stories to sell papers.

"Allow me to follow up on the question about the governor's visit," Alan says. He waits for a signal to move forward.

Three weeks had passed since the governor sat in my pickup, talking about the discovery of 1970s infrared aerial photography in the Rainwater Basin. After that meeting, I left with a smidgen of hope for wetland protection and restoration, and with the question of how I could help her. She said someone from the environmental agency would contact me. Two weeks, damn it, two weeks before someone called. They said they would get back to me. Another week slipped away and no word from the agency, further inflaming my thoughts about government agencies.

"No news. They said they would get back to me." I scan the menu, knowing I'll not venture from my usual order.

Alan cocks an eyebrow and says, "What about cancer?"

Ed bristles. "A rumor, that's all it is; at least, what I know."

The waitress brings Alan a glass and uncorks his wine bottle. "You guys are fountains of information." He waits for the wine to breathe before pouring. "You know Walter Armstead?" He waits. No response, so he continues. "While ferreting out stories, I decided to stop to visit with Walt." To Ed, he says, "You know him?"

"I do, he's a wealth of historical knowledge, if you keep him focused. He has fewer and fewer clear days. At least that's what Winnie tells me."

"Is she his third ... fourth wife?" Alan asks.

"Third, I think," Ed says.

"No matter," Alan mutters. His attention focuses on me. "Your grandfather was a friend of his, according to Walter."

"Could be," I reply. "Why this subject?"

"Walter says there are Hayman family journals." Perspiration beads form on Alan's brow. "Claims your grandfather kept records of the original settlers and the land," Alan says as he wipes his forehead.

"So, what's this have to do with anything?" This conversation sits in my gut like a heavy German dumpling.

"Your great-grandmother, Maggie, disappeared, correct?" The waitress returns for our orders. "The usual," Alan says before she asks.

"Well, according to Walter, there's mention of ... or some hint of what happened to Maggie."

That catches my interest. "Do say?"

"Yes. And he said there are diaries or logbooks or whatever about the natural area where great-grandpappy, John, settled."

I come alert from the wine-induced haze. "You're sure they exist?"

"I asked Walter the same question." Alan waits for the waitress to set the placemats and flatware in preparation for the warm plates with huge piles of steaming pasta. "They're somewhere on the Hayman land. Those journals might clear the rumors around town about your ancestors."

A young woman dressed in trekking clothes approaches our table, which stops me from answering him. She holds out her hand. "Mr. Hayman?" I look up at her. "Jamie Cameron, I'm with the state environmental agency."

Ed cocks his head, grins, and says, "Have a seat and join us for a meal." His eyes light up. "The editor here's paying."

"I couldn't," Jamie replies.

"No problem, I'm gathering information for a news story. This evening might prove interesting." Alan studies the young, athletic woman. "You might be in an article." He shifts his bulk and leans to me. "Perhaps you can save the few remaining wetlands," he pauses, gathers a thought, and winks, "and the Hayman reputation."

The next morning, I head for a visit with Mr. and Mrs. Armstead, after my wine headache fades. Winnie answers on my first knock. The soft April breeze carries a hint of rain, which the weather service predicts for late afternoon.

"C'mon in," she says, while holding open the screen door, "I've been expecting you since our visit with the paper's editor."

I step into the old-fashioned living room. Walter sits in a rocker-recliner, watching a game show. His eyes drift toward me and back to the TV. Winnie points to the chair next to Walter.

"Would you like coffee or tea?"

I glance at the TV. "Coffee's good."

She disappears into the kitchen. My decision to visit with Walter proves a smart move, he appears alert, at least mildly alert.

"Here you are." Winnie hands me a ceramic mug full to the brim.

"Thanks."

The sound of my voice near to his ear makes Walter look at me. A hint of recognition shows in his watery eyes.

"Gotta be a Hayman," he gurgles. A cough erupts from deep in his chest. Winnie steps over to help him with the second spasm.

His eyes come clear. "Damned if it ain't … Chance Hayman." He glances at the mug I hold, and motions Winnie to fetch one for him.

"Mornin', Walter," I say as Winnie seats herself near Walter's side.

He takes the mug, slurps, and looks back at me. "Shut off that damn TV. It's nothin' but nonsense."

A loose screen rattles and draws my focus away from him. My last visit occurred three years past. I came to see Walt's grandchild, with whom I graduated.

"You come to see me 'bout your grandpa's hidden treasure books?" He winks at Winnie.

I grin at him, and the smug smile vanishes.

"Well, I learned 'bout them books from one of the McFarlands or maybe the Whitlocks," he frowns, "had to think a moment." He stifles a phlegm-filled cough and moves on. "You own land with a skeeter hole and Kansas limestone bunkhouses, don't ya?"

"You're asking about our hunting preserve?" I know Walter detests the marshes. He feels it takes farm ground off the tax rolls.

He sips the coffee. An ornery twitch crosses his lips and quickly fades. "Yeah, I guess that's what it is … if you say so."

For a second, Winnie's posture becomes stiff-backed. "Walt, don't get nasty. Chance came to visit about what you might know."

Walter reaches over and pats her leg. "Fresh information of the Hayman past should liven up your church circle."

"What about the limestone bunkhouse?" I ask.

"It's good sized, no? It's got a wood floor?" He smiles at my nod. "You might look under the floorboards for some old storage cases."

"I'll do that … soon as I get a chance, thank you."

"That why they called you Chance, eh?" Walter rattles out a cough. He hands the mug to Winnie. "Your granddaddy, he had two brothers that were interesting." His eyes lose the luster.

Winnie helps him recline the chair. "You're lucky, it was one of the few moments he's been clear."

"Thanks, Winnie." I stroll back to the pickup, and wonder about my grandfather Henry and his two brothers—Calvin and Joseph.